PROMISES AND FULFILLMENT

Mark Cardozo promised Sabine a position as his wife at the very summit of the old-money Jewish aristocracy of New York—where "Our Crowd" formed a tightly closed circle of wealth and culture and influence.

Matt Ryan promised Sabine a world of danger and excitement if she took him as a lover and followed him to the hot spots of a globe exploding into war.

Bernie Ross promised Sabine the glamour and money of movieland if she allowed herself to be his "good luck piece" in the ruthless power games he played.

How could Sabine say no to any of them—hungering as she did for all that life had to offer . . . ?

A
Woman of
Fortune

𝒮

Great Novels from SIGNET

A Woman of Fortune

Will Holt

A SIGNET BOOK
NEW AMERICAN LIBRARY
TIMES MIRROR

To Dolly, my wife
and Courtney, my son
and Gisela Davidson and Gerry Waxman, my friends
who all helped form this book,

My thanks and my love.

PUBLISHER'S NOTE

This novel is a work of fiction. Names, characters, places, and incidents either are the product of the author's imagination or are used fictitiously, and any resemblance to actual persons, living or dead, events, or locales is entirely coincidental.

NAL BOOKS ARE AVAILABLE AT QUANTITY DISCOUNTS WHEN USED TO PROMOTE PRODUCTS OR SERVICES. FOR INFORMATION PLEASE WRITE TO PREMIUM MARKETING DIVISION, THE NEW AMERICAN LIBRARY, INC., 1633 BROADWAY, NEW YORK, NEW YORK 10019.

SIGNET TRADEMARK REG. U.S. PAT. OFF. AND FOREIGN COUNTRIES
REGISTERED TRADEMARK—MARCA REGISTRADA
HECHO EN CHICAGO, U.S.A.

SIGNET, SIGNET CLASSICS, MENTOR, PLUME, MERIDIAN AND NAL BOOKS are published by The New American Library, Inc., 1633 Broadway, New York, New York 10019

First Printing, November, 1981

1 2 3 4 5 6 7 8 9

PRINTED IN THE UNITED STATES OF AMERICA

Prologue

The two young men stopped at the crossroads. One signpost pointed to Vienna, the other to Berlin.

They were running from the Czar's conscription, which could swallow up thirty years of their lives—and that's if they were lucky. Behind them lay their village Pabjanice. The German-Polish border was five miles to the west.

"Come with me," Jacob urged his cousin Samuel.

Samuel shook his head.

"Not to America . . ."

"How can you not want to?" Jacob asked. "You've seen the letters they write." He started to conjure up the images. "New York . . . Electric lights . . ."

"In Vienna it is safer," Samuel countered.

"I don't want safer," Jacob shouted. "I want A-mer-i-ca—Man-hat-tan!" His voice caressed the foreignness of the words.

"Samuel Abramowitz is going to be an actor," his cousin replied. "Famous! Samuel Abramowitz speaks Yiddish, Russian, Polish, German, and only three words of English. Therefore, Samuel Abramowitz is going to Vienna!" He struck a mock-heroic pose that was indeed going to make him famous.

"You know English? What do you know in English?" Jacob asked enviously.

" 'Hello,' 'goodbye' and 'good luck' . . ."

It started to rain.

"Not coming?" Jacob asked Samuel one last time.

"Not coming."

"Then"—Jacob used the English word—"goodbye."

They shook hands and started down their separate roads. They were both handsome young men, and strong. Samuel

1

would make a good actor. Jacob had no idea what he would do with his life. But he had brought along his concertina.

A month later, the Archduke Ferdinand was assassinated in Sarajevo. That was the summer of 1914, the first summer of the First World War.

And the last time Jacob ever saw his cousin.

Chapter One

Sabine had never seen a tree.

Or a field, or lilacs. She stood in the middle of a field, the grass almost up to her shoulders. Six years old, and she had never seen anything but the spidery fire escapes, brick buildings, makeshift signs, and pushcarts that made up Rivington Street.

Now she was in a field. She had no idea what the different trees she watched so avidly were called. Some were green with leaves, some green with needles. Some were slender, with white bark, some huge enough to run around.

Her mother seemed to be sleeping, face up to the sun. Here, in this wide expanse the sun itself seemed different, hotter and brighter. The air was filled with brightly colored things that flew. They had great wings of orange or yellow-and-black, and they flew and fluttered and landed for a moment on a flower or a stalk of high grass, and then flew off again. Flies—Sabine knew flies—buzzed and zoomed. She felt like zooming, too. She ran through the tall grass, but never too far from the sound of her father's concertina. The notes were light, the music dazzled her ears, the day dazzled her eyes.

"What is that you're playing, Jacob?" Sabine's mother asked drowsily.

"Jazz," her husband answered, his voice prodding her, looking for approval. "American jazz. Do you like it, Bertha?"

"Very pretty," she said. "Could you dance to it?"

"If I had to . . ."

Jacob closed his eyes, imagining himself playing (in tails) with five musicians behind him. There were crystal chandeliers, palm trees, mirrors behind him, women smoking cigarettes, and couples dancing on the floor below the gilded

3

podium. The couples were smiling at him, nodding their approval because he was playing so well, so American . . . Gone was the feeling of rushing away . . . the memory of leaving Bertha alone in London, his fear at Ellis Island when the examining doctor had detained him—something about his heart—the fear that he might be sent back. But the music —American music—washed all that away.

Now here he was in a stranger's field near a strange town called Liberty in a strange state called New York. But his wife Bertha was with him, and his daughter Sabine (they had named her that on impulse because they considered themselves artistic and "bohemian"). And now he was trying to master "Japanese Sandman." *If you can't sell silk, sell linen,* he thought to himself.

Bertha listened to his playing. He only played the old songs on request. He concentrated on American tunes now. Perhaps he was right. Such a strange sweet land they had come to, America, and this was the first time they had left the city since their arrival. Beyond the field she could see the mountains, green and welcoming but shadowed with mysterious dark valleys. So different from the Polish plain. On the fringe of this farmer's field, were more trees than she had ever imagined could exist. Not the poplar and willow trees of the Poland she remembered—these were maple and elm and birch. Beautiful, all of it, the heat and the shade trees, the field, the stone wall, and far beyond it the white wood farmhouse with the porch and the barn, all needing a coat of paint.

One thing was like Poland: the lilacs. They were tough flowers despite their fragile, female smell. In Poland the lilacs had bloomed beside her kitchen door—a great bush, almost a tree, that in the springtime was bent over with the heavy burden of fragrant blossoms. As a child Bertha had stood in the doorway or walked into the field as far as the fence to watch the railroad trains on their way west. Twice a day the trains deigned to stop briefly at the village station before hurrying away. She was forbidden to go beyond the fence, so she would stand watching the grazing cows, which were not allowed beyond the fence either.

Sabine was skipping in time with the tune her father was playing, dancing across the field. She closed her eyes, as she twirled, and her body suddenly struck something warm and damp. She fell down on the earth. She opened her eyes. And screamed.

It was above her. Horns. Great horns and a face that was mostly holes in the nose. The mouth slobbered. Where was her father, her mother? Sabine screamed again and heard them calling her name. She could not move. It hung over her, motionless, the horns like great spears against the sun. She was too frightened to move. Then the thing groaned, made a great sound, a moaning. Finally it backed away, and Sabine was swept up in her father's arms, and the world returned to safety. But why were her parents laughing?

"Imagine," her mother was saying, "Sabine has never seen a cow."

Her father was walking toward the monster without fear.

"The cow needs milking," Jacob said. He set Sabine down, and she immediately hid behind her mother's skirts.

"Don't be afraid, darling," Bertha told her. "You shall have a treat. Jacob, where is the bucket Max keeps in his auto?"

They had borrowed the Model-T Ford that Jacob's cousin Max used for a taxi. Jacob searched through Max's tools and found a bucket, a dipper, and some tin cups.

"Are they clean?" Bertha asked doubtfully. Surprisingly, they were. She turned to the cow with authority, grasped the teats firmly, and applied pressure. The cow looked relieved.

Jacob watched with amusement. "I had no idea you were so expert."

Bertha never dropped the rhythm as she talked. "Of course I am expert. My family was *rich* in our village, and had two cows, that had to be milked."

She scooped up some milk in a tin cup and drank. "God," she said, closing her eyes in ecstasy, then bent over and handed the cup to Sabine.

"Taste this," she ordered. Sabine sniffed cautiously: she could smell the metal of the cup. What did milk smell like? She tasted. It was warm. She had never tasted warm milk. *How warm*, was her first thought. And then—*how sweet*. There was still froth around the rim of the cup. Sabine drank it all, closing her eyes in imitation of her mother. She would remember the moment for the rest of her life.

Her mother and father were talking in faraway, dreamy voices above her.

"To live in the country . . ," Bertha was saying.

"If this could only last, I'd be happy forever," Jacob agreed.

"It wouldn't be practical." They were both looking in the direction of the farmhouse.

"I'm not talking about practical. Let me dream, will you?"

"All right, dream. What would we do?"

"Raise crops . . ."

"You're not much of a farmer."

"I'm lucky. I married a milkmaid." He was laughing. But she was serious.

"It needs paint. The farmhouse."

"I could paint it." True, he had painted closets in tenements. He had painted them all peach.

"How can you tell if the foundation is solid?" Bertha continued.

"I am a carpenter. I can tell." True, he knew how to build things, was acquainted with hammer and saw and nails.

"How would we make money?" she said.

"Who knows?" He shrugged.

The talk of a *Luftmensch*, she thought, looking at him. Trying to make a living out of thin air. Her father had been a *Luftmensch* in the days when Jews had been restricted to living within the towns, and only certain towns at that. A whole army of men had frittered away their lives in the marketplace and the railroad station selling Hebrew Bibles, prayer books, fringes for prayer shawls, yarmulkes, pots and pans, wolf's teeth for good luck, amulets. Selling a little of this, trying a little of that. Not practical men, these *Luftmenschen*. Jacob talked of becoming an orchestra leader—while he ran a candy store. In Poland he had been one of the *klezmerim*, the self-taught musicians who played for the circuses and fairs, and sometimes for the nobility. Here in the New World he played at weddings, but people preferred Irving Berlin for dancing. Everybody was singing American. And Jacob was learning the saxophone. "A little of this, a little of that. If you can't sell silk, sell linen." The words of a *Luftmensch*. And yet Jacob was more than that. He was more than her father had been. Jacob had vision. He was more than a dreamer. Or was he?

"There is a way to make money," he said to Bertha and her heart leaped. "Take in boarders." Her heart sank.

"Who would come?" she asked.

"Everyone. Look around you. Everyone has a car nowadays. Everyone wants to go to the country! Like today. A place for a picnic, a little music, the children to run around in the fields. Look at Sabine. Already she looks healthier." His inspiration was growing. "They could stay overnight. The women and children stay for a week. Stay for a summer! People have money now."

"It would be so expensive."

"No *so* expensive. *Bei uns* it would be better." He was mocking the German Jews who assured the Galitzianer and Litvaks that everything German had been superior to everything Polish and Russian, particularly the Yiddish.

Jacob put Sabine on his shoulders and they strolled the field. At the far end, near the edge of the woods, was a stream. They could gaze in the water and see the sandy bottom. Downstream they discovered a rock quarry. The stream made a pool there, big enough for swimming. By now it was midafternoon, and they began to turn back.

A man approached them. "Can I help you folks?" he said, his tone friendly but reminding them that they were trespassing.

"Is this your property, sir?" Jacob asked politely.

"Yes. Sixty acres and the house. Lake, too." he added.

"We were admiring the place. I hope you don't mind," Bertha told him.

"No, don't mind at all. McNeills have loved this place a long time. My grandfather cleared most of it. This part was all woods once. Over there was the original field. His father cleared that. That's where the stones for the wall came from."

"How long have you been on this land?" Jacob asked.

The farmer counted it up. "Four generations." He looked about. "My oldest boy wants me to come west. He moved to California. That's a long way . . . . He says they got everything in California. Oranges the size of grapefruit. Everything's better there, he says."

"Another *Beiunser*," Bertha said, smiling, to Jacob.

"You Jews?" the farmer asked.

"Yes. Why?" Jacob said with an edge to his voice.

"Lots of Jews around here now—during the summer."

"Yes, well, we must be going," Jacob said. Bertha took Sabine's hand and they started off.

"You want to buy this place?" the man asked after them.

Jacob turned around. "You want to sell?"

"Give the girl some lemonade, and we'll talk."

Before three lemonades were finished, they had agreed on a price of $3,500; they would put down $450. The price included the farm, sixty acres, the lake, one cow, two horses, and a plow.

"What about the furniture?" Bertha looked around the parlor.

"No room for it in California. You want it?"

There wasn't much. On the porch there were rockers, four of them, with rush seats. Two needed reweaving. In the parlor was a sofa, an armchair, and an upright piano that could use a tuning, Jacob thought. The dining room contained an oak table, six chairs, and a sideboard full of china. Upstairs were four bedrooms, each with an iron bedstead and a chamber pot, pitcher, and washbasin.

"You have no running water?" Bertha asked.

"No. There's an outhouse. In the summer I wash in the stream. The quarry's good for swimming. You'll like it."

He gave them the furniture and the china for free. The sun was behind the mountain and the field was growing dark when they finally left. Bertha and Jacob shook hands on the deal with John J. McNeill. They were to come back with the money the following weekend. McNeill stayed on the porch as they walked away.

"It's *our* land," Jacob said, and started running, Bertha and Sabine rushing after him. He took off his shoes and socks, shocking his daughter—grownups did not behave like that. Then she caught the excitement, and as the three of them waded into the cold water of *their* stream, she took her mother's hand; it was warm with happiness.

On Monday night Jacob told his cousin Max about the farm.

The Abramowitz candy store was the meeting place for the neighborhood.

Farther uptown, near the Yiddish theaters, was the Café Royal, where the actors, the artists, the literati passed their evenings with endless glasses of tea and endless conversation. On Rivington Street the candy store was the Royal. Men came in for cigars, girls came for candy, young men came for the girls, and mothers came to look out for their daughters' reputations. Kids, candy-store comics practicing for the big time, tried out their material on the four tables that ringed the small floor. Hoofers, comics, doubles, straight men, stooges, and sidekicks polished up their patter and performance. Some of the kids had talent. Some had mothers.

Mrs. Rosen, for example, had a wonderful son, Bernard. She could never get over how wonderful he was. Bernard had been taken once, just once, to the Palace, where he had seen the comics—and could remember every word. Now Bernard was always on the lookout for a straight man. He went through straight men the way his mother went through chocolates, squashing those that didn't suit. Bernard, at eleven, possessed the voice of a bugle, and his cousin Hecky was most often straight man.

Hecky: Are oysters healthy?
Bernard: Oi! I never heard one complain.

Bernard: I sent my wife to the Thousand Islands for a vacation.
Hecky: Why the Thousand Islands?
Bernard: One week on each island.

Mrs. Rosen's giggles punctuated each joke. "I can't help it!" she would explain. "He's so humorous. Who would have thought it? He should be on the stage." Even as she was laughing, she was clocking the crowd's reaction. Was tonight better than last night? Or was it better last night? Should Hecky be replaced?

Hecky was not necessary for the finale. Bernard fell to one knee for "Mammy," which he dedicated to his mother, and Mrs. Rosen led the applause, if necessary. It was not always necessary. The Lower East Side always admired *chutzpah*. And Bernard had that.

Bernard and Hecky were not the only entertainment. Anything went. Recitations in Yiddish, vaudeville routines, songs from the Old World, the latest Tin Pan Alley hits. But the crowd had its standards. The long-winded performer often found himself surrounded by the murmur of conversation. If he persisted, he was often silenced with a peremptory "Please! People are talking!"

It was into this atmosphere that Max Abramowitz walked that Monday evening, his stint with the taxi finished for the day. It was here that Jacob approached Max, already sure of what Max's reaction would be—"Who's going to lend you the money? You want to go to Hebrew Immigrant Aid Society for another loan? You already are paying off one."

But Max surprised him. He asked no questions. His eyes flickered over the crowd and came to rest on Sabine, who was sitting by the cash register. That was her world—cash registers and comedians. Even if she couldn't recognize a butterfly, she could tell good jokes from bad. She was pale, however, always pale, and it worried Jacob, Bertha and Max.

"She looks better," Max said approvingly.

"One day—you see what it did," Jacob said. "Think what a summer would do."

"Has she seen a doctor?" Max asked. But nobody saw doctors then, unless it was too late.

Consumption was the great fear. Everyone had an absent relative, suffering from "anemia," who sent cards and mementos on the High Holy Days from far-off places. "Burn the card! Burn the money!" the fathers would command their children, who, not understanding, would wail. But the fathers prevailed. The men had worked too hard, gone through too much, to allow tuberculosis to destroy their families. Often, at Ellis Island, they had seen families split up, a son or a father—more often, a mother or daughter—ordered back to Europe to die. If the father was sick, the whole family often returned with the wage earner. If it was a daughter—well, those things happened. No wonder the cards and money were burned.

In America, they discovered the remedy—take the children to the mountains for their lungs. An industry was beginning in the Catskills: hotels.

The following Thursday, Max showed up for dinner with a woman he introduced as Leah, who was small and dark and already had circles under her eyes. But she was also lively and laughed a lot. And ate a lot. Fortunately, Bertha always made more than enough. This time, she made just enough— and watched Leah finish off the last of the English trifle.

"How do you make this?" Leah asked.

"Strawberries, fresh strawberries. I make sponge cake, a custard, and also whipped cream."

"How much sugar?"

"Enough."

"I mean measurements."

"I don't measure. I know when enough is enough."

"Is that all?" Leah wanted to know.

"Two tablespoons of rum for the flavor. I won't say where the rum came from."

Leah gave Max a nod. Max leaned back in his chair and addressed Jacob.

"You need money? I have some."

Jacob was astounded. "Why would you give it to us?" he asked.

"I wouldn't be giving. I would be coming in. As a partner."

"What would your father say?" Abraham Abramowitz was as Orthodox as Jacob and Bertha were bohemian. He wore his hat in the house, went to *shul* Friday nights, would not allow smoking in the house, would not ride in any vehicle on the Sabbath, had a wife, Rachel, who never uttered a word, and considered his nephew Jacob a bad influence on his son.

"He would say what he's been saying all along: that I'm as crazy as you are. But I don't care what he says. I brought Leah over to sample Bertha's cooking." He looked to Leah. "Tell me what you think."

"A fortune," Leah said definitively. "With her cooking, you could make a fortune; I'll tell the world."

Max and Jacob settled down to serious bargaining then. For the loan, Max wanted half interest in the boarding house and half interest in the candy store. He would get someone to run the candy store. After all, Jacob couldn't be in two places at once. It made sense. That night, in the store, the two men toasted their partnership with an egg cream.

The next Sunday, Max drove them up to Liberty in his taxi. John McNeill was sitting in a rocking chair on the porch, waiting. Jacob presented Max and they all went inside.

When the papers were signed, McNeill brought out some wine, and over the dining room table that now belonged to the Abramowitzes he made a toast.

"May you do well here," he said.

"*L'chaim*," they answered, and everyone drank.

"About the neighbors," McNeill began. "You got some good ones here. The man who owns the sawmill—downstream of you—he's Daniel Ryan, and you'll like him. He's a carpenter and he's honest and he says what's on his mind. Then you got the people who own the Mountain View House . . ." McNeill let the words hang.

"Where is that?" Max asked.

"It's the spot above you, on top of what *they* call a mountain, and I call a hill. But it does have a view all right. From there you can see sixty miles up the valley. Not that the view from here is bad."

"A hotel?" Bertha asked. "We ought to visit them."

"I wouldn't," McNeill said. "The Mountain View is just a big old wooden building, the kind they put up around the turn of the century, all turrets and verandahs. There's no point going there."

"They don't like Jews," Jacob said.

"Don't like 'em and won't take 'em," McNeill nodded. "You ought to know there's a number of people around who don't like the area getting so crowded. They feel it's bad for business."

Bertha dismissed what he said. "We won't bother them, and they won't bother us. There's room for everybody. Come, Max, inspect the property."

They went first to the kitchen. It was a big room, with a black iron range on one side and a smaller stove on the other. A wooden icebox with three doors by the opposite wall. There was a table in the middle of the room big enough for ten people to sit at. By the sink was a hand pump. The well was outside the kitchen window.

"Why two stoves?" Max asked McNeill.

"My wife used the small stove during the summer. They both work well. Now here, in this compartment by the wall, you can bake bread if you've a mind to."

"How many loaves can you put in there?" Bertha asked. She had never seen a range that size, and she looked carefully at the ten removable plates and the spiral handles.

McNeill smiled at her. "You'll like this stove. It holds the heat. It's good for baking." He opened the door to show her the oven. "My wife baked six loaves at a time, as I recall. She used to cook for ten—we had hired help during the harvest time—and she never had help."

"No help at all?"

"Well, one of my boys did the milking."

"The younger one," Bertha said.

"That's right," McNeill said, surprised. "How did you know?"

"It must be the same in all families," Bertha said, and they moved outside.

"There's the best view," McNeill said. The splendor silenced them. From the three granite slabs that served as doorsteps, they could see across the fields, where the land sloped down and then sharply dropped. Across the valley, the Catskills rose. The peaks shimmered in the sunlight.

"The town is over there." McNeill pointed. "Just beyond the glen."

"What is a glen?" Bertha asked.

"A valley."

"Is that an English word?" she asked.

"My family came from Scotland. They used it there. We always called this the glen."

"How romantic . . . a 'glen.' " Bertha smiled. "We'll call this . . ."

"Glenside," Max said.

"Not Glenside," Bertha said. "That's not quite right."

It was like naming the baby. Bertha looked down at her feet. "What do you call these rocks?"

"That's granite," said McNeill. "These slabs were hauled out of the quarry in my grandfather's time. They're the foundation of the house, and these were left over."

"Ah, I have it," Bertha said.

"Glengranite?" Jacob teased.

"Of course not. 'Glenrocks.' What do you say?" Bertha practiced saying the name. "I'm going to Glenrocks for the weekend. Have you been to Glenrocks? I hear the food is suuu-perb!"

Jacob was not certain. "Doesn't it sound a little too fancy?"

"Not a bit. Women will like it."

"Then it's settled," Jacob shrugged. "Welcome to Glenrocks."

They strolled out to the driveway, where Max had parked the taxi.

"I'll be gone by the first of June," McNeill told them.

"You needn't leave so fast."

"Oh, yes . . . I want to be gone now. I've planted the corn
and beans and three rows of lettuce and two of tomatoes.
You won't have *that* to do."

They avoided saying goodbye, but eventually they had to.

"Thank you for helping us," Bertha said as she shook
McNeill's hand.

"It was a pleasure," he answered. "This land should always
belong to someone who loves it."

On the first of June Jacob, Bertha, Max, and Sabine drove
up to Liberty with supplies and provisions from New York.
The farmhouse looked lonely. It no longer belonged to
McNeill, and yet it didn't belong to them either. Bertha hesitated before entering.

"Mama, open the door. I want some water from the
pump," Sabine said.

"All right," Bertha said, and put the key in the lock

Turning on the lights made the place seem more theirs.
Even though it was a bright day, Bertha turned on lights in
the kitchen and the parlor. She gave Sabine a glass. Sabine
held it under the spout while Bertha pumped. The water
sprang out of the pump with sparkling clarity. Sabine drank
two mouthfuls. She hadn't been thirsty. She wanted to drink
water that was *theirs*, and nobody else's.

A bell rang. The adults looked around. What was it? Who
was ringing? Where was it coming from? Somewhere inside
the house.

Max said, "I think we have a telephone."

Bertha was nonplussed. "A telephone? We have never had
a telephone." The ringing continued. They located the telephone on the wall in the front hall, and Jacob picked up the
receiver and spoke into the mouthpiece attached to the box
on the wall.

"Hello," he said, hearing at the same time another voice
saying "Hello, Mountain View House . . ."

"Hello," he said again.

"Hello, who is this?" said the other voice.

A third voice said, "Hello, I am calling the Mountain View
House. Is this the Mountain View House?"

"*This* is the Mountain View House," the second voice said.

"Hello," Jacob said again.

"Who is on the line?" the second voice said.

"This is Jacob Abramowitz."

The second voice was not pleased. "*This* is Mr. Taylor of the Mountain View House speaking. Would you please hang up the receiver?"

"The telephone rang. I answered it."

"You are on a party line. Your ring is one long, two short. The Mountain View House is one long ring. Now, kindly hang up the receiver."

"I'm sorry," Jacob said.

"What? Who is that?" The third voice was on the line again. "I am calling the Mountain View House. Who is that?"

"A local disturbance," Mr. Taylor of the Mountain View House said smoothly.

"This is Jacob Abramowitz from Glenrocks!" Jacob roared, and then he didn't know how to end it. "Goodbye!" he said at last, and hung up violently. The phone dinged in response.

"Who was that?"

"Neighbors," Jacob shouted, still angry. "Mr. Taylor from the Mountain View House. He is one long and we are one long and two short . . ."

That was their first encounter with the Mountain View House.

The next month was incredibly busy. Jacob and Max painted the house and repaired the roof while Bertha cleaned and sewed. Sheets had to be washed and ironed and put on the beds. There were countless trips up and down the stairs. Sabine followed her mother contentedly for the first four days. Then she discovered the outdoors and hated every moment she had to spend inside. Jacob and Max found some rope in the barn, tied it to a tree, and with a plank made a swing for Sabine. There were only three places she was not allowed to go by herself: the stream, the quarry, and the barn. Otherwise she was given almost total freedom. The adults were too busy to look after her. But Sabine was perfectly content to play by herself and discover the crickets that lived under the granite slabs.

At the end of the first week, after the house had been painted and the barn and shed had been cleaned, Max went back to the city to recruit customers. Bertha and Jacob were left to finish the conversion job.

Bertha got up every morning and milked the cow, then made breakfast, which Jacob allowed himself ten minutes to eat. He sat there and watched Sabine drink fresh milk, then he was off, and they didn't see him again till lunch. He had the garden to weed, and water to carry from the stream. There were chair bottoms to be rewoven, and leaks to be patched.

It was a beautiful June, cloudless and hot. Jacob, working outdoors, turned dark from the sun. Bertha lost five pounds just from cleaning and climbing the stairs. Sabine went barefoot and never stopped running except when she went to bed. At night the three of them slept with satisfied exhaustion. And the farm looked lonely no more.

On a Monday late in the month, when Jacob was in the garden, the phone rang. One long and two short—their ring. Bertha was intimidated by the telephone. She had never used one. She approached the instrument warily, then took the receiver off the hook. The black mouthpiece stuck out at her from the wooden box on the wall. She said into it timidly, "Hello."

Max's voice snapped in her ear. "I can't hear you, Bertha. Move closer." She did and yelled, "Hello!"

"That's close enough. No need to yell. I'm only in New York."

"What is it, Max?" Bertha was sure it had to be an emergency. It was.

"Are you going to keep kosher?" Max asked her.

Bertha had not thought about it. "What if I don't?"

"Then you're out of business before you open."

"Then of course I keep kosher."

Max sounded a little uncertain. "You do know how, don't you?"

"Of course I know *how*. But you know Jacob and me . . ."

"Yes. The 'free-thinkers.' "

Bertha was already going through menus in her head. "I wouldn't serve shellfish in any case. We are too far from the city."

"It means two sets of dishes."

"I know."

"Two stoves . . ."

"We have that, you know we do."

"Two sinks . . ."

Bertha did not even try to keep the excitement out of her voice. "Yes, yes. I'll figure it all out. You really have people coming? How many?"

Max named them. The Weidmans, mother, father, and daughter. The Laskys, a couple. Mr. and Mrs. Salwitz, just married. And Mrs. Rosen and son Bernard.

Bernard's lungs did not need fresh air, Bertha thought. "All these people, how did you find them?"

"Bernard and his mother are always easy to locate," Max said. "The others got into my cab. The first thing I said to the Weidmans is, you got a lovely child there, she should be out in the country this time of year. Think what a glass of fresh milk and a week on a farm would do. And they agreed, but then they wanted to know where was such a place and how expensive was it. For the weekend, fifteen dollars for the family, all meals included, I said. That's when they asked, Is it kosher?"

"Oh, and what did you tell them?"

"Of course I said, Sure. What else would I tell them? But I wanted to warn you . . ."

"That's sixty dollars," Bertha shouted into the phone. "A fortune!"

"The rest is up to you, Bertha. You have to make good."

"Of course I'll make good. When are they coming?"

"The fourth of July weekend. I'll bring them up Thursday."

"Max, order some vegetables from the Rivington Market."

"I'll bring them up with the guests."

"You're sure they won't mind?"

"Why should they mind? They'll see that everything is absolutely fresh . . ."

Another voice came on the line. "This is the Mountain View House," the voice said icily. "Would you signify when you have finished?"

Bertha panicked. "How should I do that?" she asked.

"Hang up the receiver, madam. To the right of your instrument you will see a crank. Twist it once, smartly." There was a crackle on the line. The man had hung up.

"You got that, Bertha?" Max laughed. "Twist it once *smartly*! I will see you on Thursday around six o'clock. Goodbye."

"Goodbye, Max," she said faintly. She had walked into the next room, menus on her mind, before it occurred to her that she had not signaled. She dashed back to the telephone and twisted the crank once, smartly.

Bertha sat down heavily. What would she serve these ten people (including Max) on Thursday night? The old standby, pot roast? Better still, beef stew. If she could get vegetables on Wednesday, she would make the stew and let it simmer. The flavor would be better by Thursday and it would be out of the way. Suddenly it hit her. She could not cook on the Sabbath. Everything for Saturday would have to be cooked before sundown on Friday. How could she store it all? She rushed into the kitchen and stared at the old oaken icebox. She measured the three lead-lined compartments. There was enough room there. But Jacob would have to bring in more ice from the ice house. What would she serve? Chicken. Would Velikovsky, the kosher butcher in the village, give them credit? Would the cow supply enough milk? Who would help her in the kitchen? She could not do this all alone.

When Jacob came in for lunch, he found her at the kitchen table. Lunch wasn't ready. He thought she was sick.

"What is it, my angel? What's the matter?"

"Max called," she said despondently. "He's bringing people on Thursday . . ."

"Paying people?" Jacob asked gleefully.

"Four families. Nine people."

"Wonderful."

"Two of them are Mrs. Rosen. And Bernard."

"Still wonderful! You see, we're a success right from the beginning."

"Jacob, you don't understand." Bertha tried to keep her voice controlled but it was no use. "We'll be no success because we have to keep kosher, which means I have to cook everything for Saturday the night before and who is going to help me serve and help in the kitchen, and who is going to order the food? And what if they don't show up after all, and we have all this food that goes to waste? Jacob, we could be wiped out before we have even begun!"

Jacob took her in his arms.

"How many people are coming?" he asked.

"Nine. Plus Max. And there's the three of us."

"How many chickens will you need?"

She began to calculate, and doing that immediately made her feel better.

"Ten chickens," she said.

"I will call Velikovsky."

"And where shall we feed them? In our dining room?"

"No, we need more tables. In the shed. We shall transform it."

"I'm going to need help."

"I will get it."

That afternoon he took the horse and wagon and returned three hours later with provisions, four tables, and sixteen chairs, all piled in the back of the wagon.

"Where did you get all this?" she asked him. Not one of the chairs resembled the other.

"Other people's barns. There's a great deal they don't want."

"How did you pay for them?"

"I didn't pay. They're on loan. Now Velikovsky will slaughter the chickens Friday morning. I will pick up the other meat on Thursday. Here are some vegetables. And I think I may have found some help for you. If you don't mind it being a boy."

"Why should I mind a boy?" Bertha asked him. She was so relieved she was ready to dance.

"He's fourteen."

"He will do until we find somebody steady."

"Then I will go to Daniel Ryan's tomorrow and get the boy. McNeill was right. Ryan is a good man."

That night Jacob and Bertha made love with great pleasure in the darkness of their bedroom. The country air had increased their appetite for that, too, Bertha thought contentedly, before she dropped off to sleep.

Early the next day Jacob went and fetched Matt Ryan. Fourteen years old and with a head of bright red hair, Matt was big for his age. Independent too; motherless for the past two years, he had learned to care for himself. Jacob had explained it all to Bertha before the boy came.

"Could you work in a kitchen?" she asked the boy.

"I know how to peel vegetables. I can chop up your wood for you. Do the dishes. Watch that things don't boil over. But I'm no cook myself."

Bertha was startled that so many words came out of his mouth. And so definite.

"Now Matt, here's how we begin," Bertha began. "First, make sure there's always firewood for the stove. And now comes the complicated part. These dishes here," she indicated a cupboard, "are for the meat and the vegetables. They cannot touch the other dishes *here*"—she pointed to a second cupboard—"which are for the dairy products. They must be washed separately. The first set will be washed in the sink. The second set, including the glasses for milk, will be washed in this tub. They must be dried on separate racks, using separate towels. Do you understand all that?"

"I don't understand it at all," Matt said, "but I can do it."

"Do you eat meat on Fridays?" she asked him.

"Ah no, ma'am, that's a sin."

"Exactly," she said. "And for Jews so would it be to mix milk and meat."

"Nobody ever told me exactly why eating meat on Friday was such a sin," Matt continued.

"And nobody is going to tell you about this. At least, not now," Bertha said briskly. "Just accept it. Now let me show you how to clear the tables."

"There's just one thing," Matt said. "I'd expect to be paid."

That brought a smile to Bertha's lips. "How much do you want?"

"I'd be working the weekends. Fifty cents'll do."

"A day?"

"For the whole time. Fifty cents is fair."

"Agreed," Bertha said.

They worked well together, and on Thursday they had everything ready by the time the first guests arrived with Max.

"Bertha," Max said smoothly, "this is Mrs. Weidman. And this . . ."

"When iss dinner?" hissed a voice behind him.

"Ah, Mr. Weidman. And little Ruth. Ruth, this is Sabine. She will show you where the strawberries may be picked."

"Strawberries are all gone," Sabine said definitely.

"I'll give her a razzberry!" a familiar voice trumpeted.

"Oh, Bernard, how comical!"

Mrs. Rosen and son were right behind the Weidmans.

"All right, you don't want a razzberry. You want a kiss?"

"Bernard—" Bertha continued.

"All right you don't want a kiss. You want to give me a kiss?"

"Now, Bernard—"

"You know what you can kiss. You can kiss my—"

"Bernard!"

A clap of thunder interrupted, followed immediately by a downpour of rain. It was the kind of storm the Catskills specialized in. Sudden, spectacular, and violent. A bolt of lightning struck a nearby tree. The telephone dinged. Thunder tore through the room and the house shook with the vibrations.

"Now that's what I call a hit!" Bernard cracked.

"*Bei uns*, it was louder—at Bad Ischl," Mr. Weidman shrugged.

Bertha and Jacob looked at each other. More *Beiunsers*. All weekend they were going to hear that the water was purer, the mountains more majestic in Bad Gastein, the cooking more delicious in the Alsace, and the Rhine grander than the Hudson.

Bertha sighed. "Let me go see about dinner," she murmured, and fled.

Within an hour the other guests showed up. The Weidmans were given the front bedroom; there was a cot for little Ruth. The Laskys (Mrs. Lasky a shadow of her husband, gliding into chairs, always silent) occupied the room next to the front bedroom. The newlyweds, Burt and Stephanie Salwitz, had the rear bedroom. Mrs. Rosen and Bernard occupied the spare room downstairs, across from the parlor.

By nine o'clock the guests had been fed, and an exhausted Bertha was ready to retire. So far there had been no complaints.

"Good night," she said to her guests.

"Good night," Mrs. Weidman said. Bertha and Jacob started for the stairs.

Mr. Weidman hissed, "When iss breakfast?"

They pretended they did not hear him.

Breakfast was at eight o'clock, which meant that Bertha was up at five to start baking the coffeecake and pastries that would accompany the eggs. Which meant that Matt was also up at five to chop the wood for the stoves, and Jacob was up to milk the cow, and Max was up to carry the hot water to each of the rooms, and Sabine was up because everyone else was.

By eight o'clock the aromas of baking filled the house, and by eight-ten everyone was at the table. Out came the butter that had been churned on the farm, the bakery goods fresh from the oven, the freshly ground and freshly perked coffee. And eggs—you had your choice: poached eggs, fried eggs, a cheese omelet, or boiled eggs. And there was oatmeal. And fresh cream to put on it. There was no smoked fish yet, but no one seemed to mind.

It was a beautiful day, warm with the promise of July. The moment breakfast was finished, the Weidmans took their binoculars and little Ruth and went out to stalk birds. Mrs. Rosen found a place in the shade and kept moving from spot to spot on the porch to stay out of the sun. Bernard went looking for berries and found poison ivy. The honeymooning Salwitzes disappeared for a walk, while Mr. and Mrs. Lasky stretched out on the front lawn for a sunbath.

At twelve o'clock they were all on the porch, waiting for lunch. Although the Salwitzes disappeared for long periods of time, they were always prompt for meals. Mr. Lasky was developing a tan. The mosquitos had found Mrs. Lasky and she was about to suffer sunburn. The Weidmans emptied a pitcher of milk among the three of them. The food disappeared almost as fast as the Salwitzes.

Bertha had no time to talk to anyone that afternoon. By sundown she had baked the challah, ground up the fish for the gefilte fish, and prepared the *cholent* for Saturday. The carrot and apple tzimmes had been simmering since morning.

Dinner was ready to be served.

The Salwitzes admired the gefilte fish.

Mrs. Rosen had seconds of tzimmes.

Everyone had seconds on the chicken.

Bernard Rosen ate ten slices of challah.

Bertha and Jacob collapsed that night and slept till sunrise.

On Saturday evening everyone sat on the porch to watch the fireworks display—a local ordinance prohibited fireworks on Sunday, the Fourth of July. From the village, great balls of colored light exploded in the air and showered the valley with sparks. Rockets soared toward the stars and vanished in the dark. The chatter of faraway firecrackers echoed in the hills. Sabine sat on her mother's lap and watched the dazzling lights while Bertha rocked back and forth in her chair. For a time, the five families became as one.

"Have you tried Grossinger's?" Mr. Lasky asked.

"Too big," Weidman said firmly.

"Flagler's?" Mrs. Rosen was curious.

Mrs. Weidman dismissed it. "Too far away."

They sat on a sweet summer night in rocking chairs, safe in a land of promise and contentment.

"Schindler's Prairie House?" Mr. Lasky ventured. "I hear they have a tennis court."

Mr. Weidman was definite. "Na, na. *Bei uns* it is better."

Chapter Two

Sabine had looked forward to the first day of school ever since the last guest said good-bye to the Abramowitzes. Everything had changed with the end of summer. Velikovsky had closed up shop until next season. Her father had swapped his Model T for a truck, which was more suited to the rough country roads and winter weather. There was no more Yiddish heard in the streets of Liberty. It had become just another little American town.

Sabine's school was in Liberty. On her very first day she was excited. Her father drove her to school in the new truck. Her mother had brushed Sabine's unruly black hair, buttoned her calico dress, and told Sabine she was beautiful. The truth was she was not. Someday she would be, but at the moment everything was outsize. The legs too long and gangly, the figure too skinny, the eyes too big. Only their expression was beautiful. Sabine's eyes looked out at the world with total honesty and trust.

Miss Eunice Sharpleigh was Sabine's teacher. The first four grades were contained in one room, the next four in another. The high school was in another building across the schoolyard.

Miss Sharpleigh started the day by taking attendance. It was a good opportunity for her to size up her pupils as they stood up, announced their names, and told her a bit about themselves. Abramowitz led the list, which was of course in alphabetical order. Miss Sharpleigh looked at the girl with the black hair, the knobby knees, and the calico dress.

"How do you pronounce your last name, dear?" she inquired.

"Abramowitz," Sabine answered.

"Stand up, dear, when I call your name for attendance."
Sabine obliged.

24

"Now, what in the world is that first name of yours? Sah-*been*?"

There were giggles behind Sabine's back.

"No, ma'am. It's *Say*-bine. Like fine."

"Fine. Is that another Jewish word?" Miss Sharpleigh wanted to know. Now there were more giggles, not so muffled. "Sabine Abramowitz, do your parents speak English?"

"Yes, ma'am."

"Then why did they call you Say-bine?"

"They're bohemian." Sabine repeated what she had been told. "They call me that because they were bohemians."

"I see. Will your parents allow you to salute the flag? We say prayers here. The Lord's Prayer. A *Christian* prayer. Will your parents allow you to pray to Christ?"

Sabine was confused; Miss Sharpleigh did not seem to want to know the answers.

"Sit down, Sabine Abramowitz. Next is—Adams. John Adams. Well, that's a relief. John, would you stand up please?"

Later, they did recite the pledge of allegiance. Miss Sharpleigh showed them how to stand, hand over heart, and then how to thrust it out on the word "flag." That was their assignment, to learn the pledge of allegiance. And then she asked how many of them knew the Lord's Prayer. Several confident hands shot up; a few doubtful ones hung in mid-air. Miss Sharpleigh focused again on Sabine. Therefore, all eyes were on the little girl.

"Sabine Abramowitz, I take it you do not know the Lord's Prayer?"

Sabine was silent.

"Speak up, please. I have asked you a question."

"I don't know it," Sabine stammered. She felt hot, her dress was sticking to her, it was too small, too confining, her desk was too small, too, her knees kept knocking against the iron frame.

"Do you say prayers at home, Sabine Abramowitz?"

What was she supposed to answer? Were prayers permitted at home? Who prayed? Not her father. Not her mother.

"We are bohemians," she repeated, hanging onto a lifeline that would explain everything.

"No, dear, you are Jews."

It was impossible to find the right answer. Suddenly she remembered.

"My great uncle Abraham. He prays. Every Friday he goes to *shul*!"

"Your great uncle goes to school?" The classroom rang with merriment.

"*Shul*," Sabine repeated. That was what it was called.

"What is *shul*?" Miss Sharpleigh asked, her eyes enormous behind her rimless glasses.

"Church."

"No, dear. Certainly not church. Christians attend church. Do you mean synagogue?"

Sabine had heard that word. "Yes," she said eagerly.

"I see," Miss Sharpleigh said. "Sabine Abramowitz, perhaps you would be so good as to ask your parents whether you would be permitted to learn the Lord's Prayer with us. Would you do that?"

"Yes."

"Yes, what?"

"Yes, ma'am."

The morning passed, and recess came. It was a golden day. The children filed out in order and immediately scattered into groups. They had brought lunch pails filled with peanut-butter sandwiches on white bread. Bertha had packed a hard-boiled egg, a chicken leg, hard-crusted rye bread, and an apple. Sabine ate alone and then went for some water at the fountain in the middle of the yard. A game of tag was being played to her right. She had not been invited to join. She didn't know any of the children, and kept her head down as she approached the water. A boy, much bigger than she, put his hand over the water spout.

"Abramowitz, show us your tits," he said. The game seemed to stop. More giggles. The trust was leaving Sabine's eyes.

"I want a drink of water."

"No."

"What do you mean, no?"

"I mean you can't have any. This is holy water. You can't have any holy water."

"I'm thirsty," Sabine said.

"Tough," said the boy. His hand stayed on the water spout. Where did it come from, the sudden rage she felt? She had no idea. She swelled with anger, and raised her fist and brought it down on the hand covering the water spout. The boy yowled in pain and then hit her across the head. Her ears rang. She shook her head and then hit back, not aiming anywhere, just peppering him with her fists and then with her feet. He was bigger, she knew that, but she didn't care. He was on top of her then and she fell under his weight onto dusty ground. He pulled her hair and she found a finger and bit. He screamed with pain, and pulled harder on her hair. Sabine kicked, and then there was a sudden swirl of dust and the boy was lifted off her. A scuffle, sounds she could not make out, and then a hand took her arm and someone was brushing the dirt off her face. Matt. She started to cry.

"Don't cry now," he said, horrified. "I just saved you. You're okay." He shielded her from the stares of the other children and she stopped her tears. The school bell rang. They went in to their separate buildings.

"Sabine Abramowitz," Miss Sharpleigh said when she saw the girl, "I don't know how dirty your parents are in their own home, but we do insist on minimum sanitary standards here. I shall write a note for you to take home. Do they read, your parents?"

"Yes'm."

"Good. Then will you be so good as to give them this?" Miss Sharpleigh wrote briskly, her tongue flicking out from between her narrow lips. She sealed the envelope and passed it to Sabine, then sailed on to spelling. At the end of the day, Sabine was given three books, one for spelling, one for reading (although she already knew how to read), and one for arithmetic. You will bring in a notebook with lined paper and three pencils, plus an assignment pad, she was told. Class dismissed.

Sabine left school, turned her back on it. It was a wooden building, and the windows seemed to stare at her. The high school across the yard was made of brick. She never wanted to see either place again. She hated school, hated the children, hated the yard. Her cheeks were burning. Instinctively she was making a fist. Most of the children were walking in one direction, toward town; she was headed in another. Her father had arranged to pick her up, but suddenly she found she couldn't face him. She started to run down a street, it didn't matter where. She was never going home, she was never going back to school. She was too ashamed. She felt angry at her parents. Dirty Jews, that's what they were. Her father with his silly instruments and his mustache. Foreigners. Dirty Jews. That's what she was. She hid against the bark of a tree and let the hot tears scald her face. She gasped for breath. She could not breathe *and* cry. She choked, then sat down in despair.

Which was how Matt Ryan found her—dirty, in a clump, sitting under a maple tree, cradled by the exposed roots, her hair with bits of dead leaves in it, her dress filthy, her face stained with tears, her eyes red from crying.

"You want a ride home on my bike?" he offered. She had always longed to ride his bicycle but he had never invited her before, and she had been too shy to ask. Now it was too late.

"No, I'm never going home."

"Oh. Where are you going, then?"

"I don't know. Somewhere."

"Come to my house."

She shook her head. He held out his hand. She was getting hungry, she was tired, the day had exhausted her. She looked at his hand, then took it. He helped her up, then helped brush the dead leaves off her.

"Your dress has a rip," he said. "We'll fix it."

She rode on the crossbar, and she could feel his warmth and strength surrounding her. His arms were strong, holding the handlebars. His long legs pumped the pedals. It was growing dark and the September wind cooled her face. By the time they reached Dan Ryan's house she felt better.

Mr. Ryan was surprised to see his son's guest. "Rough day, first day at school," was Matt's only explanation, and his father nodded. Matt saw to everything. He telephoned her parents.

"Sabine is with me," he said into the mouthpiece. "She misunderstood and started to walk home. I found her. She's fine. We'll bring her over in time for supper. I just didn't want you to worry." When he hung up, he looked at her.

"You want to learn how to punch?" he asked. She was silent. "You might as well learn. You were fighting okay there, but there's a few things I could show you." Fifteen minutes later Sabine found herself punching Matt's open palm savagely. He let her punch out her fury, then showed her how to jab with her left and come in with her right.

"Knee 'em if you have to," was his advice.

"Is that fair?" she asked.

"I wouldn't worry about fair. Worry about winning," he said. "Besides, you're a girl. Girls are allowed anything."

"I hate my parents," she told him suddenly.

"Why?"

"They're dirty Jews," she said.

"Who told you that?"

"Nobody had to," Sabine said. "Miss Sharpleigh—"

Matt laughed. "Miss Sharpleigh? She *smells*!" It was true—Eunice Sharpleigh did have a bad odor. "Whew!" Matt continued. "Did you ever get close to her? I bet she never takes a bath. Who would believe anything she says? She's crazy."

"She makes me feel ashamed," Sabine said, and started to cry again. Matt's arms went around her.

"Ah, no, no, no . . . Never feel that way, never. No matter what anyone does, don't you be ashamed." He was whispering the words to her, but fiercely, as though he were trying to fight all her battles for her. It surprised him to feel so protective toward this little girl, so he kissed her cheek and brushed back her hair.

"It's all right," she said. Then, "Miss Sharpleigh gave me a letter for my parents."

"Let's see it."

Sabine produced it. Matt ripped open the envelope, read the note, and crumpled it into a ball.

"Forget it," he said. "Your parents send you to school clean. I'll see that you stay that way. Come on into the house and let me sew up the rip in that dress."

Inside, he took up needle and thread; he could sew neatly. It did not surprise her. In her eyes, Matt could do anything.

Then he and his father took her home in their truck. Dan stayed in the truck while Matt led her inside, where Jacob and Bertha were waiting anxiously.

"I'm sorry," Sabine said.

"Sabine, you must never never do that again. If your father says to wait, then you wait. He will pick you up. If he says he will, he will."

"Yes, Mama," Sabine answered, but it was only a game she was playing.

Her father said, "Are you all right?"

"Yes, Papa."

"What happened?"

"Nothing, Papa. I thought I knew the way home and would surprise you." Matt choked back a sound. She was lying to her parents, protecting them. They chose to ignore the dirt on the calico dress.

"Thank you, Matt, for taking care of her," Jacob said, and Bertha added, "You must be hungry. Can I give you something to eat?"

"No, ma'am, my father's waiting outside."

"Why didn't you bring him in?"

"I told him I'd only be a minute. See you tomorrow at school, Sabine." He turned to leave.

"Say good night to Matt, Sabine," Bertha prompted. "And thank him for bringing you home."

"Thank you," Sabine said, and her eyes met his. *Something's changed*, he thought. *The expression in her eyes is different.*

Sabine had no more trouble in the schoolyard; Matt saw to that. She had no friends, but she had no active enemies either. Mostly she was ignored. And despite Miss Sharpleigh's feelings about Jews, after a week Sabine Abramowitz was called simply Sabine. Her intelligence and her eagerness to learn made her a pleasure to teach. Miss Sharpleigh grudgingly admitted that you had to hand it to them, they did want to learn.

Fall turned to winter and the storms began. The stove heated the house. Mittens were warmed on a shelf above the stove or on trivets around the stovepipe. Jacob slanted wooden planks against the house and covered them with evergreen boughs. Bertha stuffed the cracks around the window frame with newspapers and kept the oatmeal simmering on the stove. A blanket was kept over the hood of the truck, and the last thing Jacob did before going to bed was to start the motor and let it run for a minute or two. When Sabine accompanied her father to the barn to feed the two horses and Frieda, the cow, she was always amazed at the heat the farm animals gave off.

How did they know so much about winter, this kind of winter, so different from the icy winds that swept the Polish plains? They owed a great deal to Dan Ryan, who showed them how to bank the house with evergreens and gave them tips on what wood to burn (maple and apple burned slowest, and therefore were the best—pine burned faster and most of the heat went up the chimney).

In January a blizzard isolated the Abramowitzes, and the first people they saw after three snowbound days were Matt and Dan Ryan, who snowshoed over to see how they had fared. That afternoon another storm caught the Ryans in the Abramowitz house, and they were persuaded to stay the night.

That evening, as they all sat around the stove, the three parents took the time to remember their youth. Matt and Sabine were silent. Sabine was always amazed that her parents had ever had lives of their own, without her. They were more than just parents. They were Bertha and Jacob, and they had met in Paris before the Great War.

"He came into my mother's restaurant," Bertha reminisced. "He was the handsomest man I had ever seen. I was fifteen. He wore spats and a cap. *Un vrai bohème,*" she said fondly.

"She liked to recite poetry. Everyone was expected to perform in her mother's restaurant. She was terribly elegant." Jacob smiled at the memory.

"I wore spats too. And a cape. I was a sensation," Bertha laughed.

"What kind of poetry?" Matt Ryan asked her, and Bertha had to think, it seemed so long ago, more than an ocean away.

"Yiddish," she remembered. "Yes, Yiddish poetry. Mama's restaurant was famous for *la cuisine juive,* Jewish cooking. *Mama* was famous. Wasn't she?" She turned to Jacob for corroboration.

"Yes. Oh, I had heard about Mme Levinsky's food long before I heard about her daughter."

"Is she still in Paris?" Dan Ryan wanted to know.

"Of course. She is a Frenchwoman now. When the Great War came, when we were married, Jacob and I, we decided we would have to leave France."

"They gave such nasty looks because I wasn't in uniform," Jacob said.

"One day, we were sitting in a café, the day the zeppelins came over," Bertha said.

"They bombed Paris, would you believe it?" added Jacob.

"It was not dangerous. It was spectacular. From La Butte you could see these zeppelins . . ."

"What did they look like?" Matt asked.

"Like fat German sausages," Bertha said. "They were filled with gas, you know, and they floated over the city."

"What did they do?" Sabine wanted to know.

"They dropped explosives, darling."

"Why?"

Jacob had no idea how to answer that. "It was part of the war," he said lamely.

Sabine wanted to know what the people had done to be punished like that. Bertha brushed the question aside. "There was very little damage. It was just strange to sit in a café and watch these—what?—balloons, floating so slowly over the city."

"But what happened to your mother?" Dan reminded her.

"My mother? Oh, she had had enough of fleeing. She had fled the Russians and the Poles and she had no fear of the Germans. So we left without her. Jacob came to America first, and when he could"—they looked at each other then, the two years that they had spent apart still a mystery to them, Bertha in London, Jacob in New York—"he sent for me. You know what was funny?" She interrupted herself.

"What?" Dan Ryan asked.

"When we met again, after two years, we both talked to each other in English."

"What's so funny about that?"

"But you don't understand. When we parted, neither one of us knew the language."

In truth, Bertha was not smiling just because it was funny. She was remembering how on her first day in New York Jacob had proudly shown her his new candy store, and they had chattered away in English. He had assured her that it was safe to drink the tap water, he had even prepared her an ice-cream soda, and had impulsively licked the ice cream off Bertha's lips, which had led to impulsive lovemaking behind the counter.

Dan Ryan had grown up in a little village a hundred miles upstate, near the Finger Lakes.

"I remember the first automobile I ever saw. Fire-engine red and pulled right up to the dance hall. Caused some stir! We had hoss-and-buggies then. Sleighs in the winter. Roads 'were smoother. You'd take a team of horses, pack down the snow, and then wouldn't you fly along! Skim along like you was on ice. Sometimes we would ride on the ice, too. Not with the horses though. On ice boats with big sails."

Sabine sat by the warm stove, half-hearing the storm outside, and she was caught up in the world Mr. Ryan was describing. He talked of the steam boats that had plied the lake in summer, the picnics on the water, the village's centennial celebration in 1898, the Fourth of July speeches and fireworks, the livery stable where he had first worked. Such a fascinating life. The loggers would come down from the woods in the spring and tear the town apart with their exuberance. He described a brawl he had had with the loggers over a Miss Scribner, whose affections he sought. Sabine could see the little town by the lake, the white wooden houses with the green shutters, the village green and the high elms, the steamboat landing, the dirt roads, the hills, the livery stable.

"What happened?" she asked in a small voice when Mr. Ryan had stopped talking.

"Oh, what happened? The war came along. That was the Spanish-American War, and I went off to Cuba to be a hero."

"But Miss Scribner, what happened to her?"

"She married a safer investment, a banker, everything changed after that. The town . . ." He drew a breath. "I said goodbye to all that." He was silent a moment. "I guess when I went off to war, I *knew* it was goodbye."

They were all silent then, until Bertha rose. It was time to go to bed. Outside the wind howled and rattled the panes, but Sabine went to sleep with the cozy feeling of being totally protected. Everyone she loved was under one roof.

By the next morning the snow had stopped, the sun was out, and the expanse of field was dazzling, blinding white. Sabine sat at the table eating oatmeal while the two men stared out the window, their mugs of coffee steaming in the morning light.

"I'm thinking about next summer," Jacob said to Dan Ryan. "I want to expand. Do you know what I want to do?"

"What?"

"Build four bungalows there—see?—right by the line of trees."

"Would you be able to fill them?"

"Who knows?" Then, more seriously, "Yes. I think judging from last summer we could."

"Well, I might be able to help you out."

"You haven't heard it all." Jacob grew expansive. "I want to build an extension onto the house. And transform the barn into a recreation area. Build stables, riding paths, some bath houses down by the lake. Eh? What do you think?"

"Not possible. Not possible," Dan Ryan said.

Jacob flashed his grin. "You want to bet?"

And because it was the Twenties, when everything was possible, Jacob was right.

That spring Jacob, Max, and Dan Ryan built the cabins. Four cabins—all with toilets! Of course the Mountain View House complained about the added burden on the sewage system, there was talk at the Liberty town meeting of restricting further construction, but the motion was not carried.

A constant stream of people came to Glenrocks that summer. One after another, groups would sit in the rocking chairs on the front porch, making identical comments about the sunset, the stars in the sky, the fresh country air, the marvelous food. And one after another, they would leave—having made reservations for the following year.

There was never enough room. In 1923 Jacob added four cabins. In 1924 he added eight more. These were exciting times. Everyone had more money, was making more money, was reading more books, attending more films, singing more songs than ever before. Cities exploded with people, success sprouted like spring flowers. Business was good. Not good, *great!*

Jacob and Bertha seemed to thrive on all the excitement, but the rushing around took its toll. One night Jacob complained of dizziness; the next night he staggered as he was walking from the barn to the kitchen. He had to sit down. The following day, Bertha forced him to go to a doctor, who prescribed rest.

"I'm a little run down," Jacob agreed. "I will rest in the rocker."

Which of course never happened, for the moment Jacob sat down he saw all the work that had to be completed. There were cabins to be painted. Work to be done on the barn roof. The livestock to be fed. The planting season. Again Jacob rose at sunrise and worked until dark. The time for resting was always later. Plenty of time for it, later.

Sabine would remember 1924 as the summer of the radio. She spent most of her time with Matt. When he peeled potatoes, he let her empty the buckets; when he lugged in the wood, he let her carry a few sticks. At night, in his room on the second floor of the converted barn, he let her watch while he built his first crystal set.

Matt had always been fascinated by the radio, and he even knew its history. The first United States broadcast had been held on the evening of November 2, 1920, when KDKA in East Pittsburgh announced the returns of the Harding-Cox election, he told Sabine. The Dempsey-Carpentier fight had been broadcast from Boyle's Thirty Acres in Jersey City, Matt said. Sabine had no idea what he was talking about. Who was Dempsey? Jersey City she had heard of. She watched Matt's fingers as they delicately twisted copper wire and attached brass tacks along the length of an oatmeal box; he had already shellacked the box, and then had wound copper wire around it and shellacked that.

"You know what the brass tacks are for?" he asked. She didn't, of course. "You can tune into different stations, just by sliding this along. Did you know there's a radio station over in Monroe?" Monroe was a nearby town. She didn't. "Did you know they got radio stations all over the country now?" She didn't know that either. "That's what I'm going to do someday," he continued.

"Do what?"

"Talk on the radio. Work at a radio station. See this coil? One end connects to this aerial. The other to this set of earphones. Now, I take this piece of galena crystal," he picked it up to show her, "and I hook it in with this cat's whisker ..."

"Where'd you get the cat's whisker?" Sabine wanted to know.

"From a cat," he said.

From what cat? A live cat? A dead one? Did the cat object? Did he only get one whisker? There was a lot Sabine wanted to know about the cat and the whisker, but she didn't have time to ask him because he was handing her the earphones.

She put them up to her ear. It was like listening to the sea,

he said. She didn't know. She had never been to the ocean.
But she could hear a roar. It came and went. Then she
heard—music. A piano. A man's voice, singing. How faraway
it seemed. Where was it coming from? Matt moved the slide
along the brass tacks and the man singing and the piano gave
way to more sound waves, and then an orchestra was playing.
In this little stable, she could hear a whole orchestra.

The next day she told Uncle Max about Matt's set, and
that night he came to listen. It was a novelty. Why not take it
down to the guests and let them listen too?

He was as good as his word. Max made a great show of
announcing Matt's invention. A wireless set. Matt would
demonstrate it. Who wanted to put on the earphones? All the
guests were curious, more than he had imagined. Mrs. Rosen
had to be first, as always. She put on the earphones. Matt adjusted the slides. Mrs. Rosen held up a hand.

"Paul Whiteman," she breathed. "All the way from New
York!" Everyone wanted a turn. The Weidmans next,
naturally. There were not enough earphones. A fad was
born—listening to the radio. Jacob was aware of the possibili-
ties. He and Max conferred.

Reading the ad was the clincher.

SHOULD YOU OWN A RADIO?

Test yourself! Each question counts 20. A true radiophile
should score 100.

1. Do you spend time alone?
2. Do you miss some events, or have you a pair of Seven
   League Boots?
3. Are you fond of music only when you wish to listen?
4. Have you a better method of nullifying bores than turning on a radio?
5. Do you know the air is full of FREE entertainment?

That last sentence did it. Max went to New York City and
came back with a brand new Crosley radio with a magnificent cabinet. He showed it off to the guests.

"The receiving set is neutrodyne, of course," he said
proudly. "And the set is completely shielded."

Shielded? Shielded from what? Weidman worried. He

would not let little Ruth within ten feet of the set. There might be dangerous rays.

Max continued, "You can get all the signals and get them *one* at a time. And as you can see, the dial is illuminated so you can see what you are doing."

"It's wonderful, Max," Mrs. Rosen enthused. "A miracle."

"The miracle is that you don't need earphones," Max finished triumphantly. "Here, Mrs. Rosen, try it yourself." That was Mrs. Rosen's intention. She adjusted the knob. There was a squeal, a rush of static, silence, then a voice, bass and resonant.

"This is WNBC, New York," it said.

"New York!" they breathed.

"Try another station."

"Just a minute," Mrs. Rosen said firmly. From that moment she became the custodian of the radio. Will Rogers, Paul Whiteman, Walter Damrosch entered their lives. For free! Every evening.

But this also led Mrs. Rosen into difficulty. No one was interested in watching Bernard mime a record or in listening to him tell old jokes if Walter Damrosch or Will Rogers was available. The requests for Bernard's version of "Mammy" had dwindled to one: Mrs. Rosen's.

Bernard found himself offered up as the second waiter. Max and Jacob were looking for someone to help Matt. Mrs. Rosen suggested Bernard. Anything to keep him occupied.

"Let Bernard do it. Don't pay him. We'll stay for free." That was her reasoning. Bernard had no more desire to stay in the kitchen than he had to enter a snake pit, but Max had already leaped at the offer and, reluctantly, Bernard became a waiter.

Before Bernard became second waiter the service had been very respectful. Should a guest complain about the food, Matt dutifully and silently returned the plate to the kitchen and brought back another portion.

Not so Bernard.

Bernard was assigned Mr. Garfinkel's table. It started from the first breakfast, and it developed into a ritual.

Garfinkel was a man of fifty who had never married. He sniffed everything.

"Are these fresh?" he would ask Bernard, sniffing the eggs. "Na, na, they're not fresh enough. Get me fresher." And Ber-

nard, who knew he was meant for better things, would go
back to the kitchen for fresher eggs.

Garfinkel rose every morning at five to get the milk fresher
than anyone else. He was first to be seated and the last to
leave the dining hall. On the night of August 24, 1924, he
sent back the fish (too fishy) and twice sent the perspiring
Bernard back with the veal.

"This veal is not fresh. Get me fresher!" Garfinkel commanded.

"What's wrong with it?" Bernard protested.

"You ask what's wrong with it? I tell you. This veal is not
fresh. The nose knows. Don't argue with the nose. The nose
can smell fresh. Get me fresher," Garfinkel ordered, and Bernard left to find fresher. Garfinkel continued his monologue—
no one at Glenrocks complained of a lack of entertainment at
table.

"It's not like we're not paying here. We're paying good
money—to be poisoned," Garfinkel declared. "You maybe,
but not me. The nose knows. You could get poisoned. Don't
laugh, it has happened. My brother from Pilsen—you know
how they cook *there*—he ate veal once, old veal, blue veal,
the veal was older than my brother, my brother ate this veal
one night, and next morning—dead!"

Out of respect for the dead there was a moment of silence
in the dining hall, broken suddenly by a disturbance in the
kitchen. Then Bernard came through the door pulling a
year-old heifer up to Garfinkel's table.

"You want fresh?" Bernard bawled. "It doesn't come no
fresher than *this!*"

The room broke into applause. That night Bernard, who
was no dummy, discovered the key to his later success: in-
sults.

Late that summer Garfinkel had more to complain about:
the wells ran dry. There had been drought. No rain at all in
August. Hardly any in July. Perfect weather, not a cloud in
the sky. At first the guests could not have been more thrilled.

Garfinkel was the first to complain about the taste of the
water. No one paid much attention. Bernard brought him another glass. Garfinkel switched to seltzer. Then the pressure
on the flush toilets failed. Jacob examined the pipes. They
were running out of water. A hurried consultation with Max,
and then a not too confident Jacob made an announcement

at dinner. More adventure in the country! The wells were running dry. But rest assured, there would be drinking water. However, as for the flush toilets, well, it was back to the chamber pots. Fortunately, not too many of the guests were that reliant on flush toilets: very few of them had grown up with them. It was not a catastrophe. But the drinking water? Max and Jacob saw money flying out the window, until Jacob remembered the lake. Was the water pure enough to drink? They had it tested, and the results came back in three days: yes. From that moment swimming was limited to the rock quarry, and the problem was lugging the water from the lake to the house.

Sabine was pressed into helping. Like Matt and the always reluctant Bernard, she took her turn with the buckets. There had to be enough water for the cooking and for the guests to drink. Sabine started early in the morning, before the guests were up. She and her father drove the truck down to the lake. Jacob brought great big milk cans, and Sabine filled them. She was not strong enough to lift or even help lift the cans, but she could fill buckets and empty them into large containers. Three times a day they came down to the lake. Sabine developed blisters on her hands, then they callused over. She became very proud of her calluses. She was one of the workers.

Because they were all so busy, it never occurred to anyone that if Glenrocks' wells had gone dry, those of other hotels might have too. The phone rang one night. It was for Jacob.

"This is the Mountain View House," the icy voice on the other end of the wire said. "Is this Jacob Abramowitz?" The voice had difficulty with the name, naturally.

"Yes," said Jacob. "What do you want?"

The Mountain View House was now at a loss for words. "Could you—we have—well, I don't know *quite* how to say it—"

"What is it you want?" Jacob said helpfully.

"Water," came the answer. "You see, we have been hurt—as I imagine you have—by the lack of, uh, rain, and the dry wells. The fact is, we have—uh, no facilities. We are completely out of, uh, water."

"I wish I could help," Jacob said.

"You can," the voice bore down. "We would like permission to use your lake. If you would be so good . . ."

"It's Jewish water," Jacob warned, and winked at Bertha.

"Oh come now," the voice said, not understanding, "it is all *God*'s water, Mr. Abramowitz." Suddenly there was no difference; they were all God's children.

"So long as you don't mind," Jacob continued.

"No, no, no. Thank you," the Mountain View House almost gushed. Jacob hung up and rang once, smartly, to signify that the conversation had been terminated.

After that Sabine saw the crew from the Mountain View House every morning down at the lake. They never spoke to anyone from Glenrocks.

The drought ended. So did the summer. And the following winter Max went to Miami.

Chapter Three

A well-dressed gentleman flagged Max's cab right outside Pennsylvania Station.

"Good morning," said the gentleman, getting in. "I'm in a hurry."

"Where to?" Max asked.

"Florida," the man said. Max recognized a joke when he heard it. "Where to in Florida?" he asked.

"Where else would I go?—Miami!" the man said.

Max saw he was serious. "Why don't you take the train?" he asked.

"I couldn't get on it," the man answered. "I'll give you five hundred dollars plus your expenses if you'll take me to Florida."

Max did some quick calculation and said, "You're on." They stopped while Max packed a change of clothes, his toothbrush and toothpaste, a comb, and a pair of pajamas, and then they were on their way south.

"I just got back from Florida," the man told Max as they passed Newark. "I'll tell you, the bungalow is running neck and neck with the grapefruit in volume production."

"Is that so?" Max said to make conversation. But it wasn't necessary. The man could do all right by himself.

"It's a great country. Any day the sun does not shine, they *give* the newspapers away. Ford was down there, but I didn't see him. He was out fishing that day. Thomas Edison was there, too—and Roger Babson and Arthur Brisbane, four stupid people, ha, ha, ha."

"Is that so?" Max said again, caught up in spite of himself. He *knew* those names.

"They all invested their money in Florida real estate. They call it the Gold Coast down there. You want to know why?"

"Why?" Max obliged.

41

"Because you can buy a piece of real estate in the morning, sell it for more than you paid for it in the afternoon, and be very sorry tomorrow that you sold it for so little."

"All those men are rich to begin with," Max pointed out.

"You don't have to be rich. You'll find opportunities, you wait and see. Prosperity is within everyone's grasp."

The man was saying no more than anyone else did. It was 1925 and prosperity was everywhere.

Max planned to stay in Florida no longer than a week. But he stayed, and made a fortune. Miami was the right kind of town for Max. It had all the bustle of New York, plus the Southern sun. There was the din of automobile horns, and the jackhammers digging up the streets to lay pipes, or digging up the earth to lay streets. Hammers and winches built foundations. And the streets that already existed, were crowded with men rushing around with papers, the sweat pouring off their brows. They didn't wear coats or hats, and everywhere you looked there was another real estate office. There was a real estate office in the lobby of the Riviera Plaza, where Max deposited his fare. The sign in the window announced, "One Good Investment Beats a Lifetime of Toil."

Max believed it. He parked his taxi and plunged in.

He was certainly the right man at the right time. Fortunes flowered like bougainvillea under the tropical sun. The first week he was there Max made ten thousand dollars—just from investing the money he'd earned driving his taxi. He was too busy to find a place to stay, so he took up residence at the Riviera Plaza. They were glad to have him, and gave him an ocean-front room. In four months' time he never had a moment to look at the ocean.

Land was divided, then subdivided, and then that was subdivided too. If some of the lots were under water, that didn't matter. The lots would be drained. After all, man-made islands had sprung up between Miami and Miami Beach, and that land was sold off as well. Swamps had been drained. Anything was possible, and what was a little water between friends? The important thing was money. Everyone was making it.

And everyone was there. Luden's Coughdrops was there. Firestone Tires was there. J.C. Penney of the J.C. Penney Stores was there. William Jennings Bryan was there, and teaching a Bible class every Sunday in the lobby of the Riviera Plaza Hotel. President Warren G. Harding was there with his wife.

Glamour was there, and beauty. Exotic names and Everyman's dream of heaven were there. There were palaces and riches and palm trees. Women. Good health. Brochures reached Saginaw, Michigan, and Terre Haute, Indiana, telling of plantations with pine trees and palm trees, flowered and ferned, clothed in perpetual verdure, wrapped in the gorgeous folds of the semitropical sun. It was not hard to sell Saginaw and Terre Haute on that, and since Henry Ford had put the Tin Lizzie within Everyman's reach, the snowbirds descended on Florida in droves.

One look at the Gold Coast sold them on their fortune. But they were given more than one look. Tour buses took them to Coral Gables, where lakes and waterways connected Biscayne Bay to the islands. Winding avenues and plazas were built through the cool piney woods. Golf courses, country clubs, a hotel called the Miami Biltmore were all attractions. Mansions, haciendas, villas, chateaux rose. Their walls were white, their awnings striped, the roofs red tile, the foliage a brilliant green, the sky a never-ending blue. At the intersections of boulevards, fountains surrounded by tropical trees and flowers turned into wide plazas paved with coral rock. It was a long way from the Civil War monument in the town square of Saginaw.

The snowbirds came to look and stayed to buy on the spot. Max kept pen and paper handy. Sometimes he bought and sometimes he sold, but always at a profit. No one sold without making a profit. This was the procedure, make a down payment of ten percent, select a lot from the blueprint, see that the word "sold" is stamped on the receipt, and then rush out in search of a buyer.

Max had intended to stay a week. Then it became a month. But there was no point in walking away from so much money. Spring came to Miami. And then summer. The tourists never stopped coming. The boom went on.

When he had the time, Max wrote letters home begging them all to come down.

Jacob and Bertha smiled at the letters. They were busy that summer with Glenrocks. They, too, were making money. Not so fast, nor with such excitement, but they were happy. If Jacob tired easily, it was to be expected, with his heavy schedule. With Max in Florida, the job of recruiting guests fell on Jacob. By 1925 Glenrocks was staying open later in the season. It was a wonderfully warm autumn, that year, and the farm was full of guests who stayed to see the leaves turn and to sit by the wood fire with a glass of cider on cold nights. But when the leaves were off the trees and the bare branches were waiting for the snow, Bertha and Jacob finally decided to accept Max's invitation and take Sabine to Florida.

Miami's heat was as unexpected as it was welcome. They had crept onto the train on a cold gray day in New York, hurrying to get out of the wind. The first snow had started to fall on New Jersey's factories, and later it rained as they were passing through Philadelphia. But here there was heat and blazing color. Redcaps fought for their business. Great piles of luggage spilled out of the train. Wardrobes and polo ponies, steamer trunks and tennis racquets emptied out of the baggage cars. The pale Northern visitors were greeted by tanned men in white flannels and blue blazers, aggressive with good health and athletic handshakes. Everything was ultra here, bursting with health and youth, energy and ambition.

A handsome stranger approached Jacob, smiling. His blazer was the bluest, his flannels the whitest, his face the youngest and most tanned of all. It was Max.

"At last! At last!" He embraced them all. "Wait till you see what I have in store for you. Fabulous. That's the word for it—fabulous!"

Jacob and Bertha felt like greenhorns again. Max saw to the luggage, paid the redcap, flagged down a taxi. Soon they were speeding down a wide avenue, palm trees and heat to either side of them.

"How do you like it so far?" Max shouted, at ease with his life.

"I don't know," Bertha said. "It's too much to take in all at once."

"Relax. Take your time. You'll see it all."

"Where is your cab, Max?" Jacob asked.

"Gone. I sold it long ago. I have my own car now."

"You have a car?"

"A Stutz Bearcat. It's almost all mine."

"And where are you staying?"

"The same place you're staying. The Riviera Plaza. It's

right on the beach. Wait till you see it. Fabulous," he repeated. "I know the management. I got a special deal. Fabulous!" he kept repeating, as though it were a dream that might go away.

The hotel *was* fabulous. The ceiling in the lobby was at least four stories high. There was a balustrade on the mezzanine level where a string quartet played every afternoon from four to six. During the day, both entrances to the hotel were kept open. From the registration desk it was possible to glimpse the beach, the palm trees in the sand, and the breakers. White sailboats skimmed by while yachts moved majestically over the blue waters.

Their rooms were no less spectacular. The two rooms, theirs and Sabine's, were joined by a round archway. The spacious bathrooms had great mirrors that let you see all of yourself, and pink showers and bathtub and tile floors. The furniture was heavily Spanish, and antique, or almost. The hotel looked as though it had been there forever. Actually, ten years before the area had been a sand dune.

The ocean lay just beyond their balcony, stretching for three thousand miles to lands whose people would never know such luxury. The sheets on the beds, the beds that were turned down every night by invisible chambermaids, invited lovemaking.

The days were a parade of wonders. Max took them everywhere. They saw jungles and alligators, and every afternoon Bertha took Sabine to the beach and they watched the waves roll in from Europe. More than anything, Sabine loved her room at night, when her parents had gone dancing in the hotel ballroom and the sound of music wafted up to her bed. Sabine was not afraid to stay by herself. She liked to listen to the music and walk around in the room. The lamp would be lit, and the room took on a lemon color because of the yellow glass in the lampshade. Night breezes blew in from the ocean. When the orchestra stopped between numbers, the chatter of dancers reached Sabine's ears, mixed with the rhythmical slur of the surf. Each night she went to sleep lulled by the sounds of luxury.

Max tried to persuade Jacob to invest with him.

"You can buy a piece of land over a morning cup of coffee," Max told Jacob over a morning cup of coffee, "sell it at lunch for a twenty-five percent profit, and wished you'd held onto it by supper." Max repeated the litany he'd learned because he believed it.

That evening, over dinner in the ornate hotel dining room, Jacob told Bertha, "I don't understand. I have to believe Max has money. But where is it?"

Bertha watched Sabine carefully collect the fresh fruit on her spoon. "What do you mean?" she asked.

"He must have made money. He must be making it. Look where we're staying. Look where he's staying."

He gestured at the room around them. There was fourteen-carat gold leaf on the columns of the great circular dining room, and a gigantic Venetian chandelier, and mirrors and frescoes and cut crystal. Above it all was a glass dome that could slide back to reveal the night sky. There were pink shades on the individual table lights. The linen was pure white. The silver shone.

Jacob continued, "Everyone knows him. He is well-liked, respected even. They smile when he passes in the lobby. He is doing a land-office business." Jacob was proud of having learned that phrase. He used it often here in Miami, where it seemed to be true.

"But I don't see any real money," Jacob went on. "As a matter of fact, I don't see any real money anywhere. Look at us. We have paid for nothing. It is all put on a bill. We have not even paid for these clothes."

In a splurge of celebration Jacob and Bertha had bought evening clothes in one of the small, expensive shops that lined the hotel lobby. Jacob was wearing a dinner jacket and Bertha was wrapped in a white Fortuny gown, pleated all around, that flowed with the movements of her body. They looked like rich and successful people. But then, so did everyone in the room.

"Are you worried about Max?" Bertha asked.

"Not worried. Just wondering. Shall we dance?"

Sabine watched her mother and father together. On the dance floor they looked at no one but each other. The other dancers showed flickers of jealousy at such self-absorption. Jacob and Bertha were polite with each other, formal even, but the effect was that of a slow seduction on the dance floor. They knew how to move and they knew how to move each other.

Sabine sat at the table, her mouth slightly open, awed by

the perfection of her parents. They returned to the table, and suddenly Jacob was swooping Sabine up in his arms, and leading her onto the floor. Far, far above her she could see his glistening black mustache and straight white teeth as he smiled down at her. She felt beautiful. She was happier than she had ever been in her life, and her father laughed at her joy as they circled the floor one more time before returning to the table. Her mother asked Sabine to finish her dessert and then took her upstairs, put her to bed with a good night kiss, and returned to the dance floor.

That evening Max joined Jacob and Bertha, bringing along a man he introduced vaguely as a business partner.

The man's name was Mizener, and he had come to Florida to die in 1918, but had decided to build hotels instead. Jacob kept his eye on Mizener because Mizener had *his* eye on Bertha. On the dance floor, he told Bertha about his beginnings as a painter and woodcarver, and as a miner in California. He was not unaware of the romance of his tale. He had the raffishness of a successful prospector who believes in his own good luck.

"In ten years I'll be the richest man in Florida," he said.

"Doing what?" Bertha asked.

"Giving people what they want. I am responsible for the look of all this." He nodded his head at all the glitter.

"It looks like a palace," Bertha commented.

"Yes, it's supposed to," Mizener smiled. "Would you like to see more?"

"We would love to," Bertha said, deliberately including Max and Jacob. Soon there they all were, riding in Mizener's touring car. Mizener drove them to Boca Raton in the moonlight, where he had built a city of palaces with great watchtowers and thick walls. There were cloisters and arcades, three-story-high galleries, vaulted ceilings, tiled swimming pools. The eclecticism of styles appealed to Jacob, the bohemian.

"What do you call your style?" he shouted to Mizener as they raced through the night.

"Bastard Spanish. Bastard Moorish," Mizener shouted back over his shoulder.

They stopped to look at a villa that was nearing completion. "I'll show you my secret," Mizener told them as they walked from turret to turret. "You think these antique chairs are old? I take ice picks to 'em. Sometimes I shoot 'em with air rifles. I have been known to walk up and down a staircase in hobnail boots to make it look really old. Now, look at the frames on that mirror. That's my idea. You know what it is? Worm-eaten cypress. Looks antique, doesn't it? I put cypress on everything. It's become the mahogany of Miami."

"You're very sure of yourself," Bertha remarked, but she was not impressed.

"Of course. Nobody knows anything, so what does it matter? Max tells me you're thinking of moving down here."

Jacob looked at him with surprise.

"It's a wonderful life," Mizener urged them. "Where else could you be standing in fake Gothic ruins in the moonlight and making money at the same time? Max tells me you have a hotel . . ."

"Not a hotel, really. It started out as a farm."

"Yes, well, *this* started out as a garage," Mizener laughed. "We could do business. I am going to have an empire here. There's room enough for some more select people." He was looking at Bertha.

"What do you think?" he asked her when they were alone, after they had inspected a hacienda, a villa, a Tudor castle, and a palazzo.

"It's like the Café Royal," she said.

Mizener was not sure he liked that. "How so?" he asked.

"At the Café Royal, everyone is very grand. They are mostly theater people, you know, and they talk a great deal, but nobody can express himself in any one language."

"Oh." Mizener sounded offended. He was very blond and very good-looking, she thought.

"Also, they steal ideas from *everybody*," she added. "Just like you. That is why you are so successful. You are shameless."

"You're right. Will you go to bed with me?"

"I think not," Bertha said without pausing.

"Why?"

"Why should I go to bed with you when I can have Jacob?"

Mizener helped their love life. Jacob was aware of Mizener's good-humored attentions, and it made Jacob more attentive than ever. In the afternoons before teatime, after Bertha had come back from swimming in the surf, he would lick the salt off her body and then he would take her lazily in the late afternoon light. They made a game of how slowly they could move, how long they could prolong orgasm. Each of them would sense the other's oncoming climax and would stop, stop breathing even, for a moment, and then begin again. Often they would not reach a climax; they would wait until night. The evenings became deliciously excruciating. Every touch of the hand would arouse her. The brushing of knee against thigh would make him erect. They would be unable to dance and would have to sit at the table, half-listening to the conversation around them, intent only on each other's magnetism. Then, when the music had stopped and the other dancers had drifted off to their own set of dreams, Jacob would undress Bertha in their bedroom and they would stand naked at the window, letting the ocean breeze play over their bodies. He would start with the nape of her neck and descend very slowly along the lines of her body, making love with his mouth and his tongue to every indentation, finally taking her, thrusting his tongue in her until she shuddered and clutched at him. He could feel her throbbing against his face. She would cover him with kisses and lead him back to the bed. He would lie on his back and she would take him in her mouth. They were passionate lovers and very uninhibited, in an age before such things were common. Their chambermaid was delighted with them. She changed the love-tossed sheets, happy that these people were enjoying one another so much.

Max kept after Jacob. Take a flyer, take a plunge, he'd say. "How can you not invest? You're no fool. You see what's happening. It's getting better all the time. Come in with me, you'll retire early."

Jacob was hesitant. Actually, the two men already had investments together. They had a special account for Glenrocks and an agreement that either could take out money with just one signature, although it was understood that one wouldn't take money out without the other's consent. As the weeks rolled by, Max grew more and more impatient with Jacob. *He's missing the opportunity of a lifetime. He'll be sorry later, if he doesn't invest now.* Max made it sound reasonable to himself. He was doing this all for Jacob's own good. He made a few phone calls, and arranged to have money from their account transferred to *his* account. He bought binders on a few properties for Jacob. And for himself.

On New Years Eve, 1925, Mizener threw a party. Actually, the whole year had been one great party—this was the capper. Throughout Miami there was a carnival in the streets; at the Riviera Plaza they slid back the glass dome and danced under the stars. Money made them all beautiful, sleek, gorgeous creatures. A crescent moon shone over the bay and the revelers showered each other with confetti and streamers, danced on the tables and, naked, on the beaches, made love behind screens and in expensive cars. Max found two bimbos for himself, both blonde, both wearing crimson lipstick and rolled stockings. They patted Max's thigh under the table, and when their hands met at his crotch, all three of them laughed and they went to his room. Between sets he made love to both of them at once. Fifteen minutes later they were back, dancing and having at the champagne smuggled in from Nassau for the occasion.

Jacob dreamed. "Maybe I will have a hotel like this. And a yacht. I will play the saxophone on the yacht and we will take cruises to Havana . . ."

"Jacob, too much champagne," Bertha said.

"Why shouldn't I dream? Mizener dreams. What do you think? Maybe I should do business with them, with Mizener and Max."

"We'll talk about that tomorrow. Happy 1926."

"Happy 1926," he said, and kissed her. The balloons floated down, the southern breeze wafting them over the dancers. Everyone embraced, happy, happy. It was the happiest any of them would be for a long time.

The bubble burst almost immediately. First the National Better Business Bureau started investigating frauds in Florida real estate. A stock market break forced many businessmen who had come to Florida for the plunge to go back to New York.

Beneath his tan, Max was pale and evasive. He spent less and less time at the hotel or with Jacob and Bertha. His meetings with them were always hurried. He always had an appointment, somebody waiting; a glance at his watch and then he was off in his Stutz Bearcat. One day he was looking at the clock in the hotel lobby and not at his watch—it was being repaired, he said. Then so was the Stutz Bearcat. Finally, it all came out: Max had lost a great deal of money. When Jacob offered to lend him some, from their joint account, Max jumped up abruptly and dashed off without a word. This confused Jacob. *If Max needs the money, then he should have come to me,* Jacob thought. *That is how it should be with families.* Jacob decided to call New York and direct the bank to transfer money from their account for Max's use.

It was twelve noon on a mercilessly hot day in March when the call went through. At 12:05 Jacob hung up the phone, a different man. He was ruined. Max had taken all the money, *their* money, and spent it. Lost it. Everything Jacob had worked for, all those nights playing at weddings and all those hours behind the counter of the candy store. The years of doing without, abstaining, himself, walking instead of riding . . . And now, Glenrocks? Was that also gone?

Anger overwhelmed him.

"What is it?" Bertha asked, frightened. He had never looked so terrible. He was ready to kill.

"I'll be back," he said in a voice that was nothing like his own.

"Where are you going?" Bertha cried. He flung the door open and hurried down the hotel corridor. She was not dressed. She spun around and ran into Sabine's room.

"Go after your father," she ordered Sabine. "Now! Right now! Bring him back." Sabine was too startled to do anything but obey.

She looked back to see her mother, in nothing but a brassiere and panties, irrationally putting on lipstick as she watched herself in the mirror.

What was wrong? What had happened—to her mother, to her father? Sabine raced down the corridor. She caught sight of her father in the hotel lobby and called to him, but he did not hear her, or did not answer. He rushed out into the blazing street, Sabine following him. He started to walk toward Mizener's office—perhaps Max was there. He began to run. On the way he stopped to ask where Max was, He could be anywhere. Everyone, it seemed, had seen Max but no one had seen him recently. Jacob raced through the streets, his mind closed to everything except revenge. A kind of excitement drove him on.

Sabine was out of breath. Her legs ached. She called again but Jacob did not answer. The crimson of the bougainvillea, the dark green leaves, the orange stripes on the awnings, the pink garden walls, the white hats and white suits, the black canes, the blue sky—all these colors swirled in front of her. She had to stop, dizzy from the colors and the sun. She watched her father enter a dry good store. What did he want there? She followed him. Inside the store, it was cool and much darker. She was blinded momentarily. Then she heard a cry. It sounded like someone she knew, and the sound filled her with terror. She had never heard such pain before. She cried out, "Papa!" Instinctively, she knew it was Jacob, and she knew something was terribly wrong. She had no idea whether he saw her, whether he turned and looked, or spoke a word, because suddenly there was another cry and she could see a crowd of people forming. She could no longer see her father, but she knew he had fallen. It seemed to take forever to push her way through the crowd. They paid no attention to her, and she began to pummel them with her fists, fighting them, screaming. And then she saw her father, down on the floor, eyes closed and mouth open, but he was not gasping for breath. And he was not really her father. His face was all slack, gone away from her, wrenched away from her in a few seconds' time. There was this body lying there, with her father's hair and his mustache, but the color was different and his mouth had never lain open like that, slack, like a drunk's, like a stranger's. It could not be true, this was not happening. She touched him, she was down on her knees and the wooden floor scratched her knees, she was touching his shirt, she didn't dare touch his face. She was saying over and over "Papa, Papa," but he didn't answer, he didn't move. He didn't breathe. She had no idea of death, she had no idea of the finality of it, until this moment. He was gone. He would never return. He would never smile, never sing, never laugh, never hold her again as long as she lived. She would hold him now, that was what she was doing. She was holding him as though she might protect him, but he was beyond protection. His head cradled in her lap, she switched positions, vaguely aware of all the legs, trousers, skirts, and silk stockings that ringed them.

"He's dead," someone said, and then was shushed by someone else.

"No, but she must know. Get a doctor." She heard someone say that. Later she saw the man close to her, kneel beside
her, take her hand, and lift it away from her father; he was
very calculatedly trying to take one of her hands and then the
other away from her father. She clutched at her father's
sleeve. The man's hand insisted. She lost her grip. The man's
voice talked all the time, although she had no understanding
of what he was saying.

"What's your name, little girl?" the man was asking, and
Sabine suddenly panicked.

"Are you here to help my father?" she asked. "Are you a
doctor?"

"Yes," the man said, but only to the second question.
"What is your name?"

"Bertha," she lied. It was simpler. She gave all the information she could: the name of the hotel, the room number.

That was a mistake. She had given them too much information. They were separating her from her father now.
"No," she screamed. "No, leave me alone!" But they were
lifting her up. She kicked, she flailed her arms, she twisted
around. She could see them picking her father up then, oh, it
was the worst sight she had ever seen, and she never forgot it.
His head flopped back and hit the floor, his arms were life-
less, hanging down with no strength to them. The men were
picking up a body and carting it away.

"Let me stay with him," she screamed. "Please, don't take
him away. Please!" Crack! The sound of his skull hitting the
floor, she could still hear it.

"Take her home," someone whispered. "She doesn't have
to see this."

"I ain't got that kind of money," someone else protested.
"That's a *taxi* ride."

Somebody did take her home. She remembered riding in a
taxi and seeing all the bright colors from the window,
remembered seeing her mother, but why was her mother in
the lobby? Bertha was biting her lips and clutching her purse
as though she knew, and when she saw Sabine in the custody
of some stranger, she let out a little cry, just enough for the
man at the desk to look up from his work, for other guests to
turn around, not startled, merely curious. Then Bertha sank

down on the little seat, and took Sabine's hand. Bertha's hand was ice.

"Where is he?" she whispered to the stranger, and the stranger must have told her, for Bertha was out the door, leaving Sabine alone on the little seat. Sabine sat there for some time, until the desk clerk noticed her and asked if she would like to go to her room. She nodded yes, and the desk clerk took a key and led her to the suite, unlocked the door for her, and handed over the key.

Sabine shut the door and entered her parents' room. Her father's bathrobe was still on the floor where he had let it drop that morning. A wet towel was on the floor of the bathroom, from when he had taken a shower. The breakfast dishes were still on the table. The maid had not yet come. All of her father's life was now contained in this room. Some change on the dresser. Some notes he had written himself. The pencil, the one with the amethyst top in place of an eraser, lay on the bed.

Suddenly she vomited all over her new dress. There was a knock on the door, but Sabine couldn't raise herself up to answer it. She heard the sound of the key in the lock, and looked up to see the maid, who rushed the child into the bathroom, clucking over her and soothing her. Then the dress was off, and a cool washcloth covered Sabine's face. The maid put Sabine to bed, drew the blinds, cleaned up the room, and went out, leaving the door open. As she cleaned the rest of the rooms on that floor, she would return every once in a while, poking her head in the door to say a few words to the little girl.

When Bertha returned it was five o'clock, and Mizener was with her. They were discussing funeral arrangements. Mizener talking matter-of-factly and her mother nodding listlessly. Max Abramowitz was nowhere in evidence.

Jacob was buried the next day by a rabbi who knew nothing at all about him. The funeral expenses were paid by Mizener. Furtively, the rabbi asked Mizener what sort of man Jacob had been. It was the only time Sabine saw her mother release her fury.

"Don't ask him. Ask the wife. Ask the wife about the man. He was a lover!" Bertha screamed. The young rabbi, who was wearing light blue socks, with his black shoes, was startled by Bertha's intensity. He found it understandable only later, when he was told that they were not religious people, they were bohemians. Agnostics. Hardly Jews at all.

A week later Bertha and Sabine took the train back to New York. This time there was no compartment: they traveled by coach. Florida seemed like a dream to Sabine. For a time she had spent her life dining off fine china, wiping her mouth on soft linen, going to sleep in a bed as big as a room, bathing in the blue Atlantic. She had lived like the rich, and suddenly it had all been taken away. She was never going to forget that. She was never going to forget the crack of her father's skull on the wood floor, the sudden realization of death. She was never going to forget the lemon color of the bedside lamp with the Tiffany shade when she had been alone in a sumptuous suite of hotel rooms, rooms that no longer had any traces of her father.

She felt abandoned. She knew where her mother's love lay. It lay buried.

She was never going to forget that.

Chapter Four

What was Jacob's legacy to Sabine? Four things.

If you can't sell silk, sell linen.

You want to bet?

What will happen? Who knows?

And the knowledge, learned too soon in life, that warmth and love and protection can be snatched away in the time it takes for a body to sink to the floor.

Bertha and Sabine moved back to Rivington Street. It was Bertha's luck that as they were moving down in the world, Max's father and mother were moving up—and out.

"Seven rooms on Riverside Drive with a mag-nif-i-cent view," was how Rachel Abramowitz described it, careful to draw out the syllables now that she had discovered culture, and with it, the capacity for charity.

"You'll get over it," she told Bertha, who was inheriting the old Abramowitz apartment as well as total ownership of the candy store—in the Abramowitz mind, that settled all debts. "It takes time, but you'll get over Jacob's passing." (It had taken Rachel perhaps five minutes to get over it.)

Bertha, however, would not allow the name of Max Abramowitz to be mentioned in her presence. Max sent money and she sent it back. He wrote two letters. She tore them up. She would not talk about Glenrocks. That part of her life was finished. Over. The memory was too painful for her.

She lived in a silent fury, doing what she had to and leaving it at that. She took care of her daughter, ironed her daughters' dresses, washed her daughter's clothes, brushed her daughter's hair, cooked her daughter's meals, and gave nothing of herself, nothing more than a faint smile to hide the anger.

Sabine grew used to it. One day she fell in the street and cut her knee. Not a bad cut—a child's cut. Bertha washed it and put on some antiseptic and a bandage, all without saying a word. She never touched her daughter except to apply the bandage to the knee. Never put an arm around the little girl's shoulder, never gave it a pat. The next time Sabine received a cut she put on the bandage herself, and saved her mother the bother.

They each sought an escape from the world of narrow crowded streets, brick tenements, fire escapes, pushcarts, and the smell of stale cabbage.

Sabine read.

In school, she read about the War of the Roses, the population and topography of Italy, the boundaries of Poland. On the way to school, going down the stairs in the morning, the fragrance of roses in Jane Austen's well-ordered gardens banished the stink of garbage. At night she read—thank God for the free library—romances, Tom Sawyer floating down the Mississippi, Fenimore Cooper, Ernest Hemingway, and Scott Fitzgerald.

And when she worked in the candy store, counting change, ringing up the register, she read the newspapers. Bertha sold the *World*, the *News*, the *Mirror*, the *Times*. New York was bursting with the Jazz Age, and on Rivington Street Sabine lost herself in the pictures of flappers and bootleggers, oil scandals, women with bobbed hair, sensational murders, demonstrations of the Charleston.

Bertha's escape was the movies.

She let Sabine accompany her to the movie palaces. Their lobbies were four stories high (much like those in Mizener's houses) and they were built in the form of Egyptian temples, Spanish patios, or Oriental mansions. There were palm trees in great jugs, filled with sand in which patrons extinguished cigarettes. And there were great staircases, built for royalty, that led to the magic darkness where an entertainment had been prepared especially for Bertha and Sabine. There in the dark. Up on the screen.

Of course not all theater houses were palaces. The neighborhood theaters were dreary, except for the row of bulbs lighting up the marquee. But it didn't matter, because the life up there on the screen was the only thing that either mother or daughter wanted to know about.

The characters were so much larger than life, their problems so remote, that Bertha could weep at their dilemmas while remaining dry-eyed at her own. Bertha did not choose comedies. Harold Lloyd hung from ledges without her. Her taste ran to movies like *Alimony*: "Brilliant men, beautiful jazz babies, champagne baths, midnight revels, petting parties in the purple dawn, all ending in one terrific smashing climax that makes you gasp . . ."

Sabine found herself staring at Fatal Temptresses while she learned a new vocabulary mostly gleaned from gazing at the tear sheets in front of the movie houses. At home, in front of her mirror, Sabine panted. Sneered. Snarled. Smoldered. Disdained. Quivered. Invited. And waited to grow up.

Night after night, mother and daughter stumbled home through the darkened streets of the Lower East Side, holding onto the glamorous illusions in order to shut out the prospect of the silent Jacob-less rooms waiting for them on Rivington Street.

Sabine's education came, so to speak, second-hand. Love she learned from the films; the rest she gathered from reading women's magazines, pondering the discreet advertisements that described "difficult days." By the time the stock market crashed in 1929, Sabine knew all about *that* time of the month, and what to do for menstrual cramps. Black Tuesday passed and financiers leaped from office windows; Sabine couldn't be bothered. She was waiting for something more important. It finally happened one day in December. She was upstairs in the bathroom. She noticed a spot of pink on the toilet paper. The tiniest spot in the world. She treasured it. She could not believe it. A miracle. She ran with the piece of toilet paper, a banner, a flag. In her excitement she forgot whom she was showing it to. Bertha was downstairs behind the counter in the candy store.

"Look! Look! It's here! It happened!" Sabine thrust forward the piece of toilet paper.

"What are you showing me?"

"Blood. I just had my period."

"Don't be silly. Not yet. You're only—" Bertha had not reckoned the years. "You're thirteen," she said, surprised.

"It's blood, I know it is." It was hard to convince Bertha, but then again it didn't matter to Bertha. If Sabine really had her period, so be it. If she didn't, it made no difference either.

But Sabine was not to be denied her moment. Mrs. Rosen entered the store.

"Look, guess what this is!" Sabine exclaimed.

"What?" Mrs. Rosen peered at the piece of paper.

"It's blood."

"What's blood?"

"That little spot. See, there."

"That's blood?" Mrs. Rosen was dubious.

"That's blood."

"From what, a mosquito?"

"I got my period. I am a woman."

"Wonderful." Mrs. Rosen smiled, then took her hand and smacked Sabine across the face. "Welcome."

That was what Sabine needed, a little recognition. As Mrs. Rosen explained, the slap was a nice Jewish custom, woman to woman. "It's what my mother did to me. I'll remember it to the day I die. Okay, you're a woman now. *Mazel tov.* Bertha, gimme two packs of Raleigh cigarettes."

Soon after Sabine became a woman, Bertha took her to the Yiddish Theater on Second Avenue. Why did they go? Was it that Bertha sensed the possibility of comradeship? Was it some sort of celebration?

"Remember what you see. Soon this will all be over," Bertha advised as they walked into the shabby lobby, whose posters promised much gaiety. Sabine looked around. What would be over? There was dust everywhere. Colors had faded. The ushers wore no uniforms. The Yiddish Theater was no Loew's. She waited for the play to begin. The lights were dimmed, the curtain rose.

Sabine had never seen live actors. Or stage lights, props, sets. What had she expected? Something akin to the lavishness displayed in the movies. Opulent sets. Glamorous gowns. Insouciance. (Another word in her secret steamy vocabulary. It was a word that went with cigarette holders and lounging in satin wrappers.) She expected that world. She didn't expect what she saw. And she didn't understand it.

They were speaking Yiddish on the stage and she couldn't understand. All around her in the streets she had heard Yiddish; she knew the different dialects, her ear could tell the difference even though her mother and father had never spoken it. It was a language for other people. Now, in the theater, hearing it on stage, she was so annoyed she shut her ears, keeping only her eyes focused.

The patriarch had a white beard and a powerful, resonant voice. His speeches were the longest. He had two daughters. One was independent and lived away from home. The heroine was the younger daughter, who was poor and lived with her father. The young women—weren't. They were middle-aged, fat, their thighs brushing together when they walked. Their makeup was heavy, but not in a sexy way like Pola Negri's or Gloria Swanson's. And they sweated. Sabine could see the creases in their cheeks above their mouths where the powder was encrusted. The hero tended toward curly-haired melancholy. All the men in the play were poets, artists, or writers. Sabine got no sense of story, but from her experience with silent films she recognized a love triangle when she saw one.

"*Haisse, haisse Liebe!*" hissed the younger sister, thumping her breast. "*A feuer brennt!*"

"What's she saying?" Sabine asked.

"A fire's burning," Bertha whispered, caught up in the plot.

"A fire? Where?" Sabine was confused.

"In her heart, in her loins," Bertha translated.

Loins was a word Sabine immediately added to her secret vocabulary.

Following the performance, Bertha took Sabine to the Café Royal, where the tea was a long time in coming, and when it came, it came in a glass. Sabine burned her lips.

"That wasn't the best play," Bertha said defensively. "Still, it was a live play, yes?"

"Why did you bring me here? It's dirty," Sabine said.

"We brought you here when you were a baby. I remember, we said, ah no, we will not let a baby spoil our fun, there is no need to stay home every night, so we brought you with us. They loved you. You were so good, you never cried. We gave you sugar."

Sabine cast an eye on the crowded little tables, the not quite clean linen, the smoke, and the window to the outside, which reflected them all and needed washing. What had the attraction been?

"The play was silly," Sabine said, not drinking the tea. She was uncomfortable with her mother's memories.

"We won't come here again," Bertha said, rising to pay the

check. "We used to come here because it reminded us of Paris. I don't know why. It's not at all like Paris. My God, only ten years ago when we came here. And Paris, no more than fifteen. That was another life."

Bertha left a twenty-five-cent tip to old memories.

Hard times hit the rest of the country, but Bertha had already been there.

New York had changed. It was no longer the golden city; it had gone gray. There were still stylish fashions in the Fifth Avenue shop windows, but one never saw those clothes on people. Life on the dole had replaced the streets of gold.

Bertha became familiar with the installment plan. The problem was that everything went to pieces at once: the mattress that had come with the apartment, the kitchen chair that splintered and needed replacing, cups and saucers that had cracked from exhaustion, dresses that split at the seams from age and, when mended, disintegrated again in defiance. So Berthat bought on the installment plan. And owned nothing.

Except for two things. The china that came from the five-and-dime (the five-and-dime only accepted cash, and so the china was Bertha's), and Sabine's clothes, which came from the pushcarts on Hester Street. Sabine taunted Bertha by growing, and Bertha pawed over the pushcarts, grimly holding up garments to examine the fit. Sabine stood silent and blushing and wishing she were dead.

Bertha had a recurring dream of being dispossessed. Not so far-fetched, since it was happening all around her every day. Her dream was always the same. Always men would knock at the door, and she, although knowing who they were and what they wanted, always opened the door. The men shoved her aside and headed for the clothes closet, stripping the garments from the hangers while Bertha pleaded with them, down on her hands and knees. She would snatch at the clothes, and they would tear (how will I ever get them mended, she wondered in her dream). Then the men dumped the contents of all the drawers on the floor. And then they saw Sabine, and in the dream Sabine was always very young and helpless. Suddenly, Bertha understood. It was Sabine they were after. And took. Bertha would run after the men, but would get tangled in the mess of belongings littering the floor, and Sabine would disappear in their arms forever.

Oddly enough, Bertha related the dream to her daughter.

"Why am I always being taken away?" Sabine asked.

"God only knows," was her mother's answer. Bertha was a free thinker who evidently believed in God but had no good words for him.

So when she visited the men from the bank, Bertha was not surprised. In her mind, she had known they would come; after all, it was part of her dream. The men from the bank had papers, papers that Jacob and Max had signed. She looked at their signatures, the precise writing of Max, the more flamboyant scrawl of Jacob, and felt a twinge of anger. *Jacob, why are you letting this happen to me, why aren't you protecting me?* But there was no answer from the dried ink on the white paper. So she went ahead and signed at the bottom, and the candy store was turned over to the bank. She learned a new word: *foreclosure*. She had learned the word mortgage from Jacob. But "foreclosure" was new. She learned it the hard way.

After she lost the candy store, Bertha could not keep up with the bills. She was always three months behind, trying to juggle accounts, paying one to keep another away.

That was the winter of 1930. Just as winter was turning into a cold resentful spring, something happened.

It was a Saturday morning, and because it was cold Bertha was making soup. Sabine was wearing a nightgown and a sweater over it, and was standing by the living room window looking out at nothing at all when she saw a moving van pull up to the curb. Men wearing mackinaws against the cold jumped out, their collars pulled up so that it was impossible to distinguish faces. Their caps were pulled down over their ears. It reminded Sabine of her mother's dream, the dream of being dispossessed. Sabine watched the men enter the building. She heard the tread of feet on the staircase, then a knock on their door.

"Don't answer it," Sabine said to her mother. Bertha flew into a panic. The banging on the door continued, and the rough voices of the men could be heard, and Bertha knew, as she had known in her dream, that she must answer the door. Three men stood there, brawny, filling the door; once inside, they seemed to fill the apartment. One started for the kitchen.

"No," Bertha shouted, blocking the way. Had she not re-hearsed this many times in her dreams?

"We don't want no trouble," the first man warned.

"Go away from us. Get out! Get out!" Bertha kept re-peating.

"Sorry, lady." The man brushed her aside and going into the kitchen, started to collect the china.

"The china is mine!" Bertha screamed. "Nobody owns the china but me!" (Why would she want to cling to the china when she would have no table to place it on? No room for the table? No place at all in this world?)

The second man tried reason. "If it wasn't us, it would be somebody else," he said.

"Then let it be somebody else! Shame! You would be ashamed. Suppose it was your family? Suppose it was your wife?"

"If we didn't have this job, it *would* be us," the first man said.

Sabine had been watching, paralyzed at first, not believing. She watched the third man head silently for the closets. Dresses and coats came out, draped on his arm—her father's suit, the one suit her mother had saved. She thought of her father. What would he do if he were her? She knew the an-swer immediately. Improvise. He would made a scene. One evening at the Yiddish Theater had been enough. Sabine made great dramatic gestures with her arms.

"Stop!" she cried. "That's my father's suit. My father! You are taking away my father's suit. You cannot take that away. My father is dead!" Out of the corner of her eye, she gauged the reaction. The men stopped, stunned. Bertha was standing stock-still by the stove.

"Hit, Mama, hit!" Sabine urged. "Don't let them do this."

Bertha picked up a frying pan. "The china is mine!" That was all she knew, as she flailed with the frying pan. "The china is mine!" She hit away, and the heavy pan landed on an arm.

"Lady! Lady!" the first man protested. Sabine aimed for the third man's shin and connected. He yowled in pain, dropped the clothes, and grabbed her by the arm.

"No kid kicks me!" he roared.

"Sez who, buster," Sabine retorted, wondering what movie she had heard that in.

"Hands off!" Bertha commanded. "Don't touch my daughter!"

"She kicked me! Nobody kicks me!" the man protested.

"Hit, Mama, hit!" Sabine repeated, and Bertha advanced. The two of them were united in manic fury. What a release it was for Bertha—it gave her strength. *This is for Jacob,* she thought as she swung the pan once, *and this is for Sabine, and this is for me.* Then she threw the frying pan, and it bounced off the wall and clattered to the floor.

Suddenly a fourth man was standing in the open doorway, papers in hand. "What in the hell is going on here?"

"Get them out!" Sabine cried. "They want to take my father's suit. My father is dead! Hit, Mama, hit!"

"We are honest people!" Bertha was yelling. "We pay our debts. Maybe we are a few days behind, but we pay our debts. We are not bums!" Sabine cocked her fist, remembering Matt's schoolyard advice. She was ready, for action.

"Wait a minute, wait a minute," the man said, but Bertha was not to be stopped.

"A few days, two days . . . *Monday,* everything will be paid," Bertha promised. The fourth man ignored her and addressed the others.

"What are you doing on this floor?"

They looked at him in confusion.

"You got the wrong apartment," the man continued. "These ain't the people, it's the people below. Come on, get outta here!" And he herded the men out the door, they were gone as quickly as they had come.

Clothes were strewn around the room. Sabine thought they should have been forced to put everything back in place, but Bertha didn't care. She locked the door, picked up the frying pan, and went to sit down at the kitchen table, thanking God she had a table to sit down to. She and Sabine looked at each other, and burst into hysterical laughter.

"A mistake!" Bertha cried. "A mistake. That's all that kept us off the street. The men made a mistake."

"Hit, Mama, hit!" Sabine repeated.

" 'This is my father's suit,' Where did you learn that? And kicking him—where did you learn all that?"

"I don't know. Where did you learn to use a frying pan?"

The tears of laughter were flowing down their cheeks. "Hit, Mama, hit!" Bertha kept saying, as though it were the most wonderful thing that had ever been said. "I didn't know you had it in you."

"I didn't know it, either."

Suddenly sober, Bertha asked a question, no longer mother to daughter.

"What do we do now?"

"Who knows?" her daughter answered, an exact copy of Jacob. Even the grin was the same. "But it won't happen to us. You'll get a better job. And *I'll* get a job."

"You? What would you do?" Bertha laughed.

"Who knows?" Sabine repeated, this time conscious of imitating her father. "If you can't sell silk, sell linen. Right?"

It was silly, Bertha knew, to put trust in a teen-age girl, but somehow, when she looked at Sabine, she had the feeling things would turn out all right.

Bertha found full-time work through the kindness of a former candy store customer. She became a finisher for the Schneiderman shop, and so spent sixteen hours a day snipping loose threads from women's rayon panties. She worked five days a week and earned fifteen dollars; the subway ride cost her ten cents a day, so she actually cleared fourteen-fifty a week.

That left enough money for them to go to the movies twice a week—once on Saturday and once on Wednesday, when the theaters either gave away dishes or held amateur hours. One of these amateur nights was broadcast over the radio. It was called *Tune in Tonight*, which became a magical catch phrase to those on the Lower Easr Side who dreamed of being whisked off to Hollywood for screen tests. Amateur night was just the first step toward a parade of limousines and silver foxes and sequin gowns, of iced champagne and butlers who discreetly served supper for two before leaving the lovers alone in the penthouse—in short, toward the life they were viewing up on the screen.

For this, crooners and tap dancers and would-be and once-were comedians came out on stage for a desperate two minutes in the spotlight, and then walked off to anonymity again.

"You could do better," Bertha commented. Sabine didn't want to. She was waiting for the feature.

Bertha came home from the shop one day and mentioned that there had been a meeting about organizing a union.

"What happened?" Sabine said. "Are you all right?"

Bertha shrugged. "Of course I'm all right. A man came in and talked. He said we were being exploited. Maybe we are. I'd like to get more money for what I do." She said this wistfully, but with no real hope. "Then there was more talk. Then the man—his name is Simon—said he would talk to the boss, and they went in and closed the door and we went home."

That was the first time Sabine heard about Simon Davidson.

A few weeks later, Bertha came home to announce that she was now a member of Local 62 of the International Ladies' Garment Workers' Union and that she would be working only thirty-five hours a week and would be paid twenty dollars. And it would cost her thirty-five cents a week to belong to the union.

"Congratulations, Mama," Sabine said (she was just beginning to read *Generation in Chains*). "You stood up for yourself."

Bertha shrugged again. "Not me. It was Simon. Simon did it all."

Sabine continued to hear about Simon. The workers had been organized, but Simon still appeared in Bertha's conversation. He liked classical music. He particularly like Mozart. He liked string quartets more than anything. He liked the theater. He felt that David Dubinsky could push harder for social change.

"Who's David Dubinsky?" Sabine asked.

"It's his union, the ILGWU," Bertha answered.

"It's *your* union," Sabine corrected her.

"Well, he's the president. He's from Brest Litovsk."

"So what does that make him?"

"That makes him all right."

"Where is Simon from?"

Bertha blushed. "I never asked him."

Later, she announced, "Simon likes tennis."

"Where does he get to play tennis?" Sabine asked her.

Bertha was vague. "I don't know. He goes away on vacations. With his son, who is around your age."

"Is he married?"

"Was, was married. She died. She taught English in public school. Think of it. An English teacher."

"What does he look like?"

"You'll see. We thought next Saturday we would take you to the theater."

"Oh," Sabine said, and was annoyed that her mother was happy and even more annoyed that a man was making her happy. She was prepared to detest Simon Davidson. When she met him, she didn't.

Simon possessed such vitality; she hadn't expected that. She hadn't expected him to be short, either, but he was. It made no difference. He was stocky, wth heavy muscles, a long nose, a craggy face, and tight curly hair that was already turning gray. He smiled a lot and smoked a lot, one cigarette after another, and when he talked he made gestures. Anything could get him excited: the labor movement, the socialist experiment in Russia, Eugene O'Neill, Mozart, a good joke, a new restaurant. The Depression's grayness never touched him. He was aware of the poverty and the despair without ever giving in to it. Simon had plans. Simon had dreams. He was a little to the left of Dubinsky, he admitted. He was concerned because most of the unions in the American Federation of Labor were strictly segregated. He did not support the United Mine Workers, for instance. His friends were in the Trade Union Unity League, which was concentrating on organizing black coal miners.

He had told Sabine all this, and they hadn't gotten past the pasta in the basement Italian restaurant on Thompson Street. She liked the fact that he didn't talk to her, or look at her, as though she were a child. And he offered her wine. Which she accepted.

"Are you interested in the labor movement?" he asked her, and right after that, "Are you interested in the theater? What interests you?"

Sabine had never given it much thought. What was she interested in? In getting out of Rivington Street. But she couldn't tell him that.

They finished their meal. Sabine noticed that Simon was always touching. Either touching his own arm, or rubbing Bertha's hand, fondling her fingers. His hands were strong and broad and aggressive, while Bertha's seemed limp and passive. She no longer wore the wedding ring Jacob had given her. Throughout the meal she remained silent, letting Simon talk and letting him charm Sabine.

"When do I meet your son?" Sabine asked as Simon helped her put her coat on.

"He's going to join us following the performance. There's something extra tonight. Chamber music to benefit the Worker's Alliance Theater."

The play was about unionizing the black dock workers of the South.

There was a great deal of shouting. Explosive anger was the dominant emotion. Sabine remained bewildered. The shouting reminded her of her other theater experience, which had been Yiddish. This might as well have been.

During the applause and bravos that greeted the end of the play, Simon's son slipped into the seat next to them.

"This is Jerry," Simon said. Jerry held out a hand and Sabine took it. She looked at him carefully. He was dark, extremely thin, and handsome. Jerry's hair was short and very black. His eyes were black, the lashes so long they should have been a woman's. He already had a growth of beard. He shaved. She noticed this in the time it took for them to shake hands. He didn't smile.

"Did you like the play?" Jerry asked.

"It's important, very important. Powerful," Simon said.

"It's good to have vital theater," Bertha added.

"Jerry is very talented. He can do anything," Simon told Sabine. "He's going to be a great actor."

"Were you in the play?" Sabine asked Jerry. She hadn't noticed him.

"No. I'm an apprentice. I handle the props. I make sure everybody's got the right hook or the right barrel. It's a great job."

"Are you learning anything?"

"Yes, I'm learning about exploitation."

"You should hear Jerry play the piano," Simon went on. "He could be a great pianist."

"Oh," Sabine said, and because she couldn't think of anything else, asked, "Do you like Mozart?"

"*Haaaate* Mozart." Jerry wrinkled up his nose. "He's got two tunes. One major. One minor "

"Don't talk like an imbecile," His father said sharply.

Jerry seemed pleased. "Oh, I'm sorry. Mozart is an *important* composer."

The lights dimmed again for the chamber music. The string quartet entered, three gentlemen in tails and a lady in a long green evening gown. They smiled graciously and settled themselves to tune up. It was hot under the lights and the first violinist, who was almost totally bald, attracted flies. One buzzed around him and landed on his head. He brushed away the fly, then put down his bow and mopped his brow with a handkerchief. The moment he picked up the bow again, the fly made another landing. Down went the bow. Up went the handkerchief. It became a ritual. Lay down the bow. Swat the fly. Mop the brow. Pick up the bow . . . Jerry started to shake with silent laughter. Sabine glanced at him. They did not dare look each other in the eye.

Her eye caught the cellist, who was adjusting her instrument. The woman suddenly spread her legs and her knees shot out. The effect was alarming. Then she placed the cello between her legs and squeezed her knees together.

Sabine giggled.

The musicians looked up, bothered at the disturbance.

"Ssh," Simon warned them.

The musicians had raised their bows, waiting for a nod from the first violinist, when the fly again attacked. Down went the bow. *Slap!* That was too much for Jerry. He let out a laugh. The lady cellist flung out her knees in nervousness. Sabine tried to turn her giggle into a cough, a gasp, a moan of the wounded, but it remained irreverent laughter.

Jerry grabbed her hand and the two of them ran into the street, letting out the laughter. "C'mon," he said, steering her to the restaurant a few doors away. "I'll buy you a cup of coffee."

They sat in a booth.

"You were the worst," he told her.

"*You* started it," she retorted.

"Yes, but you were the worst. My father will never forgive either one of us," he said happily, and then, without pausing, "What do you think of them, my father and your mother?"

"I try not to think about them," she said.

"Why?"

"I don't know. It makes me uncomfortable."

"Women love my father," Jerry said.

"Well, he's very attractive."

"Do you think they go to bed together?"

She didn't know what to answer.

"I mean, do you think they *fuck?*"

She looked at him. He had lit a cigarette and his eyes challenged hers.

"Why don't you answer me?" he kept on.

"Why are you so angry?" she wanted to know.

"My mother killed herself," he said. "She killed herself because he was fucking around. You know what that means, don't you? Well, that's what he was doing. Anybody he could get. And my mother Rose, that was her name, used to lie in bed all day when we went on vacations and read Emily Dickinson. We would go to the mountains and she would never leave the cabin and my father went out looking for what he could get. My mother heard about it, everybody was talking about it, but she never said a word and then one night she swallowed pills and that was it. I was in the next room and never heard anything until my father found her. He came in around dawn and found her."

He took a long drag on the cigarette.

"My father went into deep mourning. Two days later he was playing Mozart on the phonograph." Jerry extinguished the cigarette. "So much for him."

When Bertha and Simon joined them, Simon now cold and disapproving, Jerry and Sabine had already become allies.

It happened all at once. She became beautiful. It was the year Roosevelt was elected, and suddenly the neck that had been too long and scrawny was graceful and aristocratic, the unruly jet black hair lustrous, and the eyes that had been too big for the face, turned large and luminous and the most remarkable color, sapphire.

She had become a leggy girl, and not large in the hips. She took long strides when she walked through the streets, and tailors, pushcart men, street-corner Lotharios, and old men in black, all panted after her. She walked with such speed in order to escape them. All she wanted from Rivington Street was *out*. She tried to close her eyes to everything. Which was how she bumped into Bernie.

"Hey, look where you're going," Bernie Rosen said automatically, and then, taking a second look. "Holy shit!"

He didn't recognize her. But she recognized him.

"Bernie! You're back in town."

"Yeah," he said cautiously. "Do I know you?"

"I'm Sabine," she said. "From Glenrocks."

"Holy shit!" he repeated, and then his attitude changed. His years of bumming around in vaudeville had not been a total loss. He had learned a lot about women—all that he felt he needed to know. Conquest was the game. Fast worker was his name. What he had learned fast in Schenectady and Shreveport, he had practiced in Pawtucket and Providence, in rooming houses, backstage, in basements, on corners. Women mistook his energy for sexuality. Actually, he didn't like women very much. Split-weeks in vaudeville had been perfect for Bernie Rosen. But now he was down and out in New York, with no prospects. Except for that very moment.

"Can I buy you a cup of coffee?" he asked. It was his automatic beginning. He smiled and gave her a look. She liked it and resented it at the same time. He always took a lot for granted. Bernie was fairly short but well put together and had that dash about him.

She agreed to a cup of coffee, and he took her arm with one hand and put his other in his pants pocket. One dime.

"How about this?" he said. "How about you buying *me* a cup of coffee?"

So she did. And told him about Jerry and the Worker's Alliance Theater.

"Is it progressive?" he asked. The word was in fashion.

"Yes," she said.

"And is there any money in it?"

"No, but they all live together and there's food."

Bernie was living with his mother at the moment, and that cramped his style. Communal living and food sounded good to him. There would be girls. There would be opportunities. He had a background in theater (Pawtucket and Providence). The rest he could improvise. After all, he thought to himself, everyone is full of shit.

"I'd like to meet them."

"I was on my way there when I bumped into you," Sabine said.

"You got money for a pack of cigarettes?" Bernie asked. She gave him a quarter and he bought a pack and kept the change and sat down in the booth—beside her now, not opposite her. She had watched him as he walked away. He tended to strut. The crease in his pants was neat. When he returned, she noticed he had taken off his tie. He looked more like a member of the proletariat.

"I know what you were thinking," he said as he sat down. "You were thinking what I would be like in bed. Want to try?"

"No, that wasn't what I was thinking." She blushed.

"Come on, that's what everybody thinks when they meet. What's he like in the sack? What's she like? It's normal."

His thigh was close to hers. She was very aware of it. They were in the back booth of the restaurant.

"Any guy ever kiss you?" he asked.

"No," she said.

"How come?"

"It never came up."

He laughed. "It never came up, huh?"

He kissed her then, deftly and professionally, and when she didn't know what to do with her lips, he opened them with his tongue, and she thought she might suffocate. And then he put her hand to his crotch.

"I'm crazy about you," he whispered into her ear. She felt something hard and stiff. He put his hand on her and rubbed.

"Bernie, I don't want to," she said, trying to free her hand.

"How do you know if you never have?" he countered.

"I know, that's all." It wasn't true. But this was not right with Bernie. Something told her instinctively: Bernie was not it.

"Are you afraid?" He was still smiling and pressing his body up to hers in the booth. His hand was stroking her thigh. "Don't that feel nice?"

It did. But she didn't want this.

"Bernie, *No.* Stop it!" she said. Her voice was louder than she had anticipated, and people turned to look at them.

Bernie shrugged and withdrew his hand.

"Okay, but will you still introduce me to your group?"

Bernard got into the Worker's Alliance Theater much more easily. In two days he had moved into the large loft off Fourteenth Street that the whole company used as sleeping quarters, meeting place, kitchen, cell unit, and home. Often also as rehearsal space. The group was hoping to get funds from the Federal Theater Project. In the meantime they lived on air and hope, and frankfurters and beans. There was no furniture to speak of. Three mattresses in the main room, chipped plates on a three-legged table in the kitchen.

Bernard found a mattress and a girl to go with it. In three weeks he caused dissension; at the end of two months there was a split, and Bernard became director of the People's Alliance Theater, which quickly became the People's Theater Alliance, cleverly taking advantage of the confusion in names with the more famous Worker's Alliance Theater.

It was Jerry who told Sabine about this. She did not see Bernie Rosen again. He had repelled her and aroused her and she became aware of the sensuality that surrounded her. He had disturbed her too much.

"Jerry," she asked one night, "have you ever kissed anyone?"

"Of course," he said, but he was lying.

"Then you understand all about these things. Kiss me."

"Why?"

"Why not?"

"All right." He sighed and reached out his hand catching Sabine around the back of her neck.

"Ow," she said.

"Sorry," he said. They came closer together; he could feel her breath on his cheek. He brought his lips to hers and pressed them there. They waited for a minute, lips tightly pressed together, and then drew apart.

"That's it?" Sabine asked, disappointed.

"That's all there is to it." Jerry felt relieved. He had no desire to kiss Sabine again. As a matter of fact, it felt foolish, uncomfortable.

Sabine preferred her fantasies.

She began *Anna Karenina* and found herself living another woman's life. Vronsky had her father's mustache, but the Lower East Side no longer existed. St. Petersburg, sleighs, and dachas presented themselves.

And she realized that she was as furious with life as her mother had been. She was denying her own life. What had she to think about? Not the present. The past.

A few things stood out in her mind: times when she had been alive. There had been the little girl, dancing among butterflies while the music of the concertina floated in the background, snowbound in a blizzard listening to the tales of her parents. Glenrocks. There had been the girl in her father's arms, dancing to society music in a hotel ballroom in Florida. She could remember the look of the place, the sound of the music, the feel of her father's arms, but Kitty and Levin were there, and Count Vronsky.

Her mind turned to Glenrocks, and that made her even angrier. That had been a wonderful life. (Conveniently forgotten were the first days of school, the schoolyard battles, the antagonism and loneliness.) Glenrocks had been people and fun and music and her father. And Matt Ryan.

The anger focused on her mother. She was stuck in a tenement existence because her mother had been too hurt and was now too proud to go back to Glenrocks. Resentment swelled inside Sabine.

She avoided Bertha. And painted her nails a defiant fire-engine red.

It was a very cold Saturday and the snow had stopped. Sabine was on Second Avenue, Anna Karenina longing for Vronsky, when Sabine heard someone call her name. Still in snowy St. Petersburg, she looked up. A brawny young man approached.

"Well, is it you or isn't it you?" he was asking. "There're not too many Sabines in this world, after all."

He looked familiar.

"It's Matt Ryan," he said. "Are you going to say you don't remember me?"

Vronsky fled; St. Petersburg melted. Sabine remembered Matt very well, but not this way. There was no more boy to him. He was a man now. The color, the copper red glow of him was the same, but he had grown taller and more robust. The grin on his face was like a bear hug. He took her by the shoulders.

"Well, look at you. Jesus Christ, I mean, *look* at you!"

"What are you doing here?"

He laughed. "Aren't you glad to see me?"

"Yes. Of course. Yes."

"Okay, then I'll tell you what I'm doing. You know how I always said I was going to work in radio? That's what I'm doing. I have my own radio show. You see that building?" He pointed toward the Broadway Central Hotel.

"Yes."

"Well, that's where the station is. WEVD. I play records. Jazz. Do you like jazz?"

Sabine wasn't even sure what it was, but she nodded.

"And I talk. Which isn't hard for me, you know that. Between records, I talk about things. Things that matter, you know. No, you don't know. Do you know what WEVD stands for?"

"No." There was a lot of information being handed out on that sidewalk.

"The initials of Eugene V. Debs."

"Oh."

"You know who *he* is."

"Yes."

"Good. What are you reading?" He examined her book. "Oh. *Anna Karenina.* I hear it ends badly."

"Don't tell me," Sabine said.

"I won't." He thought a minute. "Isn't that book a little advanced for you?"

"Tell me about Eugene V. Debs," Sabine said, to change the subject.

"He's a socialist. You know what a socialist is?" He was grinning down at her.

"Of course." Sabine said shortly. "A Bolshevik."

Matt laughed again and took her arm. "You got a lot to learn. You want to watch me do a show? You want a cup of coffee? You want to hear some jazz?"

It was yes to all of it. He took her to the cafeteria around the corner and she forgot about Anna Karenina. She let him pay for two cups of coffee and followed him to a table, where they sat down. Matt took out a pack of cigarettes to light one.

"I want a cigarette," she said.

"You smoke?" He appeared shocked.

"Of course," she said and he gave her one. She tapped the tip on her fingernail and put the cigarette to her lips. He lit it. She managed to smoke without coughing. She wondered whether Matt noticed that she was not inhaling. She considered blowing the smoke out her nostrils, but decided not to take the risk. It was quite sophisticated enough for her to be smoking at all.

Meanwhile, he talked. About the socialists and the reformers.

"They like to call us radicals, you know. If you're for the least bit of change, you're a radical. Or a Bolshie. Or a Comminist. A Red."

"You are, you know," Sabine said.

"What?" He stared at her and she blushed.

"Red. I mean, I always think of you as red—your hair is, your skin." She stopped, having said too much.

"That's me. Flaming Red. You know, all the Reds are supposed to be Jewish. I'm very confusing to them. They keep saying, What's a boyo like you doin' mixed up with the likes of them?"

"Who says that?"

"The cops, mostly. Down in Kentucky, they just scratched their heads and looked like I smelled bad. They couldn't figure out what I was doing."

"What were you doing?"

"A group of us drove down to see what was happening to the miners. Coal miners, you know."

"Yes, I know."

"They were getting their heads busted. And kicked in the belly. All because they were trying to organize a union. They work their lives away down there in the dark, bad pay, bad conditions, cave-ins, companies that don't give a damn about them when they get sick, and they get sick a lot."

He stopped. "How's your mother?"

"Fine," she said automatically.

"I'm sorry about your father. Your mother never came back to Glenrocks."

"No. Not after Papa died. She wouldn't talk about it."

"Well, they could use her, from what I hear. The hotel is still going, but not going great guns, if you get what I mean. Still, a lot of 'em closed their doors after the Crash and never reopened."

"The Mountain View House?"

"Oh, that's open, but they have had to let down their standards. There are no more groundkeepers—just one gardener, a college boy, who works summers. But they only let down their standards so far." Matt drew on his cigarette. "They still don't allow Jews."

He used the word comfortably, yet it made her uneasy. She

dodged the word whenever she could. He was asking another question.

"Do you work?"

"No, I'm still in school." She was loath to admit that, but added, "Maybe I'll have to leave if things get much worse." She hoped she sounded properly downtrodden.

"Better stick to school while you can, although it's not a bad idea to know what's going on in this strange wide world at the same time," he said, looking at his watch. "You coming with me?"

There was no question. Of course.

Before they entered the studio, Matt asked her if she had ever heard a live band before, and Sabine thought about it. There had been a dance band in Florida—she remembered that dimly. She also remembered her father playing for weddings.

"Wait till you hear this," Matt said. "Today we're doing a live session," and he swung through the door.

"Hello, Ben," he said, shaking hands with a Negro holding a saxophone. She glanced around the studio. There were fifteen musicians, some black, some white. Some were lean, almost cadaverous. One of the white men was handsome, with black hair, very young looking, a trumpet player, licking his lips. Everyone greeted Matt, and the air was thick with smoke and laughter; the men were pouring from a bottle into paper cups. There were puffs on cigarettes, sudden spurts of music, more laughter.

"This is Sabine," Matt introduced her. "I've known her ever since she was this high." He made a gesture very close to the ground. The musicians chuckled.

"Yeah . . . well . . . all *right* . . ." They were not about to believe him, but whatever he was on to, that was his business. The young trumpet player licked his lips again and brought the trumpet up, but kept staring at Sabine.

An impatient voice came from behind the glass control booth.

"You're late, you know. I hope you're ready. We're on the air in twenty seconds."

Matt waved and nodded, very cool. The musicians ambled over to their places. Matt motioned Sabine to a stool. She sat while he moved toward a microphone. A red sign flashed: ON THE AIR.

Matt started talking. It was so easy, so effortless. He had no script. He just seemed to be chatting—about the music they were going to hear, about the different musicians, about the places in Harlem where you could go to hear jazz. He mentioned Small's Paradise. And just when Sabine thought maybe he had talked long enough, he nodded and the band began to play.

Sabine almost fell off the stool. She had never heard anything like this—the enormous power and, at the same time, enormous joy. She found herself moving her body; she couldn't help it. The men played all together at first, then one by one they soared off into solos. The man called Ben, who had been very shy when speaking, rose with his saxophone and slashed across the basic beat, giving the music a country rhythm. The others grinned as they listened. Ben's saxophone played games; made jokes. They laughed, they nodded. The pianist took a turn. He was very light-skinned, with a small dapper mustache and an even smaller smile; he did not look up as he played. His playing was thoughtful, delicate; but while his right hand darted off on trips of its own, his left hand kept the music *moving*.

The trumpet player, the one who had been staring at Sabine, stood up to the mike, taking over from the pianist. After a few notes he closed his eyes, shutting out everything but the music. Sabine had never heard such intensity, and when he was through, the whole brass section delivered a series of short punches. Hit! Hit! Hit! Then all together in a driving climax. One chord, full out. As high as they could reach. And then, suddenly, very low and under, one last chord. A dip, a little comment; a breathy "Yeah" at the end. And it was over.

There was a moment's silence. Sabine could see the man behind the glass in the booth gesturing impatiently. To him, nothing was worse than "dead air." But Matt paid no attention; he just nodded his head up and down and grinned, and the musicians grinned back. They knew. It had happened.

Beautiful, beautiful, Sabine thought. How can they play like that? They look like everyone else, but then they play and everything soars.

"You liked this?" Matt said later. "You want to go to Harlem with me? How about Sunday?"

"Yes."

"Will your mother let you go?"

"Yes."

"How do you know?"

"Because I'll be with you."

He laughed. "She trusts me that much, does she?" He looked at her. "Maybe she shouldn't."

Sabine was very happy with her red nails and her lipstick and suddenly felt equipped to play the role of Fatal Temptress. She asked him for another cigarette, and touched his hand as he lit it for her, a trick she had picked up from *Flaming Passion*.

"Seventeen, huh?" Matt laughed. "Boy oh boy, you are really something!" And he took her home.

On the way he asked about Bertha. "Is she happy? Doesn't she miss Glenrocks?"

"Oh, I suppose she's happy enough. She works in a factory. There's no money in that."

"No money in anything nowadays. But wouldn't the two of you be happier in the country than here?"

They were walking through the shabbiness of the Lower East Side toward Rivington Street.

"Ah, she has too many memories," Sabine said with a trace of bitterness.

"Oh," he said, and left her on the steps. "I'll call for you Sunday at three."

She made her way up the three flights of stairs to the apartment. Bertha was having a cup of tea.

"Where have you been?" she asked.

"I met Matt Ryan," Sabine told her. "He bought me coffee and I heard jazz. Do we know any socialists?"

Bertha smiled. "Your father was."

"Papa?"

"Yes. I remember, in Paris he—" Bertha shrugged. "Your father was not always a practical man. Oh my, we were very radical. One either believed in God or socialism. But if you were socialist, you could smoke cigarettes. We were socialists."

Between that Saturday and the following Sunday Sabine tried to find out more about Eugene V. Debs. The librarian looked at her suspiciously, but gave her a book on Debs and also brought out some books by Beatrice and Sidney Webb. Now Sabine could talk about the Fabians. If it ever came up.

Bertha was a bit reluctant to let Sabine go to Harlem, even with Matt. But Simon was enthusiastic.

"Let her go," he said on Sunday when Matt arrived to get Sabine. "It will be a good experience. Where else could she hear such wonderful music?" He changed tones, looking at Matt. "You will take care of her, you know what I mean."

"Of course," Matt said. And they went to Harlem on the subway.

Sabine had never seen so many black faces. There, in the middle of the gray of winter and the sooty snow, was a kind of excitement; and a warmth. Matt took her hand. They went downstairs into a cellar nightclub. Inside it was dark; and a band was playing. People were drinking, at four o'clock in the afternoon. Everyone so sophisticated. Sabine's long red nails did little to bolster her ego.

"What'll it be?" The waitress was standing over them. Upsweep hairdo. Ruby lips. Eye shadow. Sabine could have died from envy. The waitress had purple nail polish. And earrings.

"Scotch on the rocks," Matt said, and looked at Sabine. "And what can we get for you?"

"Coca-Cola?" the waitress suggested helpfully from under her mascara.

Sabine looked up. "No. I'll have a sloe gin fizz." Had she read about it in a magazine? It sounded good, right, sophisticated. Proper for this place. The waitress raised her eyebrows slightly, and wrote down the order.

"One scotch, one sloe gin fizz," she said when she came back with the drinks. She collected the money. Each time she brought a drink, she collected the money. Matt took a drink and settled down to listen.

"What is this place?" Sabine asked.

"The Hotcha. It's just a place to go and hear jazz."

"All these people are here just for that?"

"No, well, this is a benefit."

"What's that?"

"You ever hear of the Scottsboro Boys?"

"No."

"They were these black boys, riding freight cars down

South; they got arrested, a white girl says they raped her."
Matt looked at Sabine. Did she know the word? Evidently
yes. "That's not a thing they let blacks live for in the South.
There was a trial, but it really wasn't a trial, and then there
was an appeal. Now there's a new trial . . ."

"What's this got to do with you?"

"It's just like in the schoolyard, Sabine. I swear, it's no different, except we know more words to sling at one another.
But there are still those who want to beat up people, and
those who won't stand by and let it happen."

A girl got up to sing, which was unusual. Usually there were
no vocals. She was different, though. Her mouth was slightly
pouting, her hair pulled up, her eyes little more than slits. She
closed them when she sang. Her hand touched the microphone in a loving gesture. Her other hand stayed close to her
body, but it kept time. When she sang and her eyes were
closed, her concentration was like that of the trumpet player's
in Matt's studio: total. And the voice that came out—Sabine
had never heard anything like that, either. It wasn't just singing. There was a wail and sometimes a whine, sometimes a
teasing sound. Nothing got in the way of the music, of what
the singer was feeling. She sang two numbers, one slow and
kind of mournful, one light and skimming, little darting
phrases. The applause was enormous when she finished. She
nodded slightly in acknowledgment and went back to a table
and a drink.

"Who was that?" Sabine whispered.

"Billie Holiday."

"Are there a lot like her?" Sabine asked, awed.

"There's nobody like her," Matt said with certainty.

Sabine ordered two more sloe gin fizzes. Matt looked at
her, but didn't protest. She nursed the drinks along, getting
drunk on the music. One thing was better, the next was better
than that. Small trios, then big bands, singers, raunchy comedians whose jokes she could hardly understand. What were
reefers? Sabine was discovering again—was it Matt? or was it
this exciting new world?—that she could be happy. She loved
the lights. She loved the dark. She loved the fact that outside
it was cold and the bitter traces of winter still lay on the
streets and in here, on a Sunday afternoon, now evening, edg-
ing into night, it was warm and wonderful. *Mel-low*. That
was a word floating around in the smoke and the laughter.

Mel-low. She felt mel-low. She wanted to dance, and she asked Matt. He seemed surprised, but willing.

She knew what she was doing. She wanted his arms around her. She wanted to feel what it was like, to be in his arms. Vronsky and Rudolph, and all the men crushing the ladies, suffocating them with passion—what was it like?

What it was like was crowded. On the dance floor there was no place to move. It wasn't mean-spirited; it was more like a carnival. Matt held her, and they moved their feet. That was dancing.

That was how it started. Lots of people on a dance floor, pushing together. Matt's body was close to Sabine's. She could feel him. She liked the way they moved together. She moved her body closer to him. Was he conscious of the feeling? She could feel the muscles of his thigh as they danced, she could feel the muscles in his arm as they moved. Then she could feel—what?—a rubbing. Their bodies were rubbing together. It was extremely hot and she could smell perfume and sweat, but she closed her eyes and could feel him. She could feel *him* against her thigh now. Then he moved his body away. She would not let that happen. She sought him again. They were not saying a word. They were talking only with their bodies, and again, it was a discovery for her. She became aware of every part of her body, of her breasts against his chest, of his arm, of his strength, of her hips. She began to move them against him. If he had wanted to retreat, there was no way. The floor was crowded. They let the music flow over them.

A Feuer brennt. She knew what it meant. She was burning. She could feel it inside her. She didn't know what she wanted, but she wanted to get closer to this man, and yet she didn't know how she could get any closer. She pressed against him. He was pressing against her. She loved the way he made her feel. She was happy. She knew what it was to be happy. Jubilant.

The music stopped, and Matt said, "Come on. We've had enough." Was he angry? He led her off the floor hurriedly. They sat again at the table. He didn't look at her. He fumbled for change, for a cigarette, for something to busy himself with. Then he did look at her.

"I'm taking you home, Sabine. Now."

"You're angry. Why are you angry?"

He relented then. "I'm not angry." The grin came back. "Frustrated, you might say. But I couldn't be angry. Let's just say it's time you went home."

The cold night was a shock; the grimness of Harlem at night was a shock too. Sabine tried to hold on to the warmth of the experience, but it slipped away from her. Matt would not touch her, keeping his distance on the subway ride home. When they reached her apartment he left her, hurried away, wanting to escape. "Good night," he said, and was gone.

It was cold. Cold on the street as they came home, cold in the apartment. The lights were off. Sabine didn't want light. Silently she found her way to her room in the dark. She drew a blanket around her. The apartment was silent. The street outside was silent. Then, out of the silence there came a sound.

Simon was in the next room. With her mother. Simon was in bed with her mother. She heard the muffled sounds, rhythmic sounds. Then she heard Simon.

Simon: What's the matter?
Bertha: Nothing.
Simon: You're crying.
Bertha: Yes. I had forgotten . . .

The rhythm started again. She could hear her mother—no, it was not her mother, it was the sound of somebody else, the sound of a woman—"yes," the woman was saying over and over again, "yes, yes, yes; like that, oh, yes, come, fill me, fill me, stroke me there, oh yes,"—and the sound of the bedsprings, the squeak, the rhythm like jazz, the beat like the beat Sabine had been listening to all night, the beat of sex, of jazz, of rhythm, of fucking. Sabine heard gasps now, and moans, her mother moaning with pleasure, Simon grunting. Fucking. That's what it was. That's what was going on no more that a few inches away from her, on the other side of the wall. They had not heard her come in. They were making love, and did not know she was there. Her mother was crying out with passion. Simon was silent now, stroking, moving. Faster and faster, and then they both cried out, and there was panting. Sabine could hear it all. Tears came to her eyes. She had never felt so alone. She did not move from her bed, covered with the blanket, she remained silent, the tears coursing down her cheeks. Then she heard movement again, and conversation.

"I better go," Simon said.

"Why? It's cold."

"I shouldn't stay."

"Stay. I love you."

"No. I should—"

"Stay. Come back to bed."

Silence. Then the bedsprings again. Then the sound of her mother. A sigh. Pure animal satisfaction. A man filling her again, a lover. Pleasure.

Sabine fell asleep to the sound of the bedsprings creaking. When she woke up Simon was gone, and Bertha was in the kitchen. Bertha was always in the kitchen (except for the woman who writhed on the bed).

"Sabine, I want to talk to you," Bertha said.

"No, I don't want to talk. What is that, soup?"

"Yes, soup. When did you get home last night? Did you hear Simon last night?"

"Yes." Sabine could not keep the anger out of her voice.

"I'm sorry. I didn't realize you were home." Bertha looked guilty, and blushed like a girl.

"Is he coming back?"

"I would like him to. I would like to have him back."

Sabine suddenly cried out, "How could you let him do that?"

"I was lonely."

"What about Papa?"

"Your father is *dead*."

Sabine shook her head. She didn't want to accept that, the totality of that.

Bertha continued, "You don't understand. I was lonely."

Sabine slammed her spoon on the table.

"What about me? Did you ever consider that I was lonely, too? Did you ever once put your hand on me, did you ever touch me, did you ever even ask how I was feeling?"

Bertha was not a cruel woman. It had never occurred to her that children could be lonely. To her, Sabine was a little creature who had played with dolls, looked at butterflies, waited in a hotel room, a little creature whose hand you took so she wouldn't get lost in strange railway stations, someone you had to fit with clothes . . .

Bertha's eyes filled with tears.

"Oh, Sabine." She shook her head with regret. "You don't understand. You don't understand that people are mostly . . . selfish."

"I understand that," Sabine replied roughly.

Bertha put her hand on her daughter's shoulders, seven years too late, and said, "I'm sorry."

"It doesn't matter," Sabine said, shrugging her shoulder so that her mother's hand slid off. "If you want Simon to stay here, it's all right with me."

Simon did stay. He brought a phonograph, and some John McCormack records; he preferred McCormack to Caruso.

Sabine escaped to Jerry's.

"Do your musician number," she told him. Thay had taken to improvising small bits from scenes that caught their eye. The chamber music group had started them off, and whenever Sabine was feeling down, Jerry could revive her with his pantomime of the first violinist and the fly.

"You're feeling that bad, huh?" Jerry said. Sabine nodded. "Well, you won't get cheered up around here."

The People's Theater Alliance, never on good times, had fallen on really hard times now. They had a theater (temporarily) but no money. The actors donated their time, as actors always have. And they had a director. That was Bernie. He had discovered it was better to be a director than a performer, especially a performer who depended on his mother for laughs. The director directed. The actor had to do what the director wanted. The actor had to learn lines and stand on his feet for hours in rehearsals, while the director merely walked and kept one step ahead of the actors. That was easy for Bernie. He had been doing that since he was old enough to walk. Bernie had always been just one step ahead.

"Oh, he's impossible," Jerry complained. "He had us doing all the left-over radical experimental productions that the Group Theater wouldn't touch. We have done allegories. I have been a tree. Now, Bernie wants to do the classics. He says it's because we should be well-rounded. I figure he doesn't want to pay royalties. And dead writers are easier to deal with since they don't talk back. Oh God, have you ever *read* Racine?"

"No."

"Don't. He's like Shakespeare but without the balls."

Jerry rose majestically and began to stalk the loft, spouting French and shaking an imaginary wig.

"I like that better than the musician," Sabine said. "Keep that one."

"There's more. We're on Molière now. And Bernie is trying to explain *commedia dell'arte* to us. He'll borrow anything—a little Piscator, a little Stanislavsky. You want to see a little Stanislavsky?"

Sabine said, "Later. Is this group any good?"

"Yeah, not bad. We're okay. Actually, maybe Bernie is okay too. It's just that he's such a thief. He should have remained a waiter."

When she went home that night, Sabine started to think. It was a difficult call to make, but two days later she telephoned Max Abramowitz at Glenrocks. *Poor Max*, everyone had said, *back to running his hotel since his Florida fiasco. You hadn't heard? He's penniless.*

The moment she heard his voice, her impulse was to hang up the receiver. But she didn't. She tried to keep the resentment out of her voice.

"Max, this is Sabine."

"What a surprise."

"I expect it is."

A moment's strained silence. Then he said, "I'm sorry—about your father."

Sorry? Sorry was not enough. A man runs through the streets of Florida and his heart bursts because you have stolen his future. His life has been taken. Sorry does not cover that. Sorry is too easy. No, your gut should spill over your belt and you should sweat; you should break out in rashes. Your hair should drop out. Your arches should fall. You should be a door-to-door salesman and every door should shut in your face. Women should laugh and spit on your fatness. Sorry? It's not enough for you to be sorry.

"I hear you need help," was all she said.

"Help? Who needs help?" Max parried.

"I hear you need help. Nobody cooked like my mother. People still ask after her. I hear Weidman still comes every year. And he asks after my mother."

"His wife died," Max added irrelevantly.

"I hear Lasky went to Grossinger's because of the tennis. And what about the Salwitzes?"

"You hear too damn much," Max grumbled. "Lasky will be back. He's like family. That's what we had. We had something special. Remember?"

Remember? There was hardly a day that she did not remember, and what she remembered was so strange and so isolated: the sound of the brook as it ran into the pond, the stillness of the quarry, the huge leaves of the great maple that shielded them from the sun in the summer. The clatter of dishes being set for lunch while she and Matt were still peeling the potatoes. And in the evening, the softness of the light and the sound of music. Matt. Papa. Crazy Bernard. Weidman's sigh of satisfaction.

"You need my mother. You need me. What would you pay?" Sabine's voice was steady.

"*Pay?*" Max uttered the word as though he had never heard it before. "You don't understand. We would be partners."

"We were always partners," Sabine reminded him. "You owe us a great deal of money."

"Where would I get the money?" he said.

"From your father."

"An investment? Another investment?" he asked.

"To protect his first investment," she coached him.

"Will your mother come back?"

"I don't know. It would be painful for her. There have been other offers." Sabine looked around the shabby room. Was she going too far? Other offers?

"Talk to her," he said.

"Of course," Sabine said. "And I will let you know."

"Soon." He seemed to be pleading.

"Soon," she promised, and said goodbye.

When Bertha came home that night from work, Sabine broached the subject. "I talked to Max today. He wants you to come back to Glenrocks."

"Never!"

"He was afraid to ask you himself."

"Never!" Bertha repeated. "How could he ask me? It would be too painful."

A kind of savage energy propelled Sabine. This was her one chance.

"Painful!" She threw the word back at her mother. "What do you call *this*? Do you call this a life? Do you think Papa meant for us to scratch around in this slum for the rest of our days?"

"Don't mention your father!" Bertha warned.

"Why? Is his memory so sacred?" Sabine didn't care what she said now. "You sleep with Simon and you talk about sacred memory!"

"Stop!" Bertha said.

"No. I have a chance to get out of here, and it depends on you. You are going to help me, for once you are going to help me. You don't have to talk to Max. I'll do the talking. You don't have to have anything to do with him. I'll do it all."

"You!" Bertha said scornfully. "What can you do?"

"Who knows?"

Mother and daughter looked at each other. The echo of that phrase wrung Bertha's heart. It was Jacob. Whatever was left of Jacob was in Sabine. It was impossible to deny her daughter. Bertha nodded her head in agreement.

"You won't be sorry, Mama," Sabine promised. "Something good is going to come out of this. I know it."

Ah, Bertha heard that before. She had lived through many broken promises and failures, lies that had been forgotten, dreams that had disappeared. She went into her own room and shut the door.

Glenrocks was to open, as usual, on Memorial Day. On a weekend early in May, Sabine went to inspect the premises.

"It needs paint," she told Max, echoing her parents' words from a previous decade.

"But it's still there. It's still a good hotel. So it needs a little paint and a little new spirit," Max said. He was looking to Sabine to supply both.

She inspected the rooms. There were water stains on the wallpaper from the leaks in the roof. She ate one meal. The food was Depression boardinghouse.

"Who's the cook?" she asked Max.

"I don't know her name. What difference does it make? When Bertha comes back, it will all be wonderful. This cook, she'll be out the door."

They walked the grounds, lonely now between seasons, but also lonely in spirit. In the old parlor there was a stack of phonograph records, the same records Mrs. Rosen had brought for Bernard to mime to. Nothing had changed.

Sabine looked at Max. "My mother won't be able to save this place by herself. Do you have any money to spend?"

That was the worst subject for Max. He held on to what little money he had left. What was the good of spending it?

"You're going to have to advertise."

"We never did before."

"Uncle Max, the word has gotten around. The people aren't coming. Glenrocks is like going to a funeral, am I right?"

"No. Not a funeral."

"An old age home, then."

Max was silent. But he nodded.

"You got any money?" Sabine repeated.

"You got any ideas?" Max countered.

"Of course. Or I wouldn't be here." She was thinking to herself, *Why is he trusting a seventeen-year-old girl?* But she had nothing to lose, she could take any gamble. She had only one goal in mind: to get out of Rivington Street. And she would get out of Rivington Street, if she just used her head.

"I got some money," Max finally admitted.

"Good," Sabine said, "because we're going to need it. By the way, we should have papers between us. Actually, between my mother and you."

"What kind of papers?" Max asked.

"Partnership papers. It's better to have it in writing."

Max was looking unhappy. "What do you propose to do?"

Sabine found herself making wonderful plans. She heard her own voice saying, "Tennis courts. You need some tennis courts. We'll make them. Culture. People want culture. Maybe you could have a resident theater company."

"That's expensive."

"No. All actors are out of work nowadays. You can get actors." She thought of Bernard and the People's Theater Alliance. Why not? "And dancing. You need music for dancing." Matt would be able to help her there. "How about a weekend festival of entertainment? A revue, like a nightclub. It wouldn't be so expensive. Every weekend we'd have a new show."

"You could supply that?" Max was overwhelmed.

"Absolutely," Sabine said, because she was seventeen years old and didn't know any better.

She approached Simon first.

"I want you to help me build two tennis courts," she said.

Simon was amused. "When do we start?" he said.

"As soon as you tell me what I need."

Simon listed the requirements—clay, naturally, and gravel, rollers, the drainage area.

"Do you have any flat land?" he asked her.

"Yes. Just tell me how much gravel."

"Four truckloads. Where will you get it?"

"I'll find it."

And she did. The Civilian Conservation Corps were resurfacing one of the roads leading to Liberty.

"What would it cost to get four loads of gravel?" she asked the overseer.

"What would it cost *who*?" he smiled.

"Me."

"What do you want them for?"

"I'm going to build tennis courts."

"It wouldn't cost me—I mean, we might be able to see our way clear . . . When would you need them?" he asked.

"Now, of course," Sabine said.

"We might be able to do it. How old are you?" he asked her.

"What difference does that make?"

"None. I just wonder at your guts."

"Will you help me?"

"Yes. You're gonna need some help building those things, you know."

"I know. Could you help me there too?"

"It's up to the men. Ask them."

Sabine did. Nothing could stop her. She persuaded them. She also asked Simon and Jerry up for a weekend.

"What am I doing?" Jerry asked as they shoveled off a truck. "I hate tennis."

"You are working for the good of the theater," Sabine replied. "You want a theater here this summer? Shovel!"

She had counted on Simon's enthusiasm, but not on the expertise. He knew exactly where to position the courts so that they got the greatest amount of light without the sun getting in the players' eyes. He knew exactly the amount of slope needed for drainage, the amount of gravel to use for fill, the mix of clay for the court surface. He exulted in the open air. He worked in gym shorts, shirtless. Sabine found he had a grand sense of humor, and she understood why women found him attractive. It was his vitality, a vitality that seemed to infect everyone. Even Max. The men from the CCC were costing him very little. Simon had donated his services. There was the kind of celebration about the proceedings that reminded Max of the old days, and he was happy. He had placed a few ads in the newspapers, announcing a theater, a night club—and tennis courts!!—and the response had been gratifying. Even Mr. Lasky returned from Grossinger's. Max was encouraged.

It took three weekends to finish the tennis courts.

"They're not perfect," Simon said proudly, "but you got nothing to be ashamed of. Next year you can put in four more."

Max brought out the beer. It was a balmy afternoon. The boys from the CCC gave a toast. Everybody watched Mr. Lasky and Simon play a set which Simon won easily, 6-2.

And then Sabine took Max back to the city to meet Bernard. This was part two of her plans for the summer: the theater.

Bernard had agreed to meet Max during a break in the rehearsal schedule. A few weeks before, inspiration had struck Bernard in the middle of Molière's *Le Misanthrope*. He had yawned through *Les Précieuses Ridicules*, and thumbed through *L'Avare*. The night before he had started to read (dreading it) *Le Misanthrope*, he had been rebuffed by a Park Avenue matron and her husband. They were collectors of art, and they also happened to be millionaires, and Bernard was hoping they would become patrons of the People's Theater Alliance.

Bernard had miscalculated. The couple were radical all right, but their interests lay in other directions. They wanted to finance an all-black production of Jarry's *Ubu Roi*, and, failing that, the wanted to present an evening of voodoo music on Broadway, complete with the onstage killing of chickens. They talked Expressionism, Surrealism, and even read him verses in Haitian creole. Bernard left, defeated for once, went home, and opened *Le Misanthrope*. He read of a hero who refused to lie (why hadn't *he* told the couple their

theatrical ambitions were insane, Bernard wondered). Alcinthe stood up to society!

In a flash it came to him. He would do *The Misanthrope*
as a contemporary comedy of manners, proletarian enough for
anybody. Alcinthe would be a boy from the Lower East Side.
Society would—what else? Park Avenue. Celimene, the
heroine, would be a silly little debutante. Bernard picked up a
pencil and started writing.

It took him only three days to finish his version of *The
Misanthrope*, and when Max arrived Bernard was all prepared. After Sabine made the introductions, Bernard immediately took the initiative. He turned on Max. "Are you
willing to take the dare?"

"What dare?"

"To let me present revolutionary theater. Do you think
that your audience is aware? Promise me only that. That
your audience is aware. Theater is not to entertain. It is to
enlighten. Theater should be in the streets. It should be on
the ramparts."

"I don't know," Max said weakly.

"If you don't know, then it's no good. It is bound to fail.
Unless you have faith. Have you got faith?" Max started to
turn away. Bernard clutched at his sleeve.

"Lemme tell you my project, and then you tell me whether
we should do it. You know, of course, Molière's *Misanthrope*. A classic. World famous. A comedy in the best sense
of the word. Now, what would happen if Molière had written this *today*?" Bernard was gleeful with inspiration. "Al-
ceste, my misanthrope—call him Al—has fought his way up
from the Lower East Side. He is incorruptible, uncompromis-
ing! It is his *curse* that he has fallen in love with Celimene.
We call her Cissy. What does Cissy say to you? Cissy says
'rich' 'spoiled,' 'selfish,' 'wanton.' And who is the villain, you
ask? Philinthe—Phil. Here is the man who recognizes the evil
in society and refuses to do anything about it. This society is
decadent and it must topple." He smacked the stage for emphasis.

Max was uncertain. "Is this a comedy?" he asked.

"Yes! A classic. Devastating! All we got to do is bring it
up to date. I mean, the French have *had* their revolution,
now it's our turn!"

Max was speechless. Bernard wasn't.

"You are going to see the birth of a true repertory company," he enthused. "You will be famous years from now when they write the textbooks on the theater. The People's Alliance Theater—"

"The People's *Theater Alliance,*" Sabine prompted him.

"Whatever," he said, "it will be known as the most revolutionary theater of the Thirties, and where did it start? At Glenrocks!" He smacked the stage again with the palm of his hand and dust rose. "Are we agreed?"

Max had not understood a word, but he felt that that was all to the good. Revolutionary meant new, and new was needed. Sabine became more practical.

"How many will be in the troupe?" she asked.

"Eight," Bernard said. "Nine including me. Announce the first performance for the weekend of July Fourth. We will do four plays in repertory, starting with Molière."

The rest of the company began to appear. Bernard dismissed his visitors.

"All right, to work!" he cried exultantly.

Matt was surprised to see Sabine when she appeared at the radio station, and she was surprised that she had dared to come. But she needed help. Could he arrange some concerts? She could afford to pay nothing at first; but they could split the proceeds. Of course, she had discussed none of this with Max. She decided she should get it all arranged first. And every so often she would stop and say to herself, *What are you doing? You are only seventeen years old.*

Matt agreed to three concerts toward the end of summer. He would help with the publicity. He grinned at her.

"Why are you smiling?" she asked him.

"Because you don't know what you're letting yourself in for," he said.

"It's probably better that way," she muttered. And he agreed.

Glenrocks reopened on Memorial Day weekend. And some of the old clientele came back. But there were a number of newcomers too: friends of Simon's, always ready for a tennis game, or an argument. Old Mr. Weidman was suspicious but silent—there was no room to get a word in edgewise. On the courts Simon and his friends argued about whether the ball was in, or on the line, or out. They accused each other of foot faults. Over dessert (which they ate voraciously) they argued about the system and Roosevelt, and the oncoming revolution. They quoted Thomas Paine and Karl Marx at breakfast. Stalin and Kerensky and Engels joined them on the front porch after dinner, before Simon started to play the Victrola. He had brought along his albums of Mozart string quartets and arias sung by John McCormack. His friends had brought along their girl friends and *The New Masses*.

There was bound to be a clash.

It occurred one morning after breakfast. Mr. Weidman was sitting on the rocker on the porch reading the *New York Times*. When he was finished he rather hospitably offered his paper to a wiry balding man who was sitting on the edge of the porch.

"You want the *Times*?" Weidman asked.

"I already know what it says," the man smiled.

"How could you know what it says?" Weidman asked. "I just got finished reading it."

"I don't have to read it to know what it says. It's nothing but lies."

"Lies-s-s?" Weidman hissed. "The New York *Times-s-s lies-s-s?*"

"Lies!" the man reaffirmed.

"So what is that you're reading?"

"*The New Masses*. Wanta look?"

"Thank you, no. I know your *New Masses*. Your *New Masses* lies-s-s!" Weidman was half out of his rocker with emotion.

"Your capitalist press lies!" the wiry little man encountered.

"Communist rag!"

"Fascist!"

"Bolshie!"

"Volleyball!" Simon intervened, knowing that the wiry little man loved volleyball.

But Weidman was determined to have the last word. "If you do not like it here, why do you not go back where you came from?" he cried. His English was not up to his jingoism.

The wiry little man just laughed. "I come from Newark," he said, and went off to the volleyball courts where he could brush up against young girls' bodies.

One night Sabine saw Mr. Weidman sitting alone. She asked him to dance.

"I hate dancing," he told her, and very soon went up to his room. By accident Sabine passed his door, which was half open, and she saw him, hands and arms outstretched, holding an invisible partner.

"*One* two three, *one* two three," he was saying to the ghost of Mrs. Weidman, and Sabine passed on, pretending she had seen nothing.

The People's Theater Alliance arrived the week before the Fourth of July—all of them, including four Victrolas, two violins, and three animals, plus baggage, piled into one jitney. It had been raining and the jitney's top had several tears in it, so the group was a very soggy one. They were shown immediately to their tents. "Tents?" they asked one another. In the days of the Depression one learned not to complain—but tents? While the actors inspected their tents, Glenrocks inspected the actors.

There was Henrietta, who suffered from allergies and hated the countryside. There was Sarnoff, who had once been almost-a-name in the Yiddish theater—several of the guests had seen him. He always played old men; now he required no makeup to play the parts. The juvenile was Danny, who walked with a bounce and wore a constant grin. It was he whom Bernard had chosen for his misanthrope, and a cheerier one would have been hard to find. Danny was nineteen and had dark curly hair. Through no fault of his own he would later find fame as a dancer in Hollywood. The character couple was Sam and Elspeth, and they were content with their lot, meager as it was. They had never hoped for stardom; they were happy the way they were. Elaine, a chunky girl who always wore shorts and T-shirts, was the stage manager. Another actor in the troupe was Arthur, who also constructed the sets and designed the lighting, so in spite of his horrible-looking teeth he was not only an asset to the company, he was indispensable. And, of course, there was Jerry. He took one look at the tents, one look at Sabine, and cursed. She smiled back at him.

The troupe moved on to the recreation room, which was to be their theater. The place smelled of damp wood.

"There's your stage," Bernard gestured grandly. It was no

higher than twelve feet, no deeper than eighteen, no wider than thirty. It did not allow for grand theatrical effects.

"How are we going to play Molière here?" Henrietta asked.

"Intimately," Bernard said firmly.

"When do we eat?" Elaine wanted to know.

"After rehearsal. Come, my children. We have only four days until greatness." Bernard had become accustomed to calling the troupe his children. Looking up, he saw the Glenrocks guests standing there, gawking.

"Everyone out!" he ordered. "No one allowed until opening night." The guests shuffled out and Sabine started to go with them.

"No. You stay," Bernard ordered.

"I can't stay," Sabine protested.

"Who will take notes? Stay! Take notes, get me a cup of coffee. You won't be sorry."

She was. Almost immediately, Henrietta and Bernard had artistic differences. She wanted to use a fan. Bernard differed.

"A fan—" Henrietta began.

"—ages you," Bernard finished.

Henrietta began to wheeze. She needed water. She held up her hand—no one was to help her. In her high heels, she picked her way carefully through the assortment of lumber. She left the stage. She left the recreation hall.

"Don't worry, she'll be back," Bernard told Sabine.

It rained that night. In the drizzle next morning Henrietta reappeared, her bags packed. She looked like a battered prizefighter. During the night the mosquitos had taken their toll. She was a mass of lumps and welts, with one eye practically swollen shut.

If Bernard had already been brought his morning coffee, the results might have been different. As it was, while Henrietta was limping across the dining room to Bernard's table, he was yelling at a waiter, "Where's my coffee, goddammit! Move ass!" The dining room had not filled up yet and this theatrical language was permitted. Later, Bernard would have to be reminded about restraint.

Henrietta set down her bags.

"Thith ith goodbye," she lisped coldly.

"Oh, for Chrissakes, Henrietta, use the fuckin' fan if it means that much to you," Bernard said in disgust.

"Too late," Henrietta said. "You can take your thcript and thtick it up your ath!"

The dining room was now beginning to fill up, and not just for breakfast.

Sabine looked up and saw Sarnoff shuffling across the room. She walked over to him, hoping to avert an even more dramatic scene.

"Good morning, Sarnoff," she said. "You look wonderful." He had slept in his clothes, he had a day's growth of beard on his chin, and he resembled a hobo (a dying one). And he was not to be deterred.

"I am too old," he cried at Bernard over Sabine's shoulder.

"Get me a cup of coffee somebody!" Bernard pounded his fist on the table.

Sabine snapped her fingers at a busboy, who flew to the kitchen.

"Let's all move to the sun-room," she said, "where we can talk undisturbed."

"I won't move anywhere," Sarnoff screamed. "I am too old. Too old to take this rain, and these bugs, and look, look at these wet feet. There is mold on everything. Nothing dries." He stood before Bernard like a reprimand. "This is not Art!" he declaimed accusingly.

"Coffee!" Bernard pleaded. "I would kill for a cup of coffee." He saw his whole troupe vanishing in one rainstorm.

"The coffee's coming. We'll all feel better—," Sabine began.

"Too late." Sarnoff held up a biblical hand. "Sarnoff leaves." He picked up his bags; Henrietta picked up hers.

"Never play the provintheth!" was her final warning.

"Never sleep in a tent with wet shoes," Sarnoff added.

In vain Bernard tried to invoke the spirit of Molière and, when that failed, the camaraderie of the theater. Henrietta and Sarnoff continued on their way. Finally he appealed to their loyalty to a political ideal.

Henrietta was not to be swayed.

"Let'th go!" she said to Sarnoff, and the two left, carrying their grievance along with their poor actors' luggage. The rest of the troupe watched them depart. So did the clientele of Glenrocks, who felt the urge to applaud.

Bernard turned to Elaine and said, "You will be my Cissy." Elaine was not a good choice, lacking (among other things) charm, grace, wit, and beauty. There was, in addition, the problem of replacing Sarnoff. "I will play the part," Bernard said. This, of course, made the rest of the cast more nervous. Lines were forgotten. Elaine insisted on smoking.

"Cissy would smoke," Elaine said. "All debs smoke."

"But not like that," Bernard yelled. "Elaine, you smoke like a truck driver."

"Fuck you," said Elaine, grinding out the cigarette butt with her heel.

"Fuck me? Fuck *you*!" Bernard screamed—the wit of the streets did not desert him in a crisis.

Elaine lasted ten minutes as Cissy. Bernard whirled around. "Here," he said to Sabine. "Read this."

"Me?" Sabine was astounded.

"Yeah, you. It's your ass that's at stake," Bernard said. That was reasonable. Sabine snatched up the script. She started to read.

There were several things in her favor. At seventeen she had the beginnings of elegance. Her cheekbones were aristocratic, her face had strength. Those sapphire eyes conveyed all sorts of feelings—at the present moment, fury at Bernard. But, best of all, she had talent.

"You see," Bernard said when she finished, "anyone can play that part."

Elaine was not to be humiliated. "Let anyone play it," she said, and stalked off.

Bernard turned to Sabine. "Okay. It's you or nobody. What the hell?"

"Are you crazy?" she asked him.

"Sure. So are you. I can see you're going to do it."

"No."

"What's the matter? Scared you can't learn the lines?"

"Of course not."

"I don't believe you," Bernard said, wanting desperately to believe her. "Show me."

They began a scene. Sabine had the ability to remember lines and blocking; she never had to be told twice. As Bernard watched, his excitement grew. He would have his triumph. This girl would be fresh, sweet, manageable.

"You will be my Cissy," Bernard said, smiling. "Let's face it. You have no choice."

Max reminded her that programs had already been printed,

announcements sent, ads put in the paper. Jerry felt she had nothing to lose.

"Oh, do it," he said to her, "and stop making such a scene." So she did.

Glenrocks was preparing for the weekend of the Fourth. Bertha, in her kitchen, had no time to visit Sabine. Simon gave her reports.

"She'll be fine," he told Bertha. "Jerry says she'll be first-rate." Bertha nodded and went back to her world of dumplings and briskets.

On opening night, Sabine struggled with her costume. It was white satin with very thin shoulder straps and far too big for her; the straps slipped off her shoulders. She clutched at the straps and asked for pins to fix them. Elaine, with a mouth full of pins, muttered that Sabine should find her own. Sabine got into her pumps. The heels were ridiculously high. She had the sensation of falling.

"What kind of makeup do I use?" she asked a passing Bernard.

"Debutante," he said, and was gone, hurrying off to a more pressing problem: champagne was to be served in the second scene and no one had thought to provide glasses. Bernard seized some from the kitchen.

Jerry came into the dressing room. Sabine was staring at the mirror.

"Name a debutante," she said to him.

"Carole Lombard," he said immediately.

"What kind of makeup would she wear?"

Jerry closed his eyes for a moment. "Very thin eyebrows. Lots of lipstick. Listen, everybody told me not to worry about using too much makeup. Put on lots of mascara and eye shadow. And powder," he added.

She looked at him. "What's that in your hair?"

"White shoe polish, to make me look older."

She thought he looked like a skunk.

"Are you scared?" she asked.

"I think so," he said.

"Do your musician for me. You got time?"

Jerry did a sixty-second version of the violinist and the fly. Sabine laughed.

"Thanks," she said, "I feel better."

"So do I," said Jerry. He started out the door. "Don't worry. What can happen?"

Sabine shrugged. "Who knows?" she said, and started with the makeup.

Simon watched the recreation room as the audience filtered in. Posters had filled the windows of the town's two drugstores and the meat market. Posters had been tacked to telephone poles. Ads had appeared in the papers, and Glenrocks was sold out for the Fourth of July weekend. In the dining room, during dinner, it was announced that following the performance of the play, there would be dancing and a cabaret. The audience buzzed with excitement.

Max stood in the back with his hands folded behind him. Max was satisfied—this group should also be satisfied. They were getting their money's worth: good food, recreation, entertainment.

Bernard Rosen stepped in front of the curtain, nodding and smiling. The audience applauded. He had not been a candy store comic for nothing. At just the right moment, he held up his hands to silence the applause.

"Thank you," he said. "Thank you all for allowing us to bring culture to Glenrocks. Let me tell you a little bit about the People's Theater Alliance."

And he did. The audience stirred. This was not magic. They were willing to be informed, if it didn't take too long.

It did.

Bernard traced Molière's revolutionary roots, his attacks on church and nobility, the correlation between Molière's time and the revolutionary Thirties.

"We did not choose Molière's *hilarious* comedy *lightly*," Bernard was telling an audience which had resorted to turning programs, coughing, and clearing throats. "No play more accurately depicts the schism which exists between Park Avenue and the horrors of Hoovervilles than Molière's *The Misanthrope*."

"What's a misanthrope?" a man in front of Simon whispered to his wife.

"Someone on relief," his wife answered.

Bernard bowed. More applause. The house lights dimmed. The curtains rose. The comedy began. The audience leaned forward.

Al, the misanthrope, entered with his friend Phil, and they

began to argue about friendship and insincerity. The misanthrope was wearing a tuxedo. He was elegant, but why was he wearing brown shoes? And who cared about all this talk about insincerity? They waited in silence for something to happen.

Then Sabine lurched into the blinding light.

On her entrance she had brushed by a tray, the tray with the champagne glasses Bernard had taken from the kitchen. Behind her, Sabine heard a crash. In front of her, Danny's eyes widened in horror. "Oh Christ," the misanthrope said. Sabine did not dare turn around. They stared at each other for a second.

"Choose!" Danny said. It was all he could remember.

"What?" Sabine said.

"I said, choose. Them or me!"

At this moment, Sabine's shoulder strap broke. She clutched her gown. The audience began to laugh. Sabine turned upstage.

"Oh, do hush up!" she said to the wall. She was trying to cover her front. What was her next line? She bumped into a table.

"Adorable screwball!" she said, knocking over a lamp. It shattered.

Jerry entered, as Tanner the playboy.

"Heigh ho, all," he said confidently. "Just toddled over from El Morocco."

And then he caught sight of Sabine's face. She looked like a raccoon with all that makeup. She was standing, back to the audience, clutching a gown that was slipping off, and her eyes were rolling around in her head.

"Too dull," he began and felt the urge to laugh. It was irresistible. "Too—boring." He got that much out, and then the laughter began. He couldn't help it. "Wish you could have seen Leo," he said valiantly, trying to keep up with the lines. He must not look at Sabine. But even when he was not looking at her, he could see her. "Wish you could have—ha-ha-ha—seen—omigod—seen Leo. What a fool—oh, help—oh—what a fool he made of himself!" Jerry was helpless. Worse, Sabine was approaching him. Her dress was now under control. She was coming over to him—was she supposed to? She managed to say her line.

"Too icky, dahling, too icky for words!" She got that out.

They looked at each other. A fatal mistake. They both burst out laughing. They tried to cover it by coughing, seized with fits. They turned away from one another. It was no use. They looked at Danny. The misanthrope was standing, frozen, watching them. That was worse than looking at each other.

Jerry moved. Glass crunched under his heel.

"Careful of the champagne," Sabine said, as delicately as possible. "I seem to have spilled a touch." During the course of the scene there was a great deal of traffic behind the couch where the broken glass lay, and with each step there was a distinct crunch of glass.

The fear, of course, was contagious. The other actors headed for exits that weren't there. They spilled liquids, dropped props, stepped on one another's lines, or, worse, repeated them. Doors stuck and would not open. Doorknobs came off in sweaty hands. At the end of the act, they fled to their dressing room.

No one would approach Sabine. It was as if she had the plague. Only Jerry came to see her.

"This was terrible," she said.

"Yeah," he admitted.

"Do you think anyone noticed?"

Jerry broke up again. He was almost weeping. "No. Of course nobody noticed. Everybody comes on stage, their dress falls off, they knock over tables, smash lamps. It happens all the time. No, nobody noticed."

"It's these lousy heels," Sabine said. "I couldn't walk on them."

"I noticed," Jerry said.

"What are we going to do?" Sabine said. She was filled with horror. She had to face whatever was left of an audience—face them again.

"We're going to do the second act."

Bernard lunged into the room. In costume. He was playing one of the fops.

"You," he yelled at Sabine. "Whoever said you could act?"

"You did."

"I was wrong. You have ruined everything. Let me tell you this. Your makeup is awful. I can't hear you. I have no idea what you are doing on that stage beside destroying the set. Fucking cunt, I could kill you!"

"I didn't want to do this, I told you!"

"I don't want to hear any excuses. You want to know whose ass is on the line? Yours is. Not mine."

Elaine came by at that moment. "Places for the second act," she said. She could not have been more thrilled. Both and Elaine and Bernard vanished.

"I hate him," Sabine said almost rationally.

"I hate *her*," Jerry said.

"I hate this script," Sabine said.

"Why shouldn't you? It's terrible," Jerry said.

At that moment, Max, ashen-faced, stuck his head in the door.

"We just had a telephone call. The group who was going to perform the cabaret act had a flat tire. They missed their train. They won't make it." He didn't say anything more, he just left. Sabine looked at Jerry.

"I hate him too," Sabine said. "As a matter of fact, I hate this whole night. What do you hate most?"

"Having to do the second act," Jerry said.

"You know what I hate *most* of all the things I hate about tonight? I hate these shoes." She looked at the lethal heels with fury.

"Don't wear them."

"What?"

"Don't wear them. You're supposed to be a madcap debutante. Go barefoot."

She kissed him. "You're an angel. You saved my life. Oh God, Jerry, what are we going to do about the cabaret?"

"Think about it after the show. Come on, Cissy, we're on."

They stood in the wings, waiting to go on.

"Can you imitate Bernard?" Sabine whispered.

"Of course."

"Suppose I'm a Jewish lady up here for the 'culture' that was promised in the brochure. And you—Bernard—are giving me fan lessons. Like bridge lessons. What do you think?"

"You mean you want to try it tonight?"

"Who else is going to do the cabaret?"

"Oh Christ," Jerry said, but he didn't sound really scared. "Maybe. Why not? What have we got to lose?"

"Nothing that we haven't lost already."

Sabine looked out at the stage. It amazed her. The audience was still there. They had come to see a play and they would stay until the bitter end.

Then something happened. She realized the stage was there for her to do whatever she wanted. She could make it into a Park Avenue salon if she really believed in it. Whose salon was this, anyway? It was hers. She took off her atrocious shoes and made an entrance. There was something beguiling about a young actress wearing an evening gown and carrying her shoes. The audience chuckled. Sabine tossed the shoes aside and proceeded to wind her suitor—the misanthrope—around her little finger. The audience got the point. It wasn't what Bernard had in mind. Sabine's Cissy's was no silly debutante. Her Cissy was a very shrewd female who missed nothing and knew exactly what she wanted.

This audience had missed the point of Bernard's political convictions and they were not interested in his ideas on social justice, but they could get involved with a clever young woman manipulating her lover. They were amused by her, but not by the play.

The Misanthrope was not a success. The audience applauded politely, but when the lights came on, Max faced a sea of disgruntled faces. "Bring on the band," he commanded, and hastily set up the cabaret. Rows of chairs and tables were set up. The Monticello Three, a group of college boys who were working their way through Cornell, hurried on to play. Saxophone, piano and drum, they struck up. The piano was out of tune, the saxophone had not tuned to the piano, and the drummer thumped on every downbeat. It was a lonely sound.

"Everybody dance!" Max cried out in a frenzy. A small dance floor had been carved out of the space between tables.

Nobody danced. Disaster encircled the dance floor. Max grabbed Bertha. "Dance with me," he muttered, and swept her onto the floor. They were not in time with the music, but Max didn't care. Under normal circumstances he was a rather good dancer; now, however, he was pressing—he saw profits flying out the window. The look of the faces surrounding the floor was discouraging. Women pouted; they had been cheated. They had been promised a good time and even a few laughs. Where were the laughs? Where was the good time? Was this what you called a dance? This was what you called a catastrophe. The men were yawning, thinking of bed or Parcheesi. It was getting late. Max danced faster and faster. Bertha tried to keep up with him.

"What's the matter, old folks?" Max cried jovially, to no response. "Come on and dance." They moped on the sidelines, his guests; they sat stodgily at the tables. They had been promised Comedy and Culture; they would not be taken in again so easily.

The band had started with "Old Man River," and continued with it. Nine choruses of "Old Man River," and Bertha was wondering when it would end, or if Max would keep wheeling her around the dance floor forever.

The music did stop, finally, but the silence was worse. The silence was like death. Bertha was aware that a piano was being moved onto the dance floor, but she was too tired to care. She sat down, and Simon sat beside her. The lights were dimming again. Oh God, she thought, don't tell me there's more to *The Misanthrope*. Or maybe they're going to do it all over again. No, that would be more than any person could bear. Talk about revolutions—the guests would have Bernard Rosen's head on a pike.

A spotlight hit the piano. What further torture were they going to be subjected to? Bertha and Simon stared.

Jerry walked into the spotlight. He was walking grandly, bowing to imaginary applause. (God knows it was imaginary with this audience.) Jerry's smile was humble, yet proud. Simon clutched Bertha's hand. What was Jerry up to?

The audience was very still; they, too, were wondering as they watched the boy stand for a long time, surveying the room. Then he spoke. One word.

"Culture," he said, pronouncing the word overdistinctly. The way Bernie did.

Sabine entered. Regal. A grande dame. She and Jerry nodded to one another formally. The two of them said in unison, "Culture . . .," and began their second vignette.

Jerry produced a large ladies' fan. He drew himself up (there was more than a trace of Bernard Rosen there).

"Do you know what this is?" he questioned Sabine.

She changed immediately. Gone was the artiste. In her place stood a woman who would squeeze every vegetable until she found the right one, a woman who trusted nobody in this world, and was nearsighted to boot.

"What what is?" she countered, nobody's fool.

"This." Jerry shook the fan.

" 'Sa fan." Sabine peered at it.

"Do you know what it is used for?"

"Fa fanning," Sabine said.

"Besides that . . ."

"Fa flies?"

The audience laughed tentatively.

"*Never* for flies," Jerry said severely.

"Wha for, then?" Sabine asked him.

"For expression," Jerry said grandly. He spread the fan.

"Expression?" she repeated doubtfully. "Why for expression?"

Jerry closed the fan abruptly. "It would take three hundred years of living with the classic tradition, of immersing oneself in the nuances of the glories of Versailles, the majesty of Molière, the glory of Racine . . ."

"Who? Who? Who are these people? Do they come here?"

"They're dead."

"Then they *don't* come here. So who needs them?"

More laughter.

"They gave us Culture. They established the Great Tradition. We may learn from them." Jerry pushed back imaginary glasses.

"What do we learn from them?"

"How to express oneself with a fan."

"I need *that*?" Sabine was very dubious.

"Don't you wish to be a cultured, cultivated lady of the world?" Sabine shrugged. "It couldn't hurt. So speak to me with the fan."

Jerry fluttered the fan in front of his face coquettishly.

"This," he said, "represents Desire. It says I am available, you interest me, sir, come closer and let us continue this conversation."

"I couldn't just say that?"

"Not if you want to be a lady in the classical tradition. Now this represents Rejection." Jerry tapped Sabine severely on the shoulder.

"Watch it, bud," she warned.

"Rejection," he repeated. "Try it."

"On you?" Sabine asked.

"Of course. Try it. One must not be afraid to attempt. Never fear failure. Hold the fan in your right hand, thusly. Now feel the tradition seeping into your arm, feel the history of three hundred years entering your soul. The fan is speaking to you. What is it saying?"

"It is saying, 'Kill flies!'"

"It is not!"

"It is." Sabine swatted him with the fan. "Got one!"

"No, no, no. The fan is to be used for expression!"

"Look! Look! I'm using it! This is my expression. This part is for all the fancy words you use," *flapp*, "and this part is for bringing me three hundred years of stuff I can't use," *flapp*, "and this is for being so high and mighty with all of us," *flapp*, "and look, look, this is for Culture," *flapp*. "Oh thank you, thank you for teaching me how to express myself! Hoo! Ha!" *Flapp!* Sabine chased Jerry offstage. They stood dripping with perspiration. The audence was clamoring for more. Jerry shook his head.

"We got no ending on this."

Sabine looked at him. "We'll get an ending tomorrow. Tonight, could we just take a bow?"

They did. The audience cheered and they bowed, and then the Monticello Three began to play again. This time it was "Brother, Can You Spare A Dime?" and Max rushed over to the group.

"Happy! Happy! For God's sake, something happy!" The Monticello Three segued into "I Want To Be Happy,'" and guests started dancing. Max sighed with relief.

There was a crowd swirling around Sabine and Jerry; people they did not know as well as people they did. It was exciting. The voices were full of praise.

"When did you put all this together?" Simon asked them. "The two of you are really funny." He looked at Jerry with admiration. It was the first time Jerry had ever seen that look.

Bernard Rosen appeared. "Aren't they wonderful?" he was asked.

"Yes, yes," he answered tightly. "Wonderful, wonderful."

"You're going to have something like this every weekend?" he was also asked.

"You mean like the Molière?"

"No, God forbid, not like that. I mean, like the kids." From now on they were known as "the kids." "I never saw anything so funny in my life. What did they do, make it up on the spot?"

"Oh, no, no, this took months of planning," Bernard said smoothly. "We built the show very carefully. Even the improvisations were planned." He looked at Sabine and Jerry, challenging them. They looked back. And laughed.

Most of the truly important moments in life pass unrecognized; it is only later that one can look back and say, Wasn't I happy then, or Wasn't that a success, or Wasn't life wonderful. At the actual moment one is too busy to notice—or too overwhelmed. That was true of Sabine and Jerry. All they knew was that they had performed on a little stage in a small resort hotel in the Catskills for a few minutes, and their audience had loved them. In no way could they foresee that those fifteen minutes were going to change their lives. For Jerry it meant only that his father had shown him approval for the first time in his life; for Sabine it meant that she had kept herself from being forced back into the ghetto. Entertainment had come to Glenrocks.

Bernard Rosen was no fool. He came over to add his congratulations.

"You were really good," he said.

"Oh?" Sabine looked at him. "Not a complete disgrace?"

"No. I was really surprised." He kept his smile. His eyes were ice, but he kept his smile.

"I think there will have to be changes in the play selection," Sabine said.

"Yes," Bernard agreed. "I was told that this audience was politically aware. This audience is not aware."

"No?"

"No, this audience is bourgeois."

"The audience is okay. The play stank."

"*The Misanthrope* is a fuckin' masterpiece!" Bernard exploded.

"Excuse me. *Your* version stank."

"I'll remember you said that," Bernard said, and turned away.

"I'm sure you will," Sabine called after him. She felt triumphant for maybe three minutes, and then a sudden anxiety overcame her.

"What did we *do*?" she whispered to Jerry. "I don't remember what we did."

"I remember, I think," Jerry said.

"I remember the words. But I don't understand what we did to the people."

"Whatever we did," Jerry said, looking at her, "we're going to have to do the same thing next week."

"I'll tell you what you did," a voice interrupted them. It was Matt. Sabine was both surprised and delighted to see him. In contrast to Matt, all other people paled. Was it because he was stronger, more fiery than other people, more dominant? Or because she was in love with him? There he was, looking like a movie star, dressed in seersucker, open shirt, narrow belt, expensive shoes. Her eye caught everything, but she found herself unable to speak. With Matt, she didn't have to. He kept talking.

"You two were like jazz musicians. You kept improvising," he said. "One solo was better than the next. It was like some terrific jam session. Nobody knew what was coming next. I never saw anybody do exactly what you two did. By the way, my name's Matt Ryan," he said to Jerry.

Jerry shook hands and nodded dumbly. "Thanks. We really do thank you."

They ended up taking a ride in Matt's shiny blue coupe. He was making money working in radio, despite his socialist principles, and he enjoyed spending it. The car was a convertible (of course), and Matt put the top down. They rode through the cool, triumphant evening, the three of them in the front seat, while Matt described their talent. He had a good eye and good taste.

"What it is," he was telling them, "is that you are like chameleons. Both of you can be beautiful or ugly. You make me cry. And you make me laugh. You touch me. That's because everything you do is simple. You don't waste any gestures. You don't waste any words."

Jerry and Sabine looked at each other. They had had no time to waste. That's why there were no extra words or gestures.

"Keep it that way," Matt said. "That way you hit everybody. You're not too fancy. You're not too simple-minded. Hey, you can't miss!"

They drove through the night flying on his words. They drove back to Glenrocks with music in their ears and the wind in their faces. Matt let them out, kissed Sabine, and shook Jerry's hand.

"We'll have those concerts towards the end of summer, I promise you," he said to Sabine. "Go on, get some sleep now. You two must be exhausted."

After he left them, Sabine and Jerry walked toward their respective rooms.

"What are you thinking?" Jerry asked.

"I think I'm falling in love," she said. Jerry flinched with irritation.

"Oh *shit*!" he said. "If you're going to act like that, I'm going to bed." He disappeared into the night.

Sabine wondered why he was so upset. Did he feel the same letdown she did? Was there always a letdown? Was there always loneliness on the fringe of success, waiting to creep in? She went up the stairs to bed, thinking about Matt Ryan. She fell asleep thinking about him.

Jerry did not fall asleep. He lay on top of his cot, fully dressed. He did not move. In his imagination he was watching Matt Ryan. Matt was sharing this room, moving about it, unbuttoning his shirt, unbuckling the narrow belt. Jerry touched himself; he was hard. He turned his face into the pillow and groaned.

Chapter Five

Incoherent with excitement—that's what the summer of 1934 was at Glenrocks. The feeling of creativity was almost tangible. Every weekend there was a new production of a play. Every weekend there were new revue sketches, new songs for the cabaret. Everyone was experimenting.

Once Molière had been laid to rest—*The Misanthrope* did not survive the first weekend; Bernard Rosen did not survive the second—the People's Theater Alliance discovered its affinity for the experimental plays that were being written on both sides of the Atlantic, all of them with a strong political slant. Some were realistic portraits of working-class misery, others were polemics, still others were satires whose origins were in folk tales or children's stories.

There were unexpected discoveries. Who would have thought that Danny, who as an actor was not much more than a grin, would prove to be a remarkably adept revue performer? He was terrible when he tried to *act* like a poor Lower East Side kid, but when he danced and sang he *was* that kid, with all the sass and jauntiness intact.

Who would have thought that Elspeth's rubbery face would be so appealing? Who could have conceived that Sam's worn-down Everyman possessed a kind of biting humor?

Matt Ryan lived up to his promise, and introduced Sunday night jazz concerts. At first, the older clientele at Glenrocks stayed away in droves. They rocked on the porches and sat on the verandahs, settling down to card games. The concerts began with maybe fifty people for an audience. But jazz was irresistible. By intermission every seat was taken. By the end of the concert the room was packed. Cards had been forgotten, bridge hands laid down and dismissed. There was excitement. There was magic! That was Glenrocks that summer.

Everything seemed to work. Max tried to mask his delight

that Glenrocks was making money in a Depression year, but he was not successful in hiding his pleasure.

For it was known that at Glenrocks you could get a good meal, a good tennis game, and good entertainment. You could get your money's worth. And it wasn't just what you got for your money. There was something in the air. People fell in love under a pine bough. Forgot one another in the rush of a political argument. Resolved their differences later in a hammock under the moon. People came to life at Glenrocks.

They also came because of Sabine and Jerry. It was extraordinary. It was electric. The timing was right between performer and audience. Sabine was eighteen, Jerry twenty. But they attracted all audiences. The audiences *understood*. Why? First of all, nothing escaped Jerry's eye. Or Sabine's. They saw everything and gave it the twist that made the people laugh, and understand.

Jerry looked like a long drink of water, saturnine, his black hair frizzing out as though he had just stick his finger in an electric plug. He was wonderful at playing deranged monks, mad scientists, scheming bureaucrats, and horny teenagers. But he could also portray lonely sharecroppers and old men running out of dreams.

And Sabine could look like Garbo one minute and an old crone the next. She was a chameleon, just as Matt had said, and audiences loved to watch the transformation, because it was accomplished with just a movement or two. A hat was added. A shawl. A cane. In one case, a woman's pocketbook; this was a scene that Sabine did solo.

First, she clutched the pocketbook to her side. She was an old lady walking down upper Broadway, squeezing fruit and asking prices, never content—looking for a bargain and a discussion, arguing with the grocers. "You got better? This is the best you got? What kind of price is that? Mister, I buy here all the time, you don't fool me with the prices . . . How many do I want? How many peaches? How many of me do you see? Give me one peach, 'cause that's what I am, right? One peach."

She would count out the money—pennies—carefully, careful of each precious penny. In the counting of the pennies she told it all, the desperation of the old and the poor. Then in a dazzling succession of impressions she would play the

snooty secretary being "couth," the society matron, the
middle-aged mother hiding gray hairs with debutante laughter.

Everyone worked hard that summer. New material was demanded for each weekend. Jerry and Sabine discovered gifts
they never knew they possessed. Jerry's was for languages.
They weren't real languages, of course. They just sounded
real—French, German, Oriental, Slavic; he had an amazing
ear. Sabine discovered she could sing. But never considered it
singing, because she was always imitating—a chanteuse, a
coloratura soprano, a chorus girl.

Then she found out she could write. It happened because
she wanted to describe the characters she had invented. Then
she was able to capture their dialogue. She could make them
real. Again, she used few words, but she gave life to the
scenes. She made a habit of taking notes. By the end of the
summer she had filled three notebooks. But she never showed
them to anyone, even to Jerry.

That was how they worked. Sketches, songs, blackouts
were all performed hit or miss. Do them and see how they
work. Some would fall. Some needed more developing. Some
were hilarious right from the beginning. During the week, Sabine and Jerry would sort out the material, working on some
bits and discarding others. They learned each other's timing,
discovered the effectiveness of pauses, felt instinctively the
moment when they should build, or how long an argument
should last. They learned the value of a look.

The following year refugees began streaming into the
United States from Nazi Germany. There were theater composers and directors and writers from Berlin who had stopped
for a time in Zurich or Paris, taken a breather in a little town
on the Riviera, bought English dictionaries in Madrid or Barcelona, then found their way to New York.

These were the forces of the Twenties in Germany, these
were the mad, nihilist, shocking, decadent Berliners, the talented men and women who created the milieu out of which
had come Emil Jannings, *The Threepenny Opera*, Caspar
Neher, Kokoschka. They had championed Schönberg and
Ernst Krenek, were cronies of Friedrich Holländer and Oscar
Karlweis, had worked with Weill and Lenya and Max Rein-
hardt. Five years before they had taken holidays in the Tyrol

while they talked about the theater. They had planned productions while sunning at Cap Ferrat. Their plays had been produced, their poems published, their songs recorded, their films shown all over Europe. Then suddenly they had been forced to flee, their work forbidden, their money often confiscated. They escaped Nazi Germany, but not just with two candlesticks and a Torah wrapped in a prayer shawl, like the generations that had fled Europe before them. These refugees were luckier. They bought their way out, they had friends abroad.

Glenrocks became a haven for many of them. They came for a weekend and stayed for a week or two, pounding on pianos and typewriters, arguing in two or three languages, producing skits, poems, and miniature musicals. To Bertha they resembled the inhabitants of the old Café Royal, except that these artists were much more aware of the world's turmoil than the great Yiddish artists who flocked to the Café Royal had ever been.

These artists, European Jews, warned about Hitler and the Nazis. Their audiences at Glenrocks, Jews in America, tended to shrug their collective shoulders. What could be worse than czars and Cossacks? Anti-Semitism was old news. Now the problem was job discrimination, a battle for wages, the establishment of unions. It was a time for social change. Talk about *that*!

So they did. And Glenrocks got the reputation of being radical.

Not all the refugees from Hitler were Jews. Some were socialists, others communists. It didn't matter to the Mountain View House. They classified everyone at Glenrocks as a Red and a Jew, and there was talk of free love and orgies that took place under the Glenrocks pines. Couples who were unmarried were sleeping together (that was socialistic, wasn't it?). It was well known that Jewish girls were hot stuff and easy lays. Every boy in Liberty and Monroe knew that.

What it came down to was that the staff and the clientele of the Mountain View House looked on Glenrocks with horror. And hatred.

First of all, Jews, coming in and overrunning the country. Second of all, radicals, trying to overthrow the government, and maybe even making bombs. If they weren't making bombs, they were making trouble. Third, actors. Actors never

were any good, unless they were in the movies, far enough
away so they didn't do any damage.

The Mountain View House also wasn't too fond of Matt,
the hometown boy. The Mountain View House wanted jazz
and it didn't want Jews. But Matt Ryan booked the best
bands into Glenrocks. He was also said to be somewhat of a
radical himself. He had a short temper and a big mouth, but
then he was Irish and that was expected; and his father was a
decent sort. Nobody ever said anything to Matt's face, of
course, because he was also very handy with his fists. But the
talk went on. About Jews and radicals and Reds. And Glenrocks's great popularity.

Herman Dieterl was one of the composers who had come
to Glenrocks from Berlin, via Vienna. He was a dark little
man, balding and mild-mannered, who had written two hit
songs in Germany, then latched onto composing for the
movies when sound came in. He had written tunes for the cabarets, and when Hitler came to power, Dieterl was one of
those who had fled to Vienna. Dieterl could play, he could
orchestrate, he could write music while he was holding a conversation.

He watched Sabine do her solo one night, and when she
finished he said, "*Ach Gott,* you remind me of Abrams. The
whole world could be falling part, and Sammy Abrams looks
in the mirror for gray hairs."

Sabine was intrigued. "Who's Sammy?"

"An actor in Vienna. He is like the heart and soul of the
old city, a little worn out and down at the heels, holding the
stomach in." Dieterl walked around the room stiffly. Jerry
and Sabine got the picture. "Ah, but he is *klug,* he is clever."

"So why does he remind you of me?" Sabine was not all
that pleased.

"The cleverness. He knows exactly what he does every
minute. And he takes off those parts—*ach Gott,* he is every
middle-aged gigolo in Vienna. He has captured the essence."
Dieterl smiled. "Now he makes movies. You two should be so
lucky."

Dieterl went on, "Before I left, I say to Sammy, 'Hitler has
his eye on Austria and you will see what he will do to the
Jews,' and I swear Sammy looked around as though I was
talking about someone else. 'You are Jewish,' I said, and he
turns his profile and says, 'Only from *this* side. I will only

show the Aryan profile.' I mean, it was impossible to be serious with Sammy. I tell him he should learn English, and he tells me he doesn't have time. He's getting married. Which he does. Not to a Jewish girl, by the way."

"What is all this about being *Jewish*?" Sabine said. "What does it matter?"

Dieterl was a little taken aback. "Don't ask me," he shrugged, "ask Hitler."

It was a strange coincidence that two weeks later a letter came from Vienna addressed to Jacob Abramowitz. It was a wedding announcement from Samuel Abramowitz and Gisela Horn. At the bottom, in painful English, was scrawled, "Now I marry. I learn English. How are you? Good luck."

Sabine was shocked. Didn't he know about her father? Had no one ever written? Bertha. But Bertha had been too crushed to communicate anything. It was only after a day or so that Sabine made the connection between Samuel Abramowitz and Sammy Abrams. She went to Dieterl.

"Was this the girl?" she asked, showing him the wedding announcement.

"Yes, yes, Gisi. You received an announcement? How so?"

Sabine told him the story of the two Abramowitz cousins, Jacob and Samuel, who parted at the crossroads so long ago.

"Would you write to him for me?" she asked Dieterl. "You must tell him what happened to my father. I am so sorry he did not know."

"Of course I will do it," Dieterl said.

Dieterl wrote and Sammy wrote back. In the letter he said that he was sorry to hear about Jacob. How was Jacob's family? Send pictures, please. As for himself, he was happy. He enjoyed the roles he played. Unfortunately, he could no longer work in the German cinema, but that was *their* loss.

Dieterl, reading the letter, said, "*Typisch Sammy*," but he said it very fondly.

"Send pictures." They posed out on the lawn with Glenrocks in the background. First Sabine and Bertha. Then Sabine, Bertha, Dieterl, and Jerry. Simon took the photos and Max made himself scarce while they were being taken. In the letter that was enclosed with the photos, Dieterl explained the relationships. Jerry was Simon's son. Simon was Bertha's "friend" (that relationship hardly needed explanation to a Viennese). Glenrocks was an extremely successful mountain resort, although not the kind Sammy was used to. He, Dieterl, was also doing well. Soon he might be writing a score for a show on Broadway. Surely Sammy had heard of Broadway. Love to Gisi.

Later Sammy wrote again, a little note slipped in with an eight-by-ten glossy photo of Sammy Abrams (his Aryan profile showing), hands clasped, smoke curling up from an elegant cigarette. The moment Sabine saw the photo, she knew exactly what Dieterl had meant. Sammy Abrams was the Preposterous Lover. The Rogue. A burlesque, even. And then she wondered what he was really like—was he at all like her father? Was he an idiot? No, she knew—from Dieterl—that he was not. She guessed he was a charmer—the way Jacob had been a charmer.

The note said only this: "Bressart is in Hollywood. Peter Lorre is in Hollywood. Abrams is still in Vienna. What means 'Glenrocks'?"

Dieterl had come over to the Abramowitzes for dinner. A celebration dinner. Bertha and Sabine were moving. No more Rivington Street. So Bertha invited Simon and Jerry. Sabine asked her to invite Matt. And Dieterl dropped in. Dieterl looked at the photo of Sammy.

"He thinks he is Conrad Veidt," Dieterl remarked. "But what would he do here in the American movies? Nothing. They wouldn't understand him."

Moving day was not what Bertha had had nightmares about. They were not being thrown out into the street. They were moving to an apartment on Riverside Drive that Simon had found for them. It was high up in the Nineties, and the rooms faced the street rather than the river, but it was immense compared to the three rooms on Rivington Street.

The moving men took their belongings, though to tell the truth there wasn't much to take, even after all those years. Bertha decided to leave the kitchen table and the chairs, the table she and Sabine had fought so hysterically to save. Now she left them for somebody else to use or throw away.

Saying goodbye was painful for Bertha. She saw Jacob everywhere. She remembered, in this chilly January, the heat of that day in July, her first day in America, their nervousness, the ice-cream parlor, his making love to her. How wonderful it had been, all of it. For a last moment she sat down on her suitcase, an immigrant once more, and held on to the memory of this room.

For Sabine it was a different story. Goodbye to Rivington Street, goodbye to misery, goodbye to hand-me-downs and childhood. It couldn't go fast enough. She had no memories, none she wanted to keep, of this place. Riverside Drive was different. When the wind blew like a demon off the river and the snow whipped around the corner, that reminded her of Glenrocks in winter, her real childhood, her happiness. She could not wait to leave Rivington Street.

It was time. Simon had come with a taxi. Sabine went down the stairs. It was finished.

Bertha let them go. She wanted to check. Had she left anything? Had she not! She was leaving a whole world there. The walls were bare, lighter in spots where pictures had hung. The kitchen table looked lonely without the rest of the furniture. The closets were open and empty. This was the first occasion she had time, even a moment, for reflection. She had fled Poland, fled France, left England to join Jacob, left him behind in Miami. She had never taken a moment to reflect. Now she did. And she loathed it. Better to run than to linger. Too difficult to look back on what had been. Too painful to say goodbye to the longest part of your life. Close the door and turn the key. Turn your back. Go downstairs. Leave.

Sabine did not glance back as the taxi took them away from Rivington Street. She could hardly wait to get to the new apartment. French windows that opened onto a terrace overlooking the street. From the little balustrade, you could see the trees in the park and a bit of the Hudson River. The living room was gigantic enough for two rooms. There was no dining room, but who cared? There was space, privacy, a new life there. There lay her future!

Matt came to visit and took to escorting both Sabine and Bertha to parties held mostly to raise funds—for coal miners, for farmers, for strikers, for the workers, against Fascism, against the mine owners, for the Labor Party, against one wing of the Labor Party. Sabine and Jerry were constantly called on to perform at these benefits. It amused her to watch Matt wheedle trios, jazz groups, tap dancers, comics, singers into lending their services. He was in his element, and he loved the parties. He could argue about anything. He had more facts at his command than most, and there was always that grin, and that charm.

Sabine, like most people, bowed to his superior knowledge. After all, he had been there, working on farms, hitchhiking around the country, riding the freight cars with the hobos. He had gone to Kentucky to work in the mines, and then work for the miners, organizing them. He had gone out and seen the world for himself; he had done battle—and she had done nothing.

Once, during a heated discussion—oh, there was nothing cool in those days, not the music, not the passions, not the politics—Sabine had asked what all the fighting was about. It was just after the Nuremberg Laws had been passed in Germany, the laws that had excluded Jews from citizenship. Before that they had been excluded from most professions, and then forced out of the stock exchange.

Sabine and Matt had been to the movies, one of the Cagney films that Matt so dearly loved. Any of the Warner Brothers movies with tough Irishmen was for him. He could do lovely party imitations of the movie tough guys, but Sabine secretly wondered whether he didn't sometimes play the role for real.

With two scotches behind him, his long legs stretched out, Matt started. "Oh God, Sabine. It's something like the movies. You have your good guys and your bad guys. Watch the newsreels, you'll see what I mean. The bad guys are up there on balconies screaming over microphones for more guns and more armies, they want more territory. They wear their shiny boots and their military uniforms with thick leather belts to cover up their middle-age guts.

"The good guys got their morning coats, and their little civilian hats, and they keep smiling these nervous little smiles. They mean well, I guess, but they don't want to disturb anything. They don't want to be rude, so they let things slip by, they give things away."

"You know what?" Sabine said.

"What?"

"You're not much help!"

Matt laughed and took another Scotch, and they went to another benefit and signed their names.

"What are we signing for?"

"It never hurts. It shows solidarity," Matt said. "That's the main thing. Solidarity of the working man. If we hold together, we can beat anybody."

So Sabine signed.

The situation in Spain made it all easier to understand. Civil war broke out; the rebels were Falangist, fascist, and Germany sent troops to aid them, and dive-bombers (that was a new word) to strafe (that was another new word) civilian populations. Four columns of General Franco's rebel army marched on Madrid. A fifth column (another new phrase) undermined the city from within. The rebels bombed Madrid, district by district, in an attempt to break the Loyalists' morale. They did not succeed.

What had happened? What was happening? The democracies argued, but they did not want to interfere in a civil war. Bombs tore through buildings and shattered underground stations where half the population huddled. Troops fought with ferocity in the mountains and on the hot dusty plains of Spain, while young intellectuals in New York banded together and formed groups with names like the League Against Fascism, the Young Communist League, the Supporters of Democracy. The Left sent volunteers from all over Europe to Spain—the International Brigade; Americans formed the Abraham Lincoln Brigade.

Russia sent help to the Loyalists, while the democracies continued to argue and the politicians smiled. The Duke of Alba's Palace, a great museum, was bombed and destroyed; the village of Guernica was reduced to rubble. The newsreels carried pictures. They showed the lines of refugees, with chairs and bedding piled on wheelbarrows and carts, streaming out of the cities.

The war had broken out in the middle of July. The rest of the summer was consumed in raising money to help the Loyalists.

Matt decided to do more. He wanted to be a correspondent, and decided he would go to Spain. He walked into the network's office. He had no introduction to anyone—his mouth had always been his best introduction. He talked his way past two receptionists, blarneyed his way past a much tougher private secretary, and found himself sitting in one of those corner offices where one view sweeps past the Hudson practically to San Francisco and the other stretches north beyond the skyscrapers and Central Park, beyond the valley where he grew up. These offices, the corner ones, were where power resided.

The man at the desk stared at him. His name was Boseman, and he headed the network's news bureau.

"What is it you want?" he asked. He wanted to hear Matt's voice, to have a chance to study him.

"I want to help you," Matt smiled. Bosemen didn't. "You need me. Who's there in Spain, who do you have in Europe? There's Shirer. And there's Murrow. The *New York Times* has Tolischus."

"How do you know *whom* we have?" Boseman accentuated the objective case.

"That's a correspondent's job. To find out things."

Boseman was listening. He liked the voice. Not a radio voice. Flatter, not so sonorous, but honest sounding.

"I do know you're thinking of sending Richard C. Sadler." Boseman looked at Matt sharply. Matt continued, "I also know you think there's a problem. That's why you're hesitating. Now, I don't know what the problem is—"

"Do you speak Spanish?" Boseman interrupted.

"Some. Two years in high school. I speak a little Yiddish, too."

"Are you Jewish?" Boseman asked.

"The name is Ryan. I worked in a hotel in the Catskills."

"And is that the limit of your experience?"

"No. I've been working at WEVD, I've prepared news, I've done broadcasts. I've organized jazz concerts. I've been down to the coal mines. Would you like to hear me talk about *that* for a half an hour?"

"I don't have a half an hour," Boseman said, but he was beginning to like this man.

"Could you leave in four days?" he asked.

"If you can get me a passport. I can't do that in four days by myself."

"That can be arranged."

"Fine. Then let's spend sixty seconds talking about salary."

When Matt left the corner office with the two views of the world, he had the job. He would leave after the weekend, and he didn't know what to do with his excitement. He had to talk to someone, celebrate with someone. Sabine came to mind. Why? He dialed long distance and placed a call for her at Glenrocks.

Sabine got the message and returned the call. There was something about seeing Matt's name on a piece of paper that excited her. His indifference was maddening. He would drop in at the apartment and talk to Bertha, argue with Simon, at times ignore Sabine, at other times listen carefully to her opinions.

But now he was calling her, and calling her from New York, so it must be important.

"I'm going to Spain next week," was the way he started the conversation. She could not speak.

"What do you say?" he asked. She still could not speak. "Hello, are you there?"

"Yes."

"Well, say something."

"Why are you calling *me?*" It was all she could think of to say.

He didn't know the answer. He had asked himself the same question. "I am so excited, I had to call somebody."

Somebody, she thought. *Anybody?*

"Aw, you know, it's what I always wanted," he said. "To be really on the radio, and now to be covering the war, to be in the middle of the action—"

"Will it be dangerous?"

"Oh, I should think so." He tossed it off. Everything worth doing was a little dangerous. "Aw, come on, Sabine. Be happy for me," he coaxed.

"I am," she said, trying to disguise her irritation. "I am happy. I am happy, *happy.* Will I see you before you go?"

"Of course," he said. "You and Jerry promised to do the benefit Friday night. You didn't forget, did you?"

"No, I didn't *forget,*" she snapped. "Listen, I have to go now. I'll see you Friday."

She hung up the receiver. Jerry was waiting to rehearse.

"Well?" he asked when he saw her face.

"Matt's going to Spain. As a war correspondent. He just called."

"He called you?" Jerry asked, surprised, his voice sounding odd.

Sabine looked at him. "Yes, he called me. I guess the three

thousand four hundred and eighty other people in his life were out somewhere. Let's rehearse."

They went back to their sketch and began to improvise, but it did not go well. And neither one of them could say what was really wrong.

They met Matt in Manhattan Friday night and he took them to the brownstone on West Seventy-fourth Street where the benefit was taking place. As they walked up the steps, they could hear the party inside, because the windows were open.

There was no one to make introductions. Introductions would not have helped; conversation was impossible (which stopped no one from talking). They talked at each other, and laughed a great deal. An older man took Jerry to one side. Sabine watched. For ten minutes the older man had his mouth close to Jerry's ear, and Jerry kept nodding. He held a glass in his hands, nodded, twisted the glass. There was something so unfamiliar about his actions. Sabine waited. Finally the man smiled, although it was not a warm smile, patted Jerry on the cheek, and left.

"Who was that?"

"He says he's a director."

"Is he?"

"I don't think that's what he wanted."

"Well, what did he want?"

Jerry looked at her, and then shrugged. It was over. It never happened. In his mind he asked himself, *How could they tell? How to tell from just looking at him, that he might?*

"Let's do it and get the hell out of here," he said roughly.

"Fine. Are they ready?"

"We'll tell them they have to be ready. My father's driving up to Glenrocks. I'll go with him. You need a ride?"

"No," Sabine said, and felt herself flush. She went over to Matt while Jerry prodded the host to get the entertainment started.

Sabine marveled at Matt. How did he manage it? He had come in here knowing practically nobody and already he had an audience. And a fan club.

"But of course you should," she heard a woman tell him admiringly. "I think it's the most thrilling thing in the world.

To go to Spain! Look at us. We raise a little money to buy a few guns, a few bullets. But you, you are doing the real thing! You are going over! Will they let you tell the truth?"

"What's to stop me? They censor military information, but that's all."

"Oh, my dear," a second woman said, "you are very young. You know who owns the networks, don't you? Jeremy works at CBS. He'll tell you."

Jeremy nodded wisely. "Don't be surprised when they start to blue-pencil your stuff. They will, you know."

"Who's 'they'?" Matt wanted to know.

"Oh, come on," Jeremy scoffed. "You're not *that* naive. 'They' is the same 'they' who control everything."

"Oh," said Matt, "*that* 'they.' I didn't know which 'they' you meant. Now I know."

"Aha," said Jeremy. "I knew you would. Look out for them."

"I intend to."

"By the way, it would be an enormous help if we could put your name down as part of this organization," the woman to Jeremy's right said. "You see, the names of famous people, people like you, active people, the doers of this world, they add so much. They sway the hesitant." She was smiling brightly.

"Now, which 'they' is that?" Matt asked her.

She looked puzzled, but Jeremy said quietly, "That 'they' is 'us.' "

"Oh. And which 'us' am I supporting?" Matt said.

"The League Against War and Fascism."

"That sounds like good things to be against," Matt said lightly, and signed.

The entertainment began. A friend of Matt's, a very quiet black man, sat down at the piano and played. The solemn expression on his face never changed, but the music was infectious. His left hand was a bass section all by itself. The conversation dwindled and finally stopped. It was impossible not to listen to him. When he finished, they cheered.

Then the first pianist was joined by a second. They broke into a strident sound, but the beat was even more infectious. It was a grin. It was a stomp.

"What's that?" Sabine whispered.

"Boogie-woogie," Matt answered.

The entertainment was nonstop. A huge black woman slammed out "I'm Black as a Berry But That's Only Secondary When I Get You in the Dark with Me," to great roars of laughter.

The mood soared. Hey, it was wonderful to be here and to be talented and to be listening to other talents. The music stopped only for the comedy, the comedy only for the music. Everyone was bright, and everyone was dynamic.

Sabine and Jerry were introduced. They did one song and one sketch, as scheduled, took a bow, and got off. The applause continued, as it always did.

"I'm gonna try something," Jerry said.

"Oh come on," Sabine sighed. "There are too many people on the bill. We've done enough."

"No. I feel like doing this," Jerry said, and went back on. Sabine could not believe what he was singing.

Once, when they had been at a loss for a number, she had read from the *New York Times* the names of all the generals and political leaders who had been liquidated at the Moscow Trials. Together she and Jerry had sung the names together in a merry kind of folk *Kazatski*, that went faster and faster as it named more and more men and women who had been liquidated. It had been mildly amusing at Glenrocks. It met only a silence here—the one thing you did *not* do at this sort of gathering was criticize the Soviet Union. And Jerry knew that—why was he antagonizing them, Sabine wondered, when Matt had worked so hard to get this entertainment together? The audience started to boo. Jerry turned red in the face but continued, singing faster and faster, his tongue never tripping him up. Out spilled the names, one after another, until he ended with a flourish and walked off. There was no applause.

The master of ceremonies hurried on. The last act was a Spanish flamenco singer whose name was Iglesias. He had just come from Spain, from Madrid, for the purpose of raising money for the Loyalist cause.

"Come on, I want to get out of here," Jerry said roughly to Sabine, but Matt's voice was even sharper.

"You go. We're staying."

"Suit yourself," Jerry said and Matt looked at him, really angry now.

"What's the matter with you?" Matt said.

Jerry seemed on the verge of tears. And then he did a strange thing. He kissed Matt on the cheek.

"Goodbye, Matt," he said and left before the other man had time to react.

Iglesias, the flamenco singer, was the main attraction. Beaten and exhausted and only two weeks removed from the war that had engulfed his country, he sang. They threw dollar bills at him, like fans throwing roses to a matador. The money poured in. The wealthy and the powerful opened their wallets and their checkbooks, and why not? Who would not have given, having heard the great Iglesias?

Matt wanted to shake his hand, to meet him, to thank him. But when the two men met Iglesias's gaze flickered toward Sabine, and he took her hand in both his own and smiled. Tired and depressed, he still responded to her, a man responding to a beautiful woman. And Matt responded to that, turning cold and leading Sabine away without another word.

"Why did you do that?" she said.

"I didn't like the way he was looking at you."

"And how was he looking at me?"

"The way a man—looks at a woman."

"And what's wrong with that?"

"Well, you're not a woman yet."

"Yes, I am," she replied coolly.

His look was brief but startled. "Come on. I want a drink."

"Certainly. I'll have one, too."

"You drink?"

"I can. Tonight I want one."

He nodded and ordered a double for himself (as always), and a single for her. He downed his double and ordered another; she took a sip of hers and looked at him. For a moment she thought she was going to cry, because she was already lonely: he was going away. She had never considered that possibility and didn't want to consider it now, but there it was. His face was tantalizing to her. She wanted to touch his jaw. She wanted him to touch her. It was infuriating. She drank a little more scotch. It helped her say what she wanted to.

"Were you jealous?" she asked him.

The question took him by surprise. "Jealous? Of Iglesias? Oh no, it wasn't that—"

"Why wasn't it that?"

That question stopped him for a moment. "Christ, Sabine. Iglesias is an old man compared to you. Look how young you are."

"My mother was *married* at fifteen. I'm twenty. Why don't you tell me the truth?"

"Come on, we have to leave."

Everyone in the room seemed high now, laughing, giggling, shouting.

She kissed him. She looked at his lips and wanted to feel his lips on hers. She wanted him to kiss her, but since he wouldn't, she kissed him. And felt, finally, what a man's lips were when they wanted to kiss a woman. No matter what he said, Matt wanted to kiss her. His lips were polite at first, but then he grew hungry and his tongue pressed its way until she opened her mouth and let him in. Scotch. Sexuality. *A Feuer brennt.* She wanted to feel all of his body and couldn't, wanted her hands to explore his back, but there were clothes in the way. She had to be content with the smell of sweet scotch on his breath, and his tongue in her mouth. Yes, and he was hardening, she noticed with satisfaction. She could feel him grow hard, and it was a kind of triumph for her. She pressed herself against him, almost spitefully. If he was going to leave her, at least he should be miserable. Did that make sense? She didn't understand, but she wasn't going to stop. She wanted him to notice her. No. She wanted him. Ah, well, then she did understand, after all.

He broke away and he was breathing hard. There was an almost sleepy look in his eyes and his voice was different, almost furry, when he spoke.

"That's a very dangerous game you're playing," he said, "and I don't think you know what you are doing."

But she did.

"How did you like that kiss?" she asked.

"Fine."

"Is it always like that for you?" she asked, and watched him. Was he blushing? That's the way it looked to her.

"What do you mean?"

"Haven't you been with other women?"

He had to smile. "Yes, I have been with other women."

"Is it always that good for you?" She was persistent. "When you're with other women, is it always that good?"

He was honest. "No. Not always."

She kept at it. "Is it *ever* that good?"

And he continued to be honest. "No," he said quietly. "No, I don't remember it ever being that good."

Suddenly she let go. "Listen, I shouldn't say this because it's wrong to, but you're going away, and I might never see you again—"

"Oh, Sabine, of course you will."

"Don't stop me. I want to tell you this. I have always loved you. I loved you when we were kids and you took care of me in the schoolyard. I loved you. I always wanted to be near you. I wanted you to kiss me. That's not all. I want you to make love to me."

"Please, Sabine, don't."

"I do. I want it to be *you*. I don't care if you're angry. That's how I feel and I want you to know it. And now you do. Okay. Now you can take me home."

It was dark in the crowded room which was filled with perfume that was a little tired, the musky smell of bodies, stale cigarette smoke. A few lamps were lit, but they cast more shadow than light. Matt could not move away from Sabine without an effort, and he did not make that effort. The scotch was in him and the Irish came out. He was staring at her, looking down at her, and there was a kind of anger in his eyes, but more than that, too. It wasn't until many years later that she grew to recognize the look of pain.

"I think I love you," he said. "No, I don't *think*, I know. And it is hard for me, Sabine. I'm too—" He didn't know how to finish that. "I'm on my way to Spain. My bags are already on the boat. I'm on my way to doing what I've always dreamed of doing. And I wouldn't let anything in the world stop me now. Not even you. I shouldn't have kissed you."

"You didn't. I kissed you."

"I could have stopped you." For a moment, he grinned. "I could have stopped you, Sabine, but I didn't want to. I wanted what you did. I wanted to know how your lips would feel. I was curious. Maybe more than that. And now, much more than that. I've loved you—one way or another—since you first went to school."

"But I don't want to be tied down. I want to be free to go where I want to go."

"You're *going*," Sabine said. Already the speech was too

long, and just a touch too Irish-maudlin. "Nobody's tying you down. I'm not asking for that. I don't want you to stop or give up your career. What do you think, I want to get married? I don't want to be married." She was feeling totally sophisticated. "I just felt really lonely when you called to say you were going," she said.

Something in her tone reminded him of when they were children. He put his arm around her shoulder and drew her against him, to comfort her. But they were not ready for comforting one another, for solace. He was drawn to her lips again. It was like eating peaches, drawing out the juice, tasting the sweetness. They drew away from each other, gasping. There were tears in his eyes. She blamed it on the smoke.

"I was always so sure of what I was doing," he said, shaking his head.

"Make love to me tonight, Matt," Sabine said.

"No." He was quite definite about that. If he made love to her tonight, he would never leave her.

But he did not want to be away from her either. They solved the problem by wandering around New York. They left the party to walk down the street, to sit in an empty bar while Matt had two more drinks. Their eyes would lock, and then one would turn away. Then they walked the streets, mostly dark and empty of people. They would pause. He would kiss her. He would kiss her ear and hold her, and then almost push her away from him, and they would continue to wander aimlessly. They dared not stop too long. They dared not linger in an embrace.

The moon skimmed over the silver pinnacles of the skyscrapers as they walked. The dawn rose at their backs as they walked down Fifty-second Street. The jazz joints were closing; the musicians were coming out, blinking at the light, never accustomed to daylight, it seemed, always caught unaware by that other part of the world that existed during the day. Many nodded a greeting to Matt, raised a hand in a wave, but no one stopped to chat.

Sabine and Matt continued to amble. The buildings in front of them were gold in the morning now. They could glimpse the Hudson, see the pier and the ships.

"Are you hungry?" Matt asked her.

When was she not? They went into a diner across from the pier and ordered bacon and eggs, and then pancakes, and coffee in mugs. The coffee woke them up enough for them to realize that they were both exhausted, exhausted from emotion and the night and the walking. Sabine fell asleep sitting up in the booth, her head against the side. He waited awhile, then woke her gently, his strong hand grazing her cheek. She kissed his hand and then came awake, not sure where she was, but sure somehow of him.

And then it was time to go. Sabine had slipped her shoes off under the table, and now she could not put them on again; her feet had swollen. She carried her shoes in her hand and he began to laugh. He picked both her and her shoes up in his arms and toted her across the avenue and the cobblestones.

The porters smiled. They were used to unusual behavior at sailings. These two could have been honeymooners. They were a good-looking couple, he kind of rough-and-tumble, he could have been one of them, but she—she was something special. They looked at her—only for a split second, there was not that much time—but they caught the jet black hair and the alabaster skin and the clear eyes, eyes that never looked at them, but only at the lucky stiff who was carrying her.

Matt carried her up the gangplank and then set her down gingerly, and they walked along the corridors like college kids coming in late from a frat house party, she carrying her shoes and he stumbling a bit because it was the beginning of the morning after.

In his cabin, there was a crowd.

They were all there to see Matt off. Dan Ryan. Bertha and Simon. Everyone except Jerry. They huddled together in the little cabin and they all met Richard C. Sadler, who stood a little apart. Everything about him seemed faded—sandy hair fading into almost gray and fading away from his head, eyes a faded blue, features fading into resigned tolerance laced with alcohol. Sadler was amused by Matt's friends and his family and his excitement. Sadler could not remember the last time *he* had been excited.

Simon had brought champagne, and it was tossed into chilled glasses by a steward who would get a good tip at the end of the crossing.

Addresses were exchanged. Bertha wanted Matt to visit her

mother in Paris. Simon had the names of friends. There were the usual promises to write.

There was no chance for Matt and Sabine to be alone. No place to go. Only time for a few sentences over the champagne. Both of them felt awkward.

"You don't have to write," Sabine said.

"And what if I didn't?" Matt asked.

"I'd be furious."

"Then I'll write."

They had some more champagne.

"This is a terrible time to fall in love," he said. "A terrible time."

She proposed a toast. More—a pact. "To us—for as long as we want to be together. And when we want to leave, we leave. I love you."

They clinked glasses, drank, and he kissed her one last time. When his lips left hers, she noticed her mother looking at her. Sabine closed her eyes. It was a sudden realization. She did not want to be like her mother. She did not want to, would not be so dependent on a man that her whole life flew apart at his departure. She would not be like her mother.

The gong rang. It was time. Dan Ryan stopped talking and stared at his son, then hugged him. How long had it been since he had hugged his son, how many more times would there be? The tears were hard to control. It was better just to leave. He did, waving them all goodbye. And then there was the confusion, the corridors filled with people, the messages, tears, waves, kisses, promises. A band was playing on the A deck. Simon shook Matt's hand and Bertha gave him a kiss. Sabine and Matt merely stared at each other. There was nothing to say that hadn't been said.

Then they were on the pier, all of them except Matt. Confetti and streamers were tossed in the air, and the band was still playing.

And then he was gone. Sabine went back to Glenrocks to finish out the summer.

Chapter Six

Jerry never asked about Matt. And Sabine never asked Jerry why he hadn't come to see Matt off. Matt was the subject they avoided. Instead they worked. They finished the season with the Labor Day weekend.

Two days later Sabine, who was never ill, came down with a strep throat. Bertha brought chicken soup—jellied chicken soup, since the weather was still blistering hot.

"This is the only way I know that I'm a Jewish mother," she said wryly.

"Don't say that," Sabine said irritably. "You're not a Jewish mother."

"We're Jewish," her mother laughed.

"But not *Jewish* Jewish," Sabine said. "I don't believe in all those racial distinctions." She tasted the soup. "Mmm, good. But see what I mean? What Jewish mother would serve her daughter *jellied* chicken soup?"

Bertha smiled, but she did not laugh.

In two weeks' time Sabine was well again. And she and Jerry started to work, already planning for next summer.

Sabine didn't expect Matt to write. She wanted him to, but she didn't expect it. And he didn't. There was a hasty note, saying he had arrived in Barcelona. And there was another note to Bertha, saying that he had visited her mother in Paris. All was well. That was it.

The winter passed. Work seemed to be the answer. Summer came, and Sabine was too busy to be lonely. There were times when she thought she had forgotten Matt, but that was not the case. She dreamed about him often. What disturbed her was that sometimes he would turn into someone else.

She asked Jerry, "Do you have sexual dreams?"

He appeared to be shocked. "Is there any other kind?" he responded.

Jerry was no help. He refused to take sex seriously, or anything else for that matter. Except work. When it came to work, he was totally concentrated, and ruthless. He could smell a bad idea, a sentimental word, a self-pitying attitude immediately. Out. Blue-penciled. He resisted self-pity, which was one of the reasons a great deal of his work was extremely moving. He hid the pain. Pain was something neither Sabine nor Jerry had to talk about.

Sabine never advertised her sensuality, but there was something about her. Simon noticed it.

"That's some gorgeous kid you got there," he remarked one day to Bertha. From that moment on, Bertha was careful never to leave them alone together. Bertha may not have been aware of Sabine as a child, but she certainly had more understanding of her as a woman. She decided it was time to teach Sabine the hotel business—at least the buying of food. For two months Sabine accompanied her mother to the Washington Market, to meet the wholesalers. She watched her mother in action, bargaining. This was a Bertha that Sabine had never seen. She had no shame. She used every wile, threatening, wheedling, flattering.

Sabine learned fast. She learned to smell the ripe melon and spot the sour tomato. Then one day Bertha said to her, "You go to the market tomorrow and order. I'm busy." Sabine went.

"Where's your mother?" the wholesalers asked, curious.

"Why? Is there something wrong with me?"

They grinned. "Nothing wrong with you, honey."

"Good. Then show me some lettuce."

"Sweetheart, I can show you anything you want. Lettuce? Look, here's lettuce."

"You call *that* lettuce? Give that to the Mountain View House. They won't know the difference."

"Whatsa matter with the lettuce?"

"Brown. Brown around the edges."

"Okay. You're not satisfied. Honey, I want to satisfy you. Here's a little something I got stashed away."

"Aha," Sabine winked at him. "I knew you had a little something stashed away. Yeah, that's more like it."

"I can't hide anything from you."

"Never. Never hide anything from me. We got no secrets, right? How much?"

When he named the price, she walked away. He walked after her. She shook her head. He came down on the price. She relented. Walked back. They agreed.

"And you *will* load it on the truck?" Sabine asked sweetly.

The wholesaler sighed. "You're some kid, you are," he said in appreciation.

Yes, she decided, she was. She liked doing business. She liked the haggling. It was a kind of love affair, with money the aphrodisiac. Money for goods, goods for money. You interested or not? Who wasn't interested? Sabine returned with the supplies. Bertha was pleased.

"I couldn't have done better myself," she said. From then on, Sabine dealt with the wholesalers. She used sex. It was fun.

She also helped Max with the accounts. And learned about seating arrangements, about how fast the service should be, about how much a bartender could clip before it was considered stealing.

Everything depended on the margin of profit. Bertha had learned this. Max had learned this. And now Sabine learned it. First it was a role she was playing, and then it became more than that. It was a way of life. Never something for nothing; the world did not work that way. Once Bertha had told her, "Everyone is mostly selfish," and as long as Sabine looked at the world that way, she was all right.

During the next summer it became evident that a new social hall was needed, one that would seat a thousand people, so Sabine asked Max to accompany her on a visit to Dan Ryan's mill.

Dan Ryan had helped them through rough times, had carried the accounts when Max could not afford to pay, had found workmen for them when some of the other hotels had tried to pressure the labor force to boycott Glenrocks. Dan had been their friend before, and he certainly was one now. He listened to their plans and immediately devised a method to cut the costs by one-third, promising a completion date for the following fifteenth of May. They finished their business, as always, on a handshake.

As they were leaving, Sabine glanced at Dan's desk. There was a letter there, the handwriting familiar.

"You hear from Matt?" she asked, surprised. She had assumed the blockade had stopped all mail from Spain.

"He writes when he can. Not often, once a month, maybe," Dan answered.

"Oh," Sabine said, keeping her voice even. "Well, send him our regards."

"I will."

When Sabine reached the privacy of her own room, she tossed her hat on the bed. That was supposed to be bad luck, but she didn't care. She looked at her reflection in the mirror, and told herself over and over that she didn't care. By the end of the afternoon, Sabine had convinced herself that it was she who had rejected Matt Ryan, and not the other way around.

There was little correspondence from Europe. In March, when the Nazis annexed Austria, Sabine received only two letters from Sammy, the first to reassure them that all was well under the New Order—the second to announce that production had been halted temporarily on a film of his that had been half completed.

In April, construction started on the new social hall. Sabine had little time to worry about Matt or Sammy. There were shows to be prepared for Memorial Day.

Two other events occurred at the same time. First, the Hollywood studios decided to send talent scouts to scour the country. Musicals were immensely profitable, and there must be more couples like Astaire and Rogers somewhere.

Second, Eddie Troncone came into Sabine's life.

The year before, Eddie had been just another trumpet player; Sabine recognized him from the jam session so long ago at WEVD. But this year, the Big Bands were big business. Even at the Mountain View House, everyone had heard about the Big Bands. Harry James had originally come from around Albany; he was practically a hometown boy. There were people who even knew his family. And everyone had heard Benny Goodman on the radio. And their children had his records.

Matt Ryan had persuaded these men to play at Glenrocks. Now Max was shocked to learn that these Big Bands made big money, and were mostly booked solid for the summer. He couldn't believe it. But then he had second thoughts. What did it take to make a Big Band? It took fourteen musicians, and somebody to get the arrangements, and someone the kids could idolize. Somebody like Gene Krupa.

The result was Eddie. Eddie played good trumpet, but he also had a passion for playing and a passion for living that came across on the bandstand. As far as Max was concerned, let Harry James go his own way—Max Abramowitz would replace him. So long, Artie Shaw, too bad you weren't available. Glenrocks has better.

And that was mostly true. Glenrocks had everything; and mostly better. Golf course, tennis courts, good food. Now Tuesday nights were Big Band nights. The band, like the actors, doubled and tripled, playing for the theater on Fridays, for the revues on Saturdays, and for dancing on Sundays, as well as their own concerts on Tuesdays. At Glenrocks everyone worked for his money—but had a marvelous time doing it.

Max lectured the waiters. They were picked for their looks; they were expected to dance with the ladies, whatever age. They could even go farther—Max was liberal; he didn't mind. But he was totally explicit about the dancing.

"I don't want to see one girl sitting out one Lindy," he warned, unaware that he was ten years behind the times. "I want every waiter up, even if you been waiting tables all day—and believe me, it doesn't hurt in the tip department to be dancing at night. I want you up and hopping at the dances. No long faces. I don't want to see one girl guest with a long face. That is a knife through the heart and a goodbye to Glenrocks." The waiters danced.

The heart of the resort was still the old white farmhouse where Bertha lived with Sabine. Simon had a bedroom, too, as did Jerry and the resident director. The entertainers lived dormitory style in the renovated barn, while the waiters and kitchen help lived in a new wing that connected the social hall to the dining room and kitchen. Now there were more than a hundred bungalows at Glenrocks, and each bungalow was divided in two, to accommodate two families.

Sabine never had the time to look around the grounds. She was either getting ready for a performance or rehearsing during the beautiful twilight time, which for the actors was an hour of strained nerves, shouted last-minute instructions, and, often, not-quite-prepared appearances on stage. With this kind of schedule, nothing was ever adequately rehearsed, and during the first five weeks of the season Sabine and Jerry walked around in a perpetual daze. Not only were they concocting their own skits, but they were also performing in each play. The second half of the summer was a bit easier; the programs of the first half were simply repeated.

On Tuesday nights, while the bands played, Sabine and Jerry usually met with the director and the other actors to rehearse for the weekend's production. But in the second week in June Sabine found herself free. The play that week was *Night Must Fall*, and she had refused to play old Miss Bramson and spend her entire stage time in a wheelchair. Therefore she was free until eleven o'clock when the crew (and band) would meet to discuss the revue for Saturday night.

For the first time Sabine saw part of the concert. Eddie had the audience in a frenzy, she could see that the moment she arrived. Everybody's feet were tapping. After every number the young people screamed and stomped. But Eddie wasn't like other idols. They might play for the crowd—he turned inward. When he played he shut his eyes and drew into himself; he hunched over slightly as the sound came pouring forth. He resembled a boxer more than a musician, and at the peak of a solo, when he was crouched over, you could swear he was getting ready to give the knockout punch. When he was finished with a solo, he would stand to one side, dripping with sweat, panting for breath, but never losing his concentration. At all times he was listening to that band. He got his energy from the band. And they were sparked by him.

At the end of the concert the audience tore the place apart. Max, fearing for his furniture, went from row to row, trying to quiet them. He motioned to Eddie: do something, take another bow, quiet them. Do something!

Eddie came back, thanked them all, and told them the band had played everything in the book. To be funny, someone in the crowd yelled, "Sing 'Danny Boy.' "

Eddie cocked his head, and on an impulse nodded, "Okay, 'Danny Boy' it is," and started to sing, without any accompaniment, just himself, alone there on the stage. He didn't have a singer's voice. It was a jazz musician's voice, husky, used more like an instrument than a singer would use it. The phrasing was impeccable and simple. It should have been silly, a young Italian singing an Irish ballad to a Jewish audience, but it wasn't. It was just right, and the audience was hushed. At the end, there was silence, then people murmured "Bravo," and they let him go.

Eddie had a towel around his neck when Sabine entered the dressing room. He looked up, surprised.

"You're the best thing I ever saw in my life," she said.

He admitted it. "Yeah, I'm pretty good. I'm surprised you showed up."

"So am I."

"We got a meeting now."

"Yes."

"You want to go somewhere after?"

She laughed. "Go somewhere? Yes—to bed!" She was exhausted.

He looked at her and grinned. "Okay."

She said, "That wasn't my meaning," and left him to get dressed.

She had an important meeting. Walter Gold, the Broadway producer, was coming to Glenrocks. It was hard to tell who had heard about it first. Everyone seemed to hear the news at the same time. Jamie Butler, the choreographer, had been told by a friend from New York who was a friend of Gold's, who had mentioned he was going to Glenrocks and asked how the food was. That same day three of the actors were alerted by their agents. It was official: Gold was coming to Glenrocks.

The meeting took place on the screened-in porch of the old farm house. When Sabine arrived, Jerry was lying down on the wicker couch. He thought best when he was lying down. She thought best when she paced. Jamie, the choreographer, watched the two of them.

"You know what I like about you?" Sabine said to Jerry.

He looked up at her cautiously. "No. What?"

"Pathos."

"Pathos? That's what you want to present to pure solid Gold who is coming up here to make stars of us all? He doesn't want pathos. Nobody lives on *pathos*. Listen, I am bright and fast and funny. And that's what you like about me."

"Wrong!" she said firmly. "And Chaplin lived on pathos."

"Chaplin hasn't made a movie in years. Pathos? Grim! My

God, didn't we have enough of that, all those movies about chain gangs and beaten-down bums?"

"I don't remember any movies like that!" Sabine said.

"Well I do. My father used to take me to them all. They all starred Paul Muni." And he got up to illustrate, staggering through swamplands, ball-and-chain-gang weary, round-shouldered from years in prison, and, before *that*, years in the bread lines. "Remember?"

"Let's do a takeoff on movies," Sabine said. So they did.

Eddie joined them then. He had changed. He was wearing shorts and a T-shirt, and had a towel around his neck. And he was smoking.

"I remember no movies. Only amateur nights. My mother had me play every amateur night."

"I remember society swells and hotcha music and lots of cigarettes. I don't care what the sketch is, but I want a cigarette holder," Sabine laughed.

"No, Sabine," Jerry told her.

"Why can't I—for *once*—be glamorous and dance on a table?"

"While I'm being *pathetic*? Oh no," Jerry said. They were all quiet for a moment.

"That amateur hour," Eddie said, "that was everybody's dream. They were on their way to Hollywood. The only thing they got was a set of dishes."

"Did you ever win an amateur hour?" Jerry asked him.

"Are you kidding? There was always some girl with a Shirley Temple imitation who won. But I always came in second."

"The Depression," Sabine said, and made a face.

"What was the worst thing that happened to you during the Depression?"

Sabine answered immediately, "My mother and I were almost dispossessed."

"What?" Jerry said.

"They made a mistake and came to the wrong floor, but Mama was behind in the payments—so she was sure they were after us, and she panicked. And that made them sure we were the ones. I kicked a lot of shins. She yelled. I can laugh about it now."

"Well, that's the point," Jerry said with some excitement. "We can all laugh at it now. Let's do it."

"What? A saga of the Complete Depression?"

"Why not? And we can make fun of all those movies that went with it."

"Okay, just so long as I'm glamorous. I want to be glamorous just once."

"Well, that's what a choreographer's for," Jerry said, nodding toward Jamie. "Can we have some glamorous dance sequences? But of course we have to be poor. It should be, like, our dreams."

"That's simple," said Jamie. "Silhouettes."

"I have to do a very bad tap dance," Sabine added.

"That won't be hard," Jamie smiled at her.

"What do you need me for?" Eddie asked. He had lit another cigarette. The four of them were sitting under the naked bulb. Some gnats had found their way through the screen and were crawling on the bulb. Sabine studied Eddie's face. His face was very dark, yet he never seemed to be out in the sun. And there was something still left over from the little boy he once was. Hard to tell—was it trust? Was he still trusting? He was cocky, she knew that. He saw her looking at him. He looked back, and took a drag on the cigarette. No one had spoken. Now he seemed to be directing the question to Sabine.

"What do you need me for?" he repeated.

Jerry took over. "For movie music at the beginning. Very grandiose, with lots of tympany rolls."

"We don't have tympany."

"Fake it."

"I mostly do."

"And the songs will be just with piano," Jerry continued.

"Just piano?" Eddie said, feeling a bit left out.

"And drums," Jerry added, to placate him.

"Just piano and drums . . ."

"And bass."

"Okay. That'll be okay," Eddie said.

"What's the plot?" Jamie asked.

"It'll have to be a takeoff on all those old movie plots," Jerry answered, "but I'm too tired to talk about it tonight. Sabine and I'll get together tomorrow. Yeah, let me sleep on it."

Jerry said good night and left. Jamie had the feeling of being the last guest at the party.

"Good night," he said. Sabine and Eddie murmured something. They were anxious for him to be gone.

Eddie sat across from Sabine. looking at her. He was still smoking that cigarette, blowing the smoke into the air slowly. She could tell that he was thinking about making love to her. Because that's what she was thinking. They kept looking at one another, and neither one of them made a move. It was delicious to sit on the porch and contemplate one another. He continued to smoke his cigarette while his eyes examined the various parts of her body. She found that each part was as excited by his look as if he had touched her. He focused on her breasts; the nipples became erect. His gaze traveled downward and she felt a warmth spread through her body. She wanted to cross the space that was between them. Or have him cross it. But she could not move. She was suddenly incapable of making a decision. She raised her arm to brush away an insect, but her arm was too heavy, it was an effort. She could not take her eyes off him.

Eddie had spread his legs to be more comfortable and she watched his erection grow under his shorts. They were both aware of it, and he made no effort to conceal it; he merely kept on smoking and staring. Sabine swallowed. She watched the way he breathed, the movement of his body under his shirt. She could imagine the strength of his body weighing down on her. His arm moved. He was rubbing his forearm. She could almost feel it on her own arm. She watched his hands and imagined them making love to her. She thought she was about to speak when he got up and turned off the light. Extinguished the light, extinguished the cigarette all in one gesture. And came over to her.

It was a guessing game in the dark. They were naked. She kissed hair. Lips. Belly. Thigh. More hair. She could feel muscle. Her hand grasped the cheeks of his buttocks. Strong. His hands then controlled her for the moment. It crossed her mind that someone might discover them. She would not have abandoned him now if the entire hotel entered the room. Their mouths found one another, and then he laid her on the settee and entered her. He was humping her. The wicker protested, but the sound was exciting to her—the rhythm of their movements, increasing in speed as he increased his intensity. They coupled like animals. He grunted and they slid to the floor. She pleaded with him to stop for a moment, hoping he wouldn't. He didn't. Whispers, erotic murmurs there in the dark, the moan of orgasm, the wonderful moan of lovemaking, the sound of their breathing afterwards.

"Hey," he said, surprised, "you're a virgin."

"What's wrong with that?" she wanted to know.

"Nothing's wrong with it. I mean, some girls just want to *stay* virgin."

"Whatever for?"

"For their husbands."

"Well, how do they know about making love?"

"They don't."

"You mean a man wants to marry a woman without knowing whether she is good at making love or not?"

"Guess so."

"Would you want to?"

"I don't figure on getting married," Eddie said.

"Neither do I." Sabine thought about it. "But if I did, I'd certainly want to know whether he was a good lover or not. That's just common sense."

They were quiet, together, listening to crickets.

"I could do it again," Sabine said.

"Wait a minute, will you? It takes a little while for a guy to get it up."

"Oh," she said, a little disappointed. Then she felt him open her legs, felt his mouth on her legs, his tongue between her legs. He stopped for a moment.

"You'll like this," he told her. "'It's a trumpet player's specialty."

Sabine never lied to herself. There was a moment, after Eddie had left her and she was lying in her own bed, when she thought of Matt. And she wondered why she didn't feel guilty. She didn't. She was not at all in love with Eddie.

Matt? Matt was a lost cause, and she didn't believe in lost causes. How did she get to be so practical, she wondered. *People are mostly selfish*, that's what her mother had told her. And then she thought of her father. *If you can't sell silk, sell linen.* Her father, the *Luftmensch*. Maybe that was the most practical of all. *If you can't have one, don't cry about it. Have another. Don't cry about it. Don't mourn it. Keep going.*

Mostly selfish? Yes, well, admit it. Maybe it's true. Who

knows? She lay in bed, looking out the window. There was a faint glimmer of light. Summer dawns came so soon, mixing the dark and the starlight, and she counted the things she loved. Nights. The smell of grass. Glenrocks. Performing. Jerry. She loved Jerry because he seemed like another part of herself. Matt? She stopped there. He was a part of her life, too. Had been. She could remember him from her childhood almost better than she could remember the man he had become. Troncone was next on the list. Love? No. But like, yes. She liked him. She liked sex with him. That was certain.

Then, just before sleep took over her, she wondered why she had not put her mother on that list. Neither love nor like. Not even thought of.

The next morning they all went to work. By mid-afternoon Sabine and Jerry had come up with the plot.

Joe (Jerry) is a moving man, working for a company that specializes in dispossessing families. Joe is a poor man himself and three months behind in the rent. He is married to Madge (Sabine), who spends her life in curlers and a housecoat, doing the ironing and dreaming of a future in the movies. Her best friend is Marge (to be played by a funny little snip named Audrey) who makes ends meet by having a paper route. After Joe leaves one morning, Marge, while delivering papers, persuades Madge to take the last nickel out of the sugar bowl (Madge and Joe have only one nickel saved for the month's rent) in order to buy a ticket to the Bijou Theater, where an amateur night is being held that evening. Marge convinces Madge that she will win the first prize of $100—enough to pay the three months' rent.

Of course Madge doesn't win: *Marge* does—with her Shirley Temple impression plus a military tap routine. Madge returns to the apartment, defeated, and escapes into fantasy: in a dream sequence she is in a sequin gown, dancing, dancing. She is interrupted by Joe, who comes in and starts to throw the furniture out the window. He has the court order—he must dispossess himself. When Madge protests, Joe asks her, "What do you want me to do? Lose my job?"

Joe's boss appears, ordering him to snap it up. In a frenzy of dance movement Joe tap-dances his way to the window and tosses a chair out—which lands on the head of a conveniently passing movie mogul, who "discovers" Joe and

Madge and sends them to Hollywood, while Marge shouts out the headlines announcing the good news along her paper route.

Two things happened in rehearsal.

At the beginning of Madge's dream sequence she is, of course, ironing, as always. Suddenly, a silver sequin evening gown floats by. Madge is to grab the gown and, in a moment of theatrical alchemy, be transformed into a glamorous heiress, dancing her cigarette-holdered way through life.

During the rehearsal the gown, which was on a wire and was being pulled across the stage by the crew, escaped Sabine's grasp. Desperately she reached for it, scrambling over chairs and climbing on tables. The gown drifted out of sight in the wings, the symbol of her elusive fantasy.

"Keep it in!" Jerry ordered from the back, where he was watching.

"No!" Sabine protested. "I want my moment of glamour!"

"It's much funnier if you never get it. Just keep scrambling."

"I never get to wear that gown?" Sabine asked wistfully.

"Not in this play," Jerry said cheerfully. The gown became a symbol of Madge's aberration, like a mirage haunting a dying man in the desert. No matter what was happening on stage, the moment the gown appeared in the air, Madge would stop all conversation and leap for it. Once she became craftier and sidled over to the gown, hoping to surprise it. Never stopping her conversation, she moved imperceptibly closer and closer, and then snatched—and missed—and the gown wafted out of sight again.

"At the end of the piece," Jerry decided, "*Marge* should come on, as the newsboy, wearing the gown."

"Oh, not my gown," Sabine wailed.

"Of course your gown," Audrey chirped. "What are best friends for?" Marge wore the gown.

The second idea was Sabine's. Originally, when Joe came back to dispossess himself, he lifted a chair and lazily threw it out the window.

"Say goodbye to the chair," Sabine suggested.

"What?" Jerry looked up.

"You and Madge have had this chair for ten years, and now you have to throw it away. Say goodbye to it."

Jerry thought about it for a minute. What would Joe do?

He would notice the little wooden dowel in the back that was broken. He would remember when it was broken. He would touch the chair, straighten the dowel, caress the chair, lift it. It would become a partner, he would dance with it, it would be a part of him. Then he would kiss the chair, then cover it with kisses—the legs, the legs of the chair he would gnaw on with love. Then it would be time. Time to say goodbye. One last kiss, and to the window. He could not do it—throw his loved one into the street? No, he would have one last dance, a dance of remembrance, a dance of memories. All alone, gazing at the dilapidated chair as though it were an elegant Sheraton, he would dance.

Jerry did dance. Eddie, trumpet in hand, was watching.

"Play something," Sabine suggested, and Eddie put the horn to his lips. He played a little waltz, it could have been a folk melody—it was always surprising what came into Eddie's mind. He played and Jerry danced with the chair, and the rest of the company watched with fascination.

Reluctantly, finally, Jerry went to the window. He could not look. He extended his arm, with the chair, out the window. And let go. The chair dropped. Jerry stood motionless, his head turned away from the window. There was a long moment of silence. Then an outraged "Ow!" came from outside the window.

The company broke into laughter. The spell had been broken. But this was one of those magic moments—there are so few of them—a magic moment that had been thrown together out of mixed experiences and transformed into something beautiful. They were all giddy with the success of it, Sabine and Jerry and Eddie, and they danced around together. They performed it that night for the Saturday night cabaret.

The audience was not sure what to expect. The lights dimmed, and in the dark the excited voice of an underling was heard. "Chief, chief—it's terrible! The stock market has crashed. Ten million unemployed! Starvation in the streets! What will they do?"

And a voice, so deep and sonorous, it might be the voice of God intoned, "LET THEM EAT . . . CINEMA!"

Eddie took off like a crazy person on the trumpet. The orchestra raced into the overture, and from that moment the pace never let up.

The audience recognized everything—the pathetic shabby plots, the excuses for "musical numbers," the way the movies had manipulated their emotions for years. But more than that, they understood the characters. They had all been through the same thing, trying to save a dime and not being able to, clutching at some nitwit scheme to make money and failing to, dreaming of luxury and not being able to grasp it. And, finally, having to say goodbye to so many things.

It was an odd moment. The audience roared when Joe was finally reduced to dispossessing himself in order to save his job, but they were strangely quiet when he picked up the chair.

This was Jerry's genius, to sense the moment on stage and take advantage of it. He picked up the chair carelessly. It was just a stick of furniture and he was almost at the window when he looked at it. Then he shrugged, what could he do, and made an effort to throw the chair out the window. The chair would not leave his hands. Then he really looked at the chair. And smiled to himself. Something was in his memory that he allowed the audience to share. He placed the chair and sat down in it. An uncomfortable look came over his face: there was something improper about sitting in the lap of this chair. He got up and switched places—he let the chair sit on *his* lap. Then he was satisfied, so much so that he sighed and leaned his head against the chair.

It was at that moment that Eddie felt the impulse to play. It was not as they had rehearsed it, but he followed his instinct. And Jerry went along with it. It was a strange and marvelous trio—Jerry, the chair, and the nostalgic lonely trumpet crying out for a time gone by. This time the dance was more involved. Jerry was more caught up in his own memories, and he was feeling an empathy from the audience that told him to go with it. It was an MGM waltz he performed, except the hundred strings were missing, and the chandelier and the million-dollar set. He was doing it with one chair and one trumpet and his own artistry.

When he finally let go of the chair and it disappeared out the window, he stood with his hand outstretched, his fingers open as he looked, stared, beyond the audience. Then the outstretched hand became a fist. Everyman with the clenched fist.

This was a radical audience, and the image of the clenched

fist was too powerful. They stood up and yelled, they stamped their feet, they responded with clenched fists of their own.

Jerry was stunned. He stood there, frozen in position. The crowd would not stop. The ending of the story was forgotten. There was no way to quell this. Jerry gestured and Sabine and Audrey joined him for bows. Audrey was livid; she had never gotten the chance to wear the gown. It sailed across stage now in front of their eyes; a gesture of congratulations from the crew.

Sabine kissed the dress goodbye. The house lights came on and the stage lights went off. The performers walked off the stage, but the audience did not stop applauding. Sabine, Jerry, and Audrey came back. Eddie joined them for another bow. And another. After a while they stopped counting.

It was over. And after it was over, there was the moment's sadness. Whatever had happened would never happen quite that way again.

They waited backstage for Walter Gold.

"I was right about the pathos," Sabine reminded Jerry.

"*I* was right about your gown," Jerry said. And they waited.

Everybody came backstage. There were comparisons to *The Cradle Will Rock* and *Pins and Needles*. "This definitely has to go to Broadway," they said. And "Extend it a little, build it up in the middle and it'll be a hit!" they said.

"Nobody's got your talent," they said.

And "Can I touch you now before you go to Hollywood and will never talk to us again?" they said.

They all came back. Except Walter Gold.

Walter Gold was checking out of the hotel when Sabine met him, maybe by accident the next morning.

"You're Walter Gold," she said, and he nodded.

"I am."

"Do you know who I am?"

"You're the little girl who was in the show last night."

There was silence. Sabine waited for him to say something, but he didn't, so she did.

"Well?" That was all.

"Very nice." He smiled and walked toward the car. "But too radical."

But Walter Gold was not the only one who had come to look over "Let 'Em Eat Cinema." Dieterl had been there; with another producer.

"You're gorgeous!" Dieterl said to Sabine. "I love you. You're wonderful. So talented you are."

Sabine nodded. "I didn't expect to see you here. What are you doing?" she asked.

"I am finally writing a show for Broadway."

"Oh, Dieterl, that is good news. I am so glad. When is it going on?"

"Right now. Soon. This fall, definitely. That's what they tell me. But who believes anybody?" He shrugged.

"How is Sammy?" Sabine asked.

"Interesting thought association." Dieterl smiled. "Sammy. I hear he is all right. So far. You know the first weeks after the *Anschluss* were dreadful. The Nazis had Jews down on their hands and knees scrubbing the streets. No, really; I hear the most terrible things. But now it is better. I *hear*. Sammy I do not hear from personally."

A few days later Sabine wrote to Sammy. She assured him that he could always—it was hard to choose the right words in the basic English he could understand—"work" was too menial, "find employment" too distant, "take refuge" too despairing. She finally chose "continue your career." Sammy could continue his career, and the Abramowitzes would help. She mailed the letter, and then forgot about him. And forgot about Walter Gold.

Because Jerry suddenly dropped a bombshell.

"I can't believe it. Can you imagine it?" he chattered excitedly, coming into the dressing room. "I just got a call— Dieterl. They want me for that musical!"

"They want you?" Sabine looked at him in the mirror.

"*Me*? Yes, *me*. I can't get over it. They start rehearsals in two weeks, and I'll have to leave early, I guess. How will you finish out the season? Oh, you'll think of a way."

And then he looked at her face.

"Oh, Sabine, I'm sorry. But the lady who's the star in Dieterl's show won't allow another talented female within miles."

"Oh," Sabine said.

"Should I do it? Tell me I should do it," Jerry said.

"You should do it."

"Oh, Sabine, I love you. I really do love you. And this doesn't mean the end of anything. It's just the beginning."

But Sabine had stopped listening. *People are mostly selfish.* Her mother's words kept coming back to her. What should she expect? But, underneath everything, Sabine realized that she loved Jerry much more deeply than he loved her. And that is how it would be.

He was off in two weeks amid much kissing and laughing and crying. And then Eddie left too. And Jamie and Sabine moped around and pattered through sketches and songs until the one last weekend of the season. And all the promise seemed to have disappeared, like the sequin gown that was always just beyond reach.

Chapter Seven

Jerry called from Boston on opening night. And then a week later the phone rang again at Glenrocks.

"Do you think," Jerry began in a far-away voice, "that you could possibly come up to Boston tomorrow? No—make it tonight."

"I can't get there tonight," Sabine said. "It already is night."

"Oh. I hadn't noticed. Well then, tomorrow?"

"Tomorrow."

The next afternoon she was at the Hotel Touraine waiting for him. At four-thirty Jerry knocked on her door, entered, and sprawled on the couch. He had dropped ten pounds and looked exhausted.

"You're that bad, huh?" Sabine said.

"No. That good. They want to let me go," he laughed. "Actually, *she* wants them to let me go." *She* was the lady, the star of the musical. "She hates the fact that I stop the show. Although I don't know what she's complaining about. She also stops the show every night."

Sabine interrupted. "Wait a minute—are you telling me this show isn't in trouble?"

Jerry looked shocked.

"Trouble? This is going to be a very big hit. That's why I want to stay with it. But *she* is a very insecure lady."

Oh. Sabine had expected to come up and give sustenance to a poor friend who was dying from mortal wounds. Now she was disappointed that Jerry wasn't dying. She laughed and told him that. He recognized the feeling.

"Ten years from now we can laugh, okay. Now I am in trouble."

"What's the problem?" Sabine asked.

"I don't know," Jerry countered. "You tell me."

"Let me see it, the show," Sabine said, "and then we'll talk."

"Oh," Jerry added, "one more thing. She says I'm not allowed to sing another note."

"Can you have music?"

"They don't want to pay for any more orchestrations."

"I see. So: you can't sing, and you can't have any new music. What does Dieterl say to that?"

"Dieterl has stayed away from me ever since opening night. As a matter of fact, everyone has."

Sabine looked out the window. It was a golden afternoon in Boston, and from the corner window she could view the Public Gardens. The leaves were beginning to turn. People were hurrying to the subway station on the corner. What did they care about who was stopping the show?

"I think I better see what you're talking about," Sabine said.

"Of course. I got you a ticket for tonight. It's sold out," he added proudly.

"Then we can meet after the show?"

"Back here. I don't want anyone to know you're here."

"Okay," she said, and he left. He's enjoying this, she thought. He rather likes all this turmoil. She found that annoying.

The musical was playing the Colonial Theater, which was around the corner. The moment she walked up to pick up her ticket she could tell it was going to be a hit. The customers hurried inside, anxious not to miss a moment.

The songs were marvelous, witty and sophisticated, but with heart to them. The Lady also had heart. She was effortless, and she made every moment count. The plot was flimsy. The Lady was in love with a young radical (Jerry), who was torn between political causes and true love. Simple and affecting.

Jerry came on. The audience loved him. And from the first moment, Sabine realized what was wrong. Jerry was pressing too hard—doing a solo turn. He was funny, rather like Peck's Bad Boy up there, his eyes twinkling with a joke he was sharing with the audience, but with nobody else on stage. Charming. The audience loved him. The Lady could have killed him.

During the intermission, Sabine searched in her handbag for a cigarette. Dieterl supplied her with one.

"So?" he said. "You think you can fix him, *ja?*"

"You're not supposed to know I'm here."

"Two minutes after you arrived, I heard. Everybody knows you. We all saw your revue, after all. So touching, when you clutch for the dress, yes, and it eludes you. But now, what about our friend? He is a little—pushy. Or don't you agree?"

Sabine felt disloyal, but she nodded.

"They'll have to let him go, you know. Unless—" Dieterl gave one of his Viennese shrugs and Sabine nodded again, and it was time for the second act.

The second act was short, fast, and snappy. *Too* fast. Show-stopper was piled on show-stopper. What Jerry described was true. The audience went wild when the Lady let down her hair and became a woman. And Jerry was overpowering. Dazzling. Pulling out all the stops. He knew he was good and he let them have it, yes, right between the eyes, and when he was finished rattling off his patter song, he shrugged as if to say, It was nothing, folks. And they came to their feet.

And the rest of the show didn't matter. The Lady got the radical, but who cared. All the talk, as the audience left, was of Jerry.

Back in the hotel suite, Sabine waited, and when Jerry came in he said proudly, "Well?"

Sabine looked at him. "She's right, you know. Your Lady."

"What? Are you crazy? I was incredible tonight."

"Yes, you were."

"I was particularly incredible because I knew *you* were there."

"She's still right."

"She's jealous."

"Maybe."

"*You're jealous!*"

"Probably."

"Listen to the audience. Did you hear the audience?"

"They love you here. I'm not so sure about New York."

"Audiences are audiences. The same everywhere."

They were beginning to scream at each other.

"Well, I was in the audience tonight. And I didn't love you!" she said.

"What? Of course you did."

"I didn't. You were smart-ass!"

"I was terrific!"

"But she's still right. The ending goes right out the window. The audience doesn't care what happens!"

"It's a *musical*, for God's sakes!"

"You're going to get fired!"

That stopped him. Jerry sat down. They were silent.

"Okay. What do we do?" Jerry asked after a while.

"I don't know," she said, looking at him. Not so vitalized now, he looked more than haggard. He looked the way he might when he became an old man. Some day they would both be old. The germ of an idea came to her—the idea for the number.

"Get up and dance," she said to him.

"Are you crazy? I'm exhausted."

"Good. Dance. Social dance. No, dancing school. You're at dancing school."

Jerry got up wearily and started to dance. Rebelliously, the way small boys do who hate girls and white gloves and dancing school.

"Okay, now you're fifteen and you're at Glenrocks. No, make it eighteen—the senior prom."

Jerry grinned as he understood what she was going after. He swept his imaginary partner to him. Was he smooth! Was he on the make!

"It's your honeymoon."

That startled him. He drew back, still dancing, but nervous. He had to extricate his hand from his partner's so he could wipe his palm.

"Middle-aged."

Jerry plodded. His belly protruded. His eyes glazed with boredom. He was on a treadmill.

"You're old now. And she's gone," Sabine said. Jerry kept dancing.

"Who's gone?" he asked. Sabine thought.

"Mrs. Weidman," she answered. "Remember Weidman, our *Beiunser?*"

Jerry nodded. He had seen Weidman after his wife's death, when Weidman could not sit still, when it was hard for him to concentrate on anything, when he had lost his inquisitiveness and his taste for an argument.

"What kind of music is this?" Jerry said in Weidman's complaining voice.

"A waltz," Sabine prompted gently.

"I hate waltzes," he complained more, but his tone belied it. "I hate dancing."

Sabine smiled. It was so true; he had captured the wonderful ambivalence of Weidman.

"All this time you've been dancing," Sabine coached him softly, so as not to break the mood, "you've been imagining your life with the Lady, what it would be like to be married. Now she comes in. You could live with her, or you could leave her. You have a choice. What do you say?"

It was all there in Jerry's face. The pain of living with one woman all your life, the emptiness of never living.

Jerry held out his hand to the phantom Lady.

"Marry me," he whispered.

"There's your number," Sabine said.

Jerry dropped character immediately. "It'll never work," he said. "What am I going to do out there, a *pantomime*?"

"Yes."

"And you call that a number? It'll never work."

Her voice was hard. "You want to bet?"

"Yeah! I'll bet. I'll bet you one week's salary, that is if I last another week."

"Get Dieterl," she said. "Call him."

"He's probably asleep."

"Wake him up. It's all right. He's an ally. He knows I'm here."

Dieterl, who was awake, invited them up to his suite. There Sabine, standing by the piano, outlined the number.

"It will need a line of dialogue," she said. "Something like 'She's asked me to dance; next thing you know she'll want to marry me!' "

Dieterl said, "Yes," listening carefully to Sabine.

"Then the music should begin—the beat, rather, since we can't have any *music*." Sabine looked at Jerry out of the corner of her eye. "At the beginning the beat should be one-two-three. Dancing school."

"Maybe a trumpet for the high-school prom," Jerry said.

"A saxophone is more sexual," Dieterl said solemnly.

"Then for the honeymoon . . ."

"Strings," Dieterl said.

"And for middle age . . ."

"Plonk-plonk, just like in dancing school." Dieterl was right along with her.

"And then he is alone and she is gone. An old man dancing alone," Sabine said.

"Not too sentimental here," Dieterl warned. "Back to one instrument, I think. Yes, here should be, like—a concertina."

Sabine stopped and the tears came to her eyes. The word brought forth such memories. What had she done? Who were the phantom dancers? Herself, her father? She turned away.

"Have I said something wrong?" Dieterl asked, concerned.

"No," Sabine said, "no, I think you're right. One instrument. The music should be a waltz, of course."

"Yes," Dieterl said, finally, slowly. "That should fix the moment. The one we are having trouble with. Now let me find here a tune." He lit a cigarette and went to the piano.

The director heard the idea the next morning and decided to put it in.

"When?" Sabine asked. "Next week?"

"We *open* next week. Tonight. Either it works or it doesn't."

Sabine had never seen anything like it. Dieterl completed the orchestration in an hour, smoking twelve cigarettes in the process. It was sent to the copyist while the director watched Jerry, making suggestions: "I don't understand this part," "Clear this up." They experimented. The number was put together in another hour, then rehearsed with the pianist.

"We put it in cold tonight," the director said. There was no time for an orchestra read-through. At five o'clock the conductor ran it through once with Dieterl and Jerry. The conductor nodded. Everyone agreed! Try it.

"It will work, won't it?" Jerry asked Sabine in the dressing room.

"It'll work," Sabine assured him.

"It'll work," Jerry repeated in the mirror. Then, "It won't work."

"You want to bet?" Sabine said.

"No. I don't want to bet. God, I hate *her*, I hate this business."

It was time to go on. The second act was running very fast. It had been good, but not great. The Lady's number had stopped the show, and now it was Jerry's turn.

"Oh God!" he said in the wings.

"Come on, Jerry," Sabine said in his ear. "I dare you!"

"Oh God," he repeated. And went on.

The audience laughed at his entrance. They were used to laughing at him—his hair a little wild, that's what he was supposed to be, the wild radical.

Laugh at the wild radical.

"She wants me to dance," Jerry told them, and his voice broke. The audience laughed. That was the proper response.

"Then she'll want to marry me. Dance? I hate dancing. I have always hated dancing."

And the number began. All self-assurance was gone. Jerry was suddenly the little boy struggling with the waltz step. Then the make-out artist. The saxophone began a glittery solo.

Dieterl was right, Sabine thought. Saxophones are sexier.

Onstage, Jerry went through each lightning transition. His hand was the seducer, creeping down his partner's back. It was the classic high school prom pose, and the audience identified with it. Then they laughed at the urgency and nervousness of the honeymoon period; they laughed in recognition at the boredom of middle age. And that's when the magic happened. When Jerry let her out of his arms, this imaginary woman. His arms were then free, but they were holding desperately on to—nothing. They were lost, there was the look of grief on his face. She was gone, his partner. He had hated dancing with her all these years, but she was gone. His life was gone, slipping away too, like the image of the woman he could not grasp.

Dieterl's concertina began the same waltz that had started the dance. And for a moment Jerry's face had a look of ecstasy. He was dancing with a ghost, but it was the ghost who completed the joy of a cranky old man who could say, "I hate waltzes . . . I hate dancing . . ."

There was such life affirmation in those two sentences, perverse as they were, that the audience did not laugh. They waited for what would happen next.

The Lady appeared. And Jerry looked at her.

Sabine could see from the wings the extraordinary power that Jerry possessed on stage.

"Marry me," he whispered to the Lady. "Marry me."

The Lady's smile dazzled. The play went on. Jerry had not

stopped the show. The brief final scene passed, and the curtain came down.

When Jerry stepped forward, the reaction stunned him. It was like a physical force. The audience stood and cheered. Bravos fell like bouquets. He stepped back to let the Lady through. The cheers continued. And then the Lady did an extraordinary thing—for her. She gestured to Jerry, and they shared a bow together.

The curtain closed for the last time. Backstage, the Lady motioned to the director, her husband.

"That's it," she said to him firmly. "From now on, the show is frozen. No more changes." She never said a word to Jerry.

Sabine breathed a sigh of relief. In Jerry's dressing room she hugged him, and said, "It worked! I told you it would!"

Jerry was nonchalant.

"Of course," he said. "I knew it would."

To celebrate they went for a drink at the bar of the Touraine.

"I saved your job," Sabine told him over the noise in the crowded bar.

"Yeah?"

"Yeah," she said. "They were going to fire you. Quite right. You were obnoxious." She amended that. "You *are* obnoxious." They each ordered another round. A group in the middle of the room were rehearsing football cheers. Jerry rode over that. "I will never have another number as good as that first one," he said.

"You should be down on your knees, thanking me for what I did for you," Sabine protested.

He changed abruptly. "You're right. I was a shit." And there he was, down on his knees in the bar of the Hotel Touraine. "Forgive me," he said, maudlin tears coming to his eyes. "You are my best, my only friend. I love you. Did you know that?"

Sabine was dizzy from the drinks, and she hadn't eaten dinner. The room was swirling.

"Get up off the floor," she said thickly. "I don't think you're supposed to do that."

"But I want everyone to know that I love you. Should we have another drink?"

"I don't feel very well."

"You see? You see how alike we are, the two of us? I don't feel well either." Jerry got up and lurched out of the bar, leaving Sabine with the check.

That's all right, she thought, *I'll sign his name to it. The sweet bastard, the crazy sweet selfish genius. He says he loves me, and I guess yes, he does. Where's a pencil?* She rummaged in her pocketbook, bringing forth Kleenex, lipsticks, a compact, notes, shreds of paper, littering the small round table in front of her.

He says he loves me, she repeated to herself, *but he doesn't know what that means, does he? Do I?*

"You need a little help?" The voice came from somewhere in the swirling room. It was warm and gentle, and a bit amused.

"I need a pencil," she was saying.

"Don't bother. I'll take care of the check."

"Oh, thank you," she said. The room was really racing now. She tried to find his face in the blur. She found it. She thought it was a nice face. Young. Dark hair. Curly. What else? Good smile, he was smiling.

"Why would you take care of the check?" she questioned him. "What's in it for you?" She realized she was really drunk. He laughed.

"Nothing. Obviously not tonight. No, I was over there"—he pointed to a nearby group of revelers—"and I saw you needed help."

"That obvious?" she said.

"That obvious," he confirmed.

"You a football player?" She was confused. He didn't look big enough to be a football player, but what did she know?

"God, no." He laughed again. "I'm a law student."

"I think I'm going to be sick," Sabine said.

"No you're not," he said very quietly, and took her arm. "You're going to wait."

"I'm going to wait," she repeated as he steered her across the room.

"Are you staying here? What's your room number?"

She told him. They took the elevator.

"Do you have your key?" he asked her. The elevator operator eyed them. She was oblivious; she pointed to her pocketbook.

"Shall I look?" he asked her.

"Please." She couldn't say another word. They got off on the sixth floor. He found the key just in time to unlock the door and help her to the bathroom, where she was violently ill. He wet a washcloth and put it on her brow. She noticed she had a run in her stocking. She noticed he had gentle hands. She was sick again. He stayed with her.

And that is how she met Mark Cardozo, who was going to fall in love with her and marry her.

Chapter Eight

The morning after the night before, as the saying goes, Sabine was packing to leave for New York when the phone rang. It was Mark Cardozo. He suggested breakfast, which she thought was a terrible idea.

"I'm cutting classes for you," he said.

"Today's Saturday. You don't have classes."

"Oh yes. Mornings. I'm a law student, remember."

"I thought you were a football player."

There was a moment's silence on the phone.

"Just how well do you remember last night?" he asked.

"Bits and pieces, evidently."

"I'm going to pick you up in half an hour, and then maybe you'll remember who I am," he said.

And she agreed, because she liked the sound of his voice over the telephone. She packed, left Jerry a note, and checked out of the hotel.

"The bill has been taken care of by Mr. Davis," the hotel clerk smiled sweetly.

"Who is Mr. Davis?" Sabine asked.

"Why, the star of that show at the Colonial!" the hotel clerk said, his eyebrows rising an inch above his horned rims.

Davis? Jerry Davis? Sabine had never checked the posters outside the theater. It was possible he had changed his name. Think of that! Jerry Davis.

The bellman took her luggage out to the curb. A white Packard convertible was waiting, and a young man opened the door for her. He looked vaguely familiar. She checked out everything in that first minute. He was wearing a Harris tweed jacket and a beige cashmere sweater, and a yellow button-down shirt. All very expensive. He was also wearing faded pants and white sneakers. Only the very rich could get away with that, she thought.

He gave the bellman a tip and the car keys. The bellman opened the trunk and her luggage disappeared.

The young man opened the door to the convertible and she got in.

"You *are* the person I was waiting for, aren't you?" she asked, and that made him laugh.

"You really don't remember last night, do you?"

"Not much. I think I was sick."

"That is correct. That is why the top is down. You are going to have some brisk Boston morning air, and then I'm taking you to breakfast."

She liked him. He had a very quick open smile and he was handsome. Very dark, almost Spanish-looking, and well proportioned, but slight. His fingers on the wheel were small-boned. She continued to look at him. Very good-looking, she decided. And warm and polite. She liked him. Yes.

They had breakfast at Thompson's Spa while the busboys mopped the floor with water and ammonia; it was between the breakfast and the lunch rush hours. The ammonia did wonders for her hangover.

"You're a law student?" she inquired, not believing him.

"First year."

"How old are you?"

"Twenty."

"That's young. You must be smart."

"I am."

"Why did I think you were a football player?" She looked at the size of him. "How did I ever connect you with football?"

He laughed again. "Because I was with a rather rah-rah group in the bar last night."

"Oh. Are you going to the game?"

"No," he said. "I'm driving you to New York."

It was a wonderful drive through the New England afternoon. He kept the top down, and she liked that. She liked convertibles, and all the images they conjured up. Rich was one of them. Sexy was another—and Matt flashed through her mind.

Mark told her a lot and she told him a little. He told her about his family, which was very large and had originally come from Pennsylvania, but that was around the time of the American Revolution. They lived on East Seventy-second

Street. His father did not go to work. His older brother
George handled most of the family's affairs. His mother was
terrific. They kept a lodge in Maine, a compound really.
Most of his family were there now, but he had felt a loyalty
to Harvard, and had wanted to see the game.

"My God, you're beautiful," he said suddenly.

"That's because I'm riding in a convertible," she said.
"That makes every girl beautiful."

"Oh no," he said. "No, it doesn't."

He dropped her off at the apartment on Riverside Drive
and asked if he could see her again.

"Of course," she said, and gave him her telephone number.

He turned around and drove back to Cambridge that night.

New York—Manhattan—that was the place to be in 1938.
There were luncheons and tea-dances; cocktail parties and
cotillions, literary salons, Sunday soirées, after-theater parties,
coming-out parties, and Saturday night howlabouts. There
were nightclubs. And jazz. And electric lights.

It was the life Jacob Abramowitz had dreamed of when he
stood arguing on a plain in Poland with his cousin Samuel.
And it was the life his daughter Sabine suddenly found herself living.

Jerry Davis's show had opened in New York, and it was a
smash hit. The Lady was a star returned, and Jerry was a star
discovered. Instant celebrity.

He received an invitation to every art gallery opening, every important party, every sit-down dinner. He would turn
down twenty and accept five. And Sabine would accompany
him to all five. She went because she liked being with Jerry.
It was uncomplicated. She was not required to think. The
smart talk was not smart, really—mostly the leftovers and
hangovers from the alcoholic heyday of Benchley, Parker,
and the others, gone west now to Hollywood or to rest homes
and sanatoriums. The Round Table had splintered, but the
quip remained.

And Jerry was glad to have Sabine on his arm. She was
truly stunning. She wore nothing but white, and wore no jew-
elry because she had none. She had glossy black hair and
amazing cheekbones.

Her eyes were her jewels, as an amorous and drunken investment broker, poetic on three martinis, told her. He was

correct. Her eyes were extraordinary, the color of sapphire, but it wasn't their color so much as their clarity that commanded attention. Other people's eyes, one noticed, were clouded, with smoke, dimmed by alcohol, veiled with ambition, yellowed with time. But Sabine's eyes were clear, and she saw clearly.

Her only other adornment was her laugh. She laughed like a barmaid, loud, lusty, and genuine. That was unique. She found that people were funny, and she laughed at the things they said. Only later did she discover that the man with the sharp one-liners was George S. Kaufman, that the smiling lady with the sweet zingers was Kitty Carlisle, that the attentive playboy who twice brought her champagne was a Vanderbilt; Alfred Gwynne Vanderbilt, soon to be married. She was told *that* by everyone but him.

So she saw Jerry, and he took her to parties, and on Sunday nights when he wasn't working they would sit around his place or her place and cuddle. It was all quite comfortable.

And she saw Mark. He took her to Harvard a number of times, but he never kissed her. She wondered about that, but mildly. He wasn't important enough to her for her to care all that much.

The debutante season and the Christmas holidays fell at the same time. Sabine was quite unaware of the structure of society in New York. Mark had never introduced her to his family. In a sense, she had no idea who he *was*. She knew he was a Cardozo, and that that was like being a Gimbel, a Warburg, a Kuhn, or a Loeb—one of the great families. But she really had no sense of what that meant.

Mark asked her to attend a debutante party with him at the Waldorf and she accepted. She wore white, of course. So did the deb in question, one of the minor Schiffs, who had freckles on her shoulders and red hair and was inclined to be friendly until Mother Schiff ended the conversation with an icy smile at Mark and instructions to the social secretary that Mark Cardozo was not to be received again. He was stricken from the stag list. His sin wasn't that he had brought a nobody, but that he had brought anybody at all. The ingredients at debutante parties were mixed as carefully as those of a martini. One to four—one girl to four boys. Mark had upset the mixture.

"My social career is ruined," he said gleefully. "No more fighting to get at the punch bowl."

They were walking outside the Waldorf on Park Avenue, and it was snowing.

"What did I do?" Sabine asked.

"Nothing. You were merely there. That was enough. Do you want to marry me?"

She took it as a joke.

"You haven't even kissed me yet."

"I haven't?" he said in mock surprise, and proceeded to kiss her in the snow on Park Avenue. She liked the way he kissed. It was definite, but gentle. At the same time, she found that she was analyzing it. They both felt a response, but it was crowded on the street, and in those days people did not neck in front of other people.

"I wouldn't consider marrying anyone else," she said lightly. But he pounced on it.

"Are you serious?" he asked.

"Are *you*?" She was taken aback. And then she said, "You were." He smiled and said, "And you aren't. That's all right. We've got lots of time."

He hailed a cab and took her home to Riverside Drive and kissed her quite long and well, but didn't ask to come in. He was ardent, but he didn't press. Nor did he invite her to the Cardozo home on East Seventy-second Street. She was curious, but she didn't press either.

During the winter, Jerry decided he wanted to do *more*. Just doing the show wasn't enough. Maybe they could work a nightclub. He asked Sabine. She was agreeable. Café Society and its owner, Barney Josephson, were ecstatic.

Six nights a week Jerry and Sabine performed an after-the-ater show in Josephson's café, a cellar off Sheridan Square. It was tiny and packed and smoky, and definitely the place to be seen.

Their engagement lasted until the spring, and Sabine found that she had become a kind of celebrity. Everyone came to the Village, and she was known either as herself or as "the girl who works with that fabulous Jerry Davis." It was a wonderful time. And fun.

Spring changed all that. Jerry was offered a movie contract. He told her the details. She looked at him in puzzlement.

"What's the matter with *me*?"

"You're too strong and you look too Jewish," he said. "I asked them. That's what they told me."

"Too *strong*?" She wouldn't even listen to the Jewish part.

"Don't blame me," he said.

"Too *strong*?" She felt a temper tantrum building.

"Maybe you could do a single?" Jerry suggested. That did it.

"Go fuck yourself!" she screamed at him, too angry to remember that even though she knew these words, she didn't use them.

"That's a single," he said. Unfortunately, it made her laugh. She was hurt and bewildered, but he made her laugh, and she couldn't be angry. She could never stay angry with him.

"When are you leaving?"

"First of May. My contract's up April 30."

"I'll see you off, then."

On May first Sabine stood on the platform of Pennsylvania Station with Jerry. They were surrounded by reporters and photographers. A publicity man from the studio pushed her into the background.

"No romantic attachments!" he cried out to the reporters. (He wasn't *sure* about this, not having heard from the front office. Was this Jerry Davis a new romantic bachelor or just another comic? Comics were allowed girlfriends; their fans didn't care. Once he had made a mistake with Jimmy Stewart; with those looks, he categorized the young man as a comic, not a romantic actor. Look who was wrong. Look who had lost his job. Now, he took no chances.)

"No romantic attachments!" he repeated, running along the platform in a frenzy. Jerry grabbed Sabine in a George Raft embrace.

"No romantic attachments," Jerry said, smothering her with kisses. "Say we're just good friends," he added, nibbling her neck.

"What about the children?" Sabine asked him, while the reporters poised their pencils for scandal. "What about Peppo and Bippi?"

"*They're* just good friends, too," Jerry explained. "The publicity man was not amused.

Simon arrived, late, out of breath, just in time to shake Jerry's hand before the conductor announced the train's departure.

"Goodbye," Jerry said, and then, impulsively, he really hugged Sabine. She thought she saw a tear in his eye. He looked at her and said, "*Peppo* and *Bippi?*"

They laughed together and then he was gone.

Sabine went back to Riverside Drive, and bought some novels she did not read and a radio she did not listen to. For three days she was lonely and inclined to self-pity. Then Mark Cardozo called and invited her to meet his family. They were spending the weekend at their Long Island place, he explained.

"I thought you had a place in Maine," Sabine said.

"We do. But it's too cold for Maine this time of year."

"So you have a place on Long Island in the meantime."

He didn't get the humor of it. Never mind. She accepted the invitation.

That weekend she met Mark's family.

While Jerry had his first experience in Hollywood.

It was the first time for everything. The first time Jerry had ever seen redwood. The first time he had ever *lived* in a house. His house. He was standing on the deck looking out at the view of Los Angeles. In the distance he could see Santa Monica and a thin blue line that was the Pacific.

The deck, whose redwood boards formed a railing that was also one long surrounding settee, had obviously been an afterthought. The house had been built in an entirely different style. But all the houses here were a mixture of styles.

The Hollywood Hills. So lush and private. There were so many little curving streets, with the houses hidden away above them—adobe-type haciendas, Mediterranean villas, imitation Tudor and half-timbered Norman chateaux, small New England cottages—with clumps of pine in front of the houses and, rising behind them, the mesquite and sagebrush of desert mountains where rattlesnakes sunned themselves on rocks and coyotes came down at night to hunt for cats and small dogs. Never let your animals out at night alone, McNamara had warned Jerry.

Tim McNamara was the studio's West Coast publicity man, who had met Jerry at Union Station and had arranged for the photographers and reporters to snap, question, interview, and get into print the newest name on the Hollywood scene. It was McNamara who had taken Jerry on his own *personal* tour of the studio, introducing him to important people and shielding him from unimportant ones. McNamara had his own office in the executive wing; he had his own secretary, who also had *her* own office. Several times during their meeting, McNamara leaped to answer a voice that came over a private intercom, but mostly he gave the orders while others leaped.

The studio had been more confusing than anything else about this confusing place. At first Jerry was unable to comprehend the mixture of illusion and reality—papier-mâché-and-wood mountains against a real but unreally blue California sky; the fronts of tenements so realistically New York that they gave him his first wave of homesickness, until he walked up the steps and through a door and found himself facing a blazing sun-baked alley where the grips smoked cigarettes and kicked stones at the lizards that scuttled around in the dirt. The lot sprawled for acres. There were sixteen sound stages as big as airplane hangars; when the doors clanged shut, it reminded him of the giant refrigerator in the kitchen at Glenrocks.

McNamara took Jerry on a riverboat that steamed down a three-hundred-yard Mississippi River, right by the New York tenement and over to an English pastoral village. On the way to lunch they met Jerry's new agent, whose name was Nat and who always sat a few inches apart, as though he might not be called into the conference. He nodded corroboration of everything McNamara said. In the commissary, which was disappointingly like a high school lunchroom, McNamara explained the chain of command.

It was a hard town to figure, McNamara said. Nat agreed. You had to watch your step or you could get lost; Nat found that true also. You couldn't be too careful in the beginning. Nat nodded emphatically, and tamped the tobacco in his pipe. Everyone here predicted a great future for Jerry. Nat smiled broadly. *But*—a product like Jerry had to be handled very carefully. This time Nat produced a sage nod, a knowing nod.

Jerry looked around the commissary and felt a surge of power. There were *stars* here; he recognized faces. Many of them were sitting in little conspiratorial groups. Every executive had an agent, someone at the edge of his elbow, it seemed. The other groups—larger—were more relaxed, more convivial. Ladies in Victorian period costumes puffed on Camels, and eighteenth-century buccaneers attacked the fruit salad special.

McNamara saw where Jerry's attention lay. "You're looking at one hundred million dollars worth of talent over there," he said.

Jerry was star-struck. "When do I get to meet *them?*" he asked.

"When the time comes," McNamara said, like an English nanny, and decided lunch was over. It was time to dazzle the newcomer with the new house.

"Bernard is sure you're going to like this place," McNamara said as they drove through a series of complicated winding roads, always up. "You will have to get a car. You drive, don't you?" he added.

"No," Jerry said. "I'm from New York, remember?"

"You don't drive." McNamara's voice was disappointed. (Was the contract null and void, then? Jerry wondered. Was he to be banished from Hollywood because of lack of driving skills?) "You'll have to learn how to drive. That's a must. But for the time being I'll get you a driver."

"You'll have to, because I don't know my way around," Jerry reminded him.

"You'll find your way around soon enough," McNamara said, and there was an insinuation there.

Jerry could not make out the man. His suit was beige and of lightweight fabric, a California, all-seasons fabric. Neutral. The hair was curly and sandy colored. Neutral again. The face could have belonged to Huckleberry Finn, it was so American, it was so without any apparent guile. And yet, constantly, that voice revealed hidden hints. But hints of what? McNamara gave the impression of possessing information that he was not at present at liberty to divulge.

While Nat and his pipe puffed in the back seat, McNamara maneuvered the sharp turns so capably that Jerry knew in his heart he could never learn to manipulate this roller-coaster world. McNamara was reading his mind.

"Don't worry. I'll send a driver over this afternoon. Here we are."

Jerry's first impression was of a jungle. Vines everywhere, hanging over the steep driveway. Flowers he could not name. Bushes, trees almost, covered with red purple flowers. Petals lay around the base of the tree like the aftermath of a visit by royalty. The house itself was an English cottage with casement windows, a fairytale house for a storybook life. Inside it was larger than he had expected, and cool and dark. The furniture was upholstered with slipcovers in nautical themes suitable for a Cape Cod summer rental. The exterior English, the interior Cape Cod, the deck California redwood. And the garden below? Spanish. Why Spanish? The miniature fountain that splashed so prettily was rimmed by adobe. It belonged in the courtyard of a conquistador. The gardener's shack was roofed with tile. The small swimming pool, the whole garden in fact, seemed in danger of being taken over by the vines that surrounded it.

"This will be attended to," McNamara said in horror. "I swear Bernard didn't know this place had been vacant."

"Who's Bernard?" Jerry asked. It was the second time the name had been mentioned.

"Bernard Ross. He's your producer. He used to be a comic, he handles musicals. He's from New York." Did McNamara assume that all New York Jews knew each other?

"Oh," Jerry said. "Well, listen, tell him it's not important about the yard. I mean, how much time am I going to be spending here?"

McNamara's voice was stern. "Never say that, Jerry." Nat nodded behind him. "*Never* say it's not important. Everything is important. Your car is important. Your dressing room . . ."

"Your billing," Nat added.

McNamara dismissed that. "Lawyers handle all that. But things like this garden, for instance. Don't overlook the importance of this garden. Your garden should be *successful*. You can't be too careful out here." He looked out over the deck and sighed. "Things go to seed so fast. You'll have to hire a gardener. It's expected."

"Who pays for all this?" Jerry asked, turning to Nat, who suddenly became as blank as though he were a tourist here himself.

"The studio would expect *you* to pay for the gardener," McNamara admonished the ungrateful child.

"I don't have the money to pay for gardeners," Jerry said.

"That's another thing. Never say that," McNamara lectured. "If you'll forgive me—I don't want to sound like a teacher—but you never say out here that you don't have money. You always have money out here. Isn't that right, Nat?"

"Definitely."

"Yeah? Well, skip the gardener," Jerry said.

"Now that would be a mistake." McNamara was definite about it. "Tell you what I'll do." Jerry wondered if McNamara had ever sold automobiles in a former life. "I'll try to get a kid who can double as driver *and* gardener. The studio pays for the driver, so that'll get you off the hook. How's that?"

"Sensational," Nat said for his client.

McNamara looked at his watch, which had a gold face and a gold band. "I'm due back on the set," he said. "You settle in. Call Rosemary if there's anything you want. Tomorrow we'll meet Bernard and he'll take you to see the Old Man. You'll do fine here, I can feel it. Don't you think so, Nat?"

"Would I handle a failure?" Nat gave a supporting smile, that came and went as fast as summer at the North Pole.

"Oh—do you need a girl?" McNamara asked casually. It startled Jerry.

"What"

"A girl."

"For what" Jerry was confused.

"Well, if you have to ask, I guess you don't need one." McNamara and Nat shared West Coast locker-room grins.

"Oh, I thought you meant for cleaning. Or for a secretary. I didn't understand what you meant." Jerry was making too many excuses, he could feel it. "Maybe tomorrow. I'm kind of tired from the trip."

"No problem," McNamara said as he and Nat made their way down the steep drive to the car.

As they were leaving, McNamara gave a cheery wave and Nat an intimate wink. Then Nat climbed into the front seat for the ride back down the hill.

Jerry went back into the house. His house now. Whose house had it been? Somehow they were still occupying it with their slipcovers. He walked into the kitchen. Outside the window grew a tree with lemons on it. Jerry stared, astounded. Lemons on a tree. Well, where did lemons come from if not from a tree? Before they had always come from the fruit bin, two for a dime. Now they hung on trees. How about that?

There were books in the living room, many books on self-help, on thinking positively. Two books on the craft of boat-building. Big novels. *Gone with the Wind* was there—as it is everywhere. And *Anthony Adverse*. The other books were unfamiliar titles by unfamiliar authors. Jerry decided their owners had not been successful. Had they cultivated successful gardens?

Two steps up and a corridor away was the main bedroom. The bed was huge, with a headboard but no footboard and so many pillows—throw pillows, he later learned they were called—on the bed. This bed was also lower than any he had seen. It invited lounging, relaxing, lingering. He was fascinated. French doors led to a small balcony, big enough for two canvas chairs and a small metal table. For breakfast, he thought. It overlooked the garden. Inside he noticed there was a fan on the ceiling and rattan blinds that could be let down to cover the French doors. A South Sea paradise, to go native in.

From the deck he could see no other houses. That is, he could see roofs spilling down the hills to the flatlands, but no houses, no windows. Everything was private here. And green. Bushes and vines and flowers encircled the little grass area of the garden. No people. No neighbors. He could hear nothing. No sound of automobiles climbing the hill. No voices. Truly, he was by himself.

He had not noticed the fireplace in the living room. It was small and the guard was made of a mesh. It could burn wood, but it could also be operated by turning a gas jet.

He looked down at his slacks. There was a smudge of dirt on the white material, probably from the fireplace. Never mind. He would have to buy a whole new wardrobe. He had brought nothing with him from New York. Why should he? He had nothing worth bringing. And there was nothing he regretted leaving behind. No, that was not true. He missed Sabine; he had brought her picture with him, two photos in fact. One, mock-glamorous, the two of them tangoing and holding their faces up to the light. The other shot was of Sabine alone, and she had not been aware she was being photographed. She was deep in thought, biting a nail; her eyes were wistful. The photo was mostly of her eyes, with a shadow of dark hair encircling the face. The Sabine nobody knew, except him. And maybe he didn't either. She was as private as this house. As mysterious, in a way.

There was a sound downstairs and it startled him. What was downstairs? He hadn't been there. More rooms? A garage? Was there a telephone? Could someone be breaking in? Carefully he went to the living room window.

A young man was down below. He was no burglar—he wasn't being careful enough. There was a scraping of metal. The man was gathering up a rake and clippers. The gardener. Quick service from the efficient McNamara. "Call Rosemary if there's anything you want"—what an invitation to excess. *Rosemary, bring me. Rosemary, bring me a bathtub full of strawberries. Could you run them over to me? Clothes. I don't have the time. Check wardrobe for size and bring me. Avoid red. It's the one color I don't like. Blue. Yellow. Slacks. Sportshirts.*

Jerry watched from the window. The gardener was already at work, attacking the underbrush, ripping out the vines, and cutting back the foliage. It was hot work. Soon he stopped to take his blue workshirt off and wipe the sweat off his chest with it. Jerry watched. The gardener was young, maybe his own age; his hair was different shades of blond, and tangled. Now that his shirt was off, Jerry could watch the muscular slope of shoulder, the muscular curve of arm as the gardener returned to work.

Invisible himself, Jerry was free to examine the faded work pants and wide leather belt, to watch sweat glistening on the supple back, to count the muscles from chest to belly. Jerry stood there, mesmerized, as the gardener worked. The gardener seemed unaware that anyone was watching. How would he know? There was no car in the driveway. The studio had given an order and the young man had been dispatched to clean up the grounds. Was this his driver? Jerry felt a voyeur's excitement in watching someone who is unaware of being watched. The man bent down, flexing his knees, and the muscles appeared through the tightness of the fabric of his pants. A vine resisted and the muscles in the man's arms coiled to pull harder. He tossed his head to get his eyes clear of his hair. For a moment he rested, breathing hard. Jerry watched the chest rise and fall. The arms were thick, the biceps developed, the chest developed too. In hiding, Jerry took inventory. His mouth was dry; he licked his lips, unconscious of what he was doing. Then the man returned to digging, foot on the spade, and Jerry watched the working of his buttocks.

By the end of an hour the garden had regained its shape. There was a heap of vines in the wheelbarrow, and dead leaves lay in a pile. The man took a coil of hose and began to wash down the flagstone walk by the pool. He watered the flowers while Jerry watched. Thirsty, the young man held up the nozzle and let the water fall into his open mouth. His head was bent back. The water dripped down his face and neck onto his body. Jerry watched the gardener put down the hose and take off his pants. He wore no underwear. Standing naked, he picked up the hose again and doused himself. The water slid down over the tangle of hair, down the face, down the shoulders and chest, down the flatness of belly. Down.

Jerry went down stairs he had never traveled and through a door he had never opened. He was in a garage. Empty, neat, concrete, with shelves and some carpenter's tools. A spot of black where grease had fallen from a car's engine. The garage door was up and Jerry could see the man. At the sound of Jerry's approach, the gardener turned; he did not stop watering himself, he did not hide his body.

"Hi," he said, continuing to wash himself; his right hand held the hose, his left spread the water over his chest. Jerry drew closer. He was hypnotized by the left hand's motion, spreading water over chest and down belly, carelessly fingering genitals. The young man turned away and bent over, hosing himself—spray bouncing off the calf muscles—letting the spray enter him. Then the man turned back and smiled. Jerry approached. The young man had an erection. Standing naked in the garden, hosing himself, playing with himself, aroused now, and Jerry came closer, his eyes focused on the penis that was growing and growing in front of him. He fell on his knees in front of the man and, closing his eyes, reached.

Later, the young man was matter-of-fact. His name was Zack. He said to Jerry, "You sure took your time coming out."

Jerry looked at him. "You knew I was there?"

"Of course," Zack said. They were lying on the bed in the South Sea paradise bedroom. Or rather, Zack was lying on the bed; Jerry was about to join him.

"Mr. Ross says I'm supposed to pick you up tomorrow morning at ten to drive you to the studio. You want me to come by?"

"No," said Jerry. "I want you to stay."

The first meeting with Bernard Ross, who was to be Jerry's producer, was set for ten o'clock. There was no food in the house. Zack and Jerry were both hungry. Where should they eat breakfast? Jerry suggested the Brown Derby, because he didn't know any other restaurant in Hollywood. They ate at the Brown Derby, the two of them, surrounded by clean goblets and too much silverware. They ordered orange juice and bacon and eggs, healthy American breakfasts, and they ate, Zack in his dungarees and his blue workshirt, Jerry dressed for his appointment. There had been a moment's hesitation at the restaurant entrance when Zack's dungarees were noticed, but Jerry Davis was the new name in town, and now the new face, and they were welcomed. And watched.

Bernard Ross made Jerry wait exactly fifteen minutes. Jerry sat in the outer room with Nat and McNamara. After this meeting, Jerry planned to ask McNamara where he should buy clothes and then have Zack drive him there.

"You find everything you needed?" McNamara asked him.

"Fine. Everything was fine."

"Good," McNamara said.

Nat ventured his first independent opinion. "You sleep all right? Some people don't get used to it so good," he said.

"No, I slept fine."

Then they were quiet, each of them, until Bernard Ross's secretary said, "Mr. Ross will see you now," and the three of them entered Mr. Ross's office, Nat always six inches behind Jerry.

Bernard Rosen had weathered well. He was not handsome, but it was evident in his face that he played a lot of golf at a good country club. Little of the candy store comic remained. Nothing of the experimental director was left.

There were photos on his desk (although none of his mother, who was living well in the Bronx), photos of his wife, Carol, and of their only child. It was an impressive display of pictures, denoting a loving husband and doting parent.

"Welcome," Bernard Ross (né Rosen) said from behind his desk. He did not rise. He did not extend his hand.

"Bernie!" Jerry said joyfully. "What are *you* doing here?"

"Making motion pictures," Bernard said flatly. There was to be no joyful reunion, no remembrance of youthful follies. Jerry was puzzled.

"Sit down," Bernard said. Jerry did.

"You all settled in?" Bernard inquired rather pleasantly, and Jerry nodded.

"All set to go to work?"

"Whenever you say," Jerry smiled agreeably.

"Whenever I say," Bernard repeated. He turned to Nat. "Smart client you got here."

Nat was still standing. He had not been told to sit.

"Would I work with failures?" Nat laughed.

"Would you work with queers?" Bernard asked in the same tone. What little color Nat had suddenly drained from his face.

"Whatcha talkin' about?" he stammered, suddenly all accent.

"I'm referring to your fruit of a client, this faggot here, who is sitting in a *studio* office, on *studio* property. A fucking flaming queer who's ready to suck a joint in the Brown Derby, for Chrissakes."

Now Bernard Ross refused to acknowledge that Jerry was in the room. He was screaming at Nat. McNamara sat impassively, watching Ross in action.

"Well, *you* tell him that if he so much as winks at another male in public, his ass is gonna be outta here so fast . . . We can break a contract, you know that! Nat, that morals clause is in there. You tell him all about that morals clause. He can go down on every nigger dick in LA, so long as he does it in private. I don't care. He can lick ass all the way to Frisco and back, but the moment he steps out this door, he represents the studio. He is studio property. No feelies, no ass pats, no groping. Is that clear? Now get your cocksucking faggot homoqueer client outta here before I spit in his fuckin' shit-covered face."

There was some trace of the Lower East Side left in Bernard Ross.

Jerry left in a daze; Nat pushed him out the door before he knew what was happening.

After they left, Bernard turned to McNamara.

"Did you get pictures?" he asked in a perfectly normal tone of voice.

"Yeah," McNamara said.

"Good," said Bernard. "In case he ever makes trouble."

Nat did not speak to Jerry as they maneuvered the corridors to the parking lot.

"I'll talk to you tomorrow," Nat said, hurrying away to his own car, on his way to make a few calls, to see which way the wind was blowing.

Jerry walked in the blaze of the morning sun, blinded by what he had been through, hoping to find the studio car and Zack. But when he found the car, there was another driver, a Mexican, who spoke very little English but who guided the studio car expertly up the winding road to Jerry's newly rented house, and who, once out of the car, changed uniforms and began raking up the rest of the leaves.

Chapter Nine

Sabine thought at first she would have to spend the weekend just trying to keep the names straight.

George Cardozo was the older brother. Older than Mark, just married to Paula, who was blonde and whose father was in railroads in Philadelphia. George was taller than Mark, and even thinner, and more serious.

Peter was the younger brother, just graduated from prep school and in his first year at Harvard.

Mimi was Mark's older sister, and she looked the most like him, their faces oval, their eyes dark and credulous as children's eyes. Ann, the youngest, was still at Spence.

The Cardozo family, all of it, gathered to play Beano and charades in the main house. Later on they played poker. Sabine was unused to big families, and their enthusiasms overwhelmed her at first. As did their "Long Island place."

It was an estate on King's Point, with grounds stretching down to the Sound, where two sailboats and a Chriscraft were moored. There were hills on the grounds, everything neatly manicured. *How did they mow the lawns down the hills?* Sabine wondered. The main house was white, with many sun-porches. There were two gardeners who pruned all the hedges. And in spite of all this grandeur, everything was kept casual.

George and Mark loved to play tennis. Peter was the fisherman. Ann would aquaplane if anyone would drive the Chriscraft. Mimi kept a set of watercolors and went out every morning to sketch. Mr. Cardozo had developed a craze for archery. And his wife read.

Mrs. Cardozo had curly hair and always looked as though she had just come in from a sail. She favored cashmere sweaters and shorts. Her legs were tanned, and she never bothered to wear a hat, so her face was lined with wrinkles, but it made no difference to her looks. She was hearty. She made everyone feel welcome. She stuck out her hand, four gold bracelets on her tanned wrist, to Sabine.

"Hi. Call me Sandy. That's what everyone does. They have no respect, no respect at all for old ladies," she said, obviously not old and obviously aware of the fact that her family adored her.

Sabine had taken the extended hand and so had been ushered into the group. Mark had talked about them to her, of course, as he had talked of her to them. They were not exactly strangers, yet they did not know one another. It was obvious that Mark was serious. He wanted to marry her. Everyone in the family knew that. He had written letters home from Harvard about this girl he had met in a bar.

"Oh, Julien," Mrs. Cardozo had sighed as she read one of those letters. "A bar?" The next letter talked about Sabine's involvement with the theater. "Oh, Julien, show business?" Sandy had said. "Oh, my God."

Julien Cardozo had checked out the girl and learned about her family and their hotel in the Catskills, then had returned to his charities.

"My goodness, think of her mother feeding all those people," Mrs. Cardozo had said with admiration. She never had less than fifteen at her table.

"I'm sure she has help," Julien smiled at his wife.

"I would think she would have to. How many people do they have at one time?"

"Six or seven hundred, I'm told."

"Six or seven hundred! Imagine that. Why, I could never do anything like that."

Sandy Cardozo would never have to. The Cardozos' money was old; they could trace their roots in this country back to the American Revolution, and in Spain far beyond that. In Philadelphia the Cardozo dynasty had started with a small store selling supplies to settlers on their way west. Now it was an empire of merchandising, and Julien Cardozo, its emperor, had just stepped down to make way for his son, George. George, at twenty-seven, was much more ruthless than his father, and a recent convert to the Episcopal Church.

It was hard to think of any of them as Jews. They knew no Yiddish; their second language was French, and they had all studied Latin, a required subject in every one of the private

schools the children had attended. Any taint of the ghetto
had long since disappeared in a jumble of sailing outfits, tennis whites, charm bracelets, and saddle shoes, L.L. Bean moc-
casins and heavy woolen checked lumberjackets. They spoke
with a self-mocking drawl that marked them as members of
the Spence-Chapin-Buckley-Exeter-St. Marks-Dartmouth-Vas-
sar-Harvard colony. There was a wall surrounding their Seventy-second Street house in New York, and a sign at the edge
of the dirt road leading down to the five-hundred-acre compound they kept in Maine saying Private Property. The Long
Island place had a gate. The Cardozos were well protected.

"Did you have a good trip? At least you didn't have to
take that miserable train, which is always late." Sandy
Cardozo drew Sabine inside, out of the sun. On the floor of
the den, where they stood, were Aubusson rugs.

"What are they?" Sabine asked, amazed. "And whatever
they are, what are they doing on a floor, they're so gorgeous!"

Sabine did not hide her awe. Everything overwhelmed her.
The size of the house, the space, the luxury, the casualness,
the friendliness. But she was a quick study. Ann loved to jit-
terbug. Sabine had never learned. She learned now. Peter was
her partner. Peter was crazy for the Big Bands. He had all
the records. There Sabine had some expertise. She was surprised to find Eddie Troncone's name on one of the records.
Peter was very impressed that Sabine knew Eddie.

"You actually know him? He's one of the *greats*."

"Is he?" Sabine asked delightedly.

"Is he ever! He's solid," Peter assured her.

Sandy taught her about rugs, a crash course. You examined the backing to see how tightly the threads ran on
oriental rugs. Hooked rugs were a different story. Their
unevenness was their merit. Sandy brought out twelve different orientals to test Sabine's eye. Sabine had an instinct for
the best. Sandy was impressed.

The Cardozos played tennis on Saturday afternoon. Different from Simon's, this game. First of all, everyone wore
white. They played rather silently, and there was none of that
slamming of the ball across the net and none of the triumphant victory cries of Glenrocks. The Cardozos valued
placement and strategy. They loved long rallies and hardly
seemed competitive. "Good shot," they would murmur in ap-

preciation of one another's game. It was almost British; a racket was never flung in anger, a close call never challenged. Whatever they did, they could afford to do with grace. Even lose.

During a break, Mark said very quietly to Sabine, "You've met my family. How do you like them?"

"I love them!" Sabine said, with such spontaneity that Mark was visibly disappointed.

"Well, I wish you could marry all of us, but you'll have to settle for just one."

"Doubles, Mark," Sandy cried. "You and your father against George and Peter!"

"Let's talk about this later," Sabine said, and the dutiful son ran off to his game. The women watched while the men played. The older man's expertise won him and Mark the first set. The second set was played with more concentration.

Mark's mother brought some iced tea over to the round metal table where Sabine was sitting.

"They look good, don't they?" Sandy said, taking pride in her men.

"I've never seen four more handsome men," Sabine smiled.

"Haven't you?" Sandy asked lightly. George looked over at them. He was losing, and irritated; the sound of their voices was a distraction.

"We should keep quiet," Sabine whispered.

"Nonsense. I'm his mother. I'll talk when I like," Sandy said, but she kept her voice low.

They watched the point being played. George had served, with Mark at the net. Their father had returned the serve, lobbing it over Peter's head. George drove the ball past Mark to his father, and father and son carried on a long and hard rally. Then George made one mistake. He sent the ball too close to Mark's racket. Mark hit a drive to the far corner.

"Out!" George called. It was close. Mark's look to his brother was questioning. Then he shrugged. They resumed play. Sabine, watching all this, said nothing.

Mark's mother resumed the conversation.

"Well, did Mark pop the question?" The drawl was amused.

Sabine looked around. "How did you know about it?"

"They always come to me first, as though I were the Delphic oracle."

"What did you say?"

"I told him you were a smart girl, and you would know what to answer." Sandy was looking out at the players. George and Peter had won that game. The four men shifted courts. Sabine felt uncomfortable and wondered why. Mark's mother sipped iced tea. On one of her four bracelets, the letter "S" had been engraved.

"It's for *"Sandra."* Mark's mother made a face. "An aberration on the part of my parents. Everyone else had perfectly normal names. Emily and Abigail. My brother is called Roger. But God! *Sandra.* Can you imagine? How Oriental!"

"You can say that to someone who's named Sabine?"

"Yes, what *did* happen there?" The older woman looked amused.

"My father had been reading Latin."

"Latin? Your father?" Sandy sounded surprised.

"My parents were very bohemian. He learned Latin. She recited poetry. They both wore capes and spats."

"Adorable," Sandy said.

"They were young then."

"Good shot," Sandy remarked. Mark had just won a point from George. "Funny association, Abramowitz and Latin. I never should have made it. *Disraeli* and Latin, maybe . . ."

"Why not Abramowitz?" Sabine realized she was looking at the game to avoid looking at Sandy.

"Well, it's such an out-and-out name, if you know what I mean. Did you ever think of changing it?"

"No. Why?"

"A lot of people in your business do, don't they?"

"Yes."

"Ah, but marrying a Cardozo would solve that."

"Solve *what?*"

"The Abramowitz part."

Sabine rose, realizing that two games were going on here simultaneously. And she was playing with a pro.

"I wouldn't worry about it," she said. It was hot on the court. Her face was flushed. Mark was serving to Peter. George was at the baseline. The serve hit the tape.

"Long," George said. Mark looked again at his brother but did not dispute the call.

"The serve was good," Sabine said. "It hit the line."

George was not accustomed to being contradicted.

"I called it out," he said.

"I know you did." Sabine smiled. "But you were wrong."

The game continued and she walked down the path to the main house.

There was a call waiting for her. It was Bertha. Matt had telephoned from overseas. He would call again tomorrow. It was about Sammy. Sabine told her mother she was coming home and went upstairs to pack.

The Cardozos seemed surprised when they trooped in from tennis.

"Not staying for dinner?" Sandy asked, ever hospitable.

"No. I'm sorry."

"What is it?" Mark asked.

"Family business," she explained. "It can't be helped."

Mark drove her to the station. "I don't understand," he said on the way.

"It's a friend of the family calling from Europe. He has news of the Abramowitzes." She bore down on the name, but if he noticed, he ignored it.

"I hope it's good news."

"I hope so."

"You haven't given me an answer."

"About marriage? Go talk to your mother."

"My mother?"

"I think she'd object to your marrying a Jew."

He laughed. "But we're Jewish."

"You know what? It doesn't show."

This once the train was right on time, and Sabine hurried to board it.

"We're not finished," Mark said as the train pulled out.

"Call me," Sabine said, smiling.

Chapter Ten

When the train from Zurich stopped at what had been the Austrian border, the four other occupants of the compartment watched with interest while the Nazi customs officials methodically searched Matt Ryan's luggage.

He had bought the luggage on a defiant two-day spending spree in Paris, after it was all over in Spain, after the collapse of the Loyalist forces at Teruel had wiped out the last hope for the Loyalists. After the bombardment of Barcelona from the land and the sea—Göring's aviators were practicing maneuvers with Stukas and cannon, trying out toys to see if they worked—the civilians starved and the Loyalist forces were exhausted. If he closed his eyes, Matt could still see the ghosts of people in ghosts of buildings during the Christmas bombings. Barcelona fell in January, when the resistance in Catalonia was broken. Then Madrid fell, followed by Valencia. By the end of March it was over. Matt left for Paris.

The Franco-Spanish border had been reopened, and the roads were jammed with refugees flooding into a France that had no way of sheltering them. Matt saw his first internment camp, located on the Mediterranean near Perpignan. He saw refugees whose single blanket could not help them through the icy spring nights. He saw corrugated roofs that were called shelter, and latrines that were merely holes scooped in the sand. The French government issued a daily quota of bread to keep the Spanish refugees from starving. But there were over three hundred thousand of them, without medical facilities, without hope, without a future. And no aid in sight. They had been forgotten.

The fascists had won the first round.

"Tinged with pink, that's what you are," Richard Sadler would have told him, sardonically if Sadler were still alive. But he was not. He was a casualty of the war. Drunk on the

Dutch gin he was so fond of, Sadler had fallen in front of a truck carrying soldiers to the police barracks. Since technically the war had not ended at the time, Richard Sadler had become one of the first war correspondents to be "killed in the line of duty."

When Matt reached Paris he discovered what had to be the richest, most beautiful, and seemingly most frivolous city in the world. It was the beginning of April, and the United States government had announced its recognition of the Franco regime. A month before Cardinal Pacelli had become Pope Pius XII. The Spanish refugees had been conveniently forgotten. After all, the war was over.

By a set of circumstances that could only be described as coincidental, Matt became famous for a few days. And his notoriety lasted a little longer than that.

The chief of his network's Paris bureau asked Matt to do a broadcast to the United States "wrapping up the Spanish situation," as he put it. Matt agreed. It was on the day that the United States had announced its recognition of Franco. Matt went to a bar and had a few scotches. Drinking made him either loquacious or pugnacious, sometimes both. This time both. He returned to the studio and sat down before a microphone. The light flashed. He was on the air, short-wave to the United States. And this is how he started.

"Good evening. This is Matt Ryan in Paris. Matt Ryan. Catholic. American. And, at the moment, not too proud of being either . . ."

At the time of the broadcast there was no one in the control room who spoke English. Matt's broadcast lasted no more than five minutes, no more than it could have taken to go to the men's room to fetch someone who might have stopped the broadcast. But no one went.

Matt proceeded to describe the conditions in the refugee camps. He charged that no one had come to the aid of these stateless, homeless, penniless people. That no one recognized *them*. Instead, the United States government was recognizing a regime that had taken away all rights from Spaniards.

And then he turned on the Catholic Church. There had been numerous protests from the Vatican about the atrocities committed by the Loyalists on the clergy. But the monastery of San Cristobal had been bombed by the fascists—specifically, by bombers supplied by Germany—despite the white cross painted on the roof of the building. Twenty monks and two hundred civilians who had sought sanctuary there had been killed. There had never been a protest from the Vatican. Why was that? Fascists killed priests, and the Church remained silent. Refugees were starving in camps, and the United States remained silent.

Neither the United States government nor the Vatican was silent for long after this. Protests were launched—against Matt. The broadcast was irresponsible, the charges uncalled for, the challenge to Church and diplomatic policy unacceptable: An apology was demanded.

The chief of the Paris bureau came to Matt. "It's not just your job. It's *my* job at stake. Apologize."

"Why?"

"Well, for one thing, how do you know the planes were really Fascist planes?"

"I was there. I saw them."

"It could have been a ruse on the part of the Loyalists to gain sympathy. How do you *know* the planes were German?"

"They were Stukas, dive-bombers."

The chief of the Paris Bureau looked at Matt. "The pressure is on—from the Vatican, from the States, from the network."

"I was telling the truth, for Chrissake!"

"The *alleged* truth."

"I was an eyewitness. I saw the bombing. I saw the internment camp. I was *there*."

"A war correspondent's first duty is to be *objective*," the chief of the Paris bureau said. "Can you honestly say you are objective?"

"Oh, then it's my objectivity that's in question, eh? Okay, I'll make the apology."

"Good. We'll be sending you to Vienna in May."

"Vienna? Nothing's happening in Vienna. It's already happened in Vienna."

"I know," said the chief of the Paris bureau. "That may be why you're being sent there."

Matt's apology was broadcast. And because of the headlines his first broadcast had created, a great many Americans tuned in to listen, the way they would to a Joe Louis fight.

"I have been asked to apologize for certain statements," he began. "As an American, and as a Catholic, my objectivity has been brought into question. I have been told that even an eyewitness may be deceived.

"*Allegedly*, then, there are internment camps in France for the Spanish refugees. *Allegedly*, then, they are well taken care of. Although I did not see that. *Perhaps* there is aid coming from the Red Cross. I did not see that. *Perhaps* living conditions are tolerable. I did not see that.

"I did see a monastery bombed," he continued. "Now, *perhaps* the planes in question were not Fascist planes. *Perhaps* they were merely planes with Fascist markings, painted on by the Loyalists to discredit the Fascist cause. *Perhaps* there were no Stuka dive-bombers supplied by Nazi Germany. *Perhaps* there were no German troops in Spain. *Perhaps* there were no Italian troops in Spain.

"If this be the case, as an American and as a Catholic, I apologize to the Holy Father, and to the forces of General Franco. And I apologize to Nazi Germany. If this be the case. This is Matt Ryan in Paris."

It became a very controversial broadcast. If it hadn't been for the letters, Matt might have been fired. The letters poured in, and networks read letters, they pay attention to them.

Why should an American have to apologize to Nazi Germany? the letters wanted to know. The network decided it would be foolish to fire any newsman who inspired that amount of fan mail. They would watch his activities with more interest, however. And see.

After the letters, Matt felt much better about going to Vienna. He stopped at a kiosk before boarding the train in Geneva, buying all the periodicals he could think of to while away the journey to Austria.

Now, as the customs officials fingered the five-dollar silk ties Matt had bought on the Place Vendôme, the new shirts, the wine-dark silk dressing gown, Matt Ryan just read his papers.

He noticed with satisfaction an article in the *New York Times* about help having been sent to the Spanish refugees, first by the Quakers, then the Red Cross.

Then he saw an interview in the theater section with a new star, Jerry Davis. There was his photograph. Jerry, Matt thought, Sabine's Jerry. He read the article; there was no mention of her name. The new star, however, was leaving his Broadway show at the end of the month (the papers were several weeks old) to go to Hollywood, where his career would be under the direct supervision of the most responsible of film producers. Jerry was a hot property, one requiring careful handling.

Matt yawned at the bullshit and thought about Sabine, and thinking about Sabine made him remember Sammy. Sammy Abrams was someone he meant to look up in Vienna.

He flipped the page, and the train stopped at the Austrian border.

"Have a pleasant journey," said the customs official, having neatly repacked all of Matt's luggage. "Heil Hitler!" The man was Austrian, and sounded a little uncomfortable with the salute. It did not snap out of him with the requisite fervor. Matt nodded and returned to his reading. Ten minutes later the train continued on its way to Vienna.

It was impossible, Matt thought, that Sammy Abrams had remained in Vienna. Not after the annexation. All the same, Matt planned to call the man when he arrived. Just to satisfy Sabine.

The train arrived at the Westbahnhof late in the afternoon, and Matt walked out of the station with his briefcase and his new luggage, greeting a dazzling city. He hailed a cab and directed the driver to the Hotel Bristol. Along the way he noticed the number of huge banners, the swastikas, the armbands. The swastika was on everything. On stationery, on buildings, drawn on the walls.

He spent the early part of the evening with an English journalist at the Hotel Sacher.

The man's name was Andrews and he worked for Reuters. Fortunately, he spoke German. They spent an hour listening to the conversations that went on around them in the hotel's café. Rumors in Vienna were their own harvest. The war was going to start. That was definite. It would start: (1) as soon as the French left on Bastille Day for their annual month's vacation; (2) as soon as the Balkan harvest was in, which would be around the middle of October; (3) perhaps in the first week in September, when everyone in Europe was just returning from summer holidays, still on the road, as it were.

"Do you want to talk about why were *you* banished?" Andrews asked pleasantly.

"Who says I was banished?" Matt looked up.

"Well, obviously, it doesn't do much good to station a cor-

respondent in a place where he doesn't know the language—
unless they mean for you *not* to find out things. Isn't that
true?"

"Yeah, it's true."

"You are quite well known, after all."

"What do you mean by that?"

"Well, I know you. Your broadcast did raise a stink on
both sides of the Atlantic. I'm here because I did a broadcast
about the homosexuals who have been placed in concentration camps in Germany."

"Why did you do that?"

"Quite simple. I am a homosexual. I thought it unfair."

"Oh."

"Actually there are a number of homosexuals in the Nazi
Party, but nobody talks about that. I should think it was
quite evident, though, with all those boots and whips. Something amiss there, I should say. Well, what are you going to
do about it?"

Matt's glance was wary. "About what?"

"About being in a country where you can understand nothing."

"I guess I'll have to learn the language."

"Well, that should occupy you nicely until the war is well
underway," Andrews said, and called for the check.

Back at the Bristol Matt faced the four walls, sighed, and
decided to write letters. One to his father, another to Sabine.
It was the first time in months that he had the time to write.
While the war lasted in Spain, he could only think of Sabine,
of where she was and what she was doing. Now, as he wrote,
he longed for a little of her brightness to lighten his mood, to
lighten his room. He wanted the breath of fresh air that was
Sabine.

But he could only touch on his feelings in a letter. He
wrote that he would try to contact her cousin Samuel, and
that she could answer him at the Bristol in Vienna.

He decided to call Samuel Abrams right away. He
searched through his notebook until he found the number
Dieterl had given him, then went through his German phrase-
book. He was good at languages. He spoke Spanish fluently
now, and he spoke a little French. A few of the German
words, when he pronounced them aloud, resembled the Yiddish he had heard at Glenrocks.

He asked the hotel operator to reach the number he had been given by Dieterl.

A cautious voice answered the phone, a woman's voice.

"Is this the number of Abrams—Samuel Abrams?" Matt began in halting German. The voice on the other end was hesitant, the pause over-long.

"Moment, bitte," she said, followed by more silence. Matt waited. A more robust voice, a trained voice, a man's resonant voice, came on the line.

"Hallo, wer spricht?" it wanted to know.

"Do you speak English?" Matt asked.

"A little." The voice lost some of its confidence.

"Tell me if you understand me." Matt tried to speak slowly. "I am a friend of Bertha Abramowitz from the United States. She asked me to call you."

Again, silence.

"Do you understand me?"

"Yes," the voice answered without inflection.

"My name is Matt Ryan. I am here on business, but I would like to see you. You *are* Samuel Abrams, aren't you?"

"Of course I am Abrams," the voice answered with asperity.

"Well, would it be possible for us to talk?"

"Talk?" There was caution in the voice.

"I thought perhaps we could meet at the Café Tobler."

"No, no, not the café. That is not possible. Ryan, are you not the journalist?"

"Yes," Matt said.

"Who requested the interview—the one that Ufa approved?" Abram's voice was again resonant, as though he were talking for someone else's benefit.

"Yes, of course," Matt said. "You got it."

"I beg your pardon?" Abrams said.

"I said you are correct." Matt's own voice was loud now.

"Ah, I see," Abrams said. "Would it be convenient for you to visit"—the voice was searching for words in an unfamiliar language—"to *pay* a visit to me here, at my house? It is just outside of town. Sunday afternoon, perhaps. We will take tea."

Matt was agreeable, and wrote down the directions that Abrams carefully gave him.

A taxi took Matt to the Abrams house on Sunday after-

noon. It was a rather sprawling affair in a section of town
known as Döbling. There was a wall that faced the street, a
garden behind that, and then the house. Matt paid the driver
and rang the bell at the gate in the wall. It was Abrams who
answered. It had to be, even before he introduced himself. It
was Jacob all over again, except a more flamboyant Jacob.
As a boy, Matt had always thought Jacob to be a rather sober man, except when he played his concertina—then he
relaxed. This man, as tall as Jacob but livelier, came down
the steps and shook hands through the gate even before he
opened it.

"Ah, it is you," he said. "I was worried over the phone that
perhaps it was some trick, but it is really you. I see that.
Come in, come in."

What is there about me, Matt wondered, that makes me
stand out as an American, not a police spy nor a secret
agent? When they were seated in the garden, he asked
Abrams.

"It was your cigarette. You threw it away and you had
hardly smoked it. No European would do that. And of course
you do not dress like an Austrian. So, now, tell me—is it true
what Bressart is making in America?"

Matt leaned forward across the little tea table.

"I beg your pardon?"

"His salary. I read in one of your cinema magazines that
Bressart was making one thousand dollars a week. Is that
possible? Na," Abrams answered his own question. "It is not
possible."

"I'm sorry," Matt said, "but I don't know who you're talking about."

Abrams became agitated. "Bressart! Bressart! Don't you go
to films?"

"I have been in Spain for the last two years."

"Ah well, then," Abrams said with disappointment, "then
you would not know. Bressart, Felix Bressart. He is from
here, he went in 1934 to the United States. He is now at Met-
ro-Goldwyn-Mayer, a film actor. A film star, his friends say,
but I have yet to believe that. He had talent," Abrams said
grudgingly, "but not a thousand-dollar-a-week talent. No, that
I do not believe. Then you do not know Karlweis either?"

Matt was taken aback by the man's vitality.

"No, I'm afraid I don't."

"Well, that is too bad, but I understand. Karlweis, too, I hear, is now there. In Hollywood." He pronounced it "Hollyvood," and it sounded more glamorous that way. "Would you take cake?" he asked quickly. Matt nodded and Abrams called out in his resonant voice, *"Gisi, mach schnell, und bring den Knaben mit, ja?"* A pretty girl appeared, wearing a dirndl, her hair in braids, carrying a baby.

"This is my wife, Gisela, and our baby, Freddy. How do you like that?" He was obviously pleased with his family. So was Matt. He got up and bowed. Gisela nodded. Freddy frowned.

"They are very beautiful," Matt said, and Abrams nodded.

"Yes," he said. "She is thirty years younger than I. Ha, would you believe it?"

He turned to Gisela and said in German, "Where is the tea? And the cakes? Tell Helga that the man from Hollyvood is waiting. That should speed her up." Helga was the maid, and daft for films. Her chief sorrow at the *Anschluss* was that she was not able to see American films anymore. She went faithfully to see her employer on the screen, even though he was Jewish. But he was also a film star, and everyone loved him in films. As long as they let him make films, she felt she could work in the house. She brought the cakes out now, and the tea in the Meissen teapot, along with the creamer, the delicate flowered cups, the sugar bowl, all of them on a tray holding a yellow tea rose.

Abrams talked nonstop while his young wife and the child in her lap both stared at the stranger with dark, foreign eyes. Gisela took tea with a slice of lemon, the little child ate the crumbs of the peach tart that Helga had baked, and Abrams ate and drank and wiped his mouth with the lemon yellow linen napkin and never stopped talking.

"You know the secret of my youth? I will tell you, but it is not for public knowledge. My hair is tinted. So black it is now, a gigolo black. Without the dye, I would have white hair, I swear to you, snow white hair, and what would that be to go with this face, eh? I ask you. It is not vanity, it is practicality that causes this. I am making a film now with Willy Fritsch, have you heard of him, no?"

Abrams was pleased to know that Matt was not familiar with Fritsch.

"Here if you walk on the street with him, people hiss,

'There is Willy Fritsch, Willy Fritsch.' He pretends he does not like it, but I know better. He loves it! Wait until I tell him he could walk down Hollyvood Boulevard and no one would turn. Maybe they turn and stare at Bressart, eh? That would be a joke. Yes, I like that. More cake?"

Matt was about to tell him the word was "pie" or "tart" when Abrams went on, "How do you like my English? Swell, eh? I have been practicing since five years. When Jacob and I left Poland—*mein Gott,* how many years ago was that, a lifetime ago—I knew maybe three words of English. That is why I did not go with him. It would have been better, perhaps, if I had, although, look at it this way, here I still am, the poor Jacob, he is down there, so who can tell? But is my English good enough?"

Not stopping for the answer, Abrams poured more tea. "On Monday, I am shooting at the studio. You must come visit."

"I may not have the time."

"Oh, I insist. It would be interesting for your American readers—"

"I broadcast over the radio."

"Even more so. The radio is very powerful, is it not?"

"Yes."

"We have found it so, even in this small country." His voice was tinged with bitterness. "I will not take no for an answer. You must see how we make films here, it is most interesting, and they would certainly want to meet you, an important representative of the United States."

Matt felt the tension in the sunny garden in the peaceful suburb of Vienna. The wife with the watchful, mistrustful eyes; and Abrams, selling himself too hard. Trying to charm, to please, to affect an insouciance that he clearly did not feel.

"Okay," Matt said. "Maybe there is a story there. When shall I meet you?"

"You will come for lunch?"

"Sure."

" 'Sure,' 'okay.' " Abrams savored the words. "I must listen carefully to you. Then I shall speak American."

"Keep the accent," Matt advised him. "Americans are suckers for accents."

As promised, Matt showed up at noon on Monday. The

studio was small by Hollywood standards, but there was a guard and a gate, and when Matt gave his name he was ushered through, given a guide, and taken onto the set.

Matt blinked. Another world. Chandeliers, candles, a balustrade. An orchestra. Costumes from the 1840s. Splendor. Uniforms. Mustaches. Wine goblets.

He met Abrams, who led him to a deserted makeup room where he began to daub cold cream on his face, keeping one eye on the mirror, talking very low.

"Get me out!" he said, with such quiet desperation that Matt wasn't sure he had heard correctly.

"What did you say?"

"Help me. Get me out. Do you think I have remained this long because it was my wish? No, they demanded I stay. One more film, the studio said, complete one more film and then we will help you obtain an exit visa. That is what they promised." While he was talking he took vicious swipes at his face with a paper napkin. Makeup peeled off.

"Mr. Abrams," Matt began.

"Call me Sammy. Everyone does. This whole nation is one big diminutive. Willi, Trudele, Sammy. I forbid Sammele, however. Sammy is affectionate enough."

He looked at Matt with a cynical expression. "Would you believe that I am so popular? I am so popular it could kill me." A nerve twitched in his jaw. "Now, my director Hänsl, *lieber* Hänsl, says not to worry. Why should he worry? He has his film. But I have no exit visa. And it is becoming more difficult every day. More costly. Do you know where Schuschnigg is at the moment?" Schuschnigg had been the chancellor of Austria prior to the *Anschluss*. "Schuschnigg is a prisoner at the Hotel Mètropole, which is Gestapo headquarters. The chancellor of Austria is cleaning latrines! And he isn't even *Jewish!* Have you heard of Malthausen? No? It is one of the camps."

"Internment camps?"

"Oh, *ja,* call them that. What does it matter? They are beginning to kill Jews. Relocation is the word. Sure, I believe that, "he said sarcastically. "That was correct, how I said that—'sure'—*ja?*"

"Don't worry about your English. Your English is fine," Matt said.

"Not English—*American*. I will learn American. Now, say you will help me."

"Your American is fine."

Sammy waved a towel impatiently. "Na, na, not the language. There is an Office for Jewish Emigration. It is the only agency authorized to issue permits to Jews to leave the country. You have power. You are a correspondent from the United States. You will obtain this permit for me, yes?" He smiled charmingly. "Think of it, how romantic. How romantic! An adventure! It will make a film in Hollyvood."

Is this what is meant by gallows humor? Matt thought. Sammy was almost manic.

"But you said it costs money. I have no money," Matt said.

"They will take my house. I have other property, you understand. That will pay. I am told you should see a man named Eichmann. Or Heydrich. They are the people to see."

"I'll do what I can," Matt said.

For a moment Sammy's face lost its charm. The poseur in him vanished for a minute. "Thank you," he said, and they went to join the others for lunch.

It was a relaxed and jovial affair. The other actors were careful not to tell the latest anti-Semitic jokes in front of Abrams.

Matt was surprised to see how simple the procedure was. He was told at the Office for Jewish Emigration that a permit could certainly be issued to the Jew Abrams. His dossier was brought in. The Office of Jewish Emigration knew everything about Sammy. They knew exactly the number of accounts and the amount of money in each one that Sammy possessed at the Reichsbank, formerly the Austrian National Bank. They knew about the house, the cars, the country place near Fuschl. It was *very* simple. All of them would have to be left behind, of course. And the Jew Abrams would be issued an exit visa to the land of his origin: Poland.

"Poland?" Matt repeated, stunned.

"Yes," said the official, who was neither Heydrich nor Eichmann, both of whom were extremely busy at the moment. "The Jew Abrams possesses a Polish passport. It does not apply, of course, to his wife, who is an Aryan. The child . . ." The official shrugged his shoulders. Matt noticed that no matter how the man's shoulders moved, the swastika on his armband remained immobile.

"What does that mean?"

"It means that visas for members of the German Reich must be applied for at a different office. That would take time, of course."

"There must be some way to expedite this," Matt said.

"Perhaps," said the official.

"Poland?" Sammy shouted, then ran to close the door. "Poland?" he repeated. "You think I am *verrückt*, a crazy man? I will not go back to Poland. Abramowitz in Poland? Oh no. Impossible. Utterly impossible."

"I'll do what I can," Matt said. "But it's going to cost."

"How much?" Sammy asked.

The Office of Jewish Emigration told Matt that it would cost the equivalent of fifteen thousand dollars.

Matt relayed the information to Sammy.

"It is not possible," Sammy said. "I do not have that. Not anymore. What am I going to do?"

Two days later, Sammy telephoned Matt at the Bristol.

"I have good news," he bubbled over the phone. "Our wonderful epic drama is photographing in the Tyrol this summer. I told you this was some film, eh? Spare no expense, that is what they always told me. We shall be filming in Landeck. Do you hear that? Landeck, this summer. There is a most imposing castle there. And of course, the mountains, do not forget the mountains. The mountains around Landeck are incredible. The views *herrlich*. Three weeks at the end of August, they say. You will come visit, *ja?*"

"If I can, Sammy, I would enjoy it."

"But you must. I have already rented a villa for myself and the family. It will be a holiday for you. An escape."

When Matt hung up the receiver, he decided to call Sabine. He knew of no one else who could help Sammy now. He went to the American embassy, and a call was put through to Sabine Abramowitz in New York.

When he finally reached her the next day, Sabine did not recognize the voice. There was nothing that resembled his voice. Instead it sounded like the noises that used to come from the crystal radio set Matt had built so long ago. And the message he was giving her was not clear either. Her cousin had decided on Glenrocks, he said. Could she book him, his wife and child in one of the *permanent* suites? They were not sure how long they would stay. Matt knew how difficult it was, since everyone in the world wanted to come to Glenrocks, people were even willing to pay at least fifteen thousand clams—

"What?" Sabine said, four thousand miles away.

"Clams. Simoleons," Matt shouted into the speaker, feeling extremely silly.

"Oh. Where can I contact you if a reservation is possible?"

"I can be reached at the Hotel Bristol," Matt said. "Or you can leave a message with the American consulate in Vienna. Or better still, contact the chief of the Paris bureau," and he gave her the number in Paris.

It was a most unsatisfying conversation. After so long, he had said nothing personal. She wasn't even sure what he was talking about. Sabine went to Dieterl for an interpretation.

Dieterl sighed. "Wouldn't you know Sammy would make it difficult. There must be some problem. More than his being Jewish. Obviously he needs fifteen thousand dollars to buy his way out. *Their* way out," he corrected kimself. "Gisi is not Jewish. God knows what that makes their child. Well, now, how do you propose to raise the money?"

Sabine went to her mother. Together they went to Max. Max and Bertha agreed to sponsor Sammy, but they could not get fifteen thousand dollars that quickly.

They turned to Dieterl for advice. "It is very difficult, this quota system now," he sighed. "Your United States will allow only so many Jews to enter each year. Perhaps Sammy will have to emigrate to Canada. Or Australia." He paused. "Is there no one who can help?"

Sabine's mind turned to the Cardozos. They had power and influence. And they could lend fifteen thousand dollars so very easily.

It was hard to make the telephone call. She was startled when Mrs. Cardozo herself answered the phone.

"Hello. This is Sabine Abramowitz."

There was a pause. "Yes. How are you, Sabine?"

Sandy sounded concerned. Good God, Sabine thought, she thinks I'm pregnant. Well, that's one way to get to her.

"Mrs. Cardozo, I would really like to see you and your

husband on a personal matter. And I'd rather Mark did not know about it."

She was wracking her brain for more of the script: chorus girl and family scion. There must have been thousands of movies with dialogue like this.

"Is anything the matter?" Sandy Cardozo asked. Maybe she had seen the same movies.

"I'd rather not discuss it over the phone. But it is urgent. Could we meet?"

"Well, darling, we're quite busy."

"It won't take long."

"How about tea this afternoon?"

"Thank you." Sabine hung up. *Tea?* It was too grand. She started to remove the nail polish from her right hand, and stopped. No. It's better to play your own game, not theirs. She appeared at the house on Seventy-second Street with a fair amount of lipstick, red polish on her nails, and a full pack of Camel cigarettes in her purse. She was prepared.

Except, of course, she wasn't. She wasn't prepared for Sandy's greeting. Sandy opened the door herself, with a butler hovering behind her. "Come in, come in."

Sabine stepped inside. The crystal chandelier had prisms from Czechoslovakia. The mansion itself had been designed by Stanford White; the stairway leading up to the second floor was graceful but unostentatious. And Sandy was wearing her Chanel.

"Tell Maid to serve tea upstairs in the sitting room," she informed the butler.

Sandy led the way up, past the original Degas, the Monet, the Cézanne. "Julien's father collected these early on. I don't think he paid more than a few hundred apiece, if you can believe that. Of course he had very good advice from Julien. Julien and the Lewisohns are the French specialists." Works of art stretched into every direction. On the second floor, Sandy turned and led Sabine into a small drawingroom. A large painting of straw or hay, with a weather-beaten house in the background and a stretch of sea beyond, hung over the couch.

"That's Andy's work," Sandy explained casually. "He summers in Maine on the coast, near us. Do you know Wyeth?"

Sabine shook her head. Just then Julien entered the room. They shook hands and waited for tea.

"We all have our specialties," Sandy said. "Julien collects the French school. But I'm much simpler. I collect America. You're looking well."

"Thank you," Sabine said. "Do you mind if I smoke?"

"Not at all."

Sabine was aware of their eyes watching her hands, noticing the polish, scrutinizing her body. Was anything showing? A slight bulge? There was no bulge to show.

Tea arrived, was poured, passed, sipped. Everything according to protocol. At the proper time, Julian broached the subject.

"What is the purpose of this visit, Sabine?"

"You remember I received a telephone call at your house last weekend." They frowned, perplexed. "From Vienna. A friend of mine who is a correspondent is trying to help my relatives leave the country."

"Oh, yes, I hear it is very difficult there," Julien said without any feeling.

"My friend was unable to be specific—I imagine the wires are tapped—but he told me he required fifteen thousand dollars."

"That seems like a very high price," Julien murmured.

"For what?" Sabine asked flatly, and Julien almost blushed.

"He has a family," Sabine went on. "A wife and a small boy. This is a loan, mind you. I didn't come here to ask you to buy their freedom. It is urgent that they have the money now. And I don't have any other place to go. I don't know anyone else who has that amount of money."

They were looking at her coolly. *Pushcart peddlers*, they were thinking. *Let one in and they all come. There is such a difference between us.*

"So it's money you want?" Sandy said, and the smile was elegantly cool. "Is that all?"

"No," said Sabine, letting the pushcart peddler come forth. "That is not all. You know there is a quota system for Jews. I'm sure you could arrange to have my relatives put on the list." She took a sip of tea. "Even at the head of the list."

"You're asking a large favor." Julien looked at her. "But I think it could be arranged. Only Sandy and I would like a favor in return."

Sabine looked at them.

"We'd rather you didn't see our son again."

Hondlers, too, the Cardozos. Who would have thought it? Sabine nodded her head. "Of course, if you want it that way."

Julien wrote out a check, and Sabine could not believe he was actually handing it to her. She thanked them, and left the tea unfinished. It was very quickly done, the whole affair. So why did she feel like the pushy pushcart Jew, just because she had been prepared to bargain for her cousin's life? She refused to think about it. After all, she had gotten what she wanted.

Dieterl examined the check.

"How are you going to make sure the money reaches the right hands?" he asked her.

"I have no idea."

"I think you ought to take it to Europe yourself. At least as far as the Swiss border. Mr. Ryan, perhaps, could meet you in Zurich."

The thought had never crossed her mind. Europe? She was young, rather impulsive, and at the moment—following her interview with the Cardozos—brimming with self-confidence. She could be Sammy's savior. And at the same time see Matt again. It was glamorous, intriguing, suspenseful, and better than being at Glenrocks and *not* working with Jerry.

She went to the passport office. It was amazing what the name Cardozo could do. Ease restrictions. Cut time in half—expedite, a word she picked up on her first visit and continued to use. It was so polite and, combined with the name Cardozo, so effective.

At Immigration the name was magic. Sabine did not realize how long and how patiently people had waited for their numbers to be selected under the quota system. For her there were no agonies, no anguish. If the man into whose office she was ushered seemed indifferent at first, his attitude, after two phone calls, was almost deferential. He was certain that there would be no problem. Certainly, for the proprietors of a resort as eminent as Glenrocks, coupled with the Cardozos' interest—every detail would be taken care of.

In two weeks Sabine grew to feel that she could conquer the world, although not quite Adolf Hitler's way. She was convinced that her smile melted steely hearts and that her beauty was more powerful than her passport. It was all right.

She was twenty-three and she had never been farther away from home than Florida.

She called Matt Ryan at the Bristol in Vienna. It took a day and a half for the call to be completed. She threatened and cajoled. It still took a day and a half.

"I am coming on vacation to Switzerland," she informed Matt. "I shall be in Zurich the last week in July. It would be wonderful to see you."

"I don't know if that is possible," Matt replied carefully.

"It's only for a weekend. And, by the way, I have booked that reservation at Glenrocks for Labor Day."

"Really?"

"It was expensive, but I managed. I do think we should meet *somewhere* in order to settle up the charges."

"Zurich will be okay," Matt said. "The first weekend in August." Then he added, impulsively, "I love you."

It didn't sound like something Matt would say—was it for the benefit of the wire-tappers? So all she said was, "Oh, that *is* good to know!" and then, feeling that sounded snide, she asked, "Do you really?"

He said, "Yes," and they hung up.

It was the middle of July when Sabine sailed on the *Normandie,* and there was no one to see her off. Bertha was too busy at Glenrocks, Jerry was in Hollywood, and she had left Mark Cardozo in a state of confusion. She had avoided his calls for nearly a month. He finally reached her, and asked her what he had done. Nothing, she said, it wasn't a question of that. But she thought it better if they stopped seeing one another. Was she angry? he asked. No, not angry. Busy. She knew she was hurting him and didn't know how to avoid it. The conversation ended with Sabine really being angry. But not at Mark, at his parents.

Sabine's first Atlantic crossing was not romantic. The North Atlantic weather was surprisingly cold, and the gray waves, high as cathedrals, battered the ship. The dining salon was never more than a quarter full. There were still ladies who insisted on dressing for dinner, and they entered each night, clutching the emergency ropes that had been strung all along the ship. They wore sneakers with their evening gowns and seldom stayed more than twenty minutes. There were abrupt departures amid the crashing of plates and scattering of silverware. Stewards and busboys spent most of their time with mops and pails. And there was no dancing permitted. It was too dangerous.

Sabine usually sat by herself and watched the place settings slide and the crystal smash. She ordered lobster Thermidor and Veuve Cliquot '28 and never felt sick for a moment. The waiters adored serving her, and were fascinated by the amount she could consume. They gave her extra dishes to taste. She gave them the feeling that she was a professional, and they rose to the occasion. Their service was impeccable, the food stunning. It was Sabine's first acquaintance with French cuisine. Love at first sight.

The ship's doctor was in the process of making a pass, was about to toast the beauty of Sabine's eyes, when he was summoned by a steward. A lady on D deck had broken her leg. He cursed and left, and Sabine went back to her cabin.

Not a romantic crossing. But the sight of Paris made up for it.

It was perhaps the most glittering season ever. The Republic was celebrating the one-hundred-and-fiftieth anniversary of the French Revolution, and there was dancing everywhere. There were *bals musettes* in the streets and formal dances in the Bois de Boulogne under Japanese lanterns and strings of electric lights. Soft clouds sailed through the nighttime skies, and Sabine felt she had never seen anything more beautiful.

The King and Queen of England had paid their state visit and it had been a smash, with parades and fireworks. Every Frenchman, it seemed, was cheering, his cap in the air. All the time she was there, nobody walked, nobody talked. Everyone danced, chattered, and laughed, not listening to the radio, with no time to read the headlines in the newspapers.

Sabine was very lucky to see this side of Paris, and it was due to the kindness of the chief of the Paris bureau. Naturally, he had to cover all these events, and Sabine made a striking partner. She attended all the state dinners and soirées in the elegant gardens of the different embassies.

Two days before she left for Zurich she went to visit her grandmother. She had telephoned once, but thought the operator indicated there was no such number. Anyway, it had given her an excuse to avoid the meeting. She was not sure why she did not want to meet her grandmother, but she had no curiosity. It was a duty call, for her mother's sake.

The restaurant that Bertha had described was long gone. Bertha's mother now lived alone in two rooms on the third floor of a building on rue Lepic, facing a courtyard. As Sabine entered, she noticed that the windows needed washing. She climbed the stairs and was met by the concierge, who, fortunately, spoke some English and, more fortunately, was a friend of Mme Levinsky.

Mme Levinsky was a delight. Sabine had expected a frail old lady, but her grandmother turned out to be shrewd and dominating, continually sending the concierge (who had been part of her kitchen staff during the restaurant days) into her tiny kitchen to prepare coffee or fetch cakes.

Her grandmother had strong hands, and strong eyes. Mme Levinsky asked about Bertha. Sabine described the apartment and the hotel at Glenrocks, and did not leave out Simon. Mme Levinsky had no interest in Simon.

"How is the food?" she wanted to know.

"The best," Sabine replied, and the old lady sniffed in disbelief. "But not to compare with the food here in France," Sabine added, and Mme Levinsky nodded.

"Such dreamers," she said as she looked at Sabine. "The two of them, your father and mother. Never were there two people so beautiful. But that was an age of beauty. They possessed such an air about them. They were truly lovers. I enjoyed watching them. They were so young and knew nothing. Has she been able to be happy without him?"

"She has a happy life," Sabine said, although she knew she was lying. What did it matter? Parents always want their children's lives to be happy, idyllic.

Sabine looked around the room, aware of how little either Bertha or Bertha's mother possessed for themselves. No photographs—they had been left behind in Poland. Little furniture. Only flowers seemed to be in ample supply. Mme Levinsky had pots full of flowers in the window boxes, marigolds and lacy blue flowers unknown to Sabine. Stripped of family, the old lady lavished her love on flowers.

Sabine fumbled in her purse. Somewhere there had been a snapshot. She found it finally, a bit crumpled. There for Mme Levinsky to see was her daughter Bertha, the hotel, and her granddaughter, Sabine. She handed the photo over to Mme Levinsky.

The old woman nodded, but the picture seemed to have no meaning for her.

"It is too late," she said. "I cannot see the figures. However, I will keep it if you don't mind."

It was time to leave. Mme Levinsky kissed Sabine.

"Goodbye," she said. "I am grateful you turned out to be beautiful." It seemed like a very final statement to Sabine, but she had no time to think about it. She shook hands with the concierge, thanked her, and left.

Two days later she was in Zurich.

Each day that summer was more dazzling than the last. The capitals of Europe never looked more splendid, even as they built their air-raid shelters. Take a last look, the boulevards were saying—remember us, breathe the air. Couples sat in sidewalk cafés in the afternoon sun, and lingered even longer in the twilight, watching the streetlights replace the sunlight, while the laughter of strollers under the trees echoed, soft and romantic, and the music from the little street bands wound its way through the evening.

It was that time between sun and streetlight that Sabine met Matt in a lakeside café in Zurich. It was near the railroad station. The first thing she noticed as he hurried toward her was the mustache. *He has grown a mustache. And it makes his face more boyish. And yet he is more robust. I don't remember there being so much of him.*

Matt grabbed her and hugged her and kissed her all at the same time.

They sat and took inventory of one another. *More fiery now, more fiery than rosy,* she thought.

He immediately ordered a scotch. He seemed so at ease in Europe, and Sabine marveled at that. She kept a pocket dictionary with her at all times, and had decided not to bother with verb endings—the infinitive would suffice. Matt asked her what she would like and then ordered a cup of chocolate and a packet of cigarettes.

Then they had time to look at each other. That was uncomfortable. They were not the same people they had been three years ago. *Not so boyish,* she thought now, noticing the creases around his eyes. *No longer a girl,* he thought, *but a beauty, full blown.* He looked around the café to check. Was he correct? Yes, she was without doubt the most beautiful woman in the place.

"You are so beautiful, I don't know what to say," he confessed.

"Can you stay?" she asked him, and he laughed.

"No. I have to take the next train back to Vienna because of all this madness. No one is supposed to know I'm here."

"How long do we have?" Sabine asked him.

"An hour," he said, and they sat while the daylight faded and the night came up over the Zürchersee, and the street lights flooded the promenade. He had three more scotches and she had a ham sandwich and a pastry.

"What am I going to do?" she asked him.

"Stay. I'll send instructions. I'll take the money with me. One half of it must be delivered in advance. The other half I shall give to Sammy. You have it in Swiss francs?"

Sabine nodded.

Then Matt proceeded to tell Sabine Sammy's story. The Polish passport. Sammy's refusal to be repatriated to Poland. The difficulty in obtaining a visa for Gisi, who was an Aryan. The reason for the fifteen-thousand-dollar bribe. And the plan to drive over the border to Chur from Landeck after the filming was completed. It would seem like a day's drive in the country. The border patrol in the High Tyrol consisted mostly of country boys who were champion skiers, hardly aware of the politics of the world.

"False passports, make-believe picnics—isn't that all a little melodramatic?" Sabine asked.

Matt sighed. "I can't tell you what it is like inside Nazi Germany now. Yes, it is extremely melodramatic. And I can't tell you what it is like to be a Jew."

"Thank God I'm an American," she said, and shivered. She wondered why he looked at her so curiously.

"If there should be any trouble, if things do not work out, you go to the American consul. Do you understand?"

"I feel perfectly safe," Sabine said, and showed him her passport. "You would be surprised what the Cardozo name did in the States to hurry things along."

"But you are not there now," Matt reminded her, and he rose. "I have to go."

"When will I see you?" she asked.

"I can't tell you that, but I will be in touch within a few days."

He left her at the café, and suddenly the glamour of international intrigue seemed to disappear. She was just another lonely American sitting all alone over a cold cup of chocolate.

The telephone awakened her three days later. It was Matt.

"I am going to Berlin. I have been assigned there." His voice was tense. "That upsets our weekend."

"What should I do?"

"I think perhaps you should just forget about it and go home."

"I can't do that. I had my heart set on it."

"Well, I wouldn't want you there without me."

"All the same, have the reservations been paid for?"

"Yes, all the money has been exchanged."

"It seems silly to waste a perfectly good weekend just because you can't make it. Give me the address again. I'll go by myself."

"I wouldn't advise it."

"I'm going to do it. What is the town?"

"Landeck."

She repeated the name. "Will someone from the hotel be there to meet me?"

"Yes. Someone."

"And if I need to, where can I get in touch with you?"

"At the network. Better still, the Foreign Press Club on the Leipzigerstrasse in Berlin." A moment's pause. "Sabine, I'm sorry."

"I know. It's just rotten luck."

"Oh, worse than that. Please, please be careful."

She went downstairs after the call and bought a map and found Landeck. She went for a visa, describing herself as a tourist. It was all extremely simple. She missed Matt, but didn't understand why he was so worried. Maybe his worrying meant he really did love her. Maybe it was a good sign.

She went to the railroad station and booked herself a second class ticket to Innsbruck. From there she would go to Landeck.

Sabine needn't have worried about discovering Sammy in

Landeck. In a sea of lederhosen and green Tyrolean caps, Sammy stood out. He was wearing the whitest of linen suits and the darkest of sunglasses. His hair looked suspiciously black. Freshly tinted, Sabine guessed. And he was leaning against a large touring car.

Not like my father, Sabine thought. *This man is too preposterous.* She went to him. He was surprised.

"Jacob's daughter?" he asked. *"Mein Gott, die Schönheit!"* He kissed her on the cheek and whispered, "They think you are my mistress. Why not? Everyone has a mistress here. How do you like my car? I will drive it myself," he said, and proceeded to do so. He was an atrocious driver. The roads were atrocious roads. Sabine clung to the armrests.

"Have no fear," Sammy shouted joyously as he took a curve. "Nobody dies on these roads. Except from heart failure." The peaks were a dazzling blur. Meadows, a mountain lake, tiny villages all created the same effect—illusion.

Sammy turned down a very long driveway that led to an imposing two-story villa, very Italian and the color of rust. A staircase led up to the terrace, which was ringed by a balustrade and topped by statues of marble gods; Sabine recognized the Winged Victory because of Western Union. Roses climbed up matching trellises in the arbor; golden zinnias lined the paths. Beyond the garden lay the grounds, and beyond the grounds a small lake. Beyond the lake, mountains. Beyond that, Switzerland. Sammy stood, posing, before it all.

"My chalet," he said. "Come, today we go shopping. We have lunch. Tomorrow you will come visit the film production. We are shooting, shooting, shooting. You will see history being made on film. The next day, who knows?" He smiled, and Sabine saw her father then. Was it the phrase, the gesture, the fatalistic gambler's grin?

They ate lunch under the shade of a huge plane tree at a table with a linen cloth and cut crystal. There was Sammy and his wife Gisi, and the child, Freddy, who was almost a carbon copy of his mother. They both stared at Sabine with wide dark eyes. Freddy could speak nothing at all, and Gisi knew no English, but they were content to stare. Sammy kept up constant conversation—no, a constant monologue.

The baby was perhaps six months old, and beautiful. But it wasn't the beauty that attracted Sabine. She felt a connection there. She was drawn to the child. Already he had black curly locks. Already the face was handsome, one of those faces that never changes—you can recognize the man in the baby pictures.

Sammy noticed.

"In love already?" he asked, and Sabine nodded. He laughed, and translated for Gisi. She gave the tolerant smile that a mother always gives when love is mentioned in relation to her boychild. Funny, yes, but not *that* funny.

The maid, Helga, served lunch: a cold spinach soup with sherry, and *Schinkenschnitten in Aspik,* which turned out to be ham with a sour cherry sauce. And then peaches, while bees buzzed around the table. Helga cleared the plates and disappeared. Sammy picked up a peach and savored it.

"Try and find fruit like this in Vienna," he said, and then added, "Try to find any fruit at all in Vienna." Then he whispered,

"Oh Führer, who art out host,
"Give us each day the bread you boast,
"Not just cabbage, turnip and herring.
"Give us what you eat, and what you give Göring.

"Ah, most of the cabarets are now closed," he added. "They used to mock everything. Now everything is *verboten.* I am sick of that word." He sighed and sucked on the peach and they sat there, drowsy in the heat, looking off at the view of the lake, with the heat waves shimmering just above the surface and the mountain peaks that gazed back at them, the peaks so far removed and frosty.

"Everything here is *herrlich,*" Sammy murmured. "Or 'bezaubernd,' 'magical' or 'heavenly.' No, 'enchanted' is better. And I feel it. I am making a film. About the operetta world of Strauss. The idea of a war is ridiculous. The operetta world of Strauss is not ridiculous. The past is more real than the future. The future is unthinkable. Come, let us go shopping."

They drove to Innsbruck. It was an insane journey. Sammy's mood was manic, almost defiant. He insisted on buying, buying, buying.

"Diamonds," he said to the jeweler. "We are interested in diamonds." And the jeweler was very interested in showing them. Sammy took the jeweler's loupe and inspected the stones himself. He chose the two biggest. They were also the most expensive.

"One for my wife," he said to the jeweler, laughing, and pointing to Sabine, "and one for my girlfriend. I should keep them both happy, ha?" The jeweler laughed because he had just made a sale that would keep him in business for two years.

When she understood what he was doing, or thought she did, Sabine protested to Sammy. "You can't give me a present. You mustn't do that."

"Nonsense, Schatzi. You will wear these diamonds in New York. Flash-flash. How do they look on her?" he asked the jeweler.

"*Herrlich*," the man said automatically.

They drove back to Landeck and shopped for leather goods. "What are you doing?" Sabine asked on the way.

"What do you think I can take out of this country? Nothing. Maybe what I can get away with. At present, I have three accounts the Reichsbank has not caught up with. I am changing everything. Buying everything. I will need it. Take the presents, darling. Don't worry. I ask for them back."

Sammy was recognized at the leather shop in Landeck. The shopgirl was excited and called the owner.

"Yes, yes, it's your Sammy. Would you believe it, he is here in your establishment. Na, na, it is I who am honored. Look at these goods. Sabine, what do you think of the stitching?"

"*Herrlich*," Sabine said, and he winked at her.

"You are learning," he said.

The proprietor rushed to serve Sammy.

"No, no. Your Aryan customers first, that is the rule," Sammy reminded him, while taking out his new leather wallet, which was bulging with banknotes. "Look at these shoes, so well-made. To last a lifetime . . ."

The proprietor stared at the bulging wallet. "Of course I serve you," he said to Sammy. "At once."

"So kind. We will be no time at all," Sammy said, and bought three pair of shoes for himself, five for Gisela, and two for Sabine.

"*Auf Wiederschauen*," the man gushed as they left.

"Heil Hitler," Sammy gaily reminded him, and dumped the shoes in the touring car.

That evening, as the water lapped against the shore, Sammy, Gisi, and Sabine were down on their hands and knees, their purchases stretched out on the oriental rug in front of them.

"You see what I mean?" Sammy asked Sabine. "It is the present that is so ridiculous, no?"

The following morning Sabine accompanied Sammy to his film location, where she was introduced to a man named Fortschnigg. Fortschnigg owned the medieval castle where they were filming. It had been at one time a fortress against the Huns, then a prominent way-station for the Crusaders, and subsequently a monastery; now it was a movie set. Fortschnigg had plans. He had started out as a bank teller in Munich, intelligent enough to manage the banking concerns that had been confiscated from the Jews by the Nazis. Fortschnigg's view of history was rather dim, but he had a strong money sense. He was intent on buying every available broken-down ruin in the Tyrol and restoring them all—to sell at a great profit. Already he had seen to it that this castle was chosen by the Minstry of Culture for the film. The Ministry of Culture was paying for a great part of the restoration, plus the small banker's fortune Fortschnigg charged for the rental of the castle. At the moment he could not have been happier, except for the sunburn that was peeling his brow.

He was suitably cordial to Sammy but did not offer to shake hands.

In introducing Sabine, Sammy neglected to add a last name, but explained that she was attached to the film industry in "Hollyvood." Magic word. Fortschnigg grasped Sabine's hand and shook it warmly. Could he show her around? She complimented him on his English. And Sammy left to change into costume and makeup.

While Fortschnigg gave Sabine the tour, pointing out spires and dungeons, dropping dates, he also managed to ask a great deal about films. He was a fan. He had been privileged to be included in a private screenings of *Gone with the Wind* that the Führer had ordered. "There are so many films I would wish to see," Fortschnigg said rather wistfully. "*The Wizard of Oz,* I should like to see that. I like that Judy Garland. She is most talented. She is not Jewish, is she?"

The question startled Sabine. "I have no idea," she said.

"I hope she is not Jewish," Fortschnigg continued, and went on to enthuse about Betty Grable and Alice Faye and the charm of Deanna Durbin. "A pity we shall not be seeing all those films. I shall miss seeing them," he sighed.

"Why?" Sabine asked.

Fortschnigg stammered, "Oh, because of business. I shall be forced to travel this fall. There will be no time for pleasure. One must work! Ha, ha!" And he gave a little banker's laugh. "Ha, ha, you don't believe this castle pays for itself. No, no. The old man must work to pay the rent! Ha, ha!"

That was the last "ha ha" to be heard for ten days, because the clouds camd down around the mountains and blotted out the sun. For ten days, while the actors sat around in their villas getting paid, the director and producer fumed. Soon the summer weather would be over. August was ending. In September the weather was terribly risky. They had already managed to shoot most of the interiors.

On the eleventh day Sammy was called to work. It happened to be the last day of August. Hänsl, the director, was in a frenzy. He did not want to lose time. If the sun went away again . . . He would not think about it. He assembled the actors. The technicians were out of the way. He gave Sammy instructions. Even in a crisis, these were Viennese, so there was a certain amount of banter.

"Sammy, old friend, I want another one of your famous goodbyes."

Sammy addressed the crowd. "Thirteen films, and I always lose the girl to *him*," he said, pointing to Willy Fritsch. (*Laughter.*)

"Of course. The handsome guy always gets the girl," Willy said, pointing to his famous ugly Viennese mug. (*More laughter.*)

"Listen, Hänsl," Sammy grinned, "can't we fool them this one time? Let *me* run off with the girl. Just once! Just once!" (*Laughter.*)

Hänsl shook his head tolerantly. "Next time, Sammy. Next time."

"Next time?" Sammy looked at him with a glint in his eye. "Ah, *next* time. Next time we'll really fool them. I'll run off with *Willy*." (*Much laughter.*)

Hänsl was ready for work now. "Cameras ready?"

Sammy had brought Sabine to the set, and Fortschnigg stood by her side.

"That Sammy," he chuckled, "a very funny fellow. Ha, ha!"

Sabine nodded. There was something about Sammy's attitude that disturbed her. It was the gambler's boldness. The challenge. A kind of recklessness that she wished he would subdue.

The scene began. The cameras rolled. Sammy was to bid a reluctant farewell to the lady star, and acknowledge his rival's victory at the same time. His grin was self-mocking, his gestures a bit florid to be entirely truthful. His attitude was cynical, but tinged with regret. In short, very Viennese. Sammy donned his gloves, kissed the lady's hand, and saluted Willy Fritsch, who played the rival. Sammy stood on the parapet that had seen the Crusades. His uniform perfect, his aging face handsome.

"*Tyrol, Ade,*" he said to the mountain peaks, with a rueful gesture of farewell.

"*Mein Freund, Ade,*" he looked at Willy.

"*Mein Liebchen—Ade.*" He blew a kiss, bowed, and was gone.

"Cut!" the director ordered. "That will do it. I thank you, Sammy!"

"Oh, not one more time?" Sammy said. "I do love to say '*Ade.*' "

"Na, na, this *Ade* was very moving, your goodbye. But tell me, where are you going?" There was time now for more jokes.

Sammy returned to the set, pulling off his gloves.

"Where would I go?" he asked nonchalantly. "Why—to Hollyvood!" (*Much laughter.*)

"Not so far," Hänsl said with a smile. "I may need retakes."

"Then I shall book a return ticket. See you tomorrow."

"Of course, of course. Thank you, Sammy."

"Thank *you*, Hänsl."

Sammy started to say something to Willy Fritsch, but the other actor's mind was already concentrating on the next scene, so he left with a wave.

In the touring car on the way back to the villa, Sabine was disturbed again. "Should you have mentioned Hollywood?" she asked.

"Oh God. A joke! The Viennese would die for a good

joke. And no one would take it seriously. Nobody ever would take me seriously. So, tomorrow, we go on a picnic," Sammy said.

"Do you have everything you need?" Sabine asked.

"Of course. I have the address here where the papers are waiting. And the rest of the money. Tomorrow, we go."

That evening, before bed, Sammy spent a moment with Sabine.

"Tell me about Jacob," he said.

"When I was a little girl," Sabine said to Sammy, "I spent a great deal of time by the map. I found Poland. I found the town where you both came from. I could see the roads you both took. I drew one line to Vienna, a second to Berlin, a third to Paris. And then a fourth to New York. It seemed like such an incredible distance away."

"Then what?"

"I drew his line to Florida."

"Was that where he died?"

"Yes. Yes."

"That is in the south of America."

"In the United States, yes. The line stopped there. I want your line to travel on now, from here to Zurich. From Zurich to New York. And then, to *Hollyvood*."

"Na, na, not Hollyvood. Not really *Hollyvood?* I could never succeed there," he said, wanting her to deny it.

"You want to bet?" she said.

He was serious a moment. "You must have pleased Jacob very much."

"I hope so."

"We never tell our children enough that we love them. Even I don't tell Freddy. Of course, he would not understand yet."

"He will."

"To lose a child," Sammy said, almost to himself, "that must be the worst. I can imagine nothing worse. Do you know what means the term *Judenrein?*"

"*Juden* means Jew," Sabine said.

"*Judenrein*—to be cleansed of Jews. That is what the Nazis say they want. It is silly, I know. But I do not believe the Nazis want just to force us to leave. I believe they want to kill us all."

Sabine found herself with that curious feeling again. He could not be talking about *her*. She was an American.

"Even Freddy," Sammy continued, and then rid himself of the thought. "To bed. That is enough. Good night. Sleep well."

They needed to have an early start.

Helga insisted on a proper picnic. She had roasted chickens, boiled eggs, and made sandwiches. She had sliced paperthin ham and put it between thick slices of peasant bread with three kinds of cheese. She had included two bottles of white wine and one of the Rötel, the red wine of South Tyrol. She packed a Linzertorte. And milk for the baby.

Sammy was impatient. They had packed as many of their goods as they could manage, and all of the diamonds. Sabine was wearing three diamond rings, and there were three others in her pocketbook.

"Why me?"

"You are American. They will not search you. Even for a little trip like this, they might search us. Come, let us go."

Helga continued to give instructions. "Put up the top on the car. So much sun is bad for the baby."

"Goodbye, goodbye," they waved. Freddy waved too. Helga waved back.

They drove through the sunny fields to Landeck and paused for twenty minutes for their picnic, but ate nothing. Sammy had brought his makeup case. Now he busied himself with a wig and glasses. He was very adept. It took him no time at all. Sabine hardly recognized him. When he returned, he was carrying a garment in his hand.

"My corset," he said, handing it to Gisi. "I am to be older, *ja?* Better to be fatter." They disposed of the corset by the side of the road. In another half an hour they reached Stuben, the town where they were to pick up the false passports. They stopped in front of a charming chalet that had red and white geraniums at every window.

"Please knock on the door," Sammy instructed Sabine, "and give them this." He handed her a packet. "They shall give you the passports in return."

Sabine had a sudden attack of nerves. What might happen? Would she be arrested? But she was an American. Yes, there was nothing they could do to her. She knocked on the door.

It was answered. She entered a room. There were three men,
One, the one with a mustache, held out his hand. No one
spoke. She handed the envelope to the man, who counted the
money and handed her the three passports. She examined
them. Doktor Schlegel, wife Clarissa, child Martin. Sammy
had given them one of his old photos, taken for a film years
ago. Almost convincing, she thought.

She returned to the car and they drove on. Sammy's hand,
she noticed, was trembling. He was not talking any more.
They drove in silence to the border.

The barrier was up, the swastika flying overhead. Beyond
they could see the white cross and red background of the
Swiss flag, only a short distance away.

The Austrian border guards handled their passports indif-
ferently. Two country boys, both good-natured, they eyed the
hampers of food.

"There is enough food here for an army," the taller one remarked.

"You are right," Sammy agreed. "Have some. We packed
too much. We shall never be able to eat it all. A chicken
leg?"

The guards accepted the chicken legs and the ham sandwiches, and laughed in confusion as Sammy heaped food
upon them. But they accepted the food, stamped the passports, opened the barrier, and waved them through.

"Thank God, thank God, thank God," Sammy said under
his breath as they approached the white cross with the red
background. Again there were border guards, Swiss ones.
Again, country boys, but they received their pay in Swiss
francs, not Reichsmarks. Sammy drove very slowly, careful
not to make any mistakes. The border official held up his
hand. Sammy pressed his foot slowly on the brake. The car
eased to a stop.

"How long will you be staying in Switzerland?" the guard
said.

"A few hours, only for a picnic. The baby must be back by
bedtime. Otherwise, his nurse scolds and scolds!" Sammy
chattered away. Sabine wondered why he was talking so
much.

"And what is the purpose of your visit?"

"I said, a picnic. Perhaps a bit of shopping, if there is
time." Sammy's voice sounded a trifle strained. The official

examined the passports. He was a country boy. Just a country boy. There would be no trouble now. These were the Swiss.

"You are Doktor Schlegel?" he questioned Sammy.

"Yes, yes," Sammy said irritably. The white cross with the red background flapped in the breeze. There were cows, Holsteins from the look of them, grazing on the hillside a mile down the road. A mile down the road there was a farmhouse. A mile down the road a man was walking, a hoe over his shoulder. Sabine kept her eyes on the man with the hoe. Flies were buzzing around the open picnic hamper. Gisela waved the flies away from her baby's face with her hand. Freddy stared at the shiny metal buttons on the guard's uniform. Then the guard left, with all their passports. Sabine felt perspiration trickle down her arm. She slid the three diamonds off her fingers and slipped them into her pocketbook. She didn't know why.

The guard returned.

"Follow me, please," he said, still smiling.

"Is there something out of order?" Sammy said.

"Nothing out of the ordinary. Forms to be filled out. That is all."

Sammy opened the front door and helped Gisela and the baby out of the automobile, taking Gisela's arm as they walked up the neat little flagstone path to the customs house. The guard walked behind them and in front of Sabine. When they reached the door, a second official opened it for them to enter. The first guard then turned to Sabine.

"Halt," he said. Sabine looked into the room, and into the faces of the Austrians to whom she had given the money not more than a half hour ago.

"You are Doktor Schlegel?" the man with the mustache asked Sammy pleasantly.

"Yes," Sammy said.

"No! You are the Jew Abrams. You lie!" the man screamed, and struck Sammy. The wig fell off. The glasses flew across the room.

"You can't do this!" Sabine yelled. "This is Swiss territory!" The guards looked at her blankly. Brought up in this little mountain town, they knew not one word of English. "*Verboten! Verboten!*" she said, but the Swiss guards only looked at her curiously. The baby cried out in fear. The man with the mustache grabbed Gisela by the arm and she fell, twisting her body so her baby would be protected. The man was yelling in German and Sammy was screaming back. Gisela started to rise. Her right arm hung down as though it were broken and a lock of hair fell over her forehead, the only time Sabine had ever seen a strand of hair out of place. Gisela's eyes were filled with terror.

The Swiss guards stood by. The Austrians started to drag Sammy and Gisela away.

"Stop them. Stop them. I am an American. American!" Sabine continued to shout, as though the word were magic. The Swiss continued to stare, not understanding what she wanted, taking refuge in the fact that they didn't understand her words. The man with the mustache and the two others stopped for a moment.

"This Jew is an enemy alien, trying to escape!" the official told Sabine in English.

"What do you mean, enemy alien? He is Austrian."

"He is Polish, this Jew. We are at war. Have you not heard? The Polish forces attacked this morning at dawn. We are at war. This Jew goes back."

Sammy began another struggle, and the Austrian guard hit him with the butt of his rifle, knocking him to the floor.

"Help me, help me," Sammy pleaded to Sabine. "Help me, help me," he said over and over, as he tried to crawl over to Gisela and Freddy. "Help me," he said. But there was nothing she could do, and they were taken away—Sammy and Gisela, and Freddy, still crying, Gisela trying to calm him.

"I am an American! You can't do this!" Sabine cried, and the Austrian with the mustache threw her passport at her.

"American. *Ja.* You are the Jewess Abramowitz. You are all the same," he said contemptuously. "Open your pocketbook." The Austrian stripped Sabine of her diamonds and then left her alone in the room with the two Swiss guards. She watched as the Austrian turned Sammy's automobile around. Sammy, his wife and child got in. One of the other men drove. Sabine stared after them. The Swiss guard picked up her passport and handed it to her. It crossed her mind that they had been bribed by the Germans. It crossed her mind, as they drove her to the railroad station at Settaplana, that perhaps everyone had known. The Austrian official, who had taken the fifteen thousand dollars, who after all was in touch with the Reichsbank every day; Sammy's director, needed to finish a very expensive film; the other actors, who had been so preoccupied of late.

The guards put her luggage on the train, saluted politely, and left. Country boys, she thought, who smiled and saluted. Who knew nothing.

She sat in the compartment and for a moment thought she was going to cry. The other passengers looked at her with idle curiosity and then returned to discussing the events of the day. Definitely, the war had begun.

Sabine felt like a child. A silly child at that, who had been fooled and tricked. She remembered the other train trip, the journey back from Florida, where she had abandoned her father's body to the worms.

She got up abruptly and rushed into the toilet, where she was violently ill. *The Jew Ambramowitz. I am American. The Jew Ambramowitz. I am American.*

Then she began to cry.

Chapter Eleven

Matt Ryan had cabled that he was coming home, and Sabine was waiting with Bertha and Simon in Simon's little apartment to welcome him. She found the apartment uncomfortable, small, claustrophobic. Mirrors covered one wall of the narrow living room to make it seem larger. Mirrors reflected the three of them there, sitting, waiting. Sabine could not sit still, but this apartment had no room to walk in. She picked up a lighter from the coffee table to light her cigarette and had the impulse to throw it against the wall and smash the mirror to pieces. She wanted to hear the crash, wanted to watch the jagged slivers of mirror disintegrate.

Why was she so angry? She had felt this way ever since her return from Europe. On her way back she had stopped in Paris to pay a second visit to her grandmother. That, too, had frustrated her. Mme Levinsky had been so calm.

"You must leave Paris," Sabine had told her.

"Why would I leave Paris?" her grandmother had said. "This is my home."

"You don't understand. It is not safe."

"Nonsense. The Germans will never occupy Paris. During the last war, the zeppelins came over and dropped a few bombs. Poof, your father and mother fled. I shall not."

"Grandmama,"—Sabine suddenly slipped into the term, although she had seen this woman only twice in her life—"you don't understand. The situation is much different now. I have seen the Nazis. I have just come from Austria."

"Yes," Mme Levinsky said rather drily. "Poor Sammy was never very lucky."

"They took his wife and his child. I can find no trace of them. I have been to the consulate. Nobody knows. Nobody will tell. They have vanished."

218

"It was not wise to be a Jew in Austria. Nor Poland, for that matter. But this is France, my dear."

Even the day was conspiring against Sabine. Sunshine streamed in through the windows. The flowers, freshly watered, flourished in the late afternoon light. The clock ticked peacefully on the wall. The furniture had not been disturbed in over twenty years. And in the papers one could read of the overwhelming superiority of the French army, massed on the front. The theaters and the music halls, closed on the first day of the war, had reopened. The only sign of war was the blackout, a precaution against air raids, raids that never came.

"You will stay for dinner," Mme Levinsky ordered. "There is plenty. We shall dine early because of the blackout. I shall not have you on the streets in the dark. When does your ship leave for America?"

"I take the boat train tomorrow morning," Sabine said.

Mme Levinsky threw up her hands. "Ah well, who knows when you will get a good meal again?"

"Yes, Grandmama."

They ate by the light of the fading sun. Sabine was astounded by the quality of the food. What was the secret?

"Never use salted butter," her grandmother advised. Mme Levinsky studied Sabine. "You don't resemble your mother. You resemble me when I was young. Extraordinary!"

"Have you a photograph?"

"A photograph? Of course not. Who had time for photographs? The Cossacks killed your grandfather. He was caught by chance and killed for a joke. As simple as that. The photographs were left with the books that were stacked up in piles. I grabbed your mother and ran for the train. No photographs, no."

"Cossacks?"

Mme Levinsky shrugged. "Russians, Poles, what is the difference? *Goyim.* Your grandfather knew everything. Books. Religion. Jokes. Songs. A bullet in the brain ended that." Then the bitterness disappeared as Sabine's grandmother began to reminisce about the past. "So I came to Paris. And proceeded to do what I had done all my life. Cook."

In Paris her cuisine had made her famous. *La cuisine juive* was a novelty for the Parisians. Mme Levinsky recounted the number of fleeing Jews who had found their way to Paris, dropping off bits of their lives along the way—aging parents, tubercular babies—but the strong had survived and even flourished in Paris, settling around La Butte in Montparnasse. And in the sunny days of *la belle époque,* when Offenbach's operettas were still echoing through the music halls and Bernhardt still mesmerized theater audiences, these Jews smoked and dreamed and read their poems in restaurants, found work, fell in love, buried their dead, and bore their children with a freedom they were unused to.

As Mme Levinsky talked, it was evident that she had no intention of leaving a country that had been so good to her.

"How did you get started?" Sabine wanted to know.

"I started by washing dishes. Your mother and I slept on a mattress on the floor behind the kitchen for two nights. Then I put the mattress on a table, because there were rats. I held your mother in my arms so she would not fall. We slept that way."

It all seemed so matter-of-fact, perhaps because it was so long ago. Mme Levinsky was detached from everything except the killing of her husband. That still stirred her anger.

"You must go. It is getting dark."

They parted at the door. It was awkward. Should she kiss her grandmother? Mme Levinsky was formidable. She decided to shake her grandmother's hand. Mme Levinsky laughed and drew Sabine to her, kissed her on both cheeks in the French manner, patted her on the shoulder, and let her go.

"Goodbye," Sabine said quickly, embarrassed by her own emotion.

What a strange breed we are, Sabine thought in the taxi. Grandmother, mother, and daughter, so removed from one another. Where was the warmth? Wasn't there supposed to be warmth? Or was it only toward men? So much of their lives seemed to have died with their husbands' deaths.

The following morning she boarded the boat train, and by the time she arrived back in New York, the Germans and Russians divided up Poland, and that part of the war was almost over.

Now they waited for Matt in Simon's tiny West Fifty-third Street apartment. To pass the time Simon put a recording of a Brahms piano trio on the record player, and they listened in silence to the soulfully Germanic sound of it until the doorbell rang.

Simon rose to answer it. And there he was. Matt. *Still wearing the mustache, but the grin is different. More defiant, less cocksure,* Sabine thought.

There were hugs all around and Matt's eyes took in the whole room, everything equally. He spent no more time looking at Sabine than he did at her mother. But he could feel that Sabine resisted his hug. He ignored it.

"What brings you back to New York?" Simon asked.

"I was fired," Matt said, stretching out his hands.

"Fired from your job?" Bertha said. To her that was still a Depression tragedy. "Whatever for?"

"Fighting. Brawling, you might say. It did have some elements of an Irish pub fight, except the lads were beating up two ladies. The lads were stormtroopers. The ladies—who knows?—not Jewish, I'd say. The Jews have been banned from all public places. Maybe they were—ah well, who knows, I didn't take the time to ask them. I just barged in and bloodied a few noses. Then I got arrested and was asked to leave the country. How do you like *that?*"

Nobody said anything, so he continued.

"Well, the network was not happy about it. They accused me of drinking—which wasn't wrong, God knows, there isn't much else to do in Berlin but drink. But I was being too obstreperous, so they canned me. And here I am. And how are you?"

"Fine, fine," Simon said lightly, answering for himself and Bertha, while Sabine remained still.

"And you?" Matt turned to Sabine.

"Ah well, I was not successful. I did not get Sammy and his family across the border."

"I know. I'm sorry about that."

"I could have used your fists perhaps. If you had been there."

"I'm sorry. But then, I've said that."

"Sorry is not enough. I don't accept sorry. You knew more than I did. You would have known I was walking into a trap. The stupid American girl—excuse me, the stupid American *Jew*—walked blithely into a trap, sure that her American passport would protect her. Would protect everyone. *Everyone!*"

He went to her, to give her some comfort, and she slapped him hard across the face before she knew what she was doing.

"You could have helped. You could have saved them. You could have stayed." The words came pouring out of her, and she realized she was crying.

Matt had taken her slap without a word, and he stood there, tears in his eyes, and held out his arms again. She went into them, feeling again her little-girl hurts. His arms were still there for her.

"Matt, I couldn't find a trace of them. They may be in a concentration camp. I heard about Malthausen. I heard so many rumors."

Simon spoke up. "Propaganda! Most of it is propaganda."

Matt's head spun around. "How would you know?"

"Wars use propaganda. In the last war, the Huns were butchering nuns and innocent Belgian babies. Not true, of course, but it made the Allies fight harder."

"Simon, you have no idea what is going on in Germany or Poland. No idea."

"And do you?"

"That's right. I was there. Why won't you believe me?"

The Brahms trio was cascading to a climax.

"I don't believe you because I have seen how the capitalists manipulate everything," Simon said. "War could save a collapsing economy. War means profits. The capitalists don't care who dies. I find that immoral."

"Wake up, for Chrissakes!" Matt shouted. "And turn that damned thing off."

Simon stopped the music and the two men glared at each other. Another brawl? Matt liked to use his fists. They both liked to use words. Matt decided on words.

"I forgot the party position, the Nonagression Pact."

"Are you implying that I am a member of the party?" Simon asked coldly.

"Aren't you?"

"I am not a joiner. I have never been a joiner."

"Well, I have. I was a Communist when they were fighting the fascists, but I sure as hell wouldn't stay one now that they're killing Jews."

"They are not."

"They might as well be. The Russians have closed the bor-

der to the Jews. Russia was the one escape, and that's gone.
It's mass murder now."

"I don't believe you."

"I'll name you towns. Jaroslaw. Wloclawek. Samosc." Matt
ticked them off on his fingers. "The Jews in Pultusk were
given twenty minutes to pack up and get out. Then the
houses were set on fire."

Simon suddenly dismissed the conversation. "I'm hungry.
Are we going out to dinner?"

Bertha, aware of the two men's antipathy, shook her head.
She said to Matt, "Take Sabine. You two go. Simon and I
will stay here."

And so the homecoming split in two.

"And I didn't even get a drink," Matt complained, having
had two now at Willy's Steak House, a restaurant that had
been highly recommended by several journalist cronies.

"I don't understand," Sabine said. "What happened to you
and Simon?"

"For a long time the Soviet Union was the main adversary
of the fascists. They realized that Germany would probably
attack them and they needed time to mobilize. The Russians
have always been good chess players. They figured, sacrifice
Poland and we'll have more time to prepare. So they signed
the Nonaggression Pact, and Russia and Germany split up Poland. Okay, that's their power play. I just can't stand all the
apologists, like Simon. Suddenly they're all isolationists, and
everything about Nazi Germany is a baseless rumor. Bullshit!"

He ordered another scotch to go along with the steak.

"So it's no longer just the good guys against the bad guys?"
Sabine said.

"No longer that." Matt smiled a little bit, remembering.
"No longer as easy as that. What do you think of this place?"

"There's a big waste on the vegetables," she informed him.

"What?"

"They waste a fortune on their vegetables. People come
here for the steak and the service."

"And how is the service?"

"Adequate. The bartender is clipping too much."

"How do you know that?"

"We had a drink at the bar."

"And you could tell that just from having a drink at the bar?"

"The bar was jammed. That's the best time to clip. Everyone else, but this one did too much."

"The steak?" Matt was not prepared for her expertise.

"The steak is choice. Not prime. They're getting cheated on their meats. Probably they're paying for prime and getting choice. Somebody doesn't know, or else doesn't care. Either way, they'll be out of business by Christmas."

It annoyed him that she was so confident of her own opinions.

"I don't believe you."

"You want to bet?"

"You're on. How much?"

"A hundred."

The amount surprised him. "That's a lot of money."

"If you want to bet, bet. I meant what I said. Out of business by Christmas."

She insisted on shaking hands on it.

"Where'd you come to such high stakes?" he asked her. Her face clouded over, and he guessed the answer. "Oh, yes. Sammy."

"Fifteen thousand dollars. A sucker's bet. Not even my money."

"Whose money was it?"

"It was borrowed from the Cardozos."

Matt whistled. "That's a powerful name."

"Do you know what's left of Sammy? Nothing."

"Are you giving up on Sammy?"

"I suppose you could say that. I don't know where to turn now." She was thoughtful for a moment. "It was more than Sammy, you know. It was Freddy."

"What do you mean?"

"What's going to happen to him, Matt? He's only a baby. How will he survive? I heard so many stories in Europe. Even you said—"

"I shouldn't have said those things to Simon. I have no verification."

"Don't lie to me, Matt."

"Okay, I won't. I told Simon the truth."

He took her back to the Riverside Drive apartment and came inside without being asked, taking it for granted that they were not through talking. She flung her coat over the sofa, ran her fingers through her hair, looked at him, and stopped. They became aware of each other for the first time. They were alone in the same room, not in a café nor a railroad station. Nobody else was about.

"You slapped me," he said.

"I was very angry. You're always leaving me."

"But I'm not leaving now," he said with an ambivalent smile.

"Why should you leave? You're out of a job," she retorted, and that made him laugh.

"Don't worry. I'll have a job tomorrow. Or the day after that. And I still won't leave."

She sat down. There were traces of sadness about her he had never noticed before.

"Ah, come on. You want to make a fight for Sammy, I'll fight along with you."

When he put his arm around her, his intention was to comfort her. She did not slap him this time. She took his face in her hands and kissed him. There had been so many emotions that day, the burst of feeling took them by surprise.

"I've tried not to love you," he said. "It isn't working."

"I know. I'm glad."

"I don't want to hurt you."

"Don't worry about it, Matt."

"I want to stay the night."

"I want you to."

"What about your mother?"

The phone rang. He laughed. "Good timing; maybe that's her."

But it wasn't Bertha. It was Mark Cardozo.

"Sabine, where have you been? I call and I never get an answer. Listen, I talked to my family, I found out what happened, and that was so wrong. Can I talk to you?"

"Who is it?" Matt whispered at her. She shook her head. Mark was talking, but she wasn't sure what he had just said.

"I'm sure that will be fine," she agreed, just to say something, aware, even as she spoke, that she had made a blunder.

"You mean it?" Mark's voice was college-boy eager. "Then it's a date?"

"Who is it?" Matt was more insistent, not whispering this time.

"Let me get a pencil and write it down," Sabine said into the phone.

"Write it down?" Mark's voice sounded confused. "But it's for tomorrow."

"Oh," Sabine said. She hadn't heard a word.

"Who is it, why won't you tell me who it is?" Matt said.

"Do you have somebody there?" said Mark over the phone.

"Yes, I told you about him. A friend of the family."

"Why are you saying that?" the friend of the family was roaring. "Why am I suddenly a friend of the family?"

"Mark, tell me again, please. What is it for tomorrow?"

"Lunch before I go back to Cambridge."

"Lunch," she repeated automatically, writing down the word "lunch."

"If that's all right with you. We need to talk."

"Fine." She wrote down the word "talk."

"I'll pick you up."

"No, no. I'll meet you. Tell me where."

"The Biltmore? One o'clock?"

She said the Biltmore would be fine and hung up. Matt had poured himself a drink.

"I don't share," he said. "Who're you having lunch with?"

"A boy from Boston."

"Call him up. Cancel it."

"I can't do that. I don't want to hurt him."

"Call him up."

"I don't love him, if that's what you want to know."

"Then call him."

"No."

"I don't share."

"I know. You *said* that."

He started to put on his coat. "All right, I'll leave."

Panic swept over her. "All right, I'll call him."

"Aha, you know the number!" He waved his hand at her accusingly.

"Yes, I know the number," she shouted. "It's Mark Cardozo."

Matt's manner changed abruptly. "Well, have lunch then. *Use* him, for Chrissakes."

Sabine stood with the receiver still in her hand. He replaced the receiver on the phone. "He's power. The Cardozos can help you with Sammy."

"Is that what you would do?"

"If I had to."

"Doesn't that make you a bit of a shit?"

"Perhaps. But I never lie about it. I say what I'm after." He paused. "What does it mean when you said you don't love him? Does that mean you love me?"

"Yes." She thought he knew that. Why wouldn't he know it? He gave a roar and a laugh and gathered her up in his arms.

She could feel the strength of his body. Her hands went to his mustache. For a second there was the image of her father, but that fled. Eyes closed now, she smelled the welcome maleness of him, still the aroma of tobacco and new wood. Clean and fresh. She kept her eyes closed because if she opened them she thought she would die.

Afterwards, they were in her room. She could not remember how they arrived there—the two of them lying on her bed, naked and released and breathless and so relaxed amid the tangle of the bedspread they had not bothered to take off the bed. She could remember nothing but her hunger. She had been starving all her life without knowing it. How were they naked? She could not recall the shedding of clothes. She could not remember their coupling. He had entered her, filled her, moved inside her, caused her to rock in a wonderful rhythm against him. At the time, caught up in the movement of him, in feeling his lips all over her body, in the strength of him circling her and invading her, the heat of him arousing her to a series of dizzying explosions, she thought, *This is what it's like to have a man, to have a man make love to you.* But after it was over she could not recollect when kissing turned to lovemaking, she could not remember it at all. She had been swept up in such a whirlwind of feeling, such an outpouring that now, without realizing it, the tears were rolling down her cheeks. With great concern, as he had done when she was a child, Matt asked her softly what was the matter. She shook her head. Nothing was the matter. She just wanted to look at him. And he understood that. He watched her watch him.

Man.

Woman.

She celebrated the difference.

His shoulders and neck, the thickness of neck and the play of muscle in the shoulder as his arm moved and then came to rest on his hip. Hardly hip, more haunch, more animal. Big-boned, muscled from a childhood of hard work. Hands accustomed to labor. Spatulate fingers. Hands and fingers that had been so tender, that had so aroused her, that aroused her now as she looked at them. And such a luxury of hair on his body—the hair on his chest softer than the curls on his head, darker in color than his mustache, the line of hair from chest to belly, descending below his belly to the forest of hair that surrounded his—her mind halted a moment before she could allow herself the word—cock. His cock lay in repose against his thigh. She marveled at the veins, the ridges, the head, the skin that encircled it, its color a shade deeper than the rest of his skin. Its shape reminded her of the strength of his arm, the way the veins stood out. As she concentrated on it, it began to grow again, began to fill, to stiffen. Watching it aroused her. It no longer rested against his thigh. It was pointing straight at her. Still watching it, she inched her way across the bed until she was in direct line with its force. Matt laughed softly and reached out to kiss her and enter her at the same time. This she remembered, the feeling of expanding, of opening to receive, of receiving, of thrust and withdrawal, alternating fulfillment and loneliness, in and out, there and not there, then *there* more than not there, *there* more than not. Slowly he was sliding within her, with such control, bringing her almost to the moment of overflowing and then stopping. Stretching the moment and allowing her everything, time to feel and smell, to taste his saltiness, to bury her head and rub against his furriness, his chest, feeling her breasts brushing against him, having his hair caress her. He never left her, never completely withdrew and abandoned her. At all times he was there inside her, fulfilling and completing her, and when he sensed she was ready, he increased the pressure and she felt him like a rhythmic machine increasing in tempo, never dropping tempo, increasing and drawing her with him, until she was concentrating only on the rhythm, the beat of him, responding to the beat of him, finding her own rhythm, finding their rhythm, her body needing no more instruction, knowing exactly how to respond, her hips moving against him, her body giving as he took, taking as he gave, and, when that was also changing, pounding against his maleness, moving away and then *in*, away and then *in*, away and then *in*, and then at the moment of flooding, opening her eyes and seeing his, his eyes boring in on her the way his cock was. It was the strongest moment of her life, and they came together at that exact moment, gazing into each other's eyes as the rest of their bodies rioted in orgasm.

They had taken off the spread; they lay against the pale blue sheets and the bathroom light spilled into the darkened room. She had fallen asleep.

She was incredibly beautiful to him. The curve of her shoulder was so soft and vulnerable, the fullness of her breast so opulent. He had the urge to just touch her breast again. But he knew that would never be enough, just to touch, to caress. He would have to bend his head over and circle the pink nipples with his tongue. And that would not be enough either. He would have to bury himself once more in her body, inhaling the woman perfume, sliding down toward the wonderful expanse of her hips, so much more voluptuous than his own, the slight rise of her belly, the gorgeous profusion of jet pubic hair that covered that foreign country he could penetrate but never fathom no matter how much he explored it. Tongue, nose, penis, hands, lips had conquered that territory. Pungent. Perfume. Female. His. He tossed a proprietary arm across her body and slept.

Man.

Woman.

She had forgotten about Mark again. It was almost noon when she awoke, with Matt's heavy victorious-prizefighter arm still on her. She moved and that disturbed his sleep, and then, even in half sleep, his face broke out in a grin of remembrance and he brought her down to him, and they made love again in the morning, the odor of last night's lovemaking, still salty and slightly acrid, upon their bodies. They reveled in the smell.

She was atop him this time. She called him lazy as she rode him, and in his rhythmic laziness he pulled her down; she felt she was pouring over him—that was the feeling, of melting love, melting lava, sliding down over his prick, the feeling so hot and intense his arms grabbed the bed behind

him and he groaned "Jesus" and almost came right then, but
tensed his body, sucked in his breath and stopped moving.
She stopped moving too. His body was motionless, but the
throbbing continued—she could feel the beat of him inside
her—but he did not come, did not erupt. Together they held
their breath. She was amazed to find that she too was con-
tracting. Beyond her will, she was pulsing. The moment extended. The slightest move on either of their parts would
have sent them over the edge. They were suspended. She
could feel the tick-tick-tick of their bodies until, with a flick-
ering of an eye (did he even move his head?) he granted permission and she moved, moved down him and everything
exploded—his penis, their breath, groans and cries.

She could no longer differentiate between them; they were
no longer two people. It was one lovemaking body. Theirs.
Part prick and part cunt, part breast and part muscle, part
curve and completeness, one heartbeat, one rhythm, one release that went on forever, and then not quite forever, and,
sadly, sadly, it slipped away. And when it was over she could
not, would not speak.

It was twelve-thirty then. She glanced at the clock, untan-
gled herself from him, ran into the bathroom, grabbed at her
clothes, and put them on. She was combing her hair hastily
when he came in, filling the doorway with his nakedness. She
closed her eyes against the power of his body and continued
to comb.

"Where are you going?" he asked. He had forgotten.

"I promised Mark," she said. "I'm late. I have to go."

For one moment she thought he was not going to allow her
to leave, but he did. She passed him, avoiding touching him,
found stockings, shoes, snatched her coat from the sofa,
found herself looking at him once more.

"I feel selfish," she confessed.

"Everyone's selfish," he said, still leaning against the door,
still at ease, letting her go out the door to her lunch date.
There was almost a look of triumph on his face which she
only vaguely understood.

She closed the door and thought she had left him behind.
But not really.

In the taxi, all the way to the Biltmore, she found herself
blushing. He was still with her, his smell still *on* her, on her
fingers when she put them to her lips. She was still wet from

him, and every move of her body brought him back, brought
on the blush, brought on the heat and remembrance, the
sweetness of sexuality. She could not wait for this lunch to be
over so that she could return to him, to be in bed again, to
find a place of their own, to have him inside her. She was
blushing again. She fumbled for her purse, paid the cab
driver something, she wasn't even sure how much, and rushed
into the lobby. Running from lover to suitor, her lover's sexuality still on her body, hoping her suitor wouldn't notice.

She was late, of course, but Mark took her confusion for
concern. He had ordered a drink. She grabbed at it.

They talked. No, he talked, while she made an effort to listen, but Matt's body was an obstruction; his grin, his
mustache, the odor and feel of his hands obsessed her. She
could feel him spreading her legs here, at the table, under the
table—she was fantasizing about Matt being under the table
while Mark Cardozo continued talking.

"I told her she had no right," Mark Cardozo was saying.

What was he talking about? Who had no right? She really
must listen, must concentrate.

"She did confess she had overstepped. My father kept
silent, as usual. I guess they both feel so protective . . ."

Matt was standing there. The sight of him shocked Sabine
into reality. Matt was standing over them at the table. What
was he doing, smiling, rosy and ruddy, curly hair, mustache
and grin, shaved, showered, and combed, standing over them?

Had he come to brawl? Were his fists clenched? Her mind
envisioned a duel, pistols at dawn.

Matt extended his hand. No fist.

"How do you do? I'm Matt Ryan, a friend of Sabine's
family."

"Mark Cardozo." He rose, and had a chair brought
around, ever the gentleman. Matt sat down and charmed
him. The two men chatted.

Sabine was not aware of words; she heard only the two
masculine voices chatting over cigars and brandy. What were
they talking about? Commerce? Affairs of state? Horse racing? She glanced over at Matt, so convivial, sitting there
relaxed, affable, more at ease than ever, as if nothing had
happened between them.

"I want to raise money," Matt was saying to Mark. "And
I'd like to use you."

"That's blunt enough," Mark laughed. Matt glanced at Sabine as if to say, See? That's how it's done.

"Go on," Mark said.

"I want to use your family and your name. And your house. And of course your money. It's for a good cause."

"Am I allowed to ask what the cause is?" Mark was being Ivy League amused.

Matt was Irish blunt. "Sure. The Jewish Emergency Relief Fund. That should concern you."

"There are so many causes." Mark's voice was impassive.

Matt's was not. "This isn't your everyday charity."

Mark evaded. "Yes, well, I will have to talk to my family. It is their house. And their name, you know." And more pointedly, "And their money."

"There isn't much time. The Germans are moving fast."

"Well, as I said, I'll talk to my family." He was putting it aside.

"When can I call you tomorrow?"

"I'll be back in Cambridge then."

"Then I'll call you tonight. Can you talk to them before you leave?"

Mark looked at Sabine. Slightly annoyed, but still the gentleman. "Of course," he said, and gave Matt his number. "You can talk to my mother. You'll have to anyway."

"But you'll put in a word."

"Yes, I'll do that."

"I appreciate it," Matt said, and got up. He was leaving. He smiled at Sabine, the smile of a family acquaintance, shook Mark's hand, and left.

"How did he know where we were?" Mark asked her.

"He heard me on the phone with you last night."

"You said he was a friend of the family. Who is he?"

Sabine took a deep breath and plunged in. "You asked me once if I was in love with anyone else."

"You're in *love* with him?" Mark could not consider the possibility.

"Yes."

"There's no doubt about it?"

"No doubt."

"You're very honest about it." Mark didn't know what else to say; the light was leaving his life.

"I didn't mean this . . . I didn't plan it."

"Nobody plans to fall in love, Sabine."

They sat in silence for a moment, the drinks still on the table.

"Well," he said finally, "I guess you're not hungry."

But she was. She was starving. She couldn't hide it. That made him laugh.

"When did you last eat?" he asked her.

"Maybe last night. I can't remember. How about you?"

"I ate on the train coming down. Good lord, that was yesterday afternoon."

They ordered a huge Sunday dinner. Hot rolls and ribs of beef, pink and juicy. Yorkshire pudding. Apple pie, with slices of American cheese melting against the hot pie. They had second helpings and lots of wine—they were hardly heartsick lovers.

"This is wrong, we shouldn't be doing this," Sabine muttered as she reached for another roll. He laughed so hard, people turned around.

"You're telling me this is wrong?" Mark munched on celery.

"Wrong, wrong," Sabine said, spreading the roll with butter and stuffing it into her mouth. "We'll be punished."

"I think I am eating out of frustration," Mark said, and ordered more wine. They giggled. The mood carried them through the end of the meal and they rolled out of the restaurant at four in the afternoon quite tipsy. Outside the cold air brought them to their senses and the laughter stopped.

"I have a train to catch. Want to see me off?"

"No," said Sabine. "I don't believe I better."

"I will call Sandy from the station. You see, I remember my promises." They parted on the street.

"Kiss me goodbye?" he asked. You don't ask, Sabine thought. But if you're Mark, you do. She shook her head no. He started to walk off, then turned around.

"We're not finished yet!" he yelled, and disappeared into the crowd.

When Sabine returned to Riverside Drive, Matt was waiting for her.

"That woman will never let you use her place. Or her money. I can tell you that right now," she said.

"He's good-looking," Matt said.

"Yes, he is."

"A nice guy."

"Yes, he's that."

"I'm not."

"So I gather."

"You're never going to see him again."

"Are those your instructions?"

"Correct."

"What a change. You were so smiling, so affable before. I thought he was your best friend."

"I need his money. I need his name."

"That name seems to be terribly important. His mother would kill to protect it—from the Abramowitzes."

"Then you *are* in love!"

"*He's* in love."

"Poor guy. Nice guy."

"You don't share, you said."

"That's right. I don't." Then he grinned at her. "God, you really don't know how to fight for what you want, do you? Well, I'll have to teach you." Matt had all the confidence in the world.

"You won't get their money, you won't get their house," she insisted.

"You want to bet? You want to bet?" he repeated, going to work on her neck with his mustache.

Of course, he was right. When he called Mrs. Cardozo later that evening she could not have been friendlier. The two of them chatted for half an hour before coming to terms. The Cardozos would allow a fund-raising drive to take place at their residence the following week.

Sabine could not have been more surprised. Mark had evidently told his mother that Sabine was in love with Matt Ryan. Sandy needed no further inducement: she agreed to whatever Matt Ryan wanted.

The Cardozo mansion was the size of three brownstones. There were turrets and arches. Matt Ryan was impressed. Sabine was determined not to be. He pressed the button.

The butler answered the door this time. Matt caught sight of the warm red velvet on gold leaf furniture, the circular staircase, the artworks that seemed to stretch to infinity.

"Jesus!" he exclaimed. "Are these real?"

Sandy came forward. "Isn't it embarrassing? Everyone always asks that. Yes, they're real. Come in. You're Matt? Call me Sandy. Butler will take your coats. We are meeting upstairs." She led the way.

"There must be a million dollars on this wall," Matt calculated.

"Three," Sandy corrected him.

Sabine had never thought of art in this way before. These were investments. This was like money in the bank. Maybe better. She learned fast.

"Look, a Renoir!" Matt said, poking Sabine in the ribs, using the same enthusiastic tone he had used when pointing out the new "portable" radios on the street.

Sandy led them into the main gallery. Her husband Julien made the introductions. The mansion was filling up. A hundred and fifty, maybe two hundred people were gathered here. Julien introduced them to a Loeb and a Kuhn, a Lewisohn, a Warburg, a Schiff, names that graced the wings of hospitals, art museums, and libraries, even universities, figures in banking and business, members of powerful families. Julien introduced Kuhn and Loeb to Abramowitz. Lowenstein to Abramowiz. And to Ryan. Lewisohn to Ryan. The smiles were gracious. And wary.

The Cardozo clan had come: Sandy and Julien, Peter and Ann and George. Only Mimi and Mark were missing, with apologies. One was in Bermuda, the other in Cambridge.

The butler served champagne, the maid passed sandwiches. A small group formed around Matt and Sabine and Sandy.

"Sandy," someone said, "frankly, I'm surprised you let yourself be used this way. It seems to me Roosevelt and the Congress have made it quite clear that they won't stand for any"—a sip of champagne—"pushiness."

"Oh Lenore, darling," Sandy replied, "I could not resist Mr. Ryan. He is terribly persuasive. And I do feel it's *awful* what's happened to those poor people."

"What has happened?"

Sandy took the moment to greet another guest. Sabine and Matt looked at each other. They were in agreement. Nobody knew. Nobody really knew (or perhaps did not care to know) about the situation in Germany, in Austria, in Poland.

Julien Cardozo mounted a podium and called for attention. He gave an extremely brief, polite request for funds to help feed the European refugees. The request for donations was polite and so was the response. Polite pledges. Two-hundred-dollar courtesies.

Matt grew angry. Impulsively he shouldered his way through the elegant crowd.

"Excuse me, Mr. Cardozo. You don't understand. I want to talk about *Jews!*"

They flinched.

"*Juden!*"

They bristled.

"In Germany, that's what you would be called. *Juden*. And Germany wants Europe *Judenfrei. Judenrein*. Free of Jews. *Cleansed* of Jews. I have been there. I have just come back. I have seen your children being spit at in the street and your parents forced to walk in the gutter."

He couldn't tell whether he was getting through to them. Their faces were impassive. Perhaps they loathed him. It didn't matter anymore.

"If this were Germany, you wouldn't be here. First of all, you wouldn't own this house anymore. And you could not be on the streets after eight o'clock at night and of course you couldn't have the food you have been eating, because you would not have been issued ration cards. You would have no businesses. The Nazis would have taken your banks, your stores. And if you were so lucky as to be granted an emigration permit, you would be given two weeks to get a visa. You would line up in front of the consulates and the Nazis would beat you. Your money (whatever you had) would not help you. You would be on your knees scrubbing the streets. Or you would be taken off. Where? They don't tell you. Resettlement, that is the word. You would perhaps be in Poland. In a labor camp. How many of you have ever worked out in the open twelve hours a day? I see no hands raised. Well, Jews, that's what you would be doing, if you were lucky."

He paused for breath. The room was totally silent. It made him angrier.

"Don't you understand? The Nazis want to exterminate you. Wipe you out."

Total silence.

"Has nobody ever called you that before? Jews? That's what you are. Jews. American Jews. And it looks like no one is going to help Jews. Except Jews."

Glacial silence.

"And maybe not even that. I want to thank Mr. and Mrs. Cardozo for the use of their home. I admire their taste in art. May you all enjoy a long life."

He walked into the wall of silence. And then Sandy Cardozo, in her cool detached drawl, spoke up. "The Cardozo family pledges one hundred thousand dollars."

That was the night over five million dollars was raised for the Joint Distribution Committee and the Jewish Emergency Relief Fund.

Chapter Twelve

The following Wednesday Seymour Martin, the publisher of the *New York World,* happened to meet Matt in Costello's, a bar frequented by newsmen.

"That was quite some speech you gave the other night," Seymour commented over his scotch.

"Shot my mouth off again, didn't I?" Matt smiled.

"Could you write like that?"

"What, the way I talk? The way I shoot off my mouth? Probably. Given enough money."

"And what are you doing now?"

"Having a second scotch."

"Liar. My second. Your fifth."

"Okay, my fifth. And I don't feel much of anything. Sy, you want to know what I'm doing? I'm on my way out to the World of Tomorrow with Sabine. We are going to see the wonders of the World's Fair . . ."

"How would you like to write a column?"

"For the *New York World?*"

"I can't talk for any other paper."

"Daily or weekly?"

"Daily, if you want. If you can."

"What do you mean, if I can? Of course I can. Question is, do I want to?

"Think it over at the World's Fair. And don't miss the Aquacade. Call me tomorrow."

Matt wanted to see the World of Tomorrow before it closed. So he took Sabine to Flushing Meadow later that afternoon and, in a sweet alcoholic haze, took in the 1939 World's Fair.

"Pretty fuckin' terrific!" he said. The cab driver glanced back nervously. Matt gave him a big tip and then led Sabine to the RCA Exhibition Hall, where they peered at a big box with a little blue screen on which alternated squiggles and hard-to-make-out images of people.

"What is that? On that little screen?"

"That is the future," Matt said smugly. He was in communications.

"Just tell me what it is," Sabine said.

"Television."

"Who wants to see that when you can go to the movies?"

"Look at it this way. Soon you can film anything—the war for instance—and then watch it over supper."

They proceeded to the Aquacade. It was evening now, a cold autumn evening, and the girls were freezing in their bathing costumes. They plunged into the water, forming pretty patterns as geysers shot upwards, colored lights played, and the swimmers tried to control their trembling. Sabine watched Eleanor Holm poised on the high diving board. The lights played over the perfection of her body. There she was, a goddess, standing over the world while flags of all nations flapped in the breeze and thousands watched.

"I wonder how much she's making," Sabine mused. Eleanor Holm plunged into the icy water and returned to the surface, waterproof smile undamaged.

"Not enough," she answered herself.

"I got an offer today," Matt said casually, waiting for a reaction.

"From the network?" she asked.

"No. From the newspaper the network owns."

"A newspaper?" That surprised her. "Are you serious? What would you do? Why you?" She asked in a rush of words.

"Thanks for the vote of confidence," he said. "I met Sy Martin in Costello's this afternoon—and he asked me to do a column. It all came from mouthing off at the Cardozos the other night."

"Are you going to take it?"

"It would keep me in New York."

Did he think she hadn't already thought of *that?*

"Is that what you want?" he said.

At the moment, it was. He kissed her and the Aquacade continued through the chilly night without their attention.

They left before it was over, and were in her bed by eleven o'clock.

The next morning Matt called Seymour Martin and accepted the offer.

That afternoon they went looking for an apartment. They inspected places on Riverside Drive, on the Upper East Side, in the mid-Fifties, and finally found one on Waverly Place just off Sixth Avenue, a federal period brick house with ivy still growing up the outside wall.

"What a place to spend the winter," Matt said as they looked at the outside. The apartment was a floor-through. In the back, where the bedroom was, a bow window overlooked a small garden. Around the corner was Café Society, where Sabine had once worked—the kind of place Matt felt comfortable in. The apartment would be conveniently close.

"We could be here for Thanksgiving," Matt said, looking around the apartment, picturing the cold, picturing them drinking sherry and roasting chestnuts by the fireplace with the marble mantel. He could imagine the smell of the wood fire and the snow outside.

"We?" Sabine asked.

"Yes. You'll spend Thanksgiving with me, won't you? We can have a big Thanksgiving. My father. Your mother. I won't invite Simon."

"She won't come without him."

"Then I'll invite him." Matt, flowing with holiday spirit, and went off to write his first column.

He was given free rein, he could write about anything. Besides being the cop on the beat (he called his column *"Ryan's Beat"*) he was the man who had been away and come back, and now was taking a fresh look at the most exciting city in the world. And as he thought about how easy it was for him, and how hard it was for others to reach New York, his mind turned to Sammy, and then to Freddy.

And so his first column was about the children. The Jewish children of Europe who had no place to go, who were being bartered by the members of the United States Congress for their fathers and mothers (that way the *quota* would not be increased). He quoted Eddie Cantor, writing to the president: "If these boys and girls were permitted entry into this country, they would look upon their leader as a saint." And the reply from the presidential secretary: "There is a general feeling, I believe, even among those who are most sympathetic towards the situation in which so many thousands of persons find themselves abroad, that it would be inadvisable to raise the question of increasing quotas or radical changes in our immigration laws during the present Congress. There is a very real feeling that if this question is too prominently raised in the Congress during the present session we might get more restrictive rather than more liberal immigration laws and practices."

And then Matt let them have it. He wrote about Roosevelt, who would rather play practical politics; Cordell Hull, who complained about the amount of paperwork such proceedings would create; the Allied Patriotic Societies, the American Legion, the Veterans of Foreign Wars.

"The children are going to die," his column concluded, "because of lack of action, because of words, because of arguments, because of politics, because of presidents, and because of *us*. If we do nothing about this, if we allow murder to exist, to continue—war or no war, politics or no politics, then we are all guilty. You are. I am."

The first column appeared on Monday. By Tuesday letters were pouring in—the protests, and the praise. By Thursday Matt found himself famous, and barred from certain government circles. So he wrote about *that*. It was not difficult in 1939 to find material for a column. There was too much. There were those who professed to be unaware of the situation in Europe; Matt Ryan filled them in. His style was part Cagney, part Bogart, part Warner Brothers tough guy. A pugilist of the left, they called him. He went for the solar plexus. He immediately found plenty of adversaries. Winchell, for one, who liked neither Matt's abrasiveness nor his power. Nor, most of all, his circulation. Matt was good copy to read. And sometimes to write about. Other columnists had a field day. New boy in town. They either praised him or damned him. Either way, he was getting what he had always dreamed of: power. He was now in a position of power.

Matt and Sabine never had to wait in lines. They were shown the best table. If it didn't suit, another table was found. Closer to the dance floor, closer to the entertainment. Matt never had to pay. Life itself was on the house. For a mention. For a plug. For any phrase he might choose that the restaurant, nightclub, theater producer, starlet, comic, singer might be able to reproduce and throw into an ad.

If the international situation was depressing, the theater season was incredibly brilliant. Matt and Sabine went to all the plays. They saw Tallulah Bankhead in *The Little Foxes*, Eddie Dowling and Julie Haydon in Saroyan's *The Time of Your Life*, and *The Man Who Came to Dinner*.

He wrote a column about New York being the last real diamond. And for at least two months New York became known as the Diamond.

On the fifteenth of November Sabine helped Matt move into the Waverly Place apartment. They found an oak table at a thrift shop, and two bentwood chairs and an armchair that still had its antimacassars. On Bleecker Street, in a musty little shop, they spied a mirror with a heavy carved wood frame, complete with a cherub's face, peeping out from a mass of frames stacked against it.

"How much?" Sabine asked the owner, a man as dusty as his shop.

"Ten dollars," he said.

"Too much." She shook her head.

"For you, eight."

"How do I know the rest of the frame is okay?"

"How do you know you're not going to die tomorrow?"

"I want to see the rest of the frame."

"I got no time to move all those frames."

"Come on," Matt urged, looking around the store, already impatient and ready to move on. "Obviously he's got a damaged frame or he would show it."

Sabine gave a quick estimate of the place.

"You want to bet?" she told the owner. "I'll give you five dollars, sight unseen. That's three dollars for taking a chance. Okay?"

Behind the Lucky in his mouth the man smiled—his first smile in maybe four weeks.

"It's yours," he said, and Matt and Sabine started the excavation. Sabine's instinct had been correct. There were four cherubs, one at each corner; the frame was carved and curlicued and perfect. They rushed home with the treasure and hung it over the marble mantel, then sat in their new chairs and gazed at their image in their new mirror. They were in love with each other and in love with their lives.

Three weeks later, Sabine decided to move in with Matt, so that both of them could get some sleep.

Chapter Thirteen.

The word was "swell."

As 1939 glided into 1940, smooth as a foxtrot, everything in town was swell. The music had never been hotter and you could spend a lifetime between the hours of nine at night and four in the morning, at the Three Deuces, Tony's, and Spivy's Roof on Fifty-second Street, or downtown at Café Society or the Village Vanguard or at Nick's or Eddie Condon's. You could hear boogie-woogie. You could hear Benny Goodman. Artie Shaw. Hazel Scott. Leadbelly. Billie Holiday. Music spilled into the streets. Jazz. Blues. Swing. Scat. Riff. The craze for jitterbugging was on.

Everyone went to nightclubs. They went in formals to Harlem, in top hats and taxicabs, and came home on the bus with all their money spent. There were college kids on Fifty-second Street, and prep school boys at the German American Club on Third Avenue, where nobody checked the fake ID cards. Everybody was jammed together and *that* was swell. Black tie and pearls, and college kids with leather patches on the sleeves of their jackets, and the prep school crowd with the varsity letters on their sweaters turned inside out. Their dates, wearing loafers with pennies in them or brown and white saddle shoes, with skirt and sweater combinations and a string of pearls. Everybody jammed; everyone was happy with the smoke, the booze, the music. All over town, things were swell.

Matt liked nightclubs, liked to relax at the little tables, sipping scotches or, if the day had been particularly frustrating, belting scotches. And he liked the music. Either way, frustrated or relaxed, the music mellowed him. It took Sabine time to get used to this behavior. The tiny tables and the crowds of cronies, the tons of words spilling out of their mouths, never having their own matches or their own cigarettes, always bumming a smoke between the jokes. The quips were loud, the arguments silly. Everything was in high gear. Matt ran with Sabine down streets to catch taxis to take them uptown to Carnegie Hall. He would kiss her in the taxi, scotch and cigarettes spiking his breath. Uptown, and then back down, greeting strangers in theater lobbies with a laugh and a wink. Laughter followed them like a procession of flowers.

This was Matt's time. Everyone has the time of his life, and this was Matt's. There was never enough time to make love; they made love in taxicabs and in the morning while he let the telephone ring. He drank scotch sours for breakfast and took to writing his column on the back of the Chambord menu.

Everyone knew they were lovers. Sex was a release. Matt was back in the United States, a newsman without too much news to report. There was a war, but it was a phony one. As winter came on, both Germany and France seemed to freeze behind their lines. The Germans sat on the Westwall and the French played cards, smoked, and got drunk behind the Maginot Line, going on patrol from time to time. Saturdays the French played soccer while the German troops, not two hundred yards away, applauded.

From Paris Mme Levinsky kept writing about the nonexistent war in her letters. Suddenly there was a flurry of correspondence between Bertha and her mother where before there had been none: chatty letters, filled with details of comfortable lives. Mme Levinsky complained about the rise of produce prices in Paris. In New York, Bertha was in agreement. It was criminal what a head of lettuce cost. Neither of them discussed Sammy.

Still, refugees continued to drift in from Lisbon and Montreal, circling the world to Australia or Argentina and then appearing with unbelievable stories—stories of skiing down mountains and rowing across lakes to freedom, of treachery and greed and just plain cruelty, of families separated forever. But no one seemed to believe that this separate little war, a war against the Jews, was actually taking place.

Not by accident, but because both Sabine and Matt kept questioning the refugees, they heard news of Sammy.

He had not been thrown into a concentration camp. He

had been thrown into prison in Vienna, with many other prominent Jews.

Sabine and Matt heard about Helga, Sammy's old maid, standing in line with homemade soup for her former employer.

"What are you doing, a good Aryan woman like you, making soup for a stinking Jew?" a guard had accused Helga.

Helga had had enough. In her youth she had come in from the country, and she had spent her life working. She had no head for politics; the swastika was just another emblem. But something in her exploded.

"Get away from me," she had screamed at the guard. "And watch what you're saying. I worked for many families, all of them Christian, and they beat me, they cheated me, and if I saw them now, I would spit in their faces. Only one family treated me like a human being. They were Jews. And they didn't stink either. You stink, I can smell it on you. You don't wash your feet. Keep away from me, and shut up!"

"Did anything happen to her?" Sabine asked the man who was relating the story.

"No. The guard laughed and took the soup."

"Well," Sabine continued, "were Sammy's wife and child with him?"

"Not that I know of. They continued to live at home. Only Sammy was in prison."

"Where is he now?" Sabine asked impatiently.

"*Gnädige Frau*, I have no idea. I was able to buy my way out. I had turned sixty. I signed over everything to the Nazis, and they gave me time to leave the country. The last I saw of Sammy, he was—well, what do you think he was doing? He was entertaining. Oh God, we welcomed that. Sammy kept us alive, I think. He kept us laughing. Not an easy thing to do."

So there was no word about him, really. He had been in prison. His wife and Freddy had been allowed to remain in their house. But how long would that last?

The uncertainties of the world made Matt restless. Often Sabine found him pacing the length of the Waverly Place apartment. What to write about?

He wrote about what pleased him or upset him. But big news was a waiting game. Sabine suggested they go visit Matt's father. It would give them a chance to relax. Matt agreed, and they set off for a weekend.

The town of Liberty had muffled itself up for the winter. It was three weeks before Christmas, and across Main Street strings of Christmas bulbs and giant white stars had been strung. They had arrived about five o'clock on a Friday night, and the stores on Main Street were still open.

Matt pulled over to a curb.

"I'm going to buy Dad a present. He'll get a kick out of it. You want to come?"

"No," Sabine said. "I'll wait out here."

"I won't be a minute." He smiled and walked into the drugstore. Sabine lit a cigarette, opening the car window, when the smoke began to bother her eyes.

The sounds from Main Street were very clear. There was the jangle of the sidewalk Santa Claus from the Salvation Army ringing his bell. There was the sound of laughter and clicking heels.

Then, as though she were in a dream, she heard a voice. It came from afar. She could not make out the words but there was something familiar about the sound. It made her nervous, it was irritating. She closed the window and looked out at the street. How bright the windows were in the shops. Full of promise. Small-town USA. She looked at the signs above the stores. Hetzling's. Murgenheimer's. She could hear band music.

Why was she so nervous? What was causing it? She felt she had to get out of the car. She opened the door, and the sound of the band hit her like an arctic blast. It was a German marching band. A truck turned the corner. Sabine blinked her eyes. Atop the truck stood men wearing uniforms. They were dressed like Nazis. It wasn't possible. She stood there, immobile, watching the parade, watching the signs. "Jews Get Out! Jews and Dogs Not Wanted! Franklin Delano *Joos*evelt! Hitler Is Right! America for Americans! Christians for a Christian World!"

She stood watching, stood on the sidewalk and watched it all happen again. She watched the overweight men in their uniforms. They were too fat for the brown shirts and they did not know how to wear boots, how to wear these military high-steppers. Fat grocers and clerks and garage mechanics, yelling at the pedestrians.

A hand caught her arm and she whirled. It was Matt. His face was full of fury.

"What the fuck is this?" And then he answered his own question. "The Bund! The goddamn fucking Bund!" Then, as if he couldn't believe it, because this was the town where he grew up—"*The Bund, here!*"

"Sieg *Heil!*" came from the truck with the loudspeaker.

"Sieg *Heil!*"

"Sieg *Heil!*"

Now these brown-shirted grocers and clerks were stiff-arming the Hitler salute. They had the same look, the same fury, the same screaming hysteria as in Germany. Only it was here, it was in Liberty, it was in America.

"Matt, get me out of here. I can't watch this!"

He opened the door for her and got in himself on the other side. Her hand was trembling. He put the key in the ignition. She noticed his hand was trembling too. Was he afraid?

He roared the engine and pulled away from the curb. The parade was blocking their path. Matt waited for the green light, but when it came the parade paid no heed. The parade continued, the sloppy marching men and the inflammatory slogans and the swastikas continued to block the way, and then the light turned red again and Matt honked his horn. The men looked at him, and began to yell, shaking their fists. They gave the Nazi salute.

Sabine looked across at Matt. His hands gripped the wheel and his eyes were tight with anger. He pressed his foot down on the accelerator and the motor roared, but he had not engaged the gears. They were roaring in neutral. Roaring and headed nowhere, while the swastikas continued to dance in front of them, the bifocaled paunchy Bund brownshirts vomiting out their filth.

The light changed again to green.

Matt leaned on the horn and the Bundists laughed. They laughed because they knew he would do nothing. He would wait patiently until they had finished parading.

But he didn't. Cursing, out of his mind with anger, Matt engaged the gears, slammed his foot on the gas, and headed for the group, aiming for them. He was gunning the motor and leaning on the horn, hoping to hit them, to crush them, to obliterate them.

Suddenly the yells turned to screams, and the prescription glasses were knocked to the street, the fat asses fled, the signs and swastikas flew into the air. The parade scattered and scrambled for safety, because a madman was about to kill them. They sprawled on the sidewalks and curbs of Liberty, the "Sieg Heils" lost in impotent screams of desperation.

Good, good, good—more, more! Sabine was thrilled, clutching the small triumph to herself. They did not look at each other.

"Did I hit any of them?" Matt asked.

"No," Sabine said.

"Shit! I wanted to kill them," he said. "I didn't care. They could arrest me and put me in jail. I had to do it."

"I'm glad you did it. I'm so glad you did it," Sabine said.

"I need a drink."

"Your dad will have one."

Dan Ryan had more than one. They all got not too quietly drunk, and then Matt suddenly stood up and shouted with excitement, "I've got Monday's column!" and began to scribble down notes.

The column appeared Monday afternoon. He called it "Red Light!" It did no more than describe his reactions to the Bundist parade, to the echoes of scenes he had witnessed in Nazi Germany now occurring in his own home town, and how he could no longer sit by and obey the traffic regulations. Give him a ticket, suspend his license . . .

The column drew a lot of mail but no traffic summons. Matt reveled in his power. Others were not too pleased. Winchell denounced Matt's Jewish jokes as going on "ad Nazium." Pegler felt the young Irish upstart had no business talking politics.

Matt knew he was a comer. He took to using bars, poker games, and jazz joints as backgrounds for his columns. His friends were fighters, cab drivers, drunks, and dishwashers. He observed his politics through their eyes, and his readership grew.

The first poker game of 1940 took place at their apartment. There were five players besides Matt, and he had gone out to Sheridan Square to buy delicatessen and long loaves of crusty Italian bread, enough to feed them all for seven days.

Sabine offered to help but Matt said, "No, this is men's night. I don't expect you to be a hostess, why should you wait on them? Maybe you'd like to take in a movie."

"No. I'll get in bed and read." That sounded cozy.

"But the bedroom is on the way to the bathroom."

"That won't disturb me," she said. But it obviously did disturb him. "Listen, do you want me to leave for the night?" she asked.

"No."

"Good. Because I really don't want to."

Then she had an idea. "Maybe I could watch." Matt had taught her the rudiments of poker, and she had good card sense.

"No, why don't you take the book and read? That sounds like a good idea?"

"Why? I make you nervous?"

He smiled, but he didn't deny it. She stayed and met his poker-playing buddies. Aaron Eisen, who shook her hand and looked her in the eye. She was tall enough for him, but not blonde enough. James Price, who was almost a star on Broadway and couldn't really afford this kind of game. He ignored her. Chris Mason, the network executive, in charge of the entire foreign news service. And Sam O'Brien, the publisher of a weekly news magazine. She met, shook hands, and was ready to retire when the doorbell rang, and because she was nearest to the door, she answered it.

Bernard Ross stood there.

"Hi, doll!" It was his standard greeting. "Surprised? Mason asked me to come along."

"Of course I'm surprised. I thought you'd be in Tulsa, Oklahoma." She had heard about Bernie Rosen from Jerry who called regularly to talk about life in Hollywood.

"Naw. Let the star work. He gets all the reviews."

Jerry's movie had opened for Christmas at Radio City Music Hall. Named *Champion Chump*, it had become the surprise hit of the season. Great reviews, greater business. The studio instantly decided to put all its money and energies into Jerry Davis. The picture was playing across the country, breaking attendance records, and Jerry had called Sabine forlornly from the Midwest, where he was making personal appearances.

"Where is Dubuque?" he asked. "I can't find it anywhere, and that's where they're sending me tomorrow."

"Oh come on, don't tell me you don't enjoy all this."

"No," Jerry's voice wailed over the phone. "I didn't ask for Dubuque. I didn't ask for East St. Louis. Have you ever *seen*

East St. Louis? Where am I tonight? Waterloo, Iowa. Do you know what happens in Waterloo, Iowa? Nothing. They stop room service at ten p.m. That is all that happens in Waterloo, Iowa. I am looking out the window. There is nothing out there. Nothing. I am taking a sleeping pill. And I will call you from, oh God, Wichita Falls. If I ever make it to there."

So Sabine knew where Jerry was, and she could see where Bernard was. Bernard was in hog heaven. He had become a real producer. He had produced a huge hit. And now he was enjoying Manhattan.

He bent to kiss her on the cheek. She turned so that he kissed the side of her jaw.

"Congratulations," she said. She could smell his aftershave lotion.

"Thanks." He patted her shoulder and turned his attention to the men.

"I feel lucky," he told them. "You care to deal me in?"

"Always a pleasure," O'Brien smiled. "Always a pleasure to take your money."

Bernard laughed. And Sabine thought, *Beware of men with false laughs.*

The men sat down to the game. Bernard's chauffeur waited outside, would wait all night with the motor running if that was Bernard's desire.

Sabine put on her nightgown and dressing gown in the bathroom. She was still in there when there was a knock on the door.

"Just a minute," she said.

"No hurry," said the voice from the other side. So she didn't hurry. When she came out, O'Brien, the publisher, was waiting.

He nodded, went in and closed the door; she heard the seat of the toilet knock against the tank as he lifted it. She took out the advance copy of *How Green Was My Valley* that the publishers had given Matt, in hopes of a favorable mention, and settled down on the bed to read.

"How long are you in for?" she heard Chris Mason, the man from the network, ask Bernard.

"About two weeks. Stockholder's meeting. There may be some shakeups in the New York office. That's off the record, Chris," Bernard added.

"Trust me," Mason said.

"Bet," said Matt. And Sabine went back to the Welsh coal miners. O'Brien came out of the bathroom, crossed the bedroom, and returned to the game.

"So you'll be here for two weeks," Mason was saying to Bernard. "Where are you staying?"

"The Sherry Netherland. The studio keeps a suite there." Sabine heard Bernard make just the right pause. "For executives."

"Bet," Matt said again. Bernard lost the pot. Sabine returned to *How Green Was My Valley* with satisfaction.

Aaron Eisen tiptoed through the room. "Excuse me, Sabine," he whispered. He was polite. When he went into the bathroom, he locked the door and turned on the faucet so that she couldn't hear him.

Bernard lost three more big pots, then came into the bedroom.

"Where's the can?"

She pointed. He was in no hurry.

"How's the book?" he asked.

"I like what I've read."

"Oh yeah? We turned it down. Coal miners in Wales? They're either singing or trapped in a mine. I couldn't see it."

"Mmm." Sabine kept on reading.

"Whaddya think?" Bernard asked. "You never told me what you think."

"Of what?"

"Of my success. Whaddya think of this little Jew kid who is maybe the tenth most important man in Hollywood?"

Sabine looked up from the book. "I think you are very lucky, Bernard."

"Yeah. It takes luck. And it takes balls." He tapped his head. "And *chutzpah*."

"You have all of that, Bernie," Sabine said.

"Don't call me that. Don't call me Bernie. The name is Bernard."

"I'll try to remember."

"You never did like me, did you?"

"It wasn't that I didn't like you. I just never forgave you."

"For what?" He was genuinely surprised.

"For that goddamned Molière!" She was sitting upright in bed. "For what you said to me!"

"What did I say to you?"

"Terrible things. You put me through hell!"

"Holy shit! I don't even remember that. Boy, can you ever hold a grudge."

She retreated slightly. "Aren't you holding up the game?"

"Naw. To tell you the truth, when my luck is going bad, I get out for a few minutes. To change it, you know. Sometimes that's all it takes, you know." Then he went into the bathroom, and continued talking through the half-shut door.

"I could be, very soon now, the eighth or maybe seventh most important man in Hollywood," he told her over the tinkle. In a moment he reappeared, and went back to the game.

Sabine got up out of bed and stormed into the living room.

"Flush, Bernie, flush!" she demanded.

"What's the matter?" he asked, bewildered.

"What's the matter with *you*?" Sabine said angrily. "What do you take me for? One of your starlets? You used my toilet, you can goddamned well flush it. And you can close the door next time. And I don't care if you are the *single* most important man in Hollywood, you can wash your hands when you are finished."

"I told you, its Bern*ard*, not Bernie," he said. But he was laughing. "Goddamnit, Sabine, I'm sorry," he said, and he went into the bathroom and flushed the toilet.

"Shake?" he said when he came out.

"Did you wash your hands?"

"I swear."

"I didn't hear the water running."

"You're right. I lied," he said without embarrassment. He went back in and washed his hands, then showed them to her the way a child does to a teacher.

Then he offered her his hand. She took it. "Friends?" he said, and went back to the game without waiting for her answer. He won the pot on the first hand.

Sabine had not read more than two more pages of *How Green Was My Valley* before Bernard was back in the bedroom doorway again.

"It's you," he said to her. "You're the one who did it. You're my lucky piece tonight. Come on in."

"No, I don't want to interrupt."

"I want you to." The tone of studio authority was creeping into his voice.

"Bernard, I really don't feel like it."

"Tell you what, I'll cut you in on my winnings."

She looked up. "What do you mean?"

"I said I'll cut you in. Fifty-fifty."

"How much would that be?"

"If you're really lucky for me, it could mean a thou, maybe two, for you."

She was stunned. *Those* were the stakes? "I didn't realize the stakes were so high," she said.

"Sure. Otherwise it's no fun. Come on." And Sabine left the book on the bed and let Bernard draw her into the action.

There was no objection to her being there. Bernard sat her on the arm of his chair and showed her his hands. He was a good if rather wild poker player. Sabine would never have stayed in a hand unless she had a pair of kings or better for openers. Matt had taught her that. But Bernard kept himself going, seeing and raising, bluffing on a pair of tens, then at the last moment drawing two more tens. Sabine could not believe his luck.

But Bernard obviously believed in her. While she was with him, he won five big pots. He would not let her leave, even for a cigarette. He made her sit on the arm of his chair while he played the other players superbly. It was obvious why, in all probability, he was going to head a motion picture studio. He understood other people's temperaments. He could tell about Matt. Knew, for instance, that Matt's concentration would fly away if Bernard so much as grazed Sabine's knee with his hand. So he grazed Sabine's knee and won another pot. Then, too, he noticed that Matt had a tendency to drink when he was winning, and would get careless, ending up a loser. Bernard never got careless, never got drunk—never drank, even. He played, that was all, one hand after another. Played. And won.

Mostly, that evening, it was luck. It *had* to be. By dawn, when the game broke up, Bernard had won over four thousand dollars. The players figured up their wins and losses, paid, and left.

Bernard made Sabine ask for the money. He put on his coat.

"You leaving?" she said.

"Yes, doll. Don't you think it's time?"

"I thought we had a deal," she said.

"A deal? Oh, doll, I almost forgot." And he smiled to show her he hadn't forgotten at all, peeled off two thousand in bills, and handed them over. It amused him to watch her count it, when she did; she wanted everything down to the last penny.

Matt went straight to the typewriter, his deadline only five hours away. Sabine went to bed.

That afternoon the telephone rang. It was Bernard.

"Congratulate me," he said silkily.

"What now?" She was not awake.

"Hartman's out. Greene is out. Fried is out. I am now in charge of production for the entire studio. Whaddya say?"

"Wonderful, wonderful. What does your wife say?"

"Oh shit, I forgot to call her. Goodbye." Bernard hung up and Sabine went back to sleep.

It was dark when the phone rang again. Bernard.

"What are you doing tonight? No, don't tell me. I don't want to know. This is what I want from you. I want you up here at the Sherry Netherland in half an hour."

"I can't do that," Sabine said.

"You can, you can. I want you here." His voice was alive with excitement.

"But I should talk to Matt."

"Why? He'll understand. Where is he? I'll talk to him."

"He's at the paper."

Bernard pressured her. "We'll make it the same deal. Fifty-fifty. My good-luck piece."

"Bernie—I mean, Bernard—I don't think I want to go through life being your good-luck piece."

"Listen, after what you did last night, you can call me Bernie. Call me Bubbie, I don't care."

"Bubbie?"

"Yeah. My mother called me that when I was fat."

"You are crazy, Bernard."

"I said you can call me Bernie."

"I don't want to call you Bernie."

"Lemme tell you who's in this game." Sabine recognized mogul names, executive names, and a show-business lawyer

who was featured in fan magazines, squiring beauties to pre-
mieres.

Then Bernard said, "Lemme tell you the stakes."

And when he had, she agreed. "But Bernard, one thing,"
she added. "I have to leave at three o'clock. Agreed?"

"Anything. Anything, good-luck piece. Leave at three
o'clock. My man will pick you up in fifteen minutes. Be
ready. And don't eat. I have things here."

Sabine left Matt a note saying where she was. She dashed
in and out of the shower and combed her hair. She had not
taken the time to see what the weather was, and when the
driver rang her bell, she could not locate her coat. She went
without it.

The heat was on in the limousine. There was ample space
for her to stretch her long legs. The windows were tinted.
Life was a distant blue-white, glittering past her. The driver
directed the limousine up Fifth Avenue, past the great stores
that had no rival in the world: Cartier's, Van Cleef and Ar-
pel's, Tiffany's, Bonwit's, Saks Fifth Avenue, Bergdorf Goodman. A whole avenue devoted to adorning women. What
power we have, she thought, as the limousine made its way
up the avenue. And what power there is to be had in this
world.

The limousine slid to a stop by the canopy of the Sherry
Netherland. White-gloved hands vied to grasp the handle,
open the door, help her through the revolving door, direct her
to Mr. Ross' suite. Her eye swept the lobby. Almost no one
was in a business suit, the was black tie country. Evening
gowns and tuxedo time, a world turned very handsome. Passing through the lobby, she created a stir. Even at the Sherry
Netherland the crowd was not used to that incredible combination of jet black hair, creamy skin, and sapphire eyes.
And Sabine did not walk. She strode across the lobby, her
body undulating under her simple white dress in a most pro-
vocative fashion. But she had come in out of the cold without
a coat. No mink. No fox. Who was she? It was decided she
must be very rich, someone who never had to be in the cold
long enough to need a coat. Or perhaps the coat would follow her, on the arm of a servant.

Sabine was unaware of the excitement she was creating;
her attention was on the orchestra she heard playing some-

where off the lobby. *That was my father's dream,* she thought, *to wear a tuxedo, to direct a society band. How they would have loved him.*

There was a bank of elevators, but only one that went right up to Mr. Ross's suite. It made no stops. She entered the suite. The door was open. The effect was stunning. The suite was a duplex, and the two-story living room windows overlooked everything in the world that seemed to matter. She checked the furnishings. Outsize overstuffed white chairs and sofa. Gold drapes. A fireplace bordered by black marble, containing a fire that blazed discreetly, controlled (she discovered later) by a gas jet. The grand piano was a Bechstein. The walls were hung with the best of the modern masters— Hollywood had discovered them. There was a Kandinsky, a Braque, and two Matisses, chosen to coordinate with the Chagall that faced them from the other wall.

On the immense glass coffee table, equidistant from four Steuben ashtrays, stood a tiny crystal obelisk, forming a Rond Point, a Place Vendôme. On the mantel over the fireplace, under the Cézanne, was a sculpture, dark, powerful, the body of a primitive woman, head flung back in grief.

"Hey, doll," Bernard said, and noticed where her glance was focused. "A Picasso. An important piece."

He introduced her to the other men in the room. "These are the boys."

The boys were gray, tough, shrewd. Their names were Jack and Murray, Sam and Gregg—Werner and Lefcourt, Mishkin and Newmark.

She looked at them, at their surroundings. Everyone and everything had come from somewhere else. After all, that was the story of New York. The Braques and the pre-Columbian art and the movie producers, all collected for this moment in this hotel suite, each recognizing his own and the others' value and worth and probably wondering about hers. Only Bernard, out of this entire group, had been born in New York, but a part of New York as remote as the Russian steppes from this suite at the Sherry Netherland.

"Hey, Bernard, when do we play?"

"Keep your shirt buttoned, Murray," Bernard said. The other man was older, but there was no deference in Bernard's tone. There was, rather, arrogance. Easy arrogance. That

came easy. Deference, Sabine figured, must come hard to
Bernie. Something had changed since yesterday. In his attitude toward her (there were too many "honeys" and "dolls,"
too much the impression that she was his girl of the moment), and in his attitude toward the other players. They
were all older than Bernard, and even yesterday he would not
have been quite as familiar with them as he was now. Now it
was first name and equal footing. And with some, a shade of
condescension.

"How do you like this doll? She was so eager to come she
forgot to get dressed," Bernard said and laughed. He laughed,
and then they laughed. Sabine did not.

"Bernie," Sabine said, "come help me get some dinner. Be
a good host."

His eyes flickered at the sound of the name.

"Whatever you say, doll. You are my lucky piece."

They entered a dining room dominated by Van Gogh and
no one else.

"Don't do that to me, please," she said. "I don't like it."

"Sabine," he said, "help yourself to the curry. I sincerely
apologize. Sincerely. Tonight I am a little out of my head.
Do you know what happened today, what happened to me,
what I am now? Chief of production. I am on a level with
every one of those fuckheads out there, and more powerful
than most of them. You want to know who's more important
than me, you want to know who is the only one more important? Louis B. Mayer. He is more important. Maybe Zanuck.
As of this minute. That's all. I am the third most important
man in Hollywood. What do you think of the paintings? Something, huh?" Talking nonstop, he waved a fork toward the
world outside. "Oh, Christ, Sabine, you watch me. I am going
to make movies. I am going to make classics. I got it all, I
know. I know what they want. They want what I want." The
waving fork indicated all of America outside the window and
below the window, walking through the freezing winter night.
That fork indicated the Bijous and Strands and State Theaters
in Charleroi and Moline, Cheyenne and Tucumcari, Ukiah
and Eureka, theaters he would fill up and command. It all
stretched out beyond his fork, across Manhattan and the
Hudson, across New Jersey, to Hollywood. He was going to
be lord of all this, and she was his lucky piece.

"Is this place yours?" Sabine asked.

"You kiddin'? It's the studio's. But it's here for my pleasure. For me to do what I want with it. It's reserved for the chief of production. And that's me. If you don't like curry, what do you want? I'll have them make it for you. Name it."

"Curry is fine," Sabine said, but Bernard didn't hear her.

"Hey, Beverly," he called, and almost immediately a sweet-looking blonde came in, dressed in a sequin gown that Betty Grable had worn in *Down Argentine Way* and that the studio kept in the suite, just in case. Beverly had once been in a film with Betty Grable, had been once a dancer; would be, she hoped, something more than a dancer. At the moment she was being called on to perform in other ways.

"Do me," Bernard said, unbuttoning his fly as he left the room. Sabine found herself alone with a plate of curry and Van Gogh, maybe one of the six or seven most important painters on the market.

But not for long.

The man named Murray came in, examined Sabine, examined the food.

"What is this?" he said. "The bastard wants to poison me. He knows I got an ulcer. Tell 'em to fix me some poached eggs."

"No," said Sabine, forking up some curry.

"Whaddaya mean, no?"

"I mean, tell 'em yourself."

"Who are you, anyway?"

"Not your maid," Sabine said, and then found that still wasn't enough. "What's your name—Murray? Listen, Murray, let me tell you this. I am here to do a friend a favor, a friend I grew up with, a friend who once was at my family's hotel—a hotel which, by the way, still prospers. And this friend was a waiter at that hotel."

"Oh," said Murray. But Sabine was not through.

"Now it is true that I can cook and I can manage a dining hall and I can order servants around, but I want you to understand this. I want everyone in that room to understand this, because I do believe there has been a misunderstanding here. I do not cook. I do not give orders to servants. Unless it is my pleasure."

"Oh," Murray repeated himself, and then because under the veneer of the producer lay the remains of the pushcart peddler, he began to laugh, recognizing it all, including his mistake. Murray had always admired anyone with guts, the same guts that he possessed. So he picked up one chafing dish cover—lobster Newburg. The second—chicken tetrazzini. The third—scrambled eggs.

"You think the eggs will hurt?"

"No," Sabine said, "The eggs will not hurt." So he took the eggs and then escorted her into the living room.

"Boys," Murray said, "I want you to meet a lady. Christ, I'd introduce her but I've forgotten her name."

"Boys," Sabine said, "Listen carefully. This is my name. My first name is Sabine, and I can't explain what that *means*, because my father was a romantic. My other name is Abramowitz. My father came from Pabjanice, which once was in Poland, and he died in the streets of Miami Beach."

The four men stared at her. Sat, cigars in mouth, and stared.

"Didn't anyone ever suggest that you might stand in the presence of a lady?" she reminded them.

But nobody talked to them like that. Not the starlets, who were mostly on their knees, or the stars themselves, who aimed a little higher. Not Hedda, not Louella. Nobody talked to them like that. But, like Murray, they admired her guts. It was, after all, what they themselves had lived by, lived on—guts, imagination. It went with the pushcarts. They rose one by one and shook her hand.

"What do you do?" the balding gentleman named Jack asked.

"That's not really important." Sabine gave him a dazzling smile. There was something in the atmosphere of this suite that gave her a great sense of power. "Let me tell you what I am *going* to do. Someday I am going to own a hotel—a hotel as fabulous as this one. The service may be even better. And when that day comes, I am going to ask each one of you to invest with me. And you will."

"Why would we invest with you?" Jack laughed, accustomed to making two or three million-dollar deals before lunch every day.

"Because you all are gamblers," Sabine said, and as she

said it, she knew she was right. She had them. Something in the suite—yes, she was aware it set off her black hair, her eyes. She looked beautiful here. She looked right here. And she possessed something that none of them did. She had style.

Ten minutes later Bernard returned. The game began. It fascinated only in the enormity of its stakes. Like other addicts, these movie moguls were no longer affected by small amounts. They were compelled to drive closer to the cliff and play closer to the edge, to court disaster with every hand. Tens of thousands were bet with every pot. Nobody left the table. Nobody drank. Nobody spoke except to bid, to bluff. The winners (and the winners kept changing) never changed expression. They built up their castles of chips, fortresses of red, white, and blue towers, and then watched their fortresses get dismantled, block by block, by a losing bet. They were in deadly earnest. The game never varied. Either draw or straight five- or seven-card poker. No wild cards. No crazy games.

At three in the morning, Sabine rose from her position beside Bernard's arm. "I have to leave."

"Stay," Bernard ordered.

"No. I have to leave." There was a vast castle of chips surrounding Bernard. For the last two hours he could do nothing wrong.

"I want you to stay. You stay."

"We agreed on three o'clock. It's that time."

"Stay."

"Pay up."

"Fuck off. I'll pay when I'm finished." He started to deal. "You wait."

Sabine said nothing. She went over the mantelpiece where the Picasso sculpture was standing. She took it and walked out of the room, and because it was cold she also took Bernard's cashmere topcoat from the entryway. She pressed the elevator button, went down, and had the doorman signal a cab. She went home. Matt was asleep, and she undressed quietly, seeking the warmth of his body in their bed.

In the morning Sabine told Matt what she had done and showed him the statue. He tried on the coat, but it didn't fit across the shoulders. They were on their second cup of coffee and it was approaching noon.

"When do you think he'll call?" Matt asked.

"When he gets cold enough," Sabine answered. Outside it was one of those really memorable bone-chilling, brilliant Manhattan winter days, all wind and all sunshine and all ice. No slush and no puddles. Just ice and wind and sun.

The telephone rang. Sabine, expecting Bernard, was surprised to find it was Murray.

"If he tries to con you, kid, this is the amount he won," Murray said over the phone, and told her. Sabine thanked him and hung up. The phone rang again, and Matt answered. He was cheery enough.

"Hello, there, Bernard, what's new?"

Sabine listened while Matt nodded, and then handed the phone to her.

"You took my coat. It's cold." Bernard was almost whining.

"You can have it back. Just pay up."

"I was going to pay up. You were so impatient."

"A deal is a deal."

"Jesus Christ, Sabine. You took the statue."

"It's here. You can have it."

"I mean—it's not mine, you know. It belongs to the studio. And it's priceless."

"I told you, take it back. All I want is my half of the money, which, by the way, is how much?"

"Five thousand dollars."

"That's not what I heard."

"Okay, cunt, what did you hear?"

"Now, Bernie—"

"Don't call me that."

"Don't call me cunt."

Matt looked up, ready to go to war.

Sabine continued, "I heard you won twenty-five thousand dollars last night."

"That's a lie. Who said that?"

"Everybody."

"Okay." He backed down immediately. He could do that—lie, and then admit it without embarrassment. "I got twelve-five here. Bring back the coat and the statue."

"No, Bernard. I *was* there. You bring it on down. I'll be here."

"I have meetings all day. I'll have my chauffeur bring it down."

"Not good enough. Bernard, *you* bring it down."

A moment's pause.

"Cunt."

And he hung up.

"I do believe he shall be here presently," Sabine told Matt in mock Mayfair English.

And he was. Bernard rang the doorbell, money in hand. She took it, smiling, and counted it. The bills were hundreds and she counted out one hundred and twenty-five of them while Bernard watched, not amused.

Then she gave him his cashmere coat and returned his statue.

If only he hadn't said the next word, all of their lives might have been different. But Bernard did. He called her a "cunt" again. This time Matt lunged across the room and picked up Bernard by the throat, ripping the cashmere coat but being careful not to damage the priceless statue.

"Get out of here. And never do that again. Now apologize to Sabine, or I'll smash your face in."

"Okay, okay," Bernard said, feeling the coat rip around the shoulder and wondering if it would show. "I have a meeting. I'm late. I'm sorry."

"Sorry for what?" Matt wouldn't let him go.

"Sorry I called her a cunt."

"Tell *her!*"

"I'm sorry I called you a cunt."

Sabine kept a straight face. "Bernard, that is quite all right. I accept your apology."

Bernard left for his meeting with the statue that wasn't his and the coat with the rip in it that did show. The driver was waiting to open the door for him.

"Get in the car!" Bernard yelled. He did not want the driver to notice the rip. Bernard opened his own door, and the limousine sped off.

"Oh, it's winning the little battles that gives such satisfaction," Matt said. "You should get a medal."

She received flowers instead. Five dozen red long-stemmed roses arrived from the Sherry Netherland, with a card enclosed.

"Congratulations to the champ." It was signed, "The Boys."

"That must have been some game," was Matt's comment.

"Mmm," said Sabine, who had returned to the Welsh coal miners. "It's all forgotten now."

Nothing could have been further from the truth.

Chapter Fourteen

It was at Jamie Butler's cold-water flat that Sabine realized she was just like her grandmother and her mother. She had no possessions, no photographs, not a scrap of paper to jog the mind, almost as though she had nothing to look back on.

Jamie lived on Hudson Street. Like most dancers, he had converted most of the space in his apartment into an improvised studio, with a barre and a floor-to-ceiling mirror. The other two rooms he allotted to the rest of his life; they were small and dark and crammed with photographs and showcards of musicals he had either danced in or choreographed. There were signed pictures and candid shots. Sabine found one of her and Jerry with Jamie, taken, she remembered, at Glenrocks. She looked at the photo fondly. She could see so many changes in the three of them. Jerry was now more polished, more honed down. He was sharper and more angular. And Jamie was much more intense, concentrating on a choreographer's career. And what was she? She studied the picture for a clue. She had been more carefree then. She was more beautiful now. But she had no picture of herself, no image of her life. She lived each day and tossed it away. *Goodbye to all that.* The phrase kept haunting her.

Jamie and Sabine had been meeting to sketch out the program for the following summer at Glenrocks. It was a famous spot for new talent, and the number of requests for auditions was staggering. So Jamie and Sabine started in February, lining up talent and composing the summer.

They had just finished one such session and it was about midnight when Jamie suddenly asked Sabine, "What are you going to do with your life?"

"That kind of question is for college kids, and I don't have time for it," Sabine said.

"But are you satisfied the way you are?"

"Of course," Sabine retorted and immediately realized she wasn't. So she talked a bit more rapidly as she got into her coat. "I have Matt. I keep busy. And we have another season at Glenrocks to plan."

"What about next year?"

"I don't think about next year, thank you. But I suppose I will have Matt, I will keep busy, and there will be another season to plan at Glenrocks." Jamie was looking at her. "And since you are seeing right through me," Sabine added, "I'll tell you that someday I want to take over Glenrocks. Nothing should happen to my mother or Max, of course, but I still would like to take over that hotel and—"

"You mean you don't want to perform?" Jamie was shocked.

"No, I don't want to perform. It was fun, it was always fun with Jerry, but I don't want to spend the rest of life on a stage."

"You want that hotel?" They had reached the door and she was going down the staircase. She looked back up at Jamie.

"That's right. You think that's crazy, don't you?"

"Yes," Jamie said. "Definitely. And I thought just dancers were masochists."

Sabine had bought a camera, but she had no patience with it. By the time she had found focus and range and had everything adjusted, the picture she had wanted to take was no longer there.

It was easier to make notes. She kept a book in her purse with her compact and lipstick, and jotted down impressions, scraps of conversations. That became her little scrapbook, her series of snapshots.

"Matt in nightclub," she wrote. "Out of place. Logger fresh out of woods come to town after winter. Hands too large for table. Suit confining. Times likewise."

It was a silly assumption of hers that life with Matt would go on the same way forever. But she assumed it the way her grandmother assumed that life in Paris would remain the same. Mme Levinsky wrote regularly now, because Bertha wrote to her. And she promised to pay a visit to the United States; she had even named the date. It would be after the *muguet*, the lily of the valley, had bloomed. ("What does that mean? Is she getting senile?" Bertha wondered, but Sabine, remembering the carefully tended windowboxes, knew better.

There was a plan to Mme Levinsky's life, and nothing would disrupt it.) On June 14 she would embark on the *Normandie* and spend six weeks in America. Bertha had suggested she might wish to stay longer, but Mme Levinsky had already purchased her round-trip ticket. She would return to France in August, in time to prepare for the autumn. The flowers that bloomed in the spring had to be taken care of in the fall so that they would bloom again.

Those were the plans.

It came as a shock when Sabine discovered she was pregnant. That was not part of any plan. It was not possible. In their roller-coaster world of openings and parties and newspaper articles, she had lost track of time. Then one day it occurred to her that she had not had a period for two months.

She waited two more weeks. Why? She told herself she wanted to be *sure*, she even convinced herself of that. But the two weeks passed and she still had no period. And then she went to the gynecologist and took the test, and—she recalled the punchline of some burlesque joke—"the rabbit died." She couldn't be, she insisted, but she was. She was pregnant.

It was ridiculous, but the moment it was announced—the moment it was official—she imagined she felt the life within her. She could understand that this tiny human life was inside her and growing, and he already had a personality—she was so sure it was a boy she could already picture him, with curly hair like Matt's but black like hers; she had read somewhere that the woman carried the genes for hair. Her father and Sammy all had had hair that was thick, and masculine, and triumphant.

She was sitting by herself in the Waverly Place apartment, sitting on a couch, and the leaves were beginning to flower outside on the one wan tree. She had never thought about having a child, of being a mother. She had never wanted to become pregnant, and now she was. She was surprised to find herself excited.

April was a lovely month in New York for blooming and budding and fertility. Oh, she was quite sentimental, and it was all right to be sentimental sometimes. She had had enough of the wise-cracking, finger-snapping Manhattan attitude toward life, toward the war, toward events. Sabine was suddenly the Little Mother, wondering where to put the crib, if they'd have to move out of the apartment, what Matt would think.

What would Matt think?

Would he be pleased? His son? Of course that would please him. Marriage? They had never considered it. Not true: they had considered it and said no. No ties, no commitments. Here, however, was a commitment. A baby was a commitment. How would she tell him? She could only think of the hundreds of scenes in the movies—scenes where the words "pregnant" and "having a baby" were outlawed by the Hays office, so the characters on screen fumbled through euphemistic phrases to nods of understanding. And when the dim-witted husband finally saw the light, he was awash with that crazy grin, delight, idiotic overprotectiveness. It was all there in the movies.

Matt was not delighted. He had no crazy grin. No delight. No overprotectiveness.

"Are you sure?" he said.

"The rabbit died," she said, trying to be flippant. The joke died with the rabbit.

"How far along are you?"

"Are *you?*" she thought. He is asking this as though he were detached, had no part in it.

"*I*," she said, feeling her temper rise, "*I* am three months along, perhaps a little more."

"Let's go out for dinner," Matt said, and she went with him. He took her to a rather elegant old restaurant in the Village and they both had a couple of drinks, while she played with the silverware and he looked at the menu. Like married couples, she thought to herself, who have too much to scream at each other about and nothing to say.

She continued to play with her silverware while he continued to drink, first one double, then a second. God, it is true, she thought. The Irish can drink. And maybe all the other stereotypes are true too.

"This would mean getting married," Matt said as he put down the menu. Had he made his choice of entrée?

"Oh, would it? The baby will emerge somehow, even if he doesn't see a marriage contract."

"You know what I mean. It's only fair. Why do you call it a 'he'?"

"I just do," she shrugged.

"You want this baby?" he asked.

"Yes," she said.

"I don't," he said.

The waiter came to take their order. Matt ordered brains in black butter. Sabine ordered sole meunière and a salad. Everything, every moment, seemed to be etched forever, every word was something she would carry with her to the end of her life. A part of her was looking on, observing herself and Matt, and remembering.

"You don't want the child?" she asked when the waiter had left. He really didn't want their baby?

"I don't want—I told you this, we had agreed on this—I don't want to be tied down. I don't want the responsibility. There's going to be a war, there already is a war, and I won't be around . . ."

"You won't be around?" she repeated stupidly.

"No. Not unless they end up fighting in the streets of New York. I'll go where the war is. Either London, Paris, or Moscow. That looks like the next move. That little peace treaty won't last too long. Sabine"—he left his career for a moment to look at her, to cover her hand with his—"I love you. I want you for my woman. But I am just on the verge of getting everything I ever dreamed of in terms of a career. There will be other chances—"

"For a career."

"For a child. Maybe someday we will *want* to get married. You don't want to get married now, do you?"

No, of course not. Of course she didn't want marriage, she did not want to depend on him. No matter how much they might love one another, given a choice, it was evident he was not to be depended upon.

But the baby . . .

"Listen," she said. "Let me take care of this. Don't worry about it."

"What are you going to do?"

"I'm sorry. It was silly of me to involve you."

He laughed. "But I am involved."

"No. You're not. You are not involved with this baby. You are involved with *me* and with yourself, but not with *him*."

"Stop saying *him. It.* It's still an *it*."

The entrées came, and the salad, and he ate most of his

and she ate very little of hers, and they had a bottle of wine. Red wine, which went well with the brains and not well with the sole. She felt cold and clammy and asked to be excused and went into the ladies' room, where she threw up in the toilet that smelled of piss and shit and a disinfectant that couldn't wipe out the smell of bodily functions. When she was finished, the stall smelled of her vomit too, and sour red wine. She was very neat with her vomiting and she left very little to clean up. She managed to clean that little, and then dashed cold water on her face and looked at herself in the mirror. Her eyes looked puffy. She looked as if she had a hangover.

She made her decision.

"You're right," she said at the table. "It was the wrong time. I don't know how to deal with . . . with getting rid of a baby. Maybe you do."

"I'll find out," he said, and he finished the coffee and they went back to their apartment. She had a throbbing headache and thought she might throw up again, but she didn't. She went to bed, and she slept. Slept it off, she thought the next morning.

April was beautiful that year. Sabine had trouble with all that beauty. It seemed to taunt her. She was not one to feel guilty, but endlessly she kept thinking to herself, *He will never see that sun, he will never lie in a carriage in Washington Square Park, he will never look out at that crazy tree in the courtyard and wonder what it is.*

What a time to be romantic, she thought, *Matt was right.* What kind of life would it be, bringing up a child now, saddled with all the responsibility? It could destroy her relationship with Matt. She piled up the reasons, barricades against an intruder, but the intruder entered all the same.

What would he have looked like? What kind of person would he have turned out to be?

It was Friday and Matt had found a doctor in New Jersey who would perform the abortion. It was nothing, the procedure was ridiculously simple. The doctor would let air into her cervix, and that would cause a "spontaneous" abortion. Matt explained it all to her as they passed the smokestacks, the marshes, the flatlands just west of the Hudson. The sun was grimy and there was a bitter, metallic taste in her mouth.

She wanted to brush her teeth, wash her hands, get out of the car. She wanted to talk to Matt but she didn't. She wanted to say "Turn around," but there was no way of turning around and so they kept going.

The doctor's office was comforting. It was not what she had imagined. It was not a kitchen table with newspaper spread out over it. The doctor himself had come highly recommended from a number of Matt's pals who had found themselves in similar situations. The procedure was ridiculously simple. Let the air into the cervix . . . The doctor repeated what Matt had said, which was what one of his friends had told him. The doctor was gentle and comfortingly old. *All doctors should be fathers, they should never be young,* Sabine thought. *They should always be older. Daddy.* She let his words comfort her. In a peripheral way, Sabine knew that Matt had handed the doctor money and the doctor had taken it—had he washed his hands again? She was on an examining table, she was in the stirrups, Matt was with her, and the doctor was explaining softly that in a few hours she would feel labor pains, just as though she were going to have a real baby, and then there would be blood, a gush of blood, and she would be rid of the fetus. Ridiculously simple, the procedure. However, if anything were to occur, any irregularity, call his office. At any time. There was an answering service. Of course, he expected nothing irregular to occur.

Sabine felt a sharp pain, but it went away and the doctor kept on talking in his soothing, well-modulated voice as he helped her up. She was out of the stirrups.

She was in the automobile.

She was in a hotel room, a three-story building called the Hotel Majestic.

She was in bed, lying on the bed.

She waited. Both of them were silent. The room silenced them. The day went away. Matt turned on a light. It was the overhead, a naked bulb. He quickly flicked it back off. There was a bedside lamp. He lit that. A hotel room. A lemon-colored lamp. Sabine had never felt so lonely in all her life.

The pain started, as scheduled. Labor pains. They came at intervals, and the time between pains lessened.

"Get me to the bathroom," she said to Matt and he leaped

up, took her arm, steadied her. She could feel blood trickling
down her leg. He flicked another switch. Another naked bulb,
but there was nothing to do about it. She didn't care. She sat
on the toilet and felt an enormous gush, her entire insides
falling out of her. She gasped, not from the pain, but from
the shock. There had been no sensation like this before. It
was not like fainting. Was it like dying? Emptying. Voiding.
Air out of the balloon. Deflating.

Over.

Gone.

She held out her arm. Matt took it, lifted her. She turned
and looked in the toilet bowl. Blood. The bowl was full of
blood. For an instant she thought she could see a small form,
no bigger than a finger, floating in the blood. Hardly bigger
than a clot, but it was not a clot.

Matt flushed the toilet. The blood, the entire contents of
the bowl were swept away by water. The hand of the execu-
tioner. She must not think like that. She could not think like
that. Why could she not look at him? Why did she resent his
hand on her arm? Suddenly she felt so weak she thought she
was going to collapse.

Matt helped her back to the bed.

"Rest," he said. She did not close her eyes. She stared at
the terrible little lamp by the side of the bed and felt a tear
run down her cheek. It wet the pillow, but she did not turn
her head. She did not keep herself from weeping. She didn't
have the strength. No sobs or gasps. Just the tears coming to
the surface and flowing down her cheeks.

Matt put his hand down to brush away the tears. She did
not stop him. She let him. But there was nothing his hand
could do. Brushing away tears solved nothing. It was no comfort.

She was hardly aware of the intake of breath. Matt had
seen the blood that was soaking the bed. That was not right.
He went to the phone and called the doctor's office.

He got the answering service and asked for the doctor to
call him immediately.

"I am sorry, sir, but the doctor has gone to Atlantic City
for the weekend, and there is no way to reach him."

"Atlantic City!" Matt exploded. "This is an emergency. He
said we could get in touch with him."

"He left no number. However, he will be in his office on Monday morning, if you would like—"

Matt slammed down the receiver. Dumb, stupid and dumb. When it comes to the most important things, we just convince ourselves that nothing can go wrong. Why should he have trusted a New Jersey abortionist with gray hair and a kindly face to care, to consider? *Dumb, just dumb Irish*, he thought to himself. *Like trusting in the Blessed Virgin. Kiss it and make it better. Dumb.*

He was looking for hospitals. Of course there was no directory. He called the desk, looking anxiously toward Sabine. Blood continued to flow out of her. He picked her up in his arms—it was wrong, probably all wrong, but what else could he do?—and he ran with her. She seemed light, she had no weight. He went down the staircase with her. The car was parked in front.

"Where is the nearest hospital?" he demanded of the clerk. Sabine was unconscious.

The clerk gave garbled names—Flint Street, Prince Street, Borden Avenue.

"Come with me, show me!" Matt said.

"I can't leave the desk."

"A bellboy. Somebody. I'll pay."

The bellboy, who was no boy but a man in his fifties, went out into the night with Matt. He enjoyed the drama of speeding to the hospital, giving directions—he was good at giving directions. Matt arrived at the emergency entrance and ran inside with Sabine in his arms. There was blood on his suit, there was blood everywhere. The lights were blinding bright as he came through the door, and mercifully, suddenly, there were doctors and nurses.

Oh, they knew. Their wise eyes had seen this more than once. They had seen the women come in, recover, and leave in a day. And they had seen women die from loss of blood. They had seen everything. It was Matt's first time. It was not their first, nor their last. Their eyes were angry, though. Accusing, he felt.

A young doctor, his black hair already graying, was giving orders: "Take her to the operating room." And to Matt, "There is a waiting room. I don't know how long this will take. You're lucky you brought her here this fast."

They were gone, Sabine was taken away. Matt was left alone under the bright lights. He remembered the bellboy in the car. He went out and parked the car, took out his wallet, and gave the bellboy a hundred-dollar bill.

"Call a cab," he said, "I have to stay here. I want to thank you."

"Any time," the bellboy said.

Any time? Matt thought. *Any time you happen to have an emergency, I'll be glad to help you out?*

The bellboy left and Matt found the waiting room. He sat down and stared at the pile of *Collier's* magazines that littered the round table in front of the sofa. There were two other people in the waiting room. Nobody spoke or even acknowledged the others. One was an old lady, in black, foreign-born. Italian peasant or Greek. A face like the earth. What was she waiting for? She had beads, a crucifix, was saying a rosary. He watched her fingers fumble the beads. Her lips did not move, her eyes did not focus. She traversed the life of Christ, the Holy Mysteries, with her fingers—the bead, the separation, the bead, the separation, another string.

The second person was a black man holding a magazine in his lap, not reading it. The man was enormous, his legs spread. He seemed to take up a great deal of room. He did not move. His eyes were closed but he was not sleeping.

Waiting. The three of them. Time passed.

A doctor came out, a young man Matt did not recognize. He approached the old woman. She rose, and he put his arm around her, and they started walking. The arm around her shoulder was meant to comfort, but it was condescending. It was let-me-break-this-to-you-gently time, we-have-to-suffer-loss time. The doctor was Father, the old woman Child. The doctor-father was announcing death, evidently, because the old woman stopped and paused for a second, and then there was a whimper. But the guiding arm ushered her out of earshot, did not give her time to take in her grief, perhaps found her a private place to cry out. They disappeared from view.

More waiting.

Then the prematurely gray doctor appeared. His doctor. Sabine's doctor. He beckoned. No comforting arm there, no ushering into a private spot. No word. Just a motion. Matt rose and followed.

"You're very lucky. She's very lucky," the doctor said. They were standing in the corridor. "Whoever did the job on her punctured the wall of the uterus. She was bleeding to death."

"Is she all right?"

"Yes," the doctor said. "She's all right. She'll live."

Nailing me with his eyes, Matt thought. But he also thought, gratefully, *no jargon. No "perform," no "procedure." No, this is flat-out-truth time, and it's better.*

"She'll never have another kid," the doctor stated in the same flat voice. "But maybe that's what she wanted."

"Can I see her?" Matt said.

"Yeah," the doctor said, "tomorrow. No harm in that. The harm's been done already." And he turned away and on to another case of life or death or something in between, which is what makes up the night in an emergency room.

It was a small town, and a small hospital, but Sabine was in a private room. There weren't too many patients in the place.

The next morning Sabine was awake but groggy. Everything in the room was neat, the sheets freshly laundered, the top sheet pulled back just so, the sides tucked in, the carafe of water, the paper cups on the small table, lined up. Everything was antiseptic. No trace of the blood and the violence and the horror, except in Sabine's face. And there, only a trace. There was a sadness around her mouth, fatigue in her eyes. An emptiness. Matt could barely look at her.

"I'm sorry," he managed to say.

The weakness in her voice took him by surprise.

"Look," she said, "could you just go away? And when I'm well enough to go home, come and get me. I don't want to see anyone until then. Is that all right?"

He nodded, and wanted to kiss her and didn't dare to, didn't dare disturb her, didn't want to see tears, or acknowledge regrets. He left her in the hospital room, left his New York number with the hospital staff, left the necessary funds, left the hospital, and drove back to the city. The sun was coming up and he got lost several times in strange Hoboken streets before getting back to Manhattan.

He had left her in the middle of another world. He called the hospital twice a day to check her recovery, but never asked to speak to her.

A week later he returned (he had re-covered the seat in the car, where it had been soaked with so much of Sabine's blood), and they drove back to the Waverly Place apartment. She sat by the window, watching the trees, and wondered why she still felt so weak.

A letter from Mme Levinsky, dated April 29, was waiting for them.

"No rain," she wrote Bertha and Sabine, "no rain for weeks, but the foliage is beautiful all the same. It is a pleasure to walk the streets. The youngsters already have brown faces and it is not yet May. Also the asparagus is two weeks early and delicious. The men in their uniforms are gorgeous. Men always look better in wartime. Two weeks from now I begin to pack. What does one wear in America in the summer?"

Sabine had saved all the correspondence from her grandmother to her mother, perhaps because she had no photograph. She added this letter, the last, to her collection. And turned her mind to Glenrocks. Memorial Day was to be the beginning of the season.

They had been lovers, she and Matt, who saw no need for marriage. They had been each other's warmth and protection. They had maddened each other and had been each other's main pleasure. How often had she thought of him during the day, glad that the day's end would bring them together again? No matter about the theater, the nightclub, the friends—the two of them had been together. They did not bother to say "I love you" because, perhaps, that had seemed a bit bourgeois.

They still did not say "I love you," but now they hardly looked at one another. Tears always seemed too close to the surface. It was better to continue with what life had to offer. So they told themselves.

And then, within two days, everything changed again. All their lives. Bertha's. Matt's. Sabine's. Mme Levinsky's.

The blitzkreig struck just as the *muguet* was beginning to come into full bloom. On the tenth of May, on a Friday, on an incongruously sunny day, the German armies invaded the Lowlands and France. There was no sign of war in Paris; perhaps that's what caused Mme Levinsky's downfall. She had her passport ready, and she had her ticket for June 14. She felt that the Germans would, of course, never reach

Paris. The sun would never stop shining. While battles raged and the great retreat began, she put certain clothes in mothballs and arranged sachets in her closets for her return. The *muguet* arrived in Paris. And then, unbelievably, so did the threat of a German occupation; a mass exodus began. Within one month's time nothing was valid any longer. Not her steamship ticket nor her passport. Not her world.

Millions of people attempted to flee Paris, blocking the highways. They jammed the trains until the trains stopped running. And then it was chaos. And then it was over. Mme Levinsky sent Bertha a letter, telling her daughter she might be delayed *par les événements*, but by the time she posted the letter there was no one left to collect the mail, and it never reached America.

In New York, Bertha was frantic. It was a nightmare. She went to the French embassy; no one could issue a statement, and yet everyone was talking. Orders were given and then countermanded; bulletins were received, and then no word at all. The ambassador, it was learned, could discover nothing about his own family's safety, had heard nothing of his mother and father, whose country house lay forty miles to the north of Paris.

Bertha reported this all to Sabine. Sabine had a sense of *déjà vu*—Sammy and his wife and Freddy, border guards and panic.

There was nothing to be done. Work was the best antidote. It was nearing the end of May, and Glenrocks would open as usual. Sabine (who had never mentioned her "illness") went with her mother to the hotel. The guests laughed and joked and ate, and in between meals and in between performances mother and daughter stayed close to the radio, waiting for bulletins. They read the papers for war news, studying the series of squiggly lines that showed past borders and present army positions, the bold arrows that designated the sweep of the German offensive toward Paris and the English Channel. Bertha and Sabine became very familiar with the coastline along the channel. Somewhere soon, the broadcasters announced, there would be an Allied counterattack. But there was none so far.

Following one Sunday night show at Glenrocks, Sabine was driven back to the city, where she found Matt packing.

"The British are evacuating Dunkirk. I just got a call from the network, and I'm being sent over."

"When are you leaving?" She hadn't taken off her coat.

"Tonight. Right away."

Don't sound so important, as though this was your war. Your own personal battle.

"Who is 'they'?" she asked.

"The network," he answered triumphantly. "I won. They need me."

"And what happens to the column?" she asked. Really she was asking what was going to happen to their lives.

"Seymour's arranged everything. I'll do a column once a week from over there. A report from London."

He was packing his shirts. *How well he does that,* Sabine thought. *He can certainly pack fast, neatly, a real professional.*

"Oh my God," he sighed as though released, "I thought it would never come."

"Here, let me help you pack," said Sabine, and she attacked the drawer containing his underwear and socks. The socks hit the suitcase like so many cannonballs. "I wouldn't want you to miss a plane. Or a battle. Or a scoop. Do you have enough ties? Or do they issue you a uniform?"

He was too caught up with the moment to catch the fury in her voice.

"You can stay here," he said. "As a matter of fact, the network has agreed to pay the rent, so you won't have to worry about that. And I'll write you from London. Don't expect anything for a week or two, though, because I think we are in for heavy seas over there."

"Supposing I hadn't come back tonight? Would you have left me a note on the kitchen table?"

"I would have called. What's the matter with you? You knew I was going." He tried to touch her but she turned away.

His suitcase was packed. He tightened the leather straps and then turned to Sabine.

"May I kiss you goodbye?" he asked, the man who had owned her body. *What's happened to us,* she thought, *what has made us such strangers that he must ask, and that I must think about it? Do I want him to kiss me?*

"Yes, kiss me goodbye," she said, and he did. It was unlike

any kiss he had ever given her. It was gentle. And it was un-selfish, and unlike him.

"I'm sorry," he said again, and his hand, the hand she had both loved and despised, caressed her cheek. She took his hand away and held it.

"You know I would never stop you. If you must go, you go. The same is true of me. We made an agreement. I'll live by it."

He nodded, picked up his suitcase, and left. She watched him shut the door. Outside she heard his voice hailing a taxi, heard the taxi stop, heard the door slam and the taxi take off.

He was gone. It was all so sudden.

And then the rage seized her and she had no control over it. She happened to see a number of suits in his closet. She grabbed some shears and took a gabardine, and cut it up, listening to the ripping of fabric. She grabbed another suit and slashed that through the back, stabbing at the fabric because he was gone, he had left, and she was abandoned again. Again, she thought. Why again? And the sight of her father lying on the wooden floor of the dry goods store in Florida flashed through her mind. Again. Abandoned.

She stopped because she was exhausted. She sat on the floor with the ripped remains of Matt's suits and couldn't remember how he looked in the mornings, how he looked in his bathrobe. She closed her eyes. It was hard. She could not hold onto the memory. In a panic and because she was alone, she searched for a photograph—of him, of them. Incredibly, there was none. No flash shot taken at a nightclub by the hatcheck girl. Where was the newspaper that showed them leaving the Vanguard? Gone out with the garbage, evidently. Certainly not clipped and saved. There was nothing to show that they had ever been together in their lives.

She fell asleep across the bed, wondering whether his plane had taken off, if he was safely in the air, if he thought about her.

In the morning she was still in her clothes, and her makeup had stained the bedspread and was smeared on her face. She didn't care. She made coffee and drank it alone at the table, trying to write in her notebook, wanting to write about him, but already unable to picture him. She wrote, "The first cigarette in the morning always smells the best. Coffee, Camels, and he a rumpled Winnie the Pooh." What kind of portrait was that? She closed the notebook and went in to the bedroom to collect the ripped garments.

Picking them up, she realized again that no matter how much they might love one another, she could not allow her life to depend on him.

Chapter Fifteen

If you can't sell silk, sell linen. If one thing doesn't work out, try another. Sabine, hurt and angry, turned to Glenrocks. There was plenty of work to occupy her there. Max Abramowitz seemed to be drifting in the wide open spaces, intrigued by offers to invest in Palm Springs, somewhere in California. Deals floated out there beyond the limits of Glenrocks, drifting by like mirages. He ran after them and let Glenrocks slide. So Sabine found herself taking over the management of the hotel. She checked on the guests' comfort, and checked on the amount of chlorine in the swimming pool and the number of clean towels in the bath house and the condition of the tennis courts and the regularity of transportation. It occupied her mind. It made her get up in the morning. It made her tired enough to fall asleep at night in the room that was next to her mother's. She had left their apartment—Matt's apartment—for the summer and brought her things to Glenrocks. The two women worked from dawn until eleven at night, exhausting themselves. And they never talked about the letters they were hoping for.

The news from Europe was catastrophic. The British evacuated Dunkirk and Paris fell. While Bertha and Sabine supervised the comfort of their guests, the newspapers showed Hitler dancing in front of the railroad car where the treaty ending the First World War had been signed. There was a picture of the swastika flying over the Arc de Triomphe.

One morning they were both in the kitchen, having a cup of coffee. The newspaper lay on the table.

"What was Mama like when you last saw her?" Bertha asked.

Sabine glanced at her own mother. "You know the impression I got of your mother?" Sabine said. "Strong. And she knew exactly what she was doing. I think she was a little jealous of your success. She asked about the cooking here, and was terribly disappointed when I told her how good it was."

Bertha laughed.

"So I told her that nothing could compare to her cooking."

"True," Bertha said. "There is no one to equal Mama in the kitchen." She looked at Sabine then, questioning, but afraid to verbalize what she was thinking.

"I think she's all right," Sabine said. "She had someone to take care of her. And I doubt that she ran off. She's much too sensible."

Bertha nodded, finished her coffee, dusted her hands, and went back to baking.

Matt's first column from London was about the fall of France. Sabine refused to read it.

However, she could not refuse to read the letter when it arrived. It was a small thin envelope, the precursor to V-mail, and there was not much room to write. At the bottom Matt had written "I love you," but the proof of it was in the rest of the letter. During all the chaos of the past few weeks, he had tried to contact Mme Levinsky. He had not been able to speak to her directly, but he had discovered she was well and still living in her little flat in Paris.

Sabine rushed to show the letter to her mother and then immediately wrote Matt. After that, she waited anxiously each week to read his column or hear his broadcast. That was the way the summer passed.

By fall, there was still no invasion of England. Across the channel, the Nazis massed huge amounts of artillery, and during the month of August there were great battles in the air between the Germans and the Royal Air Force.

On September 7 the night attacks on London began. Rumors of an invasion grew. Smash the city, smash the docks, reduce the country to a shambles, and then, before the winter weather begins, invade: that was what the German strategy was supposed to be. But it did not happen. The Luftwaffe barraged the largest city in the world, and thousands of civilians were killed. And the correspondents reported it all to an America that reacted with stunned disbelief. Behind the voice of the correspondents, they could hear the explosion of bombs, the shattering of glass, sometimes the shouts of the Civilian Defense and ambulance workers, sometimes the cries of the wounded. October came. By now Matt Ryan's voice was not only familiar, but famous.

"It is the seventeenth of October, the night is clear, and from where I am standing it looks like half of London is in flames, the greater part of Pall Mall and at least five fires that I can count stretching out towards St. James's Street and Piccadilly. In the opposite direction, across the river, there are other conflagrations, but the main image that remains is the dome of St. Paul's Cathedral, silhouetted against the fires behind it and the tracer bullets above it. Never in my life have I seen such destruction, and never in my life have I felt such faith in the indestructibility of England. The British people are like the dome of St. Paul's. They will not fall. They cannot be crushed. This is Matt Ryan reporting from a London in flames."

Sabine listened to the newscasts and read his columns, feeling they were losing one another. The immensity of the struggle, the importance of the war had taken over his life, while she found herself more and more involved with the management of Glenrocks.

The winter passed and she found herself facing the spring of 1941. Almost a year had gone by since Matt had left, and she had moved back to Riverside Drive. One evening in the middle of May she was surprised to hear from Mark Cardozo.

"I'm in town," he said, "and I want to come see you."

He was calling from the drugstore around the corner, and was at her door in three minutes.

"Congratulate me," he said once he was inside the apartment.

He looked more confident. Even handsomer.

"I am now a law clerk. Have you ever heard of Arthur Garfield Hayes?"

"No," said Sabine.

"Well, he's the best. And I'm working for him, and I graduated from Harvard, and what are you doing?"

"With my life or right now?" Sabine countered.

"Right now. I can't worry about the rest of your life."

"Right now I'm doing nothing."

"Then I am taking you out to dinner. Are you seeing anyone?"

"No. Matt's in London."

"Well, now you are seeing me."

He was more determined than before, and Sabine enjoyed him more. She had been lonely and now she was less so. But she also felt as though she had taken a step back in time. Mark was a beau. And having a beau was quite different from having a lover.

They talked about the future, the probability of war coming to America. He would enlist in the Navy if it came to that.

"How would your family feel?"

"It doesn't matter much what my family feels anymore," Mark answered, and it was the only time Sabine could remember a coldness to his voice.

That summer he drove her back and forth to Glenrocks. She would spend most of the week, including the weekend, at the hotel. Mark would come up and spend Saturday night, and drive her back to the city after the show Sunday.

That was the summer of Glenrocks's greatest success. From the little farmhouse that had been the nucleus, the buildings and cabins stretched out in a graceful line with a view of the valley beyond and the Catskill Mountains beyond that. The buildings were all constructed from wood supplied by Dan Ryan's lumberyard.

During that summer a number of demonstrations had flared up in the Catskills area, inspired either by the isolationists who felt America was steadily drifting toward war and blamed that on the Jews (who else?), or by the Bund meetings.

Nobody took the Bund seriously. They were a bunch of jokers, dressed up in fancy uniforms, trying to act important with flaming torches and banners. They shouted about the Protocols of Zion and hinted that the Jews were poisoning the drinking water in the area. Nobody took them seriously because everyone knew they were crazy.

But there were maybe a few accidental pushes on the streets of Liberty and Monroe when Glenrocks patrons ventured there, just the slightest hint of antagonism. One day a man in Liberty refused to make way for a group of Glenrocks guests, forcing them to walk around him. "Whaddya think?" he shouted after them. "You think you own the sidewalk? Maybe you think you own the country."

As the summer progressed, fewer guests from Glenrocks walked into the little villages. They stayed within the confines of the resort. The trickle of European war refugees looked anxiously at one another. The land of the free? They didn't always speak the language, but they recognized the signs—the stares, the rudeness.

But Glenrocks was safe. Glenrocks had a gate and a long stretch of drive leading up to the hotel itself. There was no reason for encounters; the road was used only by those coming to stay at the hotel or work in it.

Glenrocks was safe. So no one knew how the fire started. Or was started.

It was Saturday night, in the middle of summer, during a hot spell that had hung over the valley for a week. The thermometer outside the little post office in Monroe had reached 100 degrees, and there was little relief at night. There was no sign of rain.

On Saturday night there were always dances in the towns of Liberty and Monroe. The bands, groups of local merchants who made a bit of change on the side, plodded through stock arrangements of the current hits at the VFW or American Legion Hall. During intermission, the young men went out with their bottles and their girls and climbed into the back seats of Hudsons and Chevys. It was the time to get liquored up, to get a feel, perhaps to get more than that, for Saturday night work was over, it was time to let loose, the girls had finished with waiting on tables and the young men had put on the clean shirts that were soaked through with sweat before the first dance was over.

It was hot in the dance halls, it was hot outside in the cars, and the liquor and the heat made a wicked combination.

It was someone's idea to go tear-assing through the town of Liberty, leaning on the horn and yelling out the windows. Because Saturday was the wild night, and the night to go crazy. It was cooler driving seventy miles an hour, head out the window, singing at the wind or yelling, with a girl stroking your pants leg. That made you all the crazier.

Whose idea was it to go scare the kikes, to go scare the shit out of them, sitting up there in that hotels with all the money?

Whose idea was it to scare them?

Whose idea was it to go further than that?

It could have been anybody's. For it was a Saturday night, a night to go crazy. It was hot. And *somebody* had the idea.

Afterwards they said it had started in the kitchen. A spark igniting a bunch of rags. A burner that had been left on. A cigarette left burning.

But Sabine knew that was impossible. Bertha always checked the kitchen before she left for the night, and Sabine always double-checked Bertha. There was no real reason for it—it was just a habit, certainly not a fear of fires. But, automatically, before going to bed, Sabine walked through the kitchen to check.

That Saturday Max had gone to bed early—that is, by ten o'clock. He was not happy about the sounds that carried up to his room from the dance band, and since it was too hot to keep the windows closed, Max stuffed his ears with cotton and fell asleep immediately, exhausted.

The band stopped at midnight and the older guests strolled to their rooms or to their cabins. Because of the heat, some of the younger guests decided to go swimming in the pond. It was, you see, a crazy night; it was Saturday, when all wild things were possible. They wanted to go skinny-dipping. Some of the girls teased the boys, the boys dared the girls. There were giggles. And a splash. More giggles. Shouts.

Sabine listened as she walked through the corridors. The windows were all open, but there was not a breath of air on this stifling midsummer night. The sounds from the pond carried, and they made her smile at the thought of the midnight lovers and the forbidden moments. She hesitated, deciding. Should she go to the pond or not? It could be dangerous, swimming after midnight. There was no lifeguard. Suppose something happened? But then she shrugged and continued walking. Oh, let them have their fun. That's what Glenrocks was all about.

Sabine walked through the kitchen, checking the stoves. Then she passed through the recreation hall on the way up to the staff quarters, where she stayed. In her room, she poured cold water into her hands, then her face, patting her face dry. She turned off the light and went to sleep.

What woke her? The smell of smoke? She knew the minute

she woke that something was wrong. She sat up in bed. There was no sound; nothing stirred. But she went to the window, and then she thought she was dreaming. For she saw a ring of fire burning around the main building, like the border of a garden. Flowers of fire. It traced a path around the main building and the recreation hall. She was too startled to move. There was no wind to spread the fire. Why was it spreading so fast? So totally? As she watched, she saw the ring of fire burst into bloom. The wood caught in a second, and then the sounds of fire reached her. From silence there grew a crackling sound, and then flames streaked up the side of the main building, as though there had been a path of gasoline splashed on the outside.

Sabine began yelling. She ran into the hall, knocking on doors. These were the rooms with the bunkbeds where the busboys and waiters slept.

"Get up! Fire! Come on! Get help!" The corridor filled with sleepy faces.

"Go to the main building and help the people out. The hotel is on fire!" she shouted. They were staring at her, standing before them, and then she realized she was stark naked.

"Move!" she screamed. And they did. Sabine snatched up a dressing gown and ran downstairs.

There were two telephones at the hotel, one in the main house and one here. She picked up the receiver and gave the crank a vicious turn, but no operator came on the line. She continued grinding the crank until she realized that no operator was ever going to come on the line. The line had been cut.

And then she began to panic. This was more than a malicious prank. Somebody had wanted them all dead.

Sabine turned around. Fire was facing her. Her mind blanked for a moment, and then she reacted with fury. This was an invasion. This was somebody violating her, taking everything away from her, stealing her life, certainly her livelihood. She ran for a broom and began to beat at the line of flame, but the broom immediately caught fire. Where were the fire extinguishers? Where was the fire department?

Where was her mother?

She ran upstairs in a frenzy and burst through the door to find the room empty. Bertha and Simon had fled. Sabine raced down the corridor. All the rooms were unoccupied. They had all escaped.

She made her way back through the corridor and started down the stairs. Then, for a moment, it occurred to her that she might die. The fire was still contained on the first floor, but she found she could no longer breathe. She saw no flames, but she was surrounded by black smoke. Gasping, she tried to get air, but her lungs inhaled the smoke and she coughed. She might as well have been under water. She realized that she was suffocating, and that if she tried to breathe again, she would only fill her lungs with the smoke, and she would die. It was necessary for her to hold her breath and streak through the wall of flames. Was there a door—a handle? Could she touch it, turn it? Or would the blazing, searing heat burn her hand? She had no choice but to try.

Sabine closed her eyes and ran blindly, anticipating an obstacle, a closed door, a lock. But there was nothing, and stumbling down the steps she fell, panting, on the grass. Air filled her lungs. She gasped. For a moment she could not move. Then she opened her eyes.

The entire main section of the hotel was ablaze. Guests were jumping from the windows into blankets that had been stretched out. Behind Sabine a cheer rose; it was the young kids she had heard laughing down by the pond in the darkness. To them this was still another adventure, and they applauded and cheered as a middle-aged lady in a nightgown appeared in a window frame, hesitating.

"Jump!" they cried. Sabine's heart stopped beating until the woman made her decision and leaped into the dark.

"Hey, look at the building burn. It's like a skeleton," a boy behind Sabine marveled.

It was true. The bones of the building were beginning to appear. The ridgepole of the roof was like a backbone, the studs that had been carpentered so carefully formed a rib cage that was disintegrating, etched in flame.

"I bet the whole building collapses in five minutes."

"No, it'll take longer than that."

"Betcha."

Sabine looked at the gathered faces, all staring at the burning building. She saw her mother, and Simon with his arms around her. Instinctively, she looked away from the fire and caught sight of the Mountain View House, its lights blazing.

Was it possible that they had seen the fire and not called the fire department? She stood on the lawn and felt the dew on her feet. Bertha and Simon stood together. She joined them and they watched the fire engulf the main building.

And then Bertha said, "Where's Max?"

Max thought he was in hell. And he thought it curious, because he did not believe in hell. *So it is true*, he said to himself as he woke up, *there is a hell*. Then he realized he was in his own room, but it was on fire. Black muddy smoke entered his nose and, when he opened his mouth, invaded his lungs. Max touched his feet to the floor, then fell back on the bed again. The floor was scorching. He crouched for a moment on the island of his bed and was amazed to find himself crying. Weeping, because he knew he was going to die and he was frightened. Nothing had ever frightened Max. This was his first time—and his last—to know what real fear was about. He looked up at the ceiling. He was on the top floor, and as he looked the ceiling gave way, crashed down around him, and he could see the roof. And he could see flames now. Above him and around him, outside the door. He looked toward the window. Perhaps he could make it to the window. He would have to throw himself to the ground—would he break his neck? Could he endure the pain to cross the room, trying to find the window?

Fire, the pure force of it, blew open the door. The flames were roaring. Max was amazed. Fire had physical force. He could feel more than the heat, he could feel the energy.

He gave a cry and leaped from the bed, throwing himself across the room, but it was too late. Fire grasped him through the sleeve of his pajamas, searing his shoulder, running its fingers through his hair. The pain was excruciating. Unaware now of what he was or where he was going, Max beat his arms in the air, a frantic useless little dance of death, like a bug on its back waving its antennae feebly in the wind. Fire ran down Max's back. It cut like a whip, and when he opened his mouth to cry out, smoke stuffed itself in his mouth and down his throat. He was ablaze. He felt something, heard the tinkle of glass in the midst of the roaring, and then he felt the entire earth give way beneath him, and he sank through air.

Bertha was the first to see him at the window.

"Oh God, look! It's Max!" She pointed a finger and Sabine saw the crazy dancing figure, surrounded by smoke, silhouetted in flames. The kids had fallen silent now. Everyone was watching the little drama that was being played out for them—one man, his life ending, burning before their eyes. Jerkily the man moved toward the window, and fell against it. The window sash was in flames and it gave way. The body plummeted.

Several people rushed to smother the flames with a blanket. Sabine moved toward Max's body, but she knew it was too late. There was no doubt that he was dead. His face was almost unrecognizable. She stared down at him until a hand on her arm pulled her away. She resisted.

"Get away," came a voice behind her. "The roof is going to collapse."

"Save him," Sabine pleaded. Save what, save a corpse? She allowed the unseen hand to pull her away.

How light the trees looked in the fire. At first she thought the leaves had caught, but it was only the reflection of flame. Now there were more screams. Two figures appeared at a window, immobile with fear.

"Jump!"

They waited too long. The roof collapsed on them. The burning beams crashed in like frail, old bones, an old skeleton being consumed, all falling down, the building consuming itself now. An inferno. The fire's energy caused whirlpools of flame. Sabine felt the heat on her face. And in a daze, she heard the siren from the fire house in Liberty. Three blasts. And then three more.

Too late, she thought. Too late. There is nothing left to save. By the time the fire trucks arrived the main building had burned to the ground; the recreation hall, the dining room, the staff quarters were all gone. Only the cabins remained. But the heart of Glenrocks had been destroyed.

"Who notified you?" Sabine wanted to know.

"Nobody," the fire chief answered. "I was up making a cup of coffee when I saw the flames."

"Then nobody called," Sabine said.

"No. But you're lucky. Only three dead. It could have been much worse."

"Yes," she said. "It could have been. I suppose it could

have been worse." She looked up. The Mountain View House seemed to be gloating in the dawn. Sabine was tired. She wanted no more of it. The heart, the heart of it had been destroyed. Glenrocks.

The ambulance came to carry away the three bodies. Others had been injured, but no one seriously. Sabine watched the ambulance drive off. *Poor Max,* she thought. But she also thought, *Yes, he died harder than Papa. In the end, Max suffered more.*

Station wagons and pick-up trucks arrived to carry the guests to other hotels, to rooming houses. The firetrucks departed. And Simon left to find them transportation. Sabine found Bertha sitting on the three slabs of granite that had originally given the hotel its name.

It was dawn and the sweet sickly odor of smoke clung to everything. Bertha huddled in a blanket and Sabine could see that her mother's hands were trembling. She was no longer a young woman, no longer so resilient.

Sightseers on their way to work roared up the drive in their jalopies, gaped, and roared on. Sabine and Bertha took no notice. They were looking out over the fields. Sabine knew the picture in her mother's mind. Bertha was watching that first moment, so many years ago, that wondrous day in May with Jacob and his concertina, the child and the husband, the dreams—so many of them to be fulfilled, oh, the wonderful future that lay ahead for all of them on that wondrous day in May, the beauty of the day, the beauty of the marriage. And now another part of it had been swept away. Sabine glanced at her mother. For a moment she felt resentment. The older woman was shivering, was looking back over the fields, was looking at her life, and most of her life was now over.

Mother.

Mother, who had never comforted, needing comfort now. In that hot and steamy dawn, as they waited, as the sun rose—the day was going to be another scorcher, but the morning was fresh with life—the two women sat in the sweet-smelling ruins, waiting for Simon to come carry them away. As they sat there, Sabine slowly reached out her arm and drew her mother to her. To comfort.

For comfort.

On the Rocks began as the smallest of entertainments, **a** benefit to raise money for Glenrocks. The idea had been Jamie's. He had been two drinks into the Labor Day weekend and Sabine was at his place. She was not used to having time on her hands. The insurance money had been paid, but it was not nearly enough to rebuild the hotel. Bertha was on a motor trip to Canada with Simon. Sabine had only Jamie.

They sat across from each other on pillows on the floor and shared a bottle of white wine. The windows were open but there was little sound of traffic. The city had emptied for the weekend.

Jamie poured more wine into her glass.

"Do you feel the way I do?" he asked.

"How's that?"

"Like kids who have been left back at school."

"Oh, worse. I feel like two kids who weren't invited to the senior prom. The only two orphans who weren't taken on the outing. I feel like—this is *terrible* wine," she interrupted herself.

"Does it matter?" Jamie asked.

"No. Not at the moment. It serves the purpose." She lit a cigarette.

"Do you remember 'Let 'Em Eat Cinema'?" she asked him.

"Of course. I remember everything."

"You don't."

"Of course I do. I'm a dancer. We're compulsive. Disciplined. Organized. We shower a lot. Use a lot of cologne. And save everything. I have every program. I wrote down all the choreography. It's my own hieroglyphics and nobody else could decipher it." He got up. "You want to see how much we did in eight years?"

She followed him to the bookcase. There it was, everything he had collected. She started to leaf through his mementos. Forgotten performers came to life again. Routines she had even forgotten she had created. Some of the material she had performed with Jerry. It was all there, catalogued by year.

An idea came to her.

"Let's have some more wine," she said, and they settled themselves again on the pillows. "What are you doing for the next few weeks?"

"The same thing you are. Nothing."

"You want to organize a benefit? Maybe get some of the

performers who played Glenrocks?" he said. A moment's doubt. "You think anyone would want to see it again?"

"*I* would," Jamie said.

"Goddamnit, so would I. How much money do you think we could raise?"

The wine was forgotten. They decided to start at the top. They would rent Carnegie Hall. They would charge twenty-five dollars a ticket.

"Can we get away with that?" asked Jamie, who paid thirty-three dollars a month for his cold-water flat.

"Who knows?" Sabine spread her hands. "We'll see."

Then they wrote down a list of performers and decided to sleep on it.

On Monday, Sabine called Jerry in Hollywood, who agreed to fly in for the show. And then everything began to fall into place. Eddie Troncone's band was playing at the Café Rouge and he was off on Sundays; he was willing to perform with the band. Danny, the original Misanthrope, was dancing and smiling his way through the role of a ruthless charming heel on Broadway and becoming famous in the process. He offered his services. So did other performers, lesser in name but not in talent.

The performance was historic. It was sold out—at twenty-five dollars a ticket. Everyone paid the same, balcony and orchestra. There was a special kind of joy as both audience and artists looked back over a time in their lives that had been very special. Hard times—the Depression—and silly times. And good times.

The Carnegie Hall performance lasted over three hours, and at the end the audience screamed for more. The house lights came on; the audience stamped its feet. The cast assembled for one very formal bow and, on cue, all fell forward in a dead faint. They had no more to give. The performance ended on a laugh, the way all the performances at Glenrocks had.

Fifteen minutes later, still dripping with sweat and gloriously happy, Jerry entered the curtained-off area that was Sabine's dressing room and sank into a chair. Sabine was half naked, but that had never bothered Jerry. He took out a cigarette, borrowed some of her Kleenex, and sighed, "What about that? God, it felt good to perform again!"

"What are you talking about?" Sabine said. "You're performing all the time."

"Oh, you know it's not the same. Nothing is the same out there. I don't knock it and I love the money. But it's not so much fun."

"I always heard you had a terrific group out there."

"Yes, yes, it's all *wonderful*. It's *paradise*." He puffed on the cigarette. "Most of the actors are okay, but, well, it's all the other bullshit." He flicked ashes.

"If you don't like all that bullshit, why don't you come back here—and take all this bullshit?" Sabine asked.

He looked at her as though she had just come from Bulgaria, right off the boat.

"You don't understand. I'm under contract. I am *theirs*."

"Well, can't Bernard help you out?"

"Oh, Sabine I love you," he said. "You don't realize. Bernard Ross is now perhaps the *second* most important man in Hollywood."

"Why? Who died?"

"Zanuck's last film."

She threw Kleenex at him. "You have gone Hollywood," she said. " 'Film.' Film? They're not films, they're movies."

"No," Jerry said. "Warner Brothers makes movies. Zanuck makes films. And David O. Selznick, he makes films too."

"Aw gee, it's good to know the difference."

He looked at her, and they were back where they once had been. Maybe it would only be for a moment, but they both felt it. Nothing had happened. Nothing had occurred to either of them, none of those little blows that life keeps giving. For the moment they were still each other's best friend.

"Why don't you come out? We could have fun." Jerry sounded wistful.

"What would I do out there?"

"You could write. They pay a lot of money."

"Write? Movies?" She had never considered the idea.

"Well, *somebody* has to do it."

"That's what they say about funeral directors."

"You'd like California."

"Why? You don't."

"Who said?"

"You said. You just sat there and told me about all the bullshit."

"Oh, that. Honestly, that was just because I was carried away by the moment and being in front of live audiences and hearing that applause. Did you hear that applause rise just a teeny bit when I came out after you?"

"No."

"Neither did I." He laughed and lit another cigarette.

A professionally cheery voice sounded outside the curtain.

"Hey there," it said, "are you in there?" A very handsome blond young man stuck his head through. "Oh, there you are. They said you might be here," he said to Jerry.

"Oh, hi, Scott," Jerry said.

The young man grinned. Sabine thought, *Nobody is that cheerful. What a pain in the ass to wake up with someone that cheerful.*

Jerry kissed Sabine on the top of her head.

"Gotta go. I'll call you from Hollywood. Let's do this again sometime."

And he was gone with the blond young man whose name, at least for the moment, was Scott. Sabine puzzled. She knew Jerry better than anyone else, or thought she did. But he was an enigma. He could turn on and then turn off.

Later that night Sabine and Jamie went over the figures. From that one night they had cleared $65,000.

"If you can't sell silk, sell linen," Sabine muttered as she counted out the bills.

"What?" Jamie said.

"It's an expression of my father's. It means if one thing doesn't work out, try another. Things never worked out for peddlers, I take it." She looked at the figures. "Suppose we did a series of Sunday nights?"

"We could never get this cast again," Jamie said.

"I know," Sabine said thoughtfully. "But do you think the material would stand up?"

"I don't know." Jamie said.

"I don't have anything to lose. I've got no money, so all I can invest is time."

By ten the next morning, Sabine was on the phone. She made a deal with the manager of the Booth Theater. She talked to the stagehands and handled them the way she had worked the wholesalers at the Washington Market. Out of the proceeds from the Sunday benefit, she paid for two ads in the

New York Times announcing three Sunday night performances of *On the Rocks*. The first ad came out on Wednesday. The performances were sold out the next day.

The play that was booked into the Booth Theater for the rest of the week had arrived the first week in October on a Monday and left this world that Saturday night. The manager of the theater, with no other booking in hand, approached Sabine: how about presenting *On the Rocks* as a regular revue on an interim basis until he found another production? They could coproduce it.

It took Sabine one evening with Jamie and a consultation with Mark Cardozo to come to terms. Suddenly she found she was a producer. She liked it—examining every receipt, counting every ticket, questioning every bill. It was wheedle and charm—and threaten when necessary.

On the Rocks opened very quietly on a Tuesday night to an audience that perhaps had heard of Glenrocks but most certainly had never been there. They were totally unprepared for Jamie's dances, which were electrifying, and for the performers, who were not left-over summer stock but comedians with wit and bite.

And then there was Sabine. The critics did not know what to make of her. They loved her; they all said that. But beautiful women were not supposed to be funny, indeed were not allowed to be funny, except for Carole Lombard, and she was in the movies. Sabine was beautiful. And yet she made them laugh. Writers were not supposed to perform their own material, and yet Sabine did. And how did she manage to break one's heart? That was the mystery.

Except to Dieterl. The little composer took time out from writing one of his Broadway scores to write her a song. Sabine sang it as the closing number of the show. It made an interesting ending, because it was the opposite of most. Like leaves falling from a tree, one by one the performers left the stage, until there was only Sabine. She sang,

> "Home is the place that stays open forever,
> Childhood is summer slipped out of your hand,
> Friends are the people you call after midnight,
> Youth is a honky-tonk band."

The lights were disappearing, the world of Glenrocks fading. She continued,

> "Peace is the part of the park you can't find,
> Beauty's a room where mirrors lie broken,
> And life's what you're leaving behind . . ."

Chapter Sixteen

Money.

Sabine was unused to it. Other people had always taken care of it. Real money in all its different forms. Dollar bills. Stacks of twenties. Hundred-dollar bills wrapped in brown paper. Box-office statements. Accountant's ledgers. Deposit receipts. The numbers fascinated her. She delighted in the commas. Nine thousand, *comma*, three hundred dollars. And fourteen cents. Balance, sixty-five thousand, *comma*, dollars.

Each week she studied the box-office statements. Each performance included the weather report—fair or rain—the date of the show, the number of the performance. Had they really done 198 performances? Then it listed the capacity and the number of full tickets sold, separated into orchestra and balcony. Then it listed the total dead tickets. But there were no dead tickets. Every performance was sold out.

When Sabine discovered that the grosses were dropping in the first two weeks of January, she hired two checkers, who stood in the back of the theater, clocking the customers as they entered. Then she confronted her coproducer with the evidence: someone had been skimming money off the top. She expected this from bartenders, but not from gentlemen associated with the legitimate theater. Of course the possibility existed; it was a very easy trick if the house was not sold out every night. But this house was.

So the coproducer fired the treasurer, and from that moment on there was no problem. But Sabine kept an eye on everything and everyone anyway, even her coproducer.

Money meant everything at this moment in Sabine's life. It meant happy endings and it meant not having to worry, and it meant power, and it meant control. She could do what she liked. She could buy. Or she could not buy. She no longer passed the seductive windows of the great department stores.

She went in. To Bergdorf's to try on the sable, to Lilly Daché's to try on hats, to Cartier's to try on the diamonds. At one moment she had three five-carat diamonds on one finger.

"Don't you think this verges on vulgarity?" she asked the salesman, who, dreaming of a commission on the sale of $50,000 worth of jewels, assured her it did not.

"Keep them!" he urged. "Keep them for the weekend. Wear them and see how *used* you get to them. Take them!" But Sabine smiled and shook her head and left the store.

She did not change. She did not buy the furs. She moved back into the apartment she and Matt had shared. She put the money in the bank, in a savings account, and added to it each week, thrilled at the mounting total, until one evening Mark Cardozo suggested that her money might earn more money.

"How?" she asked immediately.

"By the proper investment. There are investments that offer more interest."

"What? Which ones?"

He started to name a few. Her eyes glistened. She wet her lips.

"Can I convert them to cash when the time comes?"

He laughed. "What are you planning to do, leave the country?"

"No. I'm going to rebuild Glenrocks."

"Rebuild it? How big?"

"I don't know yet."

"If your plans weren't too grandiose, you could probably get financing now."

"Yes? Tell me how."

It became a kind of lovemaking. Money excited her. Mark's talking about it excited her. How sexy the discussion of investments, planning, bonds, and income-producing properties became.

"More. Tell me more. Tell me how."

When Mark discovered this key to courtship, he became a male stripteaser, unveiling and revealing a little at a time about real estate, investments, the stock market. Arousing her.

"More."

"Later."

"Now!"

"No. Kiss me."

"Then tell me."

"Kiss me."

They were both aware of the nature of their relationship. And it amused him as much as it excited her. With his help, she began to see a structure to her own life, a world that was possible, that she could control. To rebuild Glenrocks, first there had to be an architect, then she needed building supplies, and a contractor. She thought of Dan Ryan. He would know. He would help. She called him.

On the first Sunday in December Mark drove her to Liberty to see Dan Ryan. Sabine was exultant. It was her day off, and the air in the country was bracing, the feel of winter sharper by two or three weeks than it was in the city. It was Sunday and it was good to breathe the air and look at all the places she remembered. And to remember Matt too. She closed her eyes to keep everything in her memory for a moment. But there was no time to look back on the past.

Dan Ryan opened the door, vigorous as ever, happy to see them. A pot of coffee was waiting. The three of them sat down at the kitchen table and Dan Ryan listened to the dreams in Sabine's mind, trying to convert them into reality. When he heard she wanted to reconstruct the main hotel, he had a suggestion.

"Why not build it for all four seasons?"

"All year round?" Sabine asked. "Who would want to come here in the winter?"

"You'd be surprised. Skiers."

"Oh, Dan. Nobody skis," Sabine said.

"I do," Mark said gently.

"What for?" Sabine wanted to know. In her mind, winter was going to the theater and to parties, and staying in the city. But then (how could she have forgotten it?) she remembered the glittering winter world of her childhood, and the day she, her father and mother, Matt, and Dan Ryan had all been marooned in a blizzard. She remembered the clarity of the morning following the storm, the dazzling icicles, the sparkling fields. Skiing? Skating? Why not? They had the mountains. Except for the stretch of land above them, which belonged to the Mountain View House. The Mountain View House had the highest peak in the surrounding neighborhood.

"They will never sell. Forget it," Sabine said.

"You never can tell. Fortunes change in this world," Dan replied.

"Suppose we did make this an all-year-round resort. What would that cost?"

Sabine was already imagining a huge fireplace, mulled wine, hot buttered rum. Ski weekends. Sleigh rides. Cozy suites. Should it be a hideaway for lovers, or a family resort? Which would bring in the most profit? It made sense to run a hotel for twelve months rather than three. That is, if people would come. She would have to make it attractive enough so that they would want to come.

They sat at the kitchen table, and Dan's pencil and pad roughed out the design she described, translated the dreams into rough estimates for the cost of materials and the cost of labor. Mark sat across from them, figuring out percentages, possible mortgages, rates of interest.

By two o'clock in the afternoon Sabine was able to ask, "Can we do it? Is it possible?"

Dan warned her, "If you keep it small enough at first, it's possible."

She turned to Mark. "Is there enough money in the bank to pay for all this?"

Mark smiled at her. "Sabine, you don't pay it all out at once. You don't pay in full until you're satisfied you've got what you want."

Of course, she thought. *It's the same in one industry as another. Protect yourself. Watch out. If you keep the money, you keep the power.*

"I need a loan. Can we go to the bank in the morning?" she asked Mark.

"You certainly are impatient," he said.

"I want to start. I want Glenrocks back. I want—" She stopped in confusion. "I don't want things to slip away from me."

"You can go to the bank tomorrow, if you want to," Dan remarked, leaning back in his chair, "but I can tell you, you won't break ground here until April."

"April?" Sabine asked.

"Ground's frozen solid, and there's nothing to be done about that."

Dan Ryan poured himself another cup of coffee. Mark and

Sabine rose. It was gray outside now, with the look of snow in the sky. Soon it would be dark. Night came early in December, even earlier to the valleys surrounded by mountains.

Dan poured coffee from the pot and turned on the small radio he kept over the stove.

"It's company," he explained as he snapped it on. Sabine and Mark were about to leave the house—the front door was already open—when the program was interrupted by a bulletin. That was how they learned about the Japanese attack on Pearl Harbor.

Slowly the three of them gathered around the radio, then sat down at the kitchen table as the news poured forth, incoherent announcements of bombings and official statements. Little real information, and all of it too stunning to be comprehended at once.

What Sabine did understand was this: there would be no construction on Glenrocks in the immediate future.

Mark and Sabine sat in the kitchen and listened to the broadcasts until darkness fell, and then Mark drove her back to the city. There was very little to say. Whatever there was, was being said over the radio. They listened in silence.

On Tuesday, Mark Cardozo, whose only experience at sea had been as a crew member in the Bermuda races, enlisted in the Navy and was sent to Officer's Candidate School, which did not please his mother. Mark had done this on his own initiative. And Sandy did not recognize anyone's initiative but her own.

War in America was a bit of a disappointment. There was no drama to speak of. No bomb shelters. No London blitz. Posters sprang up everywhere cautioning civilians about saboteurs and against leaking military information. There were rumors of saboteurs landing from U-boats somewhere in the Hamptons. On the West Coast there was momentary panic in the Malibu Beach area, but it never even reached the edge of Bel Air.

Very little had changed. Except for Simon—he changed. An arch-isolationist until Germany attacked the Soviet Union, he was now on many committees demanding the immediate opening of a second front. He badgered Sabine to sign petitions and send telegrams to Congress.

"What for?" she finally asked in annoyance. "The recruits

are still training with broomsticks and you want to open a second front. What are they going to shoot with? Mops?"

The war news was all bad. Within months the Phillipines had fallen. Then Bataan, Corregidor, Singapore. There was no escaping the names. They shouted from every headline, and the only good thing about the winter weather that swept across the world was that it stalled the German attack on Moscow. The Nazis had at last been halted, if only for the moment. But the thought of the freezing temperatures and the heavy snows gave Sabine great concern. She would think of Sammy and his family and wonder whether it was possible that they were still alive. And what of Mme Levinsky in Paris? How was she to survive? Sabine found herself envying Bertha, who had taken a job sewing parachutes, contributing to the war effort. Bertha, in a way, was happy.

Matt Ryan's voice, marred by static, was just that: a voice. He was becoming less and less a person to Sabine. She could remember their love, but it seemed so remote. So many events had occurred since their time together.

One night, after work, as she was walking down Forty-fifth Street looking for someone who was headed downtown to share a cab with—sharing cabs was very patriotic—Sabine noticed that the lights had gone out on Times Square. No more Camel's cigarette man blowing smoke rings into the air. No more Roseland, no Paramont. Lindy's had disappeared. The Astor was dark. The sky-high signs were dark, and the next morning's paper announced the beginning of dim-outs. In this way no ships at sea could be exposed to German U-boats.

Several of the *On the Rocks* dancers had been drafted. The replacements were inadequate, and by the middle of June, Sabine noticed that the grosses were dropping. The hit review of 1940 was now 1942's has-been.

She decided to close the show, and telephoned Jerry. He was philosophical about it.

"You made a lot of money. You made a name for yourself," he said. "Now it is your patriotic duty to come out here and kill Bernard Ross."

"Why Bernie?"

"We are making patriotic movies. With much dedication. I of course will not enter the Armed Services. I have a bad back. No one mentions the fact that I am queer."

It was the first time Jerry himself had ever mentioned it. Sabine was startled at his bitterness.

"But Bernard Ross, who should be somewhere in the South Pacific serving his country, has asthma. He may not kill the enemy, but he is coming close to killing this movie. Please, Sabine, come on out. It would be fun."

Such wistfulness. And selfishness. Jerry wanted a playmate, but she wasn't in the mood to play. She told him she would think about it.

In the meantime, in the last week of the run, a stranger in uniform caught her arm as she passed in the corridor on the way to her dressing room.

"Sabine," the voice said, and she recognized it as Mark's.

"My God," she said, hugging him. "Look at you. What are you doing here? Why didn't you let me know?"

"I didn't know myself, until I got my orders."

She felt a twinge. "Where are you going?"

"No, where are *we* going? We are going on the town."

He took her to El Morocco, because it was everyone's idea of a good time. The club was jammed, but then all nightclubs were. A kind of war fever had gripped New York. Go everywhere you can. Do everything. Work all day, dance all night. Live on energy. Don't waste time. Write V-mail letters. Conserve rubber. Sign up for sugar ration books. Let off steam.

It was okay for Mark to celebrate because he was in uniform, and nothing was too good for a boy in uniform, especially if he discreetly offered a five-dollar tip. Mark was shown to the best table. The music was loud, the food was okay at best, but who cared? There were no more steaks done the way they used to be, but still, it wasn't hash. And there was liquor. And hot music. And dancing. And that fever. Mark held her in his arms as they danced. It felt good to have a man hold her, to have a man lead her, to relax in his masculinity. She leaned her head against his shoulder because she was tired and the show was going to end soon and she wasn't sure where she was going, and seeing Mark made her lonely for all the other people in her life who were (perhaps) in scattered spots all over the globe. So he held her closer and she let him, because she welcomed it.

They ended up in bed, each surprised at the other. She was surprised at his expertise and his passion. He loved women, and there was nothing tentative about his occupation of her.

And she surprised him with her warmth and her enjoyment of sex. He had been accustomed to the rather stiff Radcliffe substitute for passion or the Scollay Square hooker's commercial imitation. He was not prepared for the real thing.

The shadows of the early morning hours made him bolder.

"Marry me, Sabine," he whispered, so softly that she was not sure she had heard it correctly.

She had never truly considered him, as a person. She looked at the clothing that was his, that had been so neatly pressed, and now was scattered around the apartment, draped over chairs and dropped on the floor. She had never really considered *him*. As if mirroring her thoughts, he said, "I have never possessed anything of my own. I don't think I have ever been anyone of my own. I have been my mother's son, my brother's brother. Your beau. Uncle Sam's ensign. I went to schools my family picked out for me and danced with girls that had been selected for me and went to a law school that my family had always gone to. The only original thing I ever did in my life was to pick you up in a Boston bar. And I don't know why I did that."

He stopped and thought. "Yes, I do. There was something lost about you. I recognized that. I responded to that. That got to me."

They were silent for a moment.

"I want someone to belong to me. Someone of my own. Sabine, I'm afraid if I lose you this time I will lose you forever, and I couldn't stand that."

She still said nothing. She was afraid to speak. The shadows of dawn were creeping away.

"Oh God, life is so lonely," he cried out, and then she was crying, glad that it was still dark, glad that he couldn't see the tears running down her cheeks. She didn't love him, but she understood his loneliness.

She said to him, "Yes, I'll marry you. I'll marry you and we will be very happy. I will make you happy." It was a time of quick romances and sudden marriages, and hers was going to be another one, because she felt sorry for him and lonely for herself, and she felt she had nothing more to offer in her life.

"Mark," she whispered as she held him in her arms, "I'll love you."

It was as much a hope as a promise.

They went to tell Mark's parents. The butler ushered them into the reception room as if they were strangers. Julien appeared and shook hands with them both. He was nervous. He asked if anyone wanted a drink. But no one did, so they sat in silence as the traffic on Seventy-second Street sizzled outside.

Then Sandy made an entrance.

She said nothing to them. Instead she told the maid, "You may bring in the tea."

Mark took over. "We're here to invite you to the wedding."

"What wedding?" Sandy asked, knowing perfectly well what Mark meant.

"Ours, Mother."

"I'm afraid we have another engagement."

"You don't even know what day it will be."

"It doesn't matter." And then she turned to Sabine. "You broke your promise. You went back on your word."

"I love her, Mother. I want to marry her."

"I understand that, Mark. I'm not talking to you at the moment. I am talking to her."

"Her name is Sabine."

"I know perfectly well what her name is. Half of New York knows what her name is. The other half won't recognize her. No, I am saying something different."

Sandy's eyes held a genteel fury. "You came to us when you needed something. You took money from us. We were glad to give it, but we did extract a promise from you. You have not lived up to that promise. I don't forgive that."

"What is it you object to?" Sabine hissed. "My name, my parents, my background? Don't tell me you're upset because I broke some silly promise. I have offered to give the money back to you and you refused. So don't tell me—"

"Where do you want me to begin, Miss Abramowitz? Do you think you will make him happy? Oh yes, I object to your background. I object to you. I think you are a conniver. I don't think you love Mark. I am sure you will not make him happy. I don't give a damn about the money. We are beyond money here!"

She had risen and the fury was evident. Sandy, who was always in control, was in control no longer.

"You're taking my son, and you want me to come to your

wedding? Where? Somewhere in Maryland, standing in line with the other soldiers? Go to your wedding? I wouldn't spit on your grave!"

And she strode out of the room.

Mark looked at his father. He gathered up his hat. "I don't want to see her again, ever," he said to Julien.

Father and son shook hands. Sabine did not offer her hand. Julien did not acknowledge her. They left. The butler did not usher them out.

They *were* married in Maryland, where there was no delay, and set off on a six-day honeymoon.

Mark wouldn't tell her where they were going. It was to be a surprise, he said, as they drove through the Poconos and headed east. She was curious—she recognized the roads, this was the way to Glenrocks. The surprise came when the car pulled up in front of the Mountain View House.

Was it some sort of joke? Did he realize where they were? Didn't he know? Sabine felt a surge of anger rushing through her. This was forbidden territory. This was the hotel that had declared itself an enemy. These were the people who had not called the fire department when Glenrocks was burning. Of course they denied knowing anything about the fire. But Sabine could not help the anger. She could only suppress it. She looked at Mark. She looked into the face of an eager, smiling, handsome bridegroom, an ensign in the U.S. Navy. *Totally innocent,* she thought.

She waited for the rejection. It was sure to come. No Jews wanted. "I'm sorry, we seem to have made an error. Your reservation was not received."

Mark was driving a Bentley, the kind of automobile that made bellboys hurry to open the door. The Bentley spelled class and royalty and big tips. (An illusion, because class and royalty hardly ever tip. But bellboys never seem to learn that.)

A bellboy in a green and white uniform with the initials MVH on the pocket rushed to take their luggage.

"We have a reservation. Cardozo," Mark said, flipping him the keys to the trunk.

"Yes *sir,*" the bellboy said, catching the keys the way he caught passes in the fall at Cornell—blond and athletic and headed for big things in life. He saluted the Navy ensign. "Yes, sir, right away, sir!"

They entered forbidden territory. On the porch were rockers, not much different from the ones at Glenrocks. Wicker rockers. The inhabitants of the rockers were mostly old. Older than the Glenrocks crowd.

Was there a difference? The men wore L.L. Bean shirts and had fewer cigars; their slacks were more neutral than those Sabine used to see at Glenrocks. The women were stringier, their hair was blue with rinse and they wore their hair in finger waves, and they sported pearls with cardigans. The *Wall Street Journal* was more in evidence. The conversations were more muffled, as though there were secrets being discussed. *They are talking about us. They are looking at us. They know*, Sabine thought. *They are waiting for us.*

The decor was green and white, green and white everywhere, on the uniforms, on the wicker upholstery. It was all peaceful, tasteful.

They approached the desk. *Here it comes*, she thought.

"Reservation for Cardozo," Mark said very casually.

"Of course, Ensign. Mr. and Mrs., is it? Of course it is; you requested the honeymoon suite. How nice to have you with us." The clerk was beaming. *I am irrational*, Sabine thought.

"How many days will you be staying with us?" the clerk asked.

"Hard to say. I have seven days' leave and there's a lot I want to see. We might leave in two days' time."

The clerk leaned over the desk confidentially.

"Don't worry, Ensign. The hotel is not filled up this summer. The war, you know."

They were shown to their suite. The view was beautiful, the decor again green and white. The bellboy opened the closets and checked the drawers until Mark tipped him. There was another salute, and then they were alone.

Sabine sat down on the bed.

"Mark, do you realize what you've done?" She began to giggle.

"What?" he said.

"Don't you know what this hotel *is*?"

"I heard you talk about it. I thought you'd like it."

"You have never stayed in one of these summer hotels?"

"No. We had the place in Maine and of course the estate on Long Island. Why stay in a hotel?"

"This hotel is restricted."

The perplexed look on his face amazed her. How could he have been so sheltered? Was it because the Cardozos were so rich? Money had never seemed to make any difference. So how was it possible that Mark had never come up against this prejudice? The look on his face gave her the answer.

"You mean they won't allow Negroes?" Ensign Cardozo was ready to be outraged. Sabine only laughed.

"Negroes!" She exploded. "Oh, them *too*. No, my darling, restricted means they won't allow Jews!"

His face was blank. He did not comprehend.

She made it more explicit. "Us."

"Suppose we told them we were Jewish?"

"They would be terribly embarrassed. And tell you there was a slip-up on the reservations."

"But the clerk admitted the place was half empty."

"Well, a convention would have been booked in. I don't know. Any excuse would do."

"What the devil did they think the name Cardozo was?"

"Spanish. Brazilian. After all, you look like a conquistador."

It was true. Mark was extremely handsome. He had fine features, a narrow nose, thin lips. No peasant blood there. He might well be the handsomest man she had ever seen. She admired the looks, the dark eyes, the determination. It was a pity that she wasn't madly in love with him.

"Are you uncomfortable here? Do you want to leave?" Mark was asking her.

"No. Let's spend the night, anyway. I've always wanted to spend a night at the Mountain View House. Let's see what the service is like."

He ordered champagne and sandwiches. The service was slow.

"The champagne is *terrific*," Sabine said. "The sandwiches are not really anything. Look at the turkey. There's not much meat there. And the lettuce is wilted."

"Should I send it back?"

"No. Let's have some more of that champagne."

They had a picnic on the bed and got slightly buzzed on the champagne.

"If we're only going to stay here one night—" Mark began.

"Please God, make it only one night or I'll starve to death," Sabine interrupted.

As it happened, a player on one of the tennis courts fell and twisted his ankle, enough to take him out of the game. A replacement was needed, and Mark volunteered. He was affable, looked good in tennis whites, and was a better player than the other three. Drinks followed four sets of tennis. The wives gossiped and compared fashions and theater, avoiding war news. Mark and Sabine were pronounced a charming couple. They were asked to join the others for dinner.

You still dressed for dinner at the Mountain View House. On the dance floor, the dark ensign in his dress whites and the glamorous raven-haired beauty, also dressed in white, looked like film stars.

The three other couples, watching them back at the table, sighed—either in remembrance or with envy. They were the "young" couples at the Mountain View House, but in truth all were near the forty mark. They glowed with health, with country club golf and tennis, but their marriages held the pallor of not enough exercise.

The evening passed pleasantly enough. The chicken had been fried, but not in good batter, the salad dressing was atrocious, and the lettuce had wilted still more. The service was polite but the waiter had dirty fingernails. Sabine checked everything. The other guests in the hotel seemed not to care. They drank a lot, and the drinks were admirable. Sabine had nothing to drink. Dessert was a long time in coming, she thought. And then it arrived.

It was a surprise: a wedding cake that the other three couples had ordered especially from the chef. And another bottle of champagne, of course, to accompany it. The trio of musicians played "Here Comes the Bride" and all the guests applauded. Mark and Sabine rose, bowed, and thanked them.

"Oh, really, we didn't expect this," Mark said, blushing under his deep tan.

"Well, one only gets married *once*," Patty Detweiler, to his right, said, and then amended herself. "Except for Bunny and me. We've each been married three times, but this is the only one that counts, isn't that right, Bunny?"

"Absolutely. I wouldn't even *recognize* my other two wives," Bunny said warmly.

"No? One of them was my sister," Henry Phillips said from across the table.

"That's right," Bunny Detweiler said, surprised. "We were brothers-in-law. My God, how time flies!"

But no one seemed to mind. The marriages had come and gone, a little flighty perhaps, but perfectly acceptable socially. There was more dancing. Bunny danced with Sabine. So did Henry. Finally they all went outside on the verandah. The lights in the valley sparkled in the summer night. It was time for a nightcap. Mark insisted that it be put on his bill.

"I never tire of this view," Patty Detweiler said. "It is so incredible how clear the stars are. And the lights."

"Perfectly gorgeous," Henry Phillips agreed.

"Restful."

"I don't know what I'd do without the Mountain View House. We've been coming here since I was a child."

"I came here with Anne *and* with Marian," Bunny remembered.

"He brings all his wives to the Mountain View," it was explained to Sabine and Mark. "It is something of a tradition."

"I like it better now that the other hotel is gone," Patty Detweiler said.

"What other hotel?" Sabine asked.

"There was a hotel halfway down the valley. Personally, I always thought it spoiled the view."

"Oh, it didn't spoil the view. You always want everything so *perfect*."

"Well, I wasn't sorry it burned down."

"We could see it from here. It made a splendid blaze. By the time we woke up and came down, the whole place was ablaze. Spectacular!"

"Did anyone send in an alarm?" Sabine asked quietly.

"I suppose someone must have. By the time we arrived it was far too late for that. Anyway, it was a Jewish hotel."

It was such a casual remark, an end-of-the-evening, over-one-last-brandy kind of comment.

"What do you mean, a Jewish hotel?" Mark asked.

"I mean it catered to Jews. Personally, I never minded them."

"Well, I did," Patty Detweiler said. "I always had a vision of purple pants. I'm glad they're gone." She took a swallow of brandy. "To me, a kike's a kike, pardon my French."

"Oh, that's a little strong," Bunny drawled tolerantly.

"No," Mark said suddenly. "No, your wife's right. A kike *is* a kike. I'm one. My wife's one."

"Oh, stop, Mark," Patty said with a giggle. "I don't find those jokes amusing."

"It's no joke," Mark said, and he stood up. "We're Jews."

"But you're in the Navy!" Henry Phillips said.

"They do *accept* Jews," Mark smiled.

"Oh yes, but so few of them seem to go."

"Really?" Mark said. "I wasn't aware of that. Every Jew that I know happens to be in the service. And I'm on my way to see action now. I've been assigned to a destroyer. I guess that means action."

"Well, I put my foot in it," Patty said, still giggling. "God knows I wouldn't have said anything—"

"But you did," Mark said. "You said it, it's been said, and it won't be *unsaid*. The only unfortunate thing about this evening was that I didn't understand. My wife did. She knows this region. She knows what restricted means. I didn't. Otherwise I wouldn't have brought her here. I brought her here as a surprise. Because, you see, it was her family's hotel that burned down. The hotel you watched burn. It was probably a mistake. I realize that now. I didn't mean to let her be hurt."

"Oh God, Mark, we really didn't know. We had no idea," Henry Phillips said. "You really are such sweet people—"

"We are, aren't we?" Mark said smiling and holding out his hand to Sabine.

"Listen," Sabine said, "You'd better enjoy the view, because as soon as I can I'm going to build that hotel again. Purple pants and all."

They went to their suite. It was dark. Before he could turn on a light, Sabine whispered to him, "Fuck me. I want you to fuck me. God, you were magnificent. I loved you for it. I want you. Fuck me. Now!"

It was such a release. Sabine had Mark fuck her on the *goyim*'s chaise, on the *goyim*'s rug, on the *goyim*'s bed. Defile the infidel. She exulted in his smooth skin, the clean lines of him. He was a passionate lover, and inexhaustible. He loved her—that helped. And if she wasn't in love with him, she loved what he had done. She loved the fact that she was married to such a man. A *mensch* even, although he probably didn't know the word. Mark was the man and she submitted to him, and out of their loneliness something bloomed that often lasts longer than love: genuine affection.

When she woke in the morning, he was inside her, moving slowly and gently, and she wanted the feel of him to last forever, it was so warm. She luxuriated in spreading her legs and opening herself to him. He was a slow lover, she found out; he did not believe in rushing things, he drew everything out. He did not give it all away. It took forever, thank heaven it took forever, before the bed began to sway with their rhythm, and he never let up. His lovemaking was as constant as his backhand. And his backhand was practically perfect.

Afterwards, when the breakfast they had ordered arrived, a card that accompanied the tray advised them that one p.m. was the check-out time and that the room had already been booked.

Mark handed her the card.

"You were right," he said. "I suppose one of our friends told the management."

"How much time do we have?" Sabine asked him. Mark looked at his watch.

"A couple of hours." He was lying naked under the sheet. Sabine took off her robe.

"Then fuck me again. Let's get our money's worth."

Chapter Seventeen

Portland, Maine, was a seaport city whose buildings were mostly red brick and whose sidewalks were either red brick or cobblestone. Casco Bay contained a vast harbor, and so in 1942 Portland was transformed into a Navy town. Not that you saw all that many sailors on the street. Portland was a refueling depot, and the destroyers that did battle with the German U-boats were fighting all the way from Maine to Key West. The Axis submarines had sunk 213 vessels since the start of the war and coastal shipping was virtually at a standstill.

Sabine found the little city strange. There were parts of it that were definitely grimy, but they were balanced by great mansions along the Western Promenade. The hotel where she was staying was—again—red brick, situated on Congress Street, the main thoroughfare in town. There were a couple of movie houses along the street, one right across from the hotel, the other and grander one a little farther along the street. Movies and cocktail lounges pretty much covered the entertainment in Portland, Maine. Unless you "belonged." But most of the Navy wives did not belong, they existed in the Lafayette Hotel, forming their own friendships, playing boring games of bridge during the hot summer afternoons.

The rooms were small. Oftentimes the hotel resembled a dormitory in college. The Navy wives would sit on the beds, their hair in curlers, and fan themselves, looking out on the dimmed-out street, and they would gossip and listen to the radio, but not really. It was only something to accompany the conversation, and the conversation was only a way of passing time until their men came back. Then the women would disband, they would belong to their husbands for the brief periods of their leave, then return to the bridge afternoons and the lonely nights.

314

They seldom even went to the movies at night. The city was packed and there was very little housing. There was a shipbuilding plant in South Portland, and in the frenzy of the summer of 1942 the shipyard workers often bought a ticket to the movies and slept there all night. When the fleet was in, horny Southern drawls and Midwestern twangs accosted every woman under fifty. The bars began to fill up at two in the afternoon. The nights in the bars were smoky and loud. There was the Hawaiian Room, with its fake palm trees and drinks in fake cocoanut shells, and all the others on down the scale. On foggy, sweltering nights the entire little New England city exuded an air of loneliness mixed with sensuality. There were sailors and whores in the back alleys. There were slipped notes and extra sets of keys, there were back seats of automobiles. There was sex in the darkened movie houses and in the shadows of Deerings Oaks, the town's largest park.

And gradually the women separated into groups. There were those who remained faithful and kept their loneliness confined to their rooms and their radios. They wrote cheerful letters and smoked too much. And there were those who became desperate, who learned to loathe red brick and cobblestones and morning fogs. They learned to tolerate the bars and the smoke and the fake South Seas decor, and they found themselves in bed with acquaintances and sometimes with strangers. They also smoked too much. Several of the marriages collapsed there at the Lafayette Hotel. The women who became too lonely or too angry, who gave up or gave in, or who were found out by their husbands, or who confessed— their marriages were soon over.

Sometimes depression set in over little things, like the Lafayette refusing to admit ladies in slacks to the dining room.

They retorted: "Don't you know there's a war going on?" and flounced out of the room. But leaving meant that one of the Navy women had given up and was going back to wherever she had called home before. She was even allowing their crummy little hotel to defeat her.

Sabine's case was different. She kept the loneliness at bay by writing. She kept a diary, filling it with her observations of wartime in a small New England city. And she sketched as she wrote. She described the shoeshine man in the barbershop next door who had come over from Greece fifty years before.

She listened to him as he talked about the rest of his family, disappearing now in the German conquest. He knew there was starvation in Greece. He was sorry, but he was American. He had three children. One was in the service, the Army. The two girls were bright. They were American. He showed pictures. They looked like their father, bright-eyed and ugly. But he was proud of them. And he talked dispassionately about the rest of the family he had lost. He was here, he shined shoes. That was his life, and what would change it? Nothing.

And there was the older woman who sat in the lobby from one to three every afternoon because she enjoyed watching the hotel traffic. It was from her that Sabine heard news. The woman asked Sabine if she wanted to read the paper. Sabine nodded and picked up the Portland *Press Herald*. There was a report of a rally in Madison Square Garden that President Roosevelt had attended. But that was not what caught her eye.

On July 17, 1942, the Berlin radio had announced the arrest and deportation of twenty thousand Jews in Paris. They were headed for resettlement in Eastern Europe.

She grew so obviously pale that the older woman asked what was the matter. "Nothing." Sabine shook her head. But already she was wondering whom to contact, how to find out about her grandmother. Already she was picturing the old lady, herded into carts, herded into trains, shouted at, perhaps beaten, perhaps starved, perhaps tortured. No, why would anyone stoop to torture a harmless old lady? But Sabine's vision filled her with terror. She rose from the couch and handed the newspaper back to the older woman and went to her room.

It was difficult making long-distance calls. The operators were disapproving. Official calls had priority. The circuits were always busy. Still, Sabine managed to speak to the head of the American Jewish Congress. He was an acquaintance of Matt Ryan's. He promised to deliver a message to Matt, but he gave Sabine little hope that she would find her grandmother's whereabouts, even find out whether Mme Levinsky was dead or alive.

"But did they just take people at random?" Sabine asked.

"Evidently. The strongest will probably be put to work in

the German factories. The others . . ." He regretted the sentence.

"How were they taken, were they taken by train? Did they have food?"

"Sabine," the man answered gently, "I would answer these questions if I could. But we have no information."

That was not exactly true. The American Jewish Congress had already received reports about the beginning of the Final Solution—the trains and the massacres, the plans to empty the ghettos, the concentration camps. The reports were in Washington. The rounding up of twenty thousand Jews in Paris was only one more statistic.

Sabine began to write about her grandmother, everything that she could remember. The strong hands, capable in the kitchen, the way she peeled a potato. The brusqueness of her manner. Her care of flowers. Her apartment. Sabine closed her eyes to remember Paris and shut out Portland, and the schoolroom map with its different colors for different countries came to her mind.

She heard nothing more from the American Jewish Congress. In September, she received a letter from Matt. He had tried to find a trace of Mme Levinsky, but he knew only that she was no longer in Paris. He had discovered that several of the trains had delivered their cargoes to camps in southern Germany, while others had continued on to Poland. He knew nothing beyond that. He was back in London, it was a hell of a war. He had heard about her marriage.

He did not offer congratulations.

The autumn cold descended on Maine, and with it the rain. The streets were slick with the damp and the red bricks became even gloomier. For days the sun did not shine. At night the fog rolled in. You could hear foghorns in the harbor.

One night, when Sabine was in the dining room, eating alone, almost enjoying the lobster bisque because it was good and made with real cream, she glanced up to see Mark entering the room. She jumped up from the table, and they embraced. The residents of the Lafayette were used to such displays of affection. Before the war, it would have seemed in bad taste. Now it seemed natural. Why not? Women were smoking cigarettes on the street and not wearing white gloves; some were doing war work in defense plants. Still, the occupants of the Lafayette Hotel always felt it was more seemly when an officer of the U.S. Navy embraced his wife than when a sailor kissed his. With sailors, it seemed, you never could tell.

They sat down at the little table and she looked at him in the light of the small lamp that shaded the worn tablecloth.

He looked haggard.

"Can you order me a drink?" he asked her. She beckoned the waitress and ordered a scotch for him.

Mark looked at her. His eyes were hard and his tone was flat; he spoke like a man she hardly recognized.

"We finally got some of them. We finally started to get to the bastards," he said. "About time, huh?"

She nodded. What could she say?

"But they took some of our best men. Is Julie here?" He looked around.

"No. She went upstairs."

"Well, you may want to drop in on her later this evening."

"Is her husband wounded?"

"Dead."

The surroundings were so strange. She could never accustom herself to this hotel and the dining room, and the polite conversations, and then these announcements of battles and deaths, and everyone walking around with secret dreads and fears locked up inside. She thought of the wives who disappeared after the terrible announcements, and wives who took the rooms of the ones who had left. It was not hard for Sabine to comprehend that her husband had been to war. The signs were obvious. As she sat opposite him, she could feel his fatigue, the strain, the emotional exhaustion. His tension, the need for company, the restlessness were obvious, as were his anger at the battles and the everyday quality of the bloodshed. She could see it all in his eyes.

After dinner she did drop in on Julie, while Mark went up to their room. But Julie had checked out of the hotel. The room was already occupied by a stranger. Sabine returned to her own room to find Mark asleep, hand stretched out to her. She kissed his hand and put it under the cover, then she undressed in the bathroom and came to bed. He did not wake up. And she did not wake him.

The next evening they went out to celebrate. The fog had rolled in and they made their way down the little narrow streets toward the docks. These were the buildings that had been erected in the nineteenth century; many of them had been abandoned during the Depression. The streets were crooked, the sidewalks were more crooked still, and in the night and the fog, it was a simple thing to twist an ankle.

But to Sabine and Mark, it seemed like fun. To Sabine it was an adventure to go out anywhere to dinner. And she was with Mark. She had been lonely for him. It was good to feel his arm around her waist as they made their way through the foggy night. As for him, he was so in love with Sabine he couldn't understand what she was doing in this strange New England port, fog-bound, house-bound most of the time. She was the most glamorous woman he had ever known, the most beautiful and the most intelligent. She had made his life suddenly bloom. He didn't care that there was a war on. He didn't care that he had to go to sea, go to battle, watch men die. Yes, it was painful, but it was also necessary. But to come back to port, to have a woman like Sabine waiting for him—that made him forget everything. He treasured the Lafayette Hotel. He worshiped that narrow little room that looked out on the yard of the Rosa E. True School. And he cherished every moment he was with his woman. He held on to her, and he was able to laugh as they poked their way through the most sinister section of Portland.

The restaurant was Boone's and it was on the Fisherman's Pier. Obviously it was a seafood restaurant, but it also served (when available) great steaks. The clientele consisted of the best businessmen in Portland and Cape Elizabeth, as well as the fishermen off the boats, the ones who could still make a living in wartime. And military personnel.

They had two drinks and a good dinner. Boiled lobster with squash and hot rolls and apple pie. And they loved every minute of it. Over coffee Mark said easily, "Sabine, I love you more than anything on earth."

Her eyes began to fill with tears and she blamed it on the martinis.

"I want to tell you something," Mark said. "I never thought I was going to be a happy man. I don't know why. I never felt happy. When I was a kid, I didn't feel happy. You know my family. Everyone's very cheery, but I never was. I had some good times, but I still never realized what happiness was. I never realized how precious life could be. I didn't understand that I could value this moment, and this dinner, and look forward to going back to that crazy hotel and making love to you. And having you there. To know that you're there. It's made all the difference."

There was a kind of finality to what he was saying, as though he were closing the chapter of a book. He finished his coffee, she finished her cigarette. Others were waiting for the table. They went back to the hotel.

They had another drink at the hotel bar. There was a pianist playing requests. They sat by the piano and listened to "Deep in the Heart of Texas" and "Blues in the Night" and then, oddly enough, a song of Dieterl's, one he had written for a movie two years ago. The movie had long been forgotten, but not the tune. And Sabine and Mark had one last drink as they listened to it, and then went upstairs to their room.

His lovemaking was more urgent that night. He enfolded her, but also clung to her. She understood the feeling. There was never enough. The sensation evaporated, the moment passed, no matter how strong the desire to prolong it. The moment passed. But how wonderful it was to make love, to listen to the foghorns outside the window, in the cold New England waters, with the chill of the night far away from them, to feel one another's bodies, to answer one another's needs. They made love, and then she began to kiss him. First the forehead and then descending. She kissed his body, all of it, and felt it relax and the tension disappear; then she felt the lust rise in him again, and she kissed him there too. She took him in her mouth. She made him come in her mouth. She absorbed him totally, and they had never felt so free, either one of them, to make love to another.

They had decided, in a more rational moment, to save one of the twin beds for sleeping, and the other for making love. The bed for love was a tangle of sheets, a sweet witness to the physicality of making love. Halfway through the night, they decided to sleep and slipped into the second bed, but the hunger of their bodies soon overcame them and in the morning's light there were two wildly tangled, wonderfully rumpled beds.

Mark had gone by the time Sabine awoke, leaving her a note. He told her to leave Portland, that he would not be back. He was not sure where he was headed (even if he knew, he could not tell her), but his ship was definitely leaving port. She read the note. "I LOVE you!" he wrote at the bottom, and then a huge "Thank You!!!" and "I love you MORE."

She had already breakfasted, packed her suitcases, and looked up the schedule of the train that left for Boston, where she would take another train to New York, when the phone rang.

It was Jerry in California.

"I don't want to hear the word 'no,' " was the way he began the conversation. "I am in desperate trouble, and after all, what are friends for? There is no one out here who can write the way you can, who can write for me. They're either too drunk or too bitter. They don't know what I want. I want real humor. I want a touch that's unique . . ."

He was already sounding like a story conference.

"You want *pathos*?" Sabine asked sweetly. It was good to hear Jerry roar with laughter three thousand miles away.

"You got it, baby. Fuckin' *pathos*. How's that for a Bernard Ross imitation?"

"Wonderful. They have a habit of listening in on the hotel switchboard."

"When are you coming out? I'll make the reservations."

"You really want me?"

"No, sweetheart—"

"I hate that word."

"I've gone Hollywood."

"Then I don't want to come out."

"Save me. From going Hollywood. Sabine, honestly, what are you doing? Can you come?"

"As a matter of fact, I can. Mark won't be coming back for some time. So I am—available."

"Well, I'm sorry, you know, about Mark. But I'm glad for *us*. Come out next week. We'll have fun. You'll see. And I'll get you fabulous money."

She liked the sound of that. As she put down the receiver, she decided that if she was going to go Hollywood, *that* was the way to do it; first class.

Chapter Eighteen

The young man who was calling out her name in Los Angeles's Union Station was blond and gorgeous. He waved at her with easy familiarity.

"Sabine! Over here! Sabine!"

She went to him. Who was he?

"I'd have known you anywhere. My name is Gregg. Two g's. Like it? It sets me off, don't you think? Anyway, Jerry sent me to pick you up. If he'd come in here, he'd have been mobbed. It's hard being famous. Where are your bags?"

Sabine had two suitcases. Gregg had commandeered four redcaps.

"This is it?" he asked incredulously. She nodded. Gregg tipped all four porters, though only one of them took the suitcases out to the automobile. A chauffeur was sitting, waiting, the motor idling.

"I shouldn't have said 'bags,'" Gregg said. "I should have said 'luggage.' Gee, I think I'll never learn."

Sabine had an idea Gregg had learned too much already.

"We'll take Miss Sabine home," Gregg instructed the chauffeur, and then joined Sabine in the back seat.

From the station the chauffeur drove out Wilshire Boulevard. There were many green lawns, surrounding pink and yellow bungalows. Then came a district of mansions and a golf course. Then more bungalows. To the right, in the cloudless sky, Sabine could see mountains, and snow on the tops of the mountains.

"What are they?" she asked Gregg.

"Mountains," he answered.

The answer didn't quite satisfy her. But Gregg's information about Los Angeles was rather spotty.

"What's this section?" she asked as they crossed Santa Monica Boulevard.

"It's Santa Monica Boulevard," he answered, glancing at the street sign.

"How long have you been here?" she asked him.

"Almost six months. It sure beats Detroit."

Sabine felt she could agree with that.

They crossed another wide thoroughfare, heading up into the hills.

"Sunset Boulevard," Sabine said.

"How did you know?" Gregg asked, impressed.

"I read the street sign."

"Oh. We're almost home."

Home? Who was he? What did he mean, home?

"Do you work for Jerry?" she asked.

"I answer his fan mail. I help out."

Suddenly there were huge pines, a whole street shadowed by gigantic beautiful pine trees. She saw a brick wall, an ornate iron gate, glimpsed a wide expanse of lawn behind it. A gorgeous flowerbed, beautifully patterned, red and orange, vivid yellow, sky blue—with flowers she could not begin to name—stretched out alongside the lawn. Mme Levinsky's small flowerboxes came to mind. She shut them out. This was California.

The iron gate opened after a signal from a buzzer. The chauffeur drove down an avenue of tall manicured cypresses. Gregg was watching her face, hoping she would be impressed. If it had cost her her life Sabine would have shown nothing. They arrived at the gravel driveway in front of the portico, and Jerry was there to greet her. He was dressed in chino pants and wore no shirt. His feet were in sandals. He was very tanned.

"Oh God, I'm too late!" Sabine rushed out of the limousine and threw her arms around him.

"What do you mean?" Jerry said.

"You've already gone and done it. I'm too late. All this expense for nothing!"

"What, my angel! What is it?"

"You've gone Hollywood." Sabine waved at the grand cypresses.

"You want them out? They'll be replaced tomorrow." Jerry soothed her.

Gregg could make no sense of this. What were they talking about? Replace those cypresses? It would cost a fortune.

Gone Hollywood? Who wouldn't go Hollywood, given the chance? The things he wouldn't do, just to go Hollywood like this. The things he had already done. Ah, thank God he was young and good-looking. He counted the people who stopped to stare at him. He counted both the women and the men. It was almost equal. He didn't care, as long as his looks attracted the attention. He knew he was going to make it. Enviously, he looked at Jerry. What did he have? It wasn't looks. There was no comparison between Jerry, whose nose was too long and whose body was too thin, and Gregg's spectacular handsomeness. He looked at Sabine. She was beautiful, she was really a knock-out. But she would never make it here. Gregg had never seen anyone who looked like her. So that meant she wouldn't make it. He couldn't imagine Sabine modeling bathing suits on diving boards. She wasn't one of those starlets. He knew plenty of them. As a matter of fact, he had gone out with a couple when he first reached Hollywood, before he met Jerry, when he was still parking cars at Ciro's. He had seen some of those girls reach the pinnacle. A spread in *Life* magazine. A studio contract. But, Gregg, was not with a studio. Jerry never allowed him in the studio. He wasn't even allowed to call Jerry at the studio unless it was with an important message. He couldn't call just to talk.

The chauffeur took two suitcases from the trunk and cast a malevolent glance at Gregg. But Gregg did not carry baggage. No more. Luggage, goddamnit—he did not carry *luggage*.

"Come on, darling, what do you want?" Jerry was saying to Sabine. "Take off your clothes. Have a swim. You want some orange juice? Have you eaten anything on the train? How about a steak?"

"You have steak?"

"Of course. What do you want? Steak and eggs? That's very western. A drink? Some vodka with the orange juice? Gregg, tell the cook to prepare something for us. We'll be down by the pool."

He took Sabine by the arm and led her down a flagstone path bordered by hibiscus.

"Do you believe this? In November? Isn't it gorgeous? How do you love it so far?"

"I'm speechless," Sabine confessed.

"Good, darling. Just don't stay that way."

The pool was azure blue. It sparkled. It blinded. There were some yellow and white canvas cabanas on the other side.

"Take a plunge. I never use it. I hate swimming," Jerry said.

"What do you mean, take a plunge? I don't have a suit."

"It doesn't matter. Nothing matters here. It's wonderful. It's free. No one can see you. Except me. Are you still as gorgeous?"

She found herself stripping off her clothes, ridding herself of the gloomy, leaden-skied, war-conscious East Coast, and she stood naked in front of Jerry.

"Oh, God, if only I wanted to," he said, "you would be the one."

She plunged into the pool, shocked to find it was warm.

"You want it colder? There's a thermostat." Jerry rose to adjust it.

"No. Forget it," Sabine told him, and stretched out, let her body laze along the gleaming sides of the pool. Nothing in life had ever been so luxurious. She was washing away four days on a train, along with the grime of the red brick, grubby New England seaport she had been stationed in. Yes, that's what she considered it. A tour of duty. Not because of Mark. Because she had been a good wife, a dutiful wife. But she had done nothing about her own life.

And she swam and could feel the heat of the sun as her arms came out of the water. She turned on her back and floated with her eyes closed for a minute.

When she opened them, Gregg was standing by the poolside holding a terrycloth robe. His eyes managed to take in the swell of her breasts, the shapeliness of her body before they traveled to her face.

"Will you need this?" he asked. He was looking at her, and Sabine never made a mistake about intentions. She was very clear about Gregg's intentions, but confused about his relationship with Jerry.

"Just leave the robe there. Thanks," she told Gregg.

"Gregg, go play tennis," Jerry said sharply from the other side of the pool. He was sitting with a script in a lounge chair. When he talked to Sabine, his voice changed. "Angel, your breakfast is here. Come, sit here beside me."

Sabine emerged from the pool and wrapped the terrycloth

robe around her. Her hair was dripping wet, but her body had never felt so alive. She was ravenous. Of course she was. She was always hungry, and Jerry knew her only too well.

"I had them make lots," he said as he watched her plunge in. The steak was thick, seared on the outside, just the right shade of pink on the inside. The orange juice was like nectar. The fried eggs had been cooked in real butter. There was toast. There was coffee and a big bowl of sugar. She looked at it all, and at the estate, and the swimming pool, and the blue sky, and the beautiful pine trees, and then she looked at Jerry.

"Don't you know there's a war going on?" she asked, making a lunge at the steak.

"Fortunately, only at the studio. It's all in the scripts. Otherwise you don't have time to notice. You get up at five and are on the lot at seven. You get home at six. It's dinner, go over lines, and time for bed."

"It's a *Modern Screen* existence," Sabine marveled. "The fan magazines tell the whole truth and nothing but the truth."

"You got it." Jerry looked at her. "Everybody's so excited that you're coming out. Dieterl wants to have a party."

"That would be nice."

"And I suppose you have to go to Bernard Ross's. He's planning something for next Sunday. It's one of those all-day just-drop-by affairs."

"What does that mean?"

"It means you drop by, you play tennis, you swim, you eat, you get drunk, sometimes you get laid, and you go home. I'm mad about Gregg, by the way." Jerry threw that in, wetting his finger to turn a page of the script he was reading.

"I guess I'm glad then," Sabine said.

"Yes, be glad. Please. It means a lot to me."

"Are you in love with him?"

"That's a very East Coast question."

"Well, what I meant was—Jerry, look at me, this is serious. I'm asking it more for myself than for you. Do you know what love is?"

Jerry looked at her for a long time, and then said, "That's even *more* East Coast. I really must say, the one thing I've learned out here is that whatever you have, enjoy it while you have it. It's a very short season here," he added, and then gestured heavenward. "Except for the weather. That's the same all year round."

The drink, the sun, the unfamiliarity of the surroundings made Sabine talkative.

"I think I'm in love. I think I always have been."

"With Mark?" Jerry looked up from the script.

"No. With Matt."

There was silence and then Jerry said, "Oh, yes. Well, I was too. Probably still am."

"You never . . ."

"Went to bed with him? Never fear. He had no eyes for me. Ah, but the number of times in my dreams that I imagined him making love to me. No. My making love to him. I was always the much more active one. Tell me, what was it like when he made love to you?"

"I don't want to tell you that," Sabine said. She backed off, and Jerry could sense it. He lightened up.

"Oh, well. Another time. When we know each other better."

"What are you reading?" Sabine asked him.

"Shit. I can't take it." He threw the script into the pool. "Don't worry. Somebody will take it out. I'll say I cried tears on every page." He lit a cigarette. "There's another war going on. And it's between the studio and myself, you see. They are sure—I mean Bernie Rosen is sure, if you know what I mean—what the public wants, and what it wants from me. And guess what? I don't want to do that anymore. I think I can do something better. More interesting. And I want you to help me."

"You have informed Bernie of all this—that you have brought me out here to do battle?"

"Of course not. I know Bernie better than that. And so do you. No, you are out here, because you are a talented writer, a New York writer, which means something. You will be brought in on story conferences, so you see how everything works, and how incredibly stupid practically everyone is. You will work on a script, I don't care what it is, or who it is with. And then, in six months, I will start. And you know me when I start. In that time I want us to come up with an idea. I want to get out of this rut of being the *schlemiel*. Once, please once, I don't want to be wacky. I would like to be in something that is not about the war. I can't stand any more

war comedies about the housing situation, the WACS, the
new recruits. And they'll never give me a chance at the *heavy*
stuff." He was up and pacing now.

Sabine gave a little sigh. Nothing was paradise.

And then it was the afternoon, and there was a get-to-
gether at Jerry's. Sabine had time only to see her room,
which was large and looked out at the pines, before people
started drifting in. Some of them had names she did not
know, but all of them seemed to know her, or know about
her. There was a very pleasant singer named Margaret Whit-
ing who was going to be married to a dark and slender actor
named Eythe. She had a sister named Barbara. Their father
was a songwriter. She was just making some records herself.
There was another songwriter named Johnny Mercer, kind of
Southern and volatile, and she liked him immediately. There
were some writers, she could tell because they looked glum
and sounded caustic and wore sweaters even in the heat of the
afternoon, as though they were perpetually chilled by the
industry that nourished them.

There were a number of stars, too, names she did recognize. The female stars were initially rather haughty and the
male stars curious. Was this new turf to be explored? But she
found Alexis Smith to be funny and not at all the ice maiden
she was always playing and Judy Garland was much more sophisticated than on screen. Judy seemed to have come with
someone but he was soon lost in the crowd. Then there was a
pianist, and in the last of the dazzling afternoon, with everyone a little buzzed from the drinks and the sunshine, they
gathered indoors and sang. They parodied one another, and
parodied one another's movies, and nobody seemed to mind.
In the midst of this, Sabine found herself a little unnerved.
There was truly so much talent, such energy around. These
were sharp people who had grown up in this territory. Some
of the songs that they were singing had been written by the
men in the room, and even as they were singing them here,
there were soldiers in barracks who were whistling the same
songs, and at the bar of the Lafayette Hotel in Portland,
Maine, some lonesome naval officer was requesting the same
tune. All over the world, the songs that filled the empty barracks and fighter squadrons, the bars and joints, USOs and
jukeboxes in small Southern towns—all came from places
like this, like Jerry's living room.

Parties broke up early in Hollywood. Monday was a work morning and everyone worked at the studio. Whatever studio it was, it was called "the studio." By seven they had all left, and the sun had disappeared behind those mountains, whatever they were called (she never did learn the name of them) and the cook-butler cleared the room and cleaned the ashtrays. Gregg helped, a little reluctantly.

"You want a fire?" Jerry asked her. "You want to snuggle, angel? And we can talk about everyone!"

"No, Jerry, I don't think so. I really want to go to bed."

"Oh, thank God you said that, because I am dead on my feet, and I have to be up at five to be Robin Hood by seven in the morning."

"Why Robin Hood?"

"It's part of one of those star-spangled films they put together where everyone does a little routine. Story: Sailor gets leave, visits studio, meets famous stars who then perform for him and his buddies before they go overseas. Don't ask me what Robin Hood is doing in the middle of this. Ask Bernie. By the way, you will come to the studio, won't you?"

"Yes, whenever you want me."

"I want you there on Tuesday. I have already set it up with Bernard. A writer's conference. Oooh," he yawned and stretched, "we're going to have fun."

Sabine went up to her room. Someone had unpacked for her. She found the dresses hung in the closets, the sweaters and underwear put away in drawers. In the bathroom there was cold cream, a new brush, a comb. She took a shower and joined the ranks of the California clean. There would never be too many showers. You could never be clean enough. When she finished the shower, she brushed her hair and put on her bathrobe.

Outside she heard strange sounds. Crickets? This was all foreign to her. But how extraordinary, the luxury of it. She had read a few pages of a book when a knock sounded discreetly at the door.

"Come in," she said. Gregg opened the door. He was also in a bathrobe, which was tied loosely in the front. He evidently had just finished his shower, because his hair was still wet. God, she thought, he looks about seventeen. How old is he, anyway? The all-American boy next door.

"I wondered if you were having any trouble sleeping," he said, smiling at her. She knew that smile.

"No," she said.

"Some people do when they first get out here," he said, loosening the tie to his bathrobe.

"No. As a matter of fact, I was just about to turn out the light."

"Well, if you ever do have trouble sleeping, just call me." He grinned at her likably, and then let his bathrobe fall open so that she could see his body. He had, of course, a beautiful body.

"Good night," Sabine said.

"G'night," he said, and closed the door. Sabine lay in the darkness and wondered. Where was he going? To Jerry's bed? Or had he come from Jerry's bed? And did he have a bed of his own?

Everyone told Sabine where she should live. Everyone had preferences. There were beach houses near Santa Monica. Those were lovely in the summer and at least ten degrees cooler, but too far if one had to commute to the studios. There was a trolley car that traveled the length of Santa Monica, but Sabine decided she did not want to be that far out. Then there were the hills above Sunset. These held estates like Jerry's—and other estates, she discovered, bigger than Jerry's. There was an old section of Los Angeles near Paramount. Lovely houses. Truly Spanish architecture. And there were wild crazy little places in the Hollywood Hills, with cul de sacs and hundreds of steps leading down from the street.

For the time being she stayed with Jerry. And she did as she was told. She had an appointment on Tuesday with Jerry and Bernard Ross. She had no idea what to expect.

She met Jerry at his bungalow on the lot and he had lunch sent in. Then he asked her the time.

She looked at her watch. "It's ten to two."

"Are you *sure?*" he asked.

"Well, more or less. I may be five minutes off."

"No, I want to be sure." He called out to one of the assistant directors to find out the exact time. The exact time was seven minutes to two.

"Thank you," Jerry said, and turned to Sabine. "We have ten minutes."

"But the appointment with Bernie is at two."

"That's what he *says*. But if you get there at two, you have to wait fifteen minutes. That's what he does. I don't play that game. So I wait until it's two o'clock and then I start for his office. Is it two yet?"

"No, it's not two yet. It's now three minutes to two."

"Then we have three minutes to kill. You play gin rummy?"

"What's the matter with you?"

"Nothing's the matter with me. I just don't like to waste time."

Precisely at two o'clock they left his bungalow.

"Phone Mr. Ross's office and tell him we're on our way," Jerry shouted triumphantly to his dresser.

They made their way through the myriad paths between sound stages, dodging bicycles and side-stepping Roman warriors. There was a neat little square, resembling a French village, and it was here that most of the executives were housed. On either side were the offices of the assistant (and lesser) producers. In the main building were the executive offices. The head offices were on the second floor. Jerry dawdled ascending the stairs, and arrived in Bernard Ross's outer office at exactly two-fifteen.

"Tell Mr. Ross we can see him now," Jerry said sweetly.

"I'll tell him you are here," said the secretary just as sweetly, and informed Mr. Ross that they were waiting.

"He will only be a few minutes," the secretary reported back to them. Jerry's eyes grew black with anger.

"We had a two o'clock appointment."

"Well, I understand, but you see, you were delayed, and Mr. Ross squeezed somebody else in," the secretary smiled.

At exactly two-thirty Bernard Ross opened the door, arms outstretched.

"Sabine, sweetheart! I never thought we'd snare you out here. Gimme kiss, gimme kiss!" He pointed to his mouth. She kissed him on the cheek.

"Come in, come in. God, how good it is to see you two together. Jerry, how've you been? The last movie was fantastic. The grosses are piling up all over the country."

They were in the office of the second most important man

in Hollywood. There was a great deal of leather. Leather couches. Leather chairs. Sabine was on the lookout for saddles and riding crops. Hunting prints hung on the walls.

Bernard consulted his watch.

"I'm sorry I couldn't give you as much time as I wanted to, but you were delayed."

"I don't like to be kept waiting," Jerry said icily.

"Who does?" Bernard smiled at him. "I believe we made the appointment for two o'clock. It is now two-thirty. That's no way to win a war."

"What am I here for, Bernard?" Sabine asked, going straight to the boss.

"To give us some class. I read the reviews of your little show. Wonderful! Wonderful! Too bad the timing was off."

"We made money."

"You coulda made a pisspot full if it hadn't been for the war."

"Well, there you have it. There is a war. What am I supposed to do about it?"

Bernard pointed a finger at Sabine.

"That's what I like about you. Directness. To the point. And a knowledge about world politics. As you know, we are not in this war alone."

Bernard was beginning a lecture. Sabine looked to Jerry for advice. Was he serious? Jerry avoided her gaze. He was watching the peasants down in the village square under Bernard Ross's window.

"The time has come for our industry to do what it can for the Soviet Union. We feel—and there have been several meetings about this in Washington—that arms, munitions, supplies are not enough. The American people must feel a solidarity with our Russian brothers. The heroic stand at Stalingrad. The siege of Leningrad. The burnt earth policy. These are a heroic people, and their story has to be told." Bernard Ross paused. "Your people were Russian, weren't they?" he asked Sabine.

"Bernie, they were Jews who were driven out by the Cossacks."

"Close enough," said Bernard. "You know the strength, the will of these people. You can sympathize with the invaders. And the oppressed. I know you can, Sabine. You are a sensitive person. You are sensitive to these people. I want you to

meet on Friday with a group. There will already be an out-
line. I want you to be the adviser. I want you to give this
project class and scope, the breadth of the Russian steppes.
The meeting will be at ten in the morning, and there will be
some famous names there. But don't be awed. One thing I
have found in this industry: names are nothing."

He turned his attention to Jerry.

"Now, Jerry, my boy, you have problems?"

"No, you have problems."

"Me, I never have problems. I *solve* problems."

"Then what are you going to do with this piece of shit?"
Jerry was holding a battered script in his hand. There were
blue pages and red pages, yellow and white pages.

"I am going to have it fixed for you, Jerry. That is my job.
That is why I arranged for this meeting. You know Ruta
White, and Jim Hinckley. You couldn't ask for better writers
than that. They are both out here now, and I have put them
back to work on it. I know that the same fanciful byplay that
made them the darlings of Broadway will solve all your problems. Shall we join them? They're in the next room."

He led them into a library. The books were bound in
leather. On closer scrutiny, Sabine observed that they were
not really books, but screenplays that the studio had produced over the years, now encased in morocco leather. A
little birdlike woman was sitting, knitting, under an Oscar. A
balding man wearing a business suit and a red bow tie was
seated in the opposite corner.

"Ruta, Jim, this is Sabine Abramowitz. I don't believe I
have to give everyone's credits," Bernard said, and then
proceeded to.

"I am not happy," said Jerry when Bernard was finished.

"What's the matter now?" Jim Hinckley sighed.

"First of all, I don't know anyone who would talk like
this."

"The Marx Brothers did," Ruta said quietly, knitting.

"How do you know?"

"Because we got it from them."

"You mean," Jerry said angrily, "you stole this from a
Marx Brothers movie?"

"Of course not." Ruta never stopped knitting. "Harpo was
over the other night for dinner. Oh listen, if it's such a big

thing we'll take it out. I mean, it was funny when Harpo said it."

"But Harpo never talks in his movies."

"I've always felt that was the one thing wrong with the Marx Brothers films," Ruta answered quietly.

"Okay," Bernard said, anxious about his next meeeting. "Can we go through this scene, line by line? Here is the rewrite. I want it shot tomorrow, so that means it must be perfect in"—again he consulted his watch—"twenty minutes. Now, Jerry, read through it."

"Okay," Jerry said. He was holding a red pencil like a vindictive sword. "First line, shit. Second and third lines, shittier. Fourth line, okay. By comparison. The girl's speech, I couldn't care less. The rest of the speeches on that page, *really* crap. The next page I have no complaints."

"You have no lines," Jim pointed out.

"That's why I have no complaints," Jerry smiled.

"The last page?" Ruta asked.

"The last page I like," Jerry admitted, and Ruta smiled over at Jim Hinckley. Obviously she had written that page.

"Okay, kids, you have fifteen minutes," Bernard said, and rose to go. In two minutes he would be late for his next appointment. Jerry and Sabine rose also.

"I thought you said twenty minutes," Jim Hinckley protested.

"That was almost five minutes ago. If you need any typing done, call Eileen. She'll do it or send someone over from the typing pool."

Bernard shut the door on Ruta and Jim. This was the Ruta White whose wit had terrorized half of Manhattan's intelligentsia, the half that was sober enough to understand what she was saying. And the Jim Hinckley who had produced three novels during the Thirties that were still studied in college English courses. Both were now trapped behind that door, on orders to satisfy Jerry's whims. And Bernard's fancies.

"See you Friday," Bernard said to Sabine and Jerry. He held out his hand to Sabine. They were back in his office now. "By the way, you haven't met my wife Carol yet. How about next Sunday? Just drop in. There'll be a few people you'd like to know."

"Just a minute, Bernie," Sabine said. "We haven't talked money."

"I don't talk money."

"With me you talk money. I want five thousand a week."

"Are you crazy? Faulkner doesn't get five thousand a week."

"As you say, names mean nothing here. I want five thousand a week. To go through what these poor people are going through, you have to make it worth my while."

"Well, I can't afford that. Suppose the other writers found out?"

"They won't find out from me."

"Nobody's ever been paid that much money."

"Then it's because nobody asked."

"You are a bitch, you know that?"

"That's right. I guess that's exactly what I am."

"All right. A year's contract."

"Five thousand whether I'm working or not."

"Jesus!" Bernard said. "I'll make sure you're working."

"You can give the contract to Jerry's lawyer to look over before the weekend." She turned to Jerry. "You *do* have a lawyer, don't you?"

"Yes," Jerry said solemnly. "And Bernard certainly knows who he is."

"Perfect. Bernard, send the contracts there," Sabine said, and then added, "And I would love to meet the woman you married."

"Carol is a doll," Bernard said, ushering them out the door. He slapped Jerry on the back. "Those changes should be back from mimeo by four o'clock. Guaranteed."

"And if I don't like them?" Jerry asked.

"We'll get new lines. Or new writers. Maybe these guys aren't right for you."

"We'll see."

Sabine and Jerry walked down the staircase and out into the brilliant afternoon sunshine. They walked sedately across the village square that resembled part of a lost France. They walked sedately because they thought they might be watched by Bernard, but once they were out of sight, behind the shelter of one of the huge sound stages, they burst into laughter.

"Do you realize I have never written a script in my life?" Sabine shouted. "And I'm getting five thousand dollars a week. Hooray for Hollywood!" she sang.

"Outrageous!" Jerry shrieked. "How did you do it?"

"After what I saw you do to those poor writers?"

"I would never do that to you."

"I'm not working for you. I'm working for him."

"But five thousand dollars? That's almost as much as I'm making."

"Bernard considers me his lucky piece."

"What?"

"It's a private joke. It has to do with poker. Where are you going now?"

"Back to the set. I have to work. I'll meet you at home tonight." He squeezed her. "I told you, we are going to have fun!"

"Uh-huh," Sabine said. On the way back to Lexington Drive she thought about Ruta White and those knitting needles. Was she knitting to cover the fact that her hands were shaking? Sabine couldn't believe it—there was no protest when whole paragraphs were cut, not even when the writers were told their work was shit.

She pitied them. She despised them.

She was twenty-six years old.

The story conference on Friday morning was conducted by Bernard Rosen. Bernard *Ross*. She must remember that.

Across from Sabine sat a man with a leather jacket and a cigar and a half-smiling face. Brecht. He was going to be one of the writers. He didn't speak English, but that was no problem. Next to him was a German writer who did speak English. He murmured translations into Brecht's ear as Bernard Ross outlined his vision of the film. Sometimes Bernard waited for the translation. Sometimes he did not bother.

"This is an important film," Bernard announced. "Not only to us but to our allies, the gallant Russian troops. What this film should depict is the extraordinary will and strength of the Russian people, the bravery of the average citizen. Also the bestiality of the Germans, of course. It is our feeling here at the studio that we have the opportunity to bring together in understanding, two cultures, the two most powerful nations in the world.

"Now for details. Start happily. The year is 1940. A bonfire, a hayride, a fall festival. The harvest is in. There is a dance. We see the lovers—"

One of the writers interrupted. "The Communists and the Nazis were still allied in the fall of 1940."

"Never say that. Never say 'Communist,' please. We are not talking about Communists. We are talking about the gallant Soviet struggle against the forces of Nazi Germany. But the other point is well taken. Begin in the spring, late spring of 1941. The crops have just been sown. We see apple blossoms. There is a dance. The peasants smile happily because there will be a record harvest. Life is good. Our lovers join the dance."

"Excuse, but Brecht does not understand. Why are lovers dancing?"

"Because they are happy," Bernard explained carefully.

"Brecht asks why, if they are lovers, they are not making love?"

"Tell him this is not one of your foreign films. Lovers dance. Period."

Everyone nodded. Brechit lit a cigar. Sabine lit a cigarette. Brecht smiled across at her.

"Pretty," he said.

"Thank you," Bernard said. "Now! I want carnage next. I want slaughter. I want the American people to see what could happen to them if the Nazi hordes ever invaded Iowa. I want barns burned. Then the resistance stiffening before Moscow. Everyone joins in. Not just the farmers. Ballet dancers, too. They should all hole up in a cave. But make sure it's a clean cave. Make a home out of it. I want pots and pans. I want earthernware. Separate rooms for the men and the women. Separate beds."

Everyone was silent, nodding.

"This has urgent priority. Straight from the U.S. government. This is to prepare us all for the second front. Now, I expect a rough draft in two weeks."

Brecht's interpreter asked, "How does one shoot the battle before Moscow?"

Bernard was quick with the answer. "Tell him not to worry. We have footage on Moscow."

Again the interpreter: "Brecht would like to know if you have footage on happy peasants?"

Brecht was not at the next story conference. Sabine went to work on the script, totally bewildered.

Carol Ross was, as Bernard had said, a "doll." She spoke in a piping doll's voice, small and penetrating. She was very proud of Bernard. She was very pleased to meet Sabine. She was very excited about the new film, whatever it was. She was very happy to be in Holmby Hills. She was very sorry to hear about Sabine's grandmother. (Who had told her?) She was very excited about her new house, and would Sabine like to see it? Sabine saw the golf tournament trophies that Bernard had won and the library, which had a great number of pictures on the walls of the hundred most important people in Hollywood. Sabine saw the lovely bedroom, with the huge bed and taffeta ruffles on the curtains and the bedspread. Carol loved each room. She was small and dark, and her eyes reminded Sabine of Gisela's. But then, everything reminded her of Gisela, and Freddy. She made a fool of herself when she met Bernard's son Harold, who was about the age Freddy would be by now, and very grown-up, shaking hands and nodding gravely. Sabine found her eyes welling with tears. She went to the powder room. There were no bathrooms in Carol's house, but there were twenty powder rooms, it seemed.

Out on the lawn she met Bernard. He was inspecting the group of guests, mingling happily on yet another beautifully manicured lawn on yet another beautifully sunny Sunday.

Bernard showed concern. "What's the matter? You're not happy here?" he asked.

"No, it's not that. It was meeting your son . . ."

As usual, Bernard misunderstood. "You writers. All the same. So sensitive. Your script got to you. But I shouldn't ask you how you do it. So long as you do it."

She left the party early, writing Mark a letter when she got home. She was very good about writing, even if it was mostly California chit-chat. What else could she write about? His family? She never heard from them, or, out here, about them. The war? He needed no reminders. She wrote about Bernard, and how funny he was, but how powerful he was too. She wrote about the detachment she felt, living in California.

She was into her second page when the phone rang. It was Matt Ryan calling from London. She did not believe she was listening to his voice, and then she did not believe what she was hearing.

"Sabine, I have bad news. Mark has been injured."

"But that's impossible. I just got a letter from him."

"He's in the hospital, Sabine. If I can swing it, can you come over?"

"To England? Now? Of course. Yes."

"Then I'll call you back. Don't leave."

She hung up the phone and found she was trembling. How deceiving feelings can be. She had thought she was numb, that she no longer had feelings, but that was not true. Her hand shook. It was getting dark, and she sat in the dark, too tired to switch on a light.

When Matt did call back, it was with instructions and numbers that she had to write down. A car would pick her up and take her to a military installation. She would fly across the country, and then to Newfoundland, and then to England. She had a day to pack.

She left Hollywood without informing anyone. *Storm Over Stalingrad* would happen with or without her slight contribution. She wrote Bernard a note explaining the situation, but she did not mail it until she was ready to leave the house. And she left Jerry a letter—he had gone away for the weekend and would not be back until Tuesday.

The doorbell rang. She pressed the appropriate buttons and saw an automobile with military insignia on it roll down the gravel drive. On her way out she grabbed three books, as though England might be bombed out of reading matter.

The entire journey seemed to be colored gray. Airports. The weather. Planes. Camouflage. Faces, On the stop in Newfoundland she descended like a sleepwalker and made her way to a makeshift shack, where she drank a cup of gray coffee without tasting it. When departure was announced, she boarded the plane like an automaton.

Over the Atlantic, someone evidently covered her with a military greatcoat; the temperature was freezing. She did not remember. Time passed without meaning, and then the plane made its descent and landed, and when the door opened, she looked out on England.

Gray again. There were gray shacks, military installations, wire fences. In a trance she walked down the steps and across the runway and then Matt Ryan's arms were around her.

Sabine did not look up. She only wanted to feel his warmth. If she looked at him, she might see that he had aged, that he had suffered, and that he was lonely. "Don't change," was what she was saying to herself. How well she understood

that phrase now. Please, let nothing change. If we hold our
breaths, nothing will. Like a photograph, we will remain constant—constantly in love, constantly happy, constantly confident of the future.

"Sabine?" His hand was under her chin, lifting her face.
She was forced to look at him. Nothing had changed. The
look in his eye was the same loving look, only more aware of
time now, the preciousness of it, the precarious amount of
time that is called life. She looked at him and realized how
much of her life had disappeared. Glenrocks gone, her father
gone, her former life gone, most of what might have been a
girlhood gone. But Matt was still here. He kissed her. It was
the kiss of two survivors, both glad that the other was still on
this earth.

Matt took her bag and led her to the jeep. "Not fancy. But
the trip isn't long," he said.

"Where is Mark?"

"In the field hospital near here. Do you want to change or
rest—or anything?"

"No, I want to see him."

"Sabine—"

"Don't say anything."

"I have to. Listen to me. It isn't just that Mark has been
injured."

"What do you mean?"

"Sabine. He lost both legs in the explosion."

"Will he be all right?" What an asinine question.

"No."

She could no longer comprehend anything. The man who
had cheerfully gone to war, who had cheerfully abandoned
everything, had been struck down in some peaceful little English hamlet. The place was as far removed from the great
battles, the howitzers and huge bombers, as a Christmas card.
And still a bomb had found him.

Matt was looking at her closely. "Can you take it?"

"Yes. Will you be here?"

"For a day or so. I will be here as often as I can."

They reached the hospital, which was no more than another series of one-story wooden barracks.

Inside, Sabine was introduced to a series of uniforms. Doctors? Military aides? She was assured a room at the White
Hart, an inn in the village. She would have to surrender her

ration books. What ration books? She would have to be issued ration books, which she would then surrender.

"Where is my husband?" she asked.

"In here," a uniformed man answered pleasantly and opened a door.

What once had been Mark Cardozo was lying in the bed, occupying only half its length. It was obvious he had no legs. The sheets were hospital smooth. The face that once had been warm with vitality, and kind and handsome, was now the color of the pillow. Gray. The world was entirely gray. His eyes were glazed with pain. Would he recognize her?

And then he smiled and she could feel her heart break. It was a phrase she had never believed in before, but something happened to her then that she would never quite recover from.

Did she smile back? She wasn't certain. He spoke her name as though it were the name of God. And she walked quickly to the part of a man who was lying on his bed. And kissed his cheek. She could smell the rot on him. Kissed his mouth then, defiantly. He put arms around her, arms that were too weak to hold on.

"Glad you came. Love you." He measured out words because there were none to waste.

"Yes, Mark, I'm here. When you're stronger I'm going to take you home. In the meantime I'm coming here every day and I'm going to yell at everyone who doesn't bring you what you need. So don't worry about anything."

"Love you," he repeated.

"Sweet-talker." She smiled at him. "Now, I want to meet all the people I'm going to have to yell at. I'll be back in a few minutes."

She found her way around, noted which orderlies changed the linen and which nurses dispensed the medication. She could see how impossibly understaffed they were. Each cubicle contained its own private horror.

After two weeks she was able to pass from one cubicle to another, listening to the screams of pain without flinching.

In those two weeks she learned to changed Mark's bandages and to cope with the incredibly foul odor of his rotting body. She learned to dissemble, to make light conversation to keep him from having to make any conversation at all. She read to him, even when his glazed eyes signified he was no longer conscious. She felt her voice assured him comfort. She managed his bedpan and cleaned up his excrement.

She spent the rest of her time in the tiny room at the White Hart, where she never truly slept, out of fear of nightmares. Often, she lay there in the late afternoon, after she had returned from the hospital, needing a change of clothes, smelling the stench of war and its wounded on herself, wondering whether she was dreaming this.

For two weeks she performed her functions and watched Mark grow weaker. But the light in his eyes when he saw her continued to grow stronger, and she passed more and more of her time by his side. Between the shots of morphine, she improvised stories about their future to distract him.

One gloriously sunny afternoon, as she was chattering away, he looked at her and said softly, "I know. I know." He said it with such finality that she found her hands shaking with terror. She looked at her watch, hoping it was time for his shot, but it was not scheduled for another hour. She cursed the British, cursed hospital schedules, cursed rigidity, and renewed her story, rushing the words a bit.

"I have thought about us," she said, "and I have decided what we shall do in six months. Because in six months you will be out of this damned hospital and we will be back in America. I think we should buy a farm somewhere close to Boston so that you can start your law practice. Boston has been a good town to us. Remember how we met in Boston? The first time I was ever drunk? Oh, you were so gallant—I *think*. Were you gallant? You were always that way. Remember the drive back to New York that weekend? What we will *do,* we will buy one of those old Colonial houses with a center hallway and run around the countryside picking up antiques for next to nothing. In the summer we can go sailing."

The pain was contorting his face.

"Go on. I like it," he managed to say.

"Let's see. I'll badger your mother into giving us one or two of her paintings. And we will entertain, but not too often and not too many people at one time. And in the summer we will take a month's vacation because we will be terribly rich."

"We *are* terribly rich," he laughed, but he was unable to keep the bitterness out of his voice. Sabine struggled to continue.

"We will go to the compound in Maine and stay with your

family and then in two years—it'll give us time to be together—"

"Please." He interrupted her, because he could not bear the
pain any longer.

"I'll be right back," she promised him and left the room,
careful not to run. But the moment she was in the corridor
she raced to find the nurse on duty.

"My husband needs his shot. Now."

"The name, madam?" The nurse was very cool.

"Cardozo."

The nurse consulted her records. "No. I'm afraid not for
another hour."

"Don't tell me another hour. He's in pain. Give him his
shot now."

"I'm afraid that is impossible, madam."

"Why impossible?"

"There is always the danger of addiction."

Sabine thought she must be losing her mind.

"Addiction? He's dying and you're worried he might turn
into a dope fiend? He's dying and he's in pain and give him
his fucking shot, you lousy bitch!"

"Please control yourself!" So precise, so correct, the re-
proving voice.

"I won't control myself. I will sit right here and I will
scream until one of you takes care of him."

"You *may not* disturb the other patients."

"I don't give a fuck about the other patients. Give my husband his shot!" The tears of rage were running down her
face. The fracas brought a doctor.

"Here, here, what's this?" he asked.

"This woman demands we give her husband more morphine than is indicated," the nurse said righteously.

"Give him the shot!" Sabine heard herself screaming.
"Give him the fucking shot. What does it matter? He's dying."

The doctor grabbed her firmly. "Stop that!"

"I'll stop when you give him the shot."

"This is intolerable behavior."

"Give him the *shot!*"

"I assure you this situation will not reoccur."

"Give him the shot!"

The doctor made his decision. Turning to the nurse, he asked in a clipped tone, "Room number?"

"168."

Briskly now, physician, nurse, and Sabine walked down the barracks corridor, past the makeshift cubicles. They approached Mark's door. Sabine became suspicious.

"You have the morphine?"

"Yes, we have everything, Mrs. Cardozo." The physician was white-lipped with fury.

They opened the door. Mark was lying in the bed, but his face was no longer contorted with pain. His face no longer belonged to him. He had died, and in the agony of his dying his sphincter muscles had let go, so that he had died in his own excrement. He had died while she was screaming outside in the corridor. She had never said goodbye to him. It was no way for him to have died.

She turned on the doctor and the nurse. "I hope you are happy. I hope you die the same way, I hope you die in agony, I hope you die in *more* pain . . . Get out!"

They left, but she did not linger. She was not one to linger with corpses.

They buried him the next day, the way they buried everyone—hurriedly. Hurried words spoken over the grave, then the casket was lowered, with no one remaining to watch the hole filled with earth. The curate had already proceeded to the next service. There were so many dying.

As she was leaving the military cemetery, running away from the raw hole in the ground, the thought haunted her, *Not one, not one of them have I been able to save. Papa . . . Sammy . . . Freddy . . . Gisela . . . Grandmama . . . Mark . . .*

Sabine had nowhere to go with her anger. She was standing in the tiny public room of the White Hart Inn when she was told there was a trunk call from London for her.

It was Matt.

"Mark is dead," she said.

"What are you going to do?"

"I don't know. I suppose I shall go back to the States and do what I have been doing. Nothing. After all, what is anybody doing in this goddamned war? Nothing. Mostly nothing." She could not help the hysteria. She could hear it in her voice, and she knew there was nothing she could do to stop it.

"You come to London," Matt ordered. "You'll stay at my flat for a few days. And then we'll see. You know the address. I'll tell the landlady you're coming. She has the key, in case I'm not in. I can't talk anymore now. I'll see you tomorrow."

And he hung up before she could say no, or even say let's see, let's think about it. He had made the decision for her. She was grateful. It was so much easier to check train schedules and leave the hotel. And leave Mark.

Sabine entered the world of wartime London, where eggs were more prized than diamonds, and oranges rarer than that; where there were queues for everything and ration books and tickets, but not much in the stores to buy. Where there were mounds of rubble and shells of buildings, where even the railroad station seemed propped up.

She had never been to London before the war, so she had nothing to compare it to. Everyone marched, bustling with determination. That much reminded her of New York. However, in London there was much striding and shouldering others out of the way, with a careless "Sorry!" thrown back over the shoulder. There were uniforms everywhere. Royal Navy. RAF. And terribly efficient women with sensible shoes. WREN? Every so often, there was the welcome surprise of a U.S. uniform.

A taxi driver helped her with her luggage and maneuvered through the jumble of streets. Even before the bombings, London was very different from New York's sensible numbered street system, but now, with the detours and the shell holes, the route was a maze that Sabine lost track of. Matt's place was close to Jermyn Street and just off the Strand. The landlady welcomed her, the taxi driver brought her luggage upstairs. When she gave him some of the incomprehensible English money, he handed her back change.

"Shouldn't I give you more? Did you take out something for yourself?" she asked.

"Yes, indeed, mum. I took out what was right. But there's those who mightn't. Learn the currency," he admonished her, and went down the stairs.

"Make yourself comfy," said the landlady. "If you need anything, I'm just down the stairs. I don't go out much."

Sabine found herself alone, in a strange country and a

strange room. She took off her hat and looked around. Matt was not a neat man: this room belonged to someone who was always in a hurry—where the sofa and comfortable armchairs were not used for sitting but for throwing clothes on. Suit jackets, trousers, shirts were strewn about. In the kitchen, cups and saucers were scattered every which way. She stacked them in a pile and thought of washing them, but then thought *To hell with it,* and returned to the living room to sit down. In passing she caught sight of the view from the front window. She could glimpse a bit of the Thames, thanks to the buildings that had been leveled. It was a glorious day. Even the Thames looked blue. It was a poet's day, clean and blue-skied. No doubt the poets' birds, larks and finches were trilling somewhere.

Suddenly her legs could no longer support her and Sabine sat down with her back to the window and the day. She did not move Matt's clothing. She sat on Matt's pants. She thought of the day he had left her, that Sunday night on Waverly Place. She touched the fabric of the jacket that had been flung over the arm of the sofa, and she thought of Mark.

Her mind could not comprehend Mark's death. No more jackets for him to wear. For him, no more sunny days. No smiles. He had been erased.

She had not loved him; she hoped he had never known that. She hoped she had made him happy. She had truly given herself to him. That is, she had given him everything but her heart, because that had not been hers to give. Ah yes, she guessed that was the connection. Touching Matt Ryan's jacket, she thought of the man she loved who was still alive. And then thought of the man who had loved her who was not.

That was how Matt found her, sitting on his pants, on the sofa, sitting amid the ruins of his clothes with her hat off but her coat still on.

"Did you just get here?" he asked, surprised. "I thought—"

"No," Sabine said, "I've been here a while."

She did not move. Matt had come from a busy day, and his energy was still on a high work level, his mind on the rumors about Mussolini and Churchill's announcement about the effectiveness of the air strikes on Germany. He had expected that they would go out to eat, to a good place he had found, it would be like the Village in the old days. But she was sitting on the couch, shell-shocked, he thought. She was so far away from him.

He went over to her and took her hand. She looked at him.

"I didn't realize . . ." he began, and then she truly saw him for the first time since he had come into the room. In this foreign country, this strange city, in this world of war and widowhood and hospitals and funny currency, his eyes were—home. His eyes were of her childhood, and comforting. She began to cry silently, because she had seen his eyes and because she was in love with him. She knew, as she had always known, that no matter what happened in their lives, this was her man. This was the only man she would ever love. *Had* ever loved. The boy who had fought for her in that long-ago schoolyard and was taking her hand now in a London flat, seemed to understand everything about what she was feeling, more than she did herself.

"There's nothing to eat here. Are you hungry?" he asked.

Through her tears, she nodded yes. Some things never changed—she would always be hungry.

"Come," he said. "We'll get a bite to eat. Tomorrow you'll have to get a ration book. No, don't worry. I'll see to it."

"I'll see to it" was like a warm overcoat placed over her. She was so weary.

They ate in silence. It was all right. She didn't need to ask him about his work. And they needn't talk about her life. They dined without words, comfortable with one another. He knew the owner (he knew everyone in the world), who brought them a good red wine. It was a welcome to Sabine. They drank the wine, and then walked to his flat through the clear London night air. It was intensely dark because of the blackout. Figures appeared out of the night, bumping into them—there was the ubiquitous "Sorry." And then they were home.

Sabine was too tired to undress, too weary from the wine. She went into the bedroom and lay down on the bed. She could feel herself drifting off into sleep. The curtain had not been drawn. Half asleep, she saw the sliver of a moon rising over the rubble out the window. How peaceful, she thought, and then because she was buzzed on the wine, she imagined the moon sailing over the world. She saw the graveyard where Mark's body lay, and then, too late, two thoughts came into her mind, about the same moon shining on Freddy, Sammy, and Gisela, and that strange little hotel in New Jersey where she and Matt had gone for her abortion. Did the moon ever shine there? Did the stars ever come out? Or was it eternally dark, with bloody mattresses and the taste of metal in the mouth? Ah, what they had done to one another, she and Matt, what they had done with their love? Doomed to be childless children now.

He entered the room then.

"Do you want to be alone?" he asked.

No, she did not want to be alone with the moon and the graves and the bits and pieces of her past that she could not get rid of. No, not alone.

"No," she said. "Don't leave me, Matt."

And he lay down beside her and cradled her in his arms. It was too much for her to bear. The moon was like a silver knife, accusing her. She was there, safe, and *they* were not, they were no longer on this earth. And the anger that emerged surprised her, overwhelmed her.

"Take me," she said to him. "Oh, fuck me, Matt. Oh God, do it to me." She was shocked; she was talking like some whore, and she meant it. She wanted it. She wanted him. She wanted to use him.

Where was the energy coming from? She had no idea. She threw off her clothes, and he ripped off his, and they were in bed, and all she could feel was his body. His body, the feel of his hair and the strength of his chest; she knew how strong his arms were when they embraced her, she knew the seduction of his hands and his fingers, how they could arouse her. She knew his tongue. She could feel him rising between her thighs. She grabbed him. Oh, he was warm, and he was hard, and she was crazy from needing him inside her. She could not get him inside her fast enough. She climbed on him. She wanted him to fill her and overwhelm her and he was doing that, and she came, and it was still not enough, she needed more. The moon was still there, still at her back, she could not shut out the eye of the moon. And she kissed him then. She had not kissed him. They had been making love and she still had not kissed him. She did now and ran her tongue over his mustache, took his lips in her mouth, took his tongue as she had taken his penis. Possess him, she wanted to possess him. He understood, and because he was the man he was, he let her, allowed her whatever she needed.

Nothing was enough for her. She took his penis in her mouth, she licked his body with her tongue, she slid over his hardness with her softness, enveloping him. She had orgasms, and then they shared orgasms and the special beating pulsation that comes from coming together locked them for a few moments, immobile, and then she had to start again. The tears streamed down her face. He could feel them on his chest, on his face, when she bent over him.

And then, when she was exhausted, he made love to her. So gently, almost like rocking a baby, so gently, so tenderly. The storm was over. She was alive, she had survived, and the others had died. Through him, she had undergone such pain, through him she had lost—he could not say how much. But he now gave her love and understanding. He let his body love hers, he soothed her, and then with the power that was his, he aroused her until she clasped him in a shudder, and could feel his power coursing through her, his strength giving her strength. She fell asleep almost immediately, and he stayed inside her for the rest of the night. They slept that way. Spent children.

London was brisk that spring. Sabine had very little time to think of herself. It was just what she needed.

"There's someone I want you to meet. You'll like him," Matt said one day, and they arranged to have tea with a gentleman who arrived in a stiff British Army uniform.

"This is Peter Wurmann. My friend, Sabine."

They shook hands.

"How do you take your tea?" she asked.

"Black, please." He was not British. He had an accent. Wurmann acknowledged her look. "No, I am not English."

Over tea, he told his story. He was from Vienna. In 1939, when the war broke out, he managed to reach England, where he was immediately put in an internment camp.

"It was—as most events are in war—ridiculous. There we were, all of us—Nazis and Jews together—in an internment camp, until the British could sift us out. The Nazis constantly pretended to be Jews. But listen, it's not so easy to be a Jew. I always wanted to play the joke, you know, the reverse of the pogroms. 'Take down your pants and let's see whether

you are circumcised!' Ah well, after a time we Jewish refugees were allowed out of the camp, but of course there were
very few jobs in London. All of London seemed to be full of
Viennese Jews. So I was advised to go to Brighton. That's a
resort on the channel. A Mrs. Werner would allow me to be
a—what is the word—dustman? No, that is not quite correct."

"Handyman?" Sabine suggested.

"That sounds correct, if American," Wurmann smiled. "So
I went down, and she gave me a room in her basement, and
enough money to live on and I did the chores. She instructed
her daughters, who I must say were not the greatest beauties
of this world"—that was the Viennese male in him
emerging—"never to speak a word to me. And I never spoke
to them. Then, of course, the British Armed Forces needed
doctors, and that is what I was in Vienna, and so I am now a
major. I went back to Brighton to visit the Werners. Mrs.
Werner was shocked, she was furious. She saw the uniform
and medical corps emblem. She looked at the two unmarried
daughters. Right then, she shrieked at them, 'Why did you
never speak to him?' 'Because you told us not to.' 'But how
was I to know he was a *doctor?*' "

Wurmann leaned back and chuckled. "The war has had its
compensations—although very few."

Sabine was laughing. It felt good. They discussed tea—in
Vienna it would have been coffee, but in England it had to be
tea. They talked of the different pastries, none of which were
available anymore, certainly not in London. And then it was
time for Wurmann to go.

"May we see you again?" Sabine offered her hand.

"Of course. What a pleasure this has been," Wurmann
smiled.

That evening Matt and Sabine strolled through a primrose
evening. The weather was soft and the war seemed far away.
As they walked, Sabine had the feeling Matt was also far
away.

"What's the matter?" she asked him.

"Oh, nothing. I'm just edgy." They were silent a moment
"Nothing gets done. People just talk. I just talk."

"Tell me."

"No, it's too beautiful a night to waste it." But they did
waste it because he was never quite with her. She had

thought they might stroll. His impatience kept them from ever walking *together*.

When they returned to his flat the phone was ringing, and he rushed to answer it.

"Yes," he said into the receiver. "Of course, it's not too late. Come now."

Sabine watched him pace after he hung up.

"Who was that?"

"A man named Zygielbojm—don't ask me how to spell it. He's a Pole—rather, a Jew, who's Polish. He was in the Jewish Socialist Bund in Warsaw, and he lost his wife and family there. He managed to escape, I don't know how, but he showed up in London last year and made an appeal on the BBC about the extermination of the Jews. I did an interview with him—"

"What do you mean, extermination?" Sabine asked.

"Just that. Extermination. He says, and God knows there's proof enough, that the Nazis are planning to wipe out every Jew in Europe. Last year they had mobile vans and they used to gas ninety Jews at a time. Just select them and gas them, or shoot them. He said all that on the radio, everybody heard it, but nobody did anything. Nothing happened. Now, evidently, it's gotten worse. He's on to some more information and he doesn't know what to do with it, so he's coming here. Except I don't know what to do with it either."

Sabine's mind was not with him. Grandmama. Sammy. Gisela. Freddy.

"What do you mean, nothing's being done?" she said.

"I'll give you an example. This guy Zygielbojm made a broadcast almost a year ago. This week, finally, they've set up a conference in Bermuda between the United States, England and some of the neutral nations. It's taken a whole year for them just to sit down and say, What do we do with the Jews? Where do we put them? Who wants them? I know for a fact that Sweden has offered to take in refugees, but the U.S. and England haven't figured out where the funds would come from. For Chrissakes, everyone bloody well knows there isn't a Jewish agency in the States that wouldn't put up all the money! But no, they have to confer, examine, set up an agenda. You want to know something? I get the feeling that there is a lot of pressure from somewhere *not* to do anything. Six thousand Jews a day are being killed while they confer.

And there's always an excuse. Now they say that any action 'might further enflame the Nazis.' Bullshit!"

Sabine a little timid in the face of his anger, said, "Matt, we don't know about all this in the States."

"You've been in Hollywood for a year, where they're still talking about all-star musicals to pep up the boys' morale. The *government* knows."

"Well, don't get angry with me. I didn't know."

"Well, now you're learning." The doorbell rang. "We both are, I guess. I'm not angry with you, Sabine. I'm angry with everything." He went to answer the door.

A slight dark man entered. The two men embraced, and Matt introduced Sabine. The man nodded, bowed, and immediately directed his talk toward Matt.

"News is not good," he said, in broken English. "The uprising in Warsaw is now finished. Three days they thought to kill us Jews. Four weeks later, and we died with guns in hands. At least that, at least. But now, over. Now, all the time talking, and not listening, Matt, not listening. Somebody must listen, Matt. Maybe you. You hear of Oswiecim, a town south Poland? They now have"—he searched for the word—"a crematoria, to burn."

"Burn people? Alive?" Sabine asked.

"No. Gas. Zyklon B. They build—*Fabrik*, factory . . . *Badeanstalten*."

Matt tried to help out. "Public baths."

"Yes, but *gas*, they *gas* the Jews by the thousands, then burn them. By the thousands. Every day. By the thousands."

"Are you sure?"

The man was tired, he was weary with the struggle, with the strange language, with the need to explain, with the fact that what he was talking about was so unbelievable.

"Matt, is true. Centers. *Ausrottung*. You know what means—extermination."

Matt looked to Sabine. She could do nothing but stare. She could not comprehend.

"Who?" she finally said, her mind on her grandmother, Sammy, Freddy, Gisela.

"*Who?*" The man was impatient. Why didn't they understand? "Jews. Everyone. Old, young, babies, women. Everyone."

"How many already?" Matt asked him.

"In January, seven hundred thousand. Now? Now it is May. Now, I don't know."

"Well, I tell you, and maybe it's of no help, but at the Bermuda Conference they're trying to liberalize the immigration laws to America as well as get some Jews to Sweden." Matt felt ashamed of himself. Nothing but words, and these words passed by the dark little man, who could not understand them. He rose to his feet.

"Oswiecim!" He shouted. "Dachau! Maidanek! Terezin! Belsen! Death camps! Why they waiting? Death camps!"

Then he sat down again. "Matt, can you help?" He had practiced these words, obviously, before he had come. He had made sure that these words were perfect. They came out perfectly.

"I will do what I can. I will call Washington. I will broadcast. Do you have any evidence with you?"

"Reports, only reports. No photos." The man repeated again. "Reports."

"Today is the fifth of May. Can I call you in two days?"

"In two days, I call you," Zygielbojm said. "Is easier. By night." And the man left, again nodding at Sabine. She found herself unable to react, to smile, to nod. She simply stared. The door shut.

"What are you going to do?" she asked Matt.

"Just what I said. Call Washington. Do a broadcast."

But it was not that simple. The power, *his* power, was of no use. There were three calls to Washington—no results on two of them, a bit of information on the third. Negotiations were in progress. Any emphasis, any broadcast could be damaging. The word "fatal" was used. *"Fatal,"* Matt thought, *how can they throw that word around concerning negotiations?* "Fatal" against *Ausrottung.* How pallid the English word seemed, like some Victorian disease. He spent most of one night and part of the next day writing copy, and the rest of the day trying to persuade the network to let him broadcast it. Total frustration. He found himself censored.

Two days later Zygielbojm telephoned. The conversation was brief. Matt admitted defeat, but only temporarily, he assured Zygielbojm.

Now it was the eleventh of May. Sabine and Matt had a date with Peter Wurmann.

Instead of tea, Wurmann asked for scotch. All correspondents were kept well supplied—that was one sign of power. Matt poured the drinks.

"She sent me a clipping from a weekly called *Aufbau*, a refugee paper. It says that in just one Polish town, Kolomier, the Nazis took twelve intellectuals—would you believe a town that size had twelve intellectuals?—then hanged them all. And then took all the pregnant women and slit their bellies."

Sabine did not dare think. She would not let a thought enter her mind.

"Perhaps it is not true. Perhaps it is only a rumor," she said. Wurmann looked at her.

"My cousin in New York said she did not believe it. Her sister, who lives in Kolomier, was eight months pregnant . . ."

He poured himself another scotch and changed the subject.

"And you, what are your plans?" he asked Sabine. "Are you going to stay in London?"

She had not looked ahead more than a day at a time, but surely there was finally no place for her in London. What was she to do? Take up space, eat precious rations? There was no need for her here, beyond Matt.

"No, I imagine I will return to California," she said, "when Matt can find a flight."

"You are from California? Your family is there?"

"No. My mother is in New York."

"Sabine has a cousin in Vienna. Sammy Abrams," Matt said.

Sabine recognized the change that came over Wurmann's face. It was a look of delight and remembrance that usually occurs only when somebody famous is mentioned.

"Oh, I remember Sammy. I remember his films. Do you know, by coincidence, my father was even in jail with him."

Suddenly, Sabine was alert.

"You mean he's still alive? What jail?"

"Oh, well, after the *Anschluss*, a great number of Viennese Jews were rounded up and sent to jail. Not a concentration camp, a jail. My father was released after several weeks."

"And Sammy?"

"I do not know. That was 1939, a long time ago. There was a rumor that he had been sent to Theresienstadt—Terezin, they call it. That's the concentration camp for artists."

"And his family?"

"I don't know. Maybe it's not true, maybe he did not go." It was an echo of the conversation a minute ago, lies to cover up fears.

"There was a boy, Freddy, Sammy's son," Sabine said. "He was just a baby when I last saw him."

"Perhaps he survives," Wurmann said, drinking his third scotch. Then he left. Matt and Sabine were silent. Neither of them was quite sober.

"Why is Freddy so important to you?" Matt asked slowly, and Sabine closed her eyes.

"Because he's the last—," and it was out before she knew it. "He's the last in the line. There's me, and there's him."

"You're blaming me," Matt said. "And I *am* to blame for the fact that you can't have children, isn't that right?"

"I don't want to talk about it," Sabine said. "I don't want to talk about what happened. Freddy was such a sweet little boy, and . . . and . . ." She didn't finish.

"I'll see what I can wangle in terms of a plane ride," he said.

They went to bed.

The next morning, just before noon, Zygielbojm shot himself in the head in front of Parliament, his final protest to a world that wouldn't listen. The report of his suicide made the early editions of the evening papers, but not the finals.

Chapter Nineteen

When she returned to New York on her way back to California, the first thing Sabine discovered was that she was rich. Under the terms of Mark Cardozo's will, she had inherited over twelve million dollars.

She telephoned the Cardozos, but the butler said they were out. So she wrote them a letter, lying, lying, describing Mark's death, how peaceful it had been, how happy he had been at the end. How he had asked her to send them his love.

She also included in the letter the amount of money the Cardozos had lent her for Sammy Abramowitz's abortive flight from Austria. She licked the envelope, placed a stamp on it, and mailed it. That part of her life was finished.

While she was in New York she made a few other calls. The first was to an official of the Joint Distribution Committee, the second to a member of the American Jewish Congress whom she had met in the fund-raising days of 1940.

Harstein of the Joint Distribution Committee corroborated all Zygielbojm's allegations. Yes, there was a deliberate policy of annihilation of the Jews. The second man was more cautious, but also more explicit.

"The Germans do not use the word *Ausrottung*," he said. "We have received reports directly from the German Ministry of Foreign Affairs in Berlin. They refer to a Europe that is *Judenfrei*."

"I know what the word means," Sabine said. "But what is the policy?"

"Well," said the official bitterly, "since there is no place to send these Jews—and since Europe is to be cleansed of them—what do you suppose the policy would be?"

Question for question. "What about Sweden? What about the neutrals?" she asked. "What does the State Department intend to do?"

356

"They have requested that we withhold this information from the American people."

"Why?"

"I suggest you ask them."

"You sound so angry," Sabine said.

"Wouldn't you be?" came the reply.

Yes, she would be. Yes, she was. It confused her. She heard rumors, but none of them made sense. A decision on the Jewish question—always a question!—would be forthcoming on August 12. And then it was postponed until October 11. Was that possible? She made several more calls. This time she called a friend of Matt's in the State Department. He talked to her, gave his regards to Matt, but refused to divulge any information.

Anger and frustration began to mount. Sabine donated a great deal to the American Jewish Congress, but she could see that money wasn't helping either. Nobody was telling the public what was happening.

Then it came to her. It was simple: make a movie. My God, there were propaganda movies about everything. The home front. Our boys overseas. The French underground. *Storm Over Stalingrad*. She even had a screen credit, and *Storm* was a big hit. She flew to California.

She found herself in Bernard's office. She had even waited the requisite ten minutes before being shown into the Ross inner sanctum.

"You want to make an important film?" She was choosing her words carefully.

"Every film is important," he corrected her.

"But this is a film on a subject that has never before been put on the screen." *Oh, let his ego sway him.* "You could be the first!"

"Go on," Bernard said, intrigued but suspicious.

And Sabine described the Pole she had met in London, his description of the Warsaw ghetto, the extermination camps, the number of Jews dying every day, the callousness of the Allied Governments. Finally, she described Zygielbojm's suicide.

"This is an entertainment medium," Bernard said.

"What was it that got you? The suicide? The camps? What don't you like?" Sabine asked. She wanted to throttle him.

"A movie about Jews?" he asked. "Who would come?"

"Everybody, if you make it exciting enough." Sabine could not believe what she was saying. She was talking about some musical, some crazy war adventure epic that would guarantee twenty million in receipts.

"Listen to this. I tried to smuggle my uncle Sammy, his wife and child over the border—"

"Smuggling over the border?" Bernard considered that. Good. Suspense.

"—but they were caught, thrown into a concentration camp, this old man, his young wife and little son."

"Frank Morgan, Norma Shearer, and Freddie Bartholomew—or Roddy McDowall." Bernard was already casting it. "Or, if Morgan's not right, how about Felix Bressart?"

"Wonderful." Sabine trampled past the stars' names. "The resistance starts, just like the French Resistance, only this time it's the Jews. A handsome young man joins the others, a beautiful young girl is his sweetheart. They learn about the concentration camps and decide to organize a group to release the prisoners who are being sent to their deaths."

"This is getting very heavy," Bernard warned.

Sabine improvised. "At Purim, there is a dance. Listen, it is a dance of defiance, a protest against the oppressor. There is a surprise attack from the Nazis. The girl is killed. But the plan goes on. They attack the concentration camp. There can be a terrific battle scene—"

"This is *very* heavy, Sabine."

"You never have to see the inmates. No starvation. Just Nazis being killed. At the end, the hero is dying, and he tells the other partisans to get the message to the world. Tell everyone about the camps." Sabine could tell from the look on Bernard's face that she was not winning.

"You don't like that, huh? How about this?" (What was she doing? She was playing Hollywood, to get her message across.) "Our hero learns that the Nazis plan to obliterate the ghetto, and he mobilizes the Jews. He realizes they will all die, but at least they will die with honor. There is one tunnel to the outside. The Germans attack and are repulsed. The Jews have won a battle! But they know they cannot resist forever. The girl and the hero say goodbye; he tells her to leave by the tunnel and somehow—somehow—get the message to the world, telling them what is happening to the Jews. She leaves, and he faces the Nazis, first with the weapons he and his comrades have been able to purchase from the black market, and then finally with his fists. He fights against the Germany army with his fists!"

"How long will it take to write this?" Bernard was interested.

"Two weeks," she said impulsively.

"Two weeks?" he repeated. "Be very careful on accuracy. We don't want to get nailed."

Nailed? By whom? For what?

"Do you know any place that has a basement?" she asked.

"A basement? In Southern California? What do you need a basement for?"

"To write in. I want to get away from the sun."

Bernard considered it. "I don't know anybody with a basement. Would a wine cellar do?"

It did fine. Sabine found herself back at Jerry's house (he had gone to Mexico for two weeks). She set herself a regime. At eight in the morning she would descend to the wine cellar and there, among the dusty Burgundies and Bordeaux, she would immerse herself in a world that she could only imagine from reports she had heard third-hand. She stayed until five o'clock in the afternoon, when she would emerge into the unreal world of Beverly Hills—late golden sunshine, fresh breezes, desert and far-off mountain peaks. She would make herself a simple dinner, listen to the war news and go to bed. Each day she followed the same schedule, and exactly two weeks later she placed a script in front of Bernard Ross. He put it to one side of his desk.

"Read it," she said.

"Of course I'll read it," he assured her.

"Read it now, Bernard."

"What's your rush, doll?"

"Read it." And because he had always admired her guts, he gave in and read. And got involved, as she knew he would. When he was done he rose, walked around his desk, and kissed her.

"Thank you," he said, as he was ushering her out the door. "Thank you for creating a masterpiece."

"When will it go into production?"

"Give me a day. Two days."

"With you behind this film, Bernard, I know it will be given top priority."

"I will call you within the week."

He called the following day. "Where's Jerry?" he asked.

"I guess still in Mexico."

"You know where?"

"No."

"Sabine, you have to do me a favor. A big one. Jerry has already turned down five scripts. They want to put him on suspension."

"Who's 'they'? I thought *you* ran the studio."

"Don't kid yourself. I have people to answer to. I am trying to avoid trouble. The columnists are already making innuendos—"

"Oh?" Sabine asked. "About what?"

"About everything. His patriotism, why he isn't married, why he isn't in the army."

Sabine did not understand. Every word, every bit of publicity about Jerry was handled by the studio. If items had been planted in the columns, the studio had to have done it.

"I want him to go on a War Bond tour," Bernard said, "cross-country. And I want you to go with him. You're his friend. You can keep him out of trouble. If you're there, it won't cause talk. *And,* I want you to come up with an idea for a film. You know him. Come up with a really knockout musical idea."

"What about the movie I just wrote?"

"There's nothing in that for Jerry."

"But what's going to happen to it?"

"It's already in production! I'm going to work on it while you and Jerry are running around the country. I envy you. I wish I could get away. You leave Friday."

That night, she received a note from Sandy Cardozo.

How good of you to write us about Mark. We had, of course, received the news from the War Department, but your personal touch was appreciated. Your kindness to our son will be remembered. You made him happy, which is, perhaps, all that mattered.

> Julien joins me in
> fond regards, Sandy
> (Mrs.) Julien Cardozo

Sandy had written a thank-you note. Sabine almost laughed, but then she read the note again, and recognized the self-protection that marks a survivor.

Jerry Davis was all right until they reached Kearney, Nebraska. By then the weather had turned raw, and he was tired of the public, of having his every meal invaded by autograph hunters poking paper napkins and menus in front of him, wanting to touch him, finding any excuse to hover near.

That week *Life* magazine was devoting four valuable pages to Bob Hope and his overseas tour, with Frances Langford and Jerry Colonna.

Jerry hurled the magazine across the room in the New Conant Hotel.

"Look at that!" he screamed at Sabine. "Four pages. The studio could have sent me overseas, but no! Hope gets four pages in *Life* and I get the front page of the *Weekly Sentinel*. Is that fair? Is that right? I hate these little towns, I hate these little papers, I hate these little people."

He got up.

"Where are you going?" Sabine asked anxiously.

"Out. Walking. Do you think there are any sailors in Kearney, Nebraska?"

"Wait a minute. I'll go with you."

They walked out into the street.

"I hate Bernard Ross," Jerry said. "I hate Walgreen's," he said as they passed. "And the First National Bank."

Sabine, walking along beside him, said nothing.

"Do you know why he's punishing me? Because I don't want to be the Great Schlemiel anymore. I refuse to go to my grave like Joe Penner—'Wanna buy a duck?' No, let me die here in Kearney, Nebraska."

It was time to go home to Beverly Hills.

One evening on their way back Sabine, impatient and restless, left Jerry and went to the observation car. The train was passing through a valley that reminded her of the Hudson. And, for no reason at all, it again occurred to Sabine that she, like her mother, like her grandmother, had no keepsakes. What a strange word. Her mind was flooded with memories then, of her father and Dan Ryan sweating on the roof as they shingled, of her father and mother, snowbound with Matt and Dan Ryan, snowbound and cozy in lives that had yet to be lived out, lives that were important with promise. The countryside raced by and darkness began to come down. She lit a cigarette and was joined by an army corporal who politely asked for a light. She gave him her cigarette to light his.

"Nice," he said, nodding at the scenery. "I grew up in country that looked like this."

They watched in silence as the night drew on. He flipped his cigarette on to the tracks. The sparks bounced away into the night.

"I keep looking at this country and I say, 'Don't change,'" the corporal said. "Ridiculous, right?"

"No," Sabine smiled. "Not ridiculous."

"I'd just like it to be what I remembered—when I come back," the corporal added as he left her.

Keepsakes. The way things were. Sabine realized she had discovered the idea for Jerry's next film.

In the summer of 1943, battles raged around the world, and inside the studio. Perhaps it was Bernard Ross's preoccupation with the power struggle that elicited a speedy okay to Sabine's project for Jerry. It gave Bernard more time to busy himself with his own offensive now that the old man who ruled the studio had suffered a stroke that totally paralyzed his right side, allowing him to spew obscenities only from the left side of his mouth. Along with his ability to move, the old man had also lost a great deal of his power, and Bernard's concentration was focused on gaining it. So *Goodbye to All That*, the script Sabine wrote for Jerry, came into being.

The film was, in a way, a goodbye to childhood, but it was also a salute, a fond one, to the kind of innocence that had preceded this war. The film, even if only an illusion, became the symbol of what the American servicemen were fighting for. Sabine had drawn on Dan Ryan's stories of growing up in the middle of New York State, the skating parties and summer loves, the end of the horse-and-buggy days and the excitement of a new era of horseless carriages.

The story line was fairly simple. It was about a small-town boy (schlemiel enough so that Jerry's audiences would recognize their character) who desperately longs for his father's approval. But his father has no kind words for a son who can do only two things—play a cornet like an angel and fix horseless carriages. The usual series of predicaments follow. The boy is fired from his job as a clerk because he is too honest. He is too shy to ask the girl of his dreams, who plays piano in the dance band, to go out with him. But life continues, in a celebration of small-town pleasures—a sliding sequence with the first snow, sleds careening down the hill past a flicker of homes, and in the end the Fourth of July, when the dreamer hero unexpectedly wins the horseless carriage race. Fired up by the speeches about the Spanish-American War given by the Civil War veteran orators, the dreamer enlists in the army—the first volunteer, off on the train to Cuba. And suddenly, in a rush, it all comes together. The girl of his dreams confesses her love. She was also shy. His father, confessing that he never knew how to express his feelings, embraces his son. And the train leaves the tiny station for the world. The countryside rolls by and the hero realizes that he is leaving the small town and the small-town ways, the green of New York State, the hills, the beauty, his girl, the families, and it is one continuous band of memory seen through his eye, with the almost mournful sound of the cornet echoing over the hills, the remnants of all the Saturday night dances—"Good Night, Ladies"—and under his breath, as the dreamer passes, he utters everyone's feeling:

"Don't change."

Nobody paid much attention to *Goodbye*. The film was completed in four weeks and Bernard Ross never walked on the set once during the filming. A preview was planned in a little theater near Encino, and Bernard Ross did not show up. But an associate of Bernard's who did go noticed, perhaps halfway through the movie, a clearing of throats, the click of handbags opening and closing, the rustle of handkerchiefs. What was happening here? The studio's leading comic had this audience weeping. There must be some mistake. It took the associate some time to figure this out.

And it took Bernard no time, once he heard about it, to figure that if he opened the film in New York with little publicity, maybe in one of the smaller movie houses, he might get good reviews. In fact, the New York reviews were ecstatic, the crowds even more so. In the midst of all the battle pictures and epic war dramas, a small musical that recalled the American way of life became a symbol of home, and hope.

More than that. A hit.

Power came with a hit. Sabine could feel it. She was solicited, sought out, flattered, partied, propositioned, wheedled.

Bernard bought her lunch, at the Brown Derby, where there was not a trace of war. The steaks, roast beef, all kinds of fish, and sugary confections brought to mind a world of so long ago. The chatter was high, the mood optimistic, and Bernard benevolent.

"This service is certainly efficient; I wonder who trains them," Sabine, the ex-hotelier, remarked.

"Who cares?" Bernard Ross shrugged. "That's one thing I'll never have to do again—wait on tables. Christ, it nearly killed me. Remember Garfinkel?"

"Who could forget?" Sabine said.

Two days later, Jerry called her.

"Bernie's made an idiot out of you," he spat into the phone.

"What do you mean?"

"Your other script, about the Polish Jews. You better visit the studio. See the dailies. Or whatever has been edited already. You're in for a shock."

He hung up and Sabine headed for the studio.

She burst through a door that had a No Admittance sign on it, confronting a surprised Bernard Ross and several underexecutives in the midst of a screening.

"Sit down, doll," Bernard said, "and watch!" She did. She saw bits and pieces of her script about the Warsaw ghetto, no more than that. The basic story was there, but it was no longer about Jews. There were no Jewish names, no Stars of David, there was no ghetto. There were only two lovers battling the Nazi horde, Polish patriots fighting and dying for a free Poland.

The lights came on. Bernard Ross rose and dismissed the underlings.

There was perfunctory applause, followed by handshakes, as they filed out of the screening room.

"What did you do?" Sabine screamed.

"I filmed your script," Bernard screamed back.

"That's not my script, and you know it. That's got nothing to do with what I had in mind. You changed it. Poles! You turned them into Poles!

"There's nothing wrong with Poles."

"Nothing wrong with Jews, either," she said. "Why, Bernie? Why did you do this?"

"Shut up and stop screaming, cunt!" Ah, this was the old Bernard. This was the Bernard she knew.

"Let me tell you something," he said. "It is the policy of this studio and of every other studio in town to make movies which aid our war effort and demonstrate Americanism. We can show how hideous the Nazis are, but we cannot show Jewish atrocities."

"Why?"

"One, it won't sell. Two, we in the industry do not want to be accused of special interests."

"I don't believe you. You've shown everything: saboteurs, traitors, war crimes, island epics. How come you could show the Czechs being shot, but not the Jews?"

"It's all backed by official rules," Bernard said loudly. "We can make films about refugees, but not specifically Jewish ones. We cannot raise the question of religious faith or race, or ask for or promise U.S. aid. There are to be no specifics concerning the Jewish problem. And that is official!"

"You—*you* are official. *You* are the number one man in Hollywood, or at least that's what you've been boasting about all this time. Now you tell me you have no power, you have no control. Jews are being exterminated and you cannot even raise your voice in protest. All I'm asking you to do is to tell the truth!"

He faced her angrily. "Then I will tell you the truth. When it comes to Jews, the American people don't care!"

That took her breath away.

"I don't believe you," she said weakly.

"Believe me," he yelled at her. "Don't you think I don't hear it every day—that *we* are being blamed for this war, that if it wasn't for *us*, American boys wouldn't be dying in Europe." Suddenly his fury was real. "It's the same shit I been hearing all my fuckin life, that it's *our* fault, *our* fault, *my* fault."

"I don't believe you. You turn these tantrums on and off."

"Go to the State Department and ask them. Go to the President and watch him go into a state of shock: 'So many Jews, I had no idea, oh my!' "

She turned away. "If you wanted this movie to be made, you would have made it. Don't blame it on the government."

"I don't risk my neck, I don't risk the studio's neck on Jewish propaganda. Where are you going?"

"To find someone with more guts than you have."

He ran after her toward the lot. The buildings were huge blazing white blocks; extras, grips, and messengers sauntered along.

"Go. Go with my blessing!" Bernard was screaming as she walked down the street to the parking space that still had her name on it. "No one in town will let you make a movie like that. You better get wise to that!"

His rage caused a stir among the ranks. Indians turned war bonnets to listen to the screeching; Brigadier generals from central casting stopped in their tracks.

"Liar! Cheat!" the beautiful girl with the raven hair was yelling at the head of the studio.

"You'll never work again!" The head of the studio was screaming at the beautiful girl with the raven hair, who was getting into her convertible.

"Oh, yeah? Go live with yourself!" the girl shrieked in a rage as she tore out of the parking lot.

"Never work again! Get wise to that!" The head of the studio shook his fist at the receding convertible. Then he turned back to his office. The Indian chiefs, admirals, and generals continued on their way to their own epics.

Chapter Twenty

Sabine retreated to Glenrocks, where there was no hotel. She may have been the only person in America who felt a sense of defeat.

It was the end of January, 1944. The war news was encouraging. The Allied invasion was imminent, the war in the Pacific was turning in favor of the Allies, and it finally looked like the beginning of the end.

For a month following her clash with Bernard Ross, Sabine had sat in Los Angeles, reading the papers, listening to the news, relieved to hear the sound of Matt Ryan's voice from London. His voice sounded weary and yet exultant, and it was the only comfort she had.

At night she dreamed the same dream, and it never went away and it never changed. She saw lines of people, and in the background nothing but stumps of trees. Beside the lines of people there were the dead carcasses of animals. Then she realized that these carcasses were human; some of the rib cages had been torn open and children were feeding on the corpses, while their parents mutely looked on. The carcasses were riddled with maggots. Sabine screamed to the children, but they paid no attention to her. The parents looked and said, "Too late."

Too late. That was her feeling and the cause of her anger. Again she had been too late and too weak, and she had been tricked and lied to.

So one day in January she went home. Not to New York, not to Bertha, not to the apartment on Waverly Place. To Glenrocks.

She rented a house just outside Liberty. The house reminded Sabine of her childhood. It was winter, and there were chores to be done, constantly. The wooden house was small. It contained a good-sized kitchen with a wood range for

367

cooking, a pump by the kitchen sink, a parlor with a small
kerosene stove that heated the two bedrooms if you kept the
doors open. The smaller bedroom was no more than a closet,
except for the narrow little window that looked out on a
black and white combination of snow and bare branches.

It was a one-mile walk to the village of Liberty, where she
shopped for groceries, and a mile in the other direction to the
stone pillars that marked the entrance to Glenrocks. Sabine
bought a jalopy for fifty dollars that was good for nothing
except to take her into town. But it had a heater and defrost-
er, and a rumble seat that reminded her of better and happier days.

She went to the gas rationing board, where an A-sticker
was affixed to her windshield, allowing her five gallons of
gasoline per week.

Five gallons was more than enough. Armed with her ration
books for sugar and meat, she drove the old car into Liberty
once a week for groceries, then returned to her little house.

The one thing she ran out of was cigarettes. They became
increasingly difficult to buy as the war went on. She rummaged around ashtrays for butts and took to smoking brands
with names like Marvels and Wings (when she could find
those). She bought boots for walking and a red-and-black-
checked wool jacket, the kind the hunters wore, and she
bought a radio. That was the extent of her purchases. She
had no telephone. She had brought books with her, and at
night she read or listened to the radio. Dinner was to the tune
of Fred Waring and his Pennsylvanians, an apple went with
"I Love a Mystery." In bed she listened to the Lux Radio
Theater.

She drove to Liberty, but she always walked to Glenrocks.
She'd poke around the ruins where the kids had smashed windows. Inside one of the remaining cabins she noticed used
rubbers. Glenrocks was now the make-out place for teenagers,
the hang-out for boys who had not yet gone to war or were
home on leave, making out with the little cock-teasing town-
ies who didn't want to go all the way, but did anyway. No
babies needed. Stolen sex was so delicious. Sabine hated these
young lovers. She wore her bitterness like a shroud.

One day she noticed fresh tire tracks in the snow. Someone
had been there the previous night. She walked toward the

barn and looked at the charred remains of the farmhouse, now mostly covered by snow.

Glenrocks was a graveyard, and still she was drawn to it, so that she would circle the ruins and the world she had once known could come back to haunt her. Matt, doing the chores and peeling the potatoes. The craziness of the boarders. Her father playing the concertina. Her mother in the kitchen. The smell of bread baking, the warmth of summer and the sound of bees. At times she would sit on the granite slabs that had been the entrance to the farmhouse and just stare at the white field that stretched beyond.

She felt barren and desolate, full of self-loathing and self-pity. Aware of it and unable to lift a finger to help herself. So she went back to her little house and vented her anger on the woodpile, welcoming snow and wind, hoping to be snow-bound again as she once had been when Matt and his father—and her father—were all at Glenrocks.

Time passed, but the passing of time did not help decrease the bitterness, did not lessen the anger. The trips to Glenrocks became a daily ritual: she walked there to see the shuttered arrogance of the Mountain View House, now closed for the duration. She lowered her head, to visualize every stone of Glenrocks, and she stayed, thinking of nothing, until the sun had gone behind the mountains.

Twice the sheriff's car drove up while Sabine was visiting Glenrocks. The first time he wanted to ask who she was—actually to order her off private property, until she convinced him the property was hers. The second time was a month later; he wanted to see if she was all right. She assured him she was.

In March the days dripped and the nights froze. Icicles came and went; the season was changing. Patches of bare brown appeared. What were frozen puddles at dawn turned to small ponds by noon and returned to ice at night.

Spring—or that last awkward pause before it—was the most desolate season of all. The snow was vanishing. In her heart, Sabine dreaded what was coming. She could live with winter; she was not certain she could abide spring—buds and beginnings, births.

One night she had a new dream. This one had to do with the soil. She could not remember what she was digging, but she always ended up weeping and then would awake dry-eyed, unsure of what had caused her tears, but positive that she had been crying. *Of course, digging means a grave*, she thought; *yet there is no body. There is no feeling of loss.* The dream disturbed her.

One afternoon, when the weather turned suddenly cold, Sabine returned from Glenrocks to find—of all people—Jerry, standing on her little porch, stamping his feet in their thin leather city shoes that did nothing to keep out the cold.

"Don't think this has been easy," he said, as his breath frosted in front of him.

"Oh God!" Sabine said in dismay. "How long have you been here? You must be freezing."

"These feet have been in California. They are not used to snow."

"Why didn't you go in? I never lock the door."

"You mean I could have just walked into the house?"

"I never lock the door. There's nothing to lose here," she said.

"I could have died from exposure!" he said indignantly, and then, "Aren't you glad to see me?"

"Of course!" It took her a moment too long to say it. He was intruding. "Come, I'll make you some tea, and you can tell me why you're here."

"I'm here to save you, obviously," he said as they went inside. He sat right by the range in the kitchen and accepted the steaming cup of tea she brought him.

"Jesus, you look terrible," he observed. "You're up for an Oscar."

"I don't give a shit."

"I wasn't even nominated. And it was the best thing I've ever done."

"Yes, it was," she agreed. How far away all that seemed.

"Are you going back for the presentations?"

"No. I never want to go back there." She looked at him. "What do you mean, you came here to save me?"

He dodged the question. "This is a wonderful place to spend the rest of your life," he said, looking around. "I gather you have two bedrooms? I take it that little space is a bedroom."

"Yes, two bedrooms. But you can't close the door if you want any heat. And there's no bathroom."

"What is there, then?"

"Chamber pots, and a privy out in the stable. I don't recommend the privy. It's too cold out there."

"I have come to a monastery. What's for dinner, gruel?"

"Bacon and eggs."

"Oh, that sounds good." He brightened, then said as an afterthought, "What do I do with my chamber pot? Afterwards, I mean."

"Empty it into the privy."

He went into the tiny bedroom. "Oh my God," she heard him saying, "I'm staying one night, maybe two. That's it. I have to get back to California. I'll make something *urgent* come up."

But Jerry didn't leave. He learned to use the chamber pot and to empty it, and he helped chop the wood. And every day he walked with Sabine to Glenrocks and watched her (when she was not aware of it) and wondered what he could do to help.

One night, after the dishes and before "Your Hit Parade," he asked, "What are you going to do after the war?"

"I have no idea," she told him.

"Stay here?"

"Maybe."

"You're not serious."

"I told you, I don't know." Her voice had a touch of asperity.

"Well, you can't just sit here and mourn for the rest of your life."

"I'm not mourning."

"What are you doing?"

"I'm pulling myself together."

"Sabine, my love—and you are my love—you are not pulling yourself together, you are running away, and I don't know from what. I can't believe it's because of one fight with Bernie. I mean, you've been fighting with him most of your life. So have I."

She turned her back on him. So he continued. "And you'll forgive me if I say I don't believe it's grief over Mark's death. So what is it? Matt?"

She still didn't answer.

"Sabine, it's time you stopped moping around. Get up and get out! Get married, have kids. Open the hotel!"

"Shut up!" she said to him. "Shut up! What do you know

about anything? That son of a bitch didn't want to get married! Oh God, we were always going to be free. That free, bohemian spirit. No ties. Free to go, free to stay! He wanted it that way!"

"And you?"

"All right, *I* wanted it that way. I didn't want to be like my mother. Look how she dried up after my father died."

"Until she met my father."

"Yes, and I don't want that. I *didn't* want that." She had begun to cry, and she no longer realized he was in the room. "I wanted that baby. I wanted to have that baby and he didn't want it. Oh, God, I wanted that baby."

"You'll have another one," Jerry said softly.

"I can't have another baby!" She turned around furiously. "I left whatever there was of me in some toilet bowl in New Jersey! Some fucking creep butcher cut into me wrong. And took off for Atlantic City for the weekend. And that's that!" The tears were streaming down her face.

"You blame Matt?"

"Yes, I blame Matt."

Jerry was very quiet for a moment. "Sabine, we all do terrible things to the people we love."

"I don't!"

"Well, you're lucky then. You haven't had to make that choice. I hope you never do."

She was quiet now, though the tears were still coursing down her cheeks. She gave a sigh. He opened his arms, and she came into them, sitting on his lap.

"You know what I think you should do?" he asked. "You should go back with me to California."

"Never!" she said vehemently.

"Listen, it was a suggestion, not a proposal of marriage." They sat in repose for several minutes. Then he had another idea.

"Why not reopen Glenrocks?"

"What for?"

"Well, answer me this. Why did you come back here, of all places?"

She had to think about that. "I'm not sure. Somehow, I always had the impression my father built Glenrocks for me. In my mind, it was like the beginning of a dynasty."

"Like *Elizabeth the Queen*, or *The Foxes of Harrow* . . ."

"Yes. Handed down, generation to generation." Sabine laughed. "My God, look at it. Some dynasty! I'm it! The last of the Abramowitzes!"

"Well, maybe not."

"Oh come on, Jerry. I've really given up hope about Sammy and his family."

He dismissed that. "Last of the Abramowitzes or not, you ought to reopen Glenrocks. After all, the last of the Abramowitzes inherited twelve million dollars."

"Cardozo money," she reminded him.

"*Your* money now," he reminded her. Then she began to laugh, a welcome sound.

"What's funny?"

"Just think," Sabine said, "if I wanted to, I could say, 'The family Cardozo invites you to Glenrocks.' "

"Mass apoplexy on Seventy-second Street."

"It's almost worth it for that alone."

"Whatever—Sabine, I'm leaving tomorrow. I can't stand the chamber pot situation another day."

But, actually, it was not Jerry's friendship that forced Sabine back into life. It was Dan Ryan's death.

The sheriff's car appeared for the third time the following morning, while Jerry was packing to leave.

"I didn't know who to tell, Miss," the sheriff explained, "but I knew you and he were friends. And you and Matt. And well, we found Dan last night, in bed. Nobody had seen him, and you know him, always up and around, so we checked and there he was."

Sabine called London, but Matt was not there, and the network could provide no information, only a promise to relay to Matt the news of his father's death. It was up to Sabine to make funeral arrangements.

Jerry sighed. And unpacked. Three more days to spend in the little house with the wood range and the chamber pots. Together, Jerry and Sabine visited the funeral home, picked out the casket, planned the funeral.

"When is the burial?" Sabine suddenly thought to ask the funeral director.

"Directly following the first thaw," the man answered. "He'll keep in the ice house till then."

Sabine could hear Jerry stifle a laugh. They left quickly. In a little bar called Rusty's, which was no more than a neon sign and four bar stools, two or three tables, and some Irish goodwill, they drank to Dan Ryan.

It was in Rusty's that Sabine learned about the auction at the Mountain View House.

"Oh, sure," said the bartender, "they haven't been able to pay their taxes now going on three years."

"You mean, the whole package is up for auction? The hotel, the lands, everything?" Sabine asked.

"Kit and kaboodle," the bartender said with satisfaction.

"When?" Sabine asked.

"Friday," the bartender answered.

"I am *not* staying," Jerry said firmly.

"Yes, you are. I'm not going to that auction alone," Sabine said.

Jerry stayed. There were not too many buyers at the auction. After all, it was wartime, it was winter, it was the Catskills, and nobody had too much interest in a hotel that was falling apart and in 1,500 acres that needed taxes paid.

It was cold in the rambling hotel. Of course there was no heat. The auctioneer, who was in a hurry, kept rubbing his hands together. Mr. Taylor, the son of the original owner, stood in one corner and watched, expressionless, as the bidding sputtered and fluttered, and watched things go for next to nothing. What did he care? He was going to Oklahoma. He had prospects. This whole hotel could go to hell. Was going to hell.

A few antique dealers bought a few of the brass beds. A hotel in Albany bought the china. A girls' school in Poughkeepsie got the kitchenware. And the beautiful young woman with the very dark hair and very white skin just sat silently until the place itself, the lands, came up for sale.

A chilly sunlight filled the room. Taylor waited for the bidding to reach a hundred thousand. For Christ's sake, that was the least you could expect. His father had built the cleanest, most Christian, the swankiest, the most elegant—

The black-haired beauty bid ten thousand dollars. Taylor could not believe it. He flashed a look at the auctioneer. Give it some hustle, he thought. The Mountain View House had been the *swankiest*, the most *elegant*—

"Twenty thousand," he called out.

From his childhood Taylor could remember the carriages, the finery. He remembered the first Daimler—

"Thirty thousand." said the beauty. And then there was silence. The auctioneer waited for bids. Thirty thousand—that was nothing for the Mountain View House, the verandahs, the view, the reputation.

"Sold for thirty thousand dollars to—." The auctioneer pointed the gavel in the direction of the beauty.

Sabine rose.

"Abramowitz," she said very clearly, coming down heavy on the *tz*. She presented the treasurer with her check and her credit references.

It was over and done with. The Mountain View House was gone. Taylor gave a last look. Fuck it, he was going to Oklahoma, and he never wanted to see this place again as long as he lived.

They met outside.

"Hello, Mr. Taylor," Sabine said pleasantly, extending her hand. "We are taking over the neighborhood."

He nodded and got in his station wagon.

"I hope you come back some day for a stay. We would surely welcome you at Glenrocks."

Mr. Taylor gave a brief nod of his head, said nothing, and drove off.

"That," she said to Jerry, "is known as a payback."

"Okay," Jerry said. "Now that you have fifteen hundred acres of land, what are you going to do with it?"

"Wait for the war to finish, so I can start building. You want to take a stroll around the property?"

"No," Jerry shivered. "I want to get back to L.A. Listen, this is my last mission of mercy."

She kissed him on the cheek. "I love you," she said, and he said, "Of course."

Chapter Twenty-One

Nothing could happen fast enough.

D-Day—the invasion was successful. Sabine followed the news reports. She had written to Matt about his father (and also about the sale of the Mountain View House), and she was a little surprised when he replied quickly. It was a short letter.

Thanks for the note. As you can imagine, there hasn't been much time for sitting down and figuring things out. But there will be time for that later. I love you. I always have. I always will.

Matt

Sabine kept reading the papers. The United Nations had established a War Crimes Commission, but the Commission moved with the maddening slowness of all official bodies. Meanwhile, the trains were still carrying Jews to the extermination camps. Was there nothing that could be done? Sabine devoted her energies to the American Jewish Joint Distribution Committee. Finally, through the Red Cross, food packages were allowed into some of the camps. And then Eisenhower issued a statement warning the Germans that they would be held responsible for the maltreatment of forced laborers and prisoners in the camps.

And still nothing was done.

Why not bomb them? Sabine asked herself. *Was that such a cruel thing to do, to stop the extermination?* The papers answered her rhetorical question: the most positive solution to the plight of those in concentration camps, they said, would be the earliest possible victory over Germany.

"Bullshit!" Sabine said. She continued to work, worked even harder, but nothing really assuaged her frustration. She worked and she planned for the future. And then, in May, it was suddenly all over. Hitler was dead, the Russians spilled into Berlin. Auschwitz was liberated, and the Americans and British opened up the horrors of Buchenwald, Dachau, and Belsen. As the spring thaw reveals the ravages of winter, so the victory brought to light, bit by bit and camp by camp, the totality of the horror.

Matt was being sent to cover the proceedings that would lead to the trials of the war criminals in Nuremberg.

"It's already started," he told Sabine on the telephone. "Wait and see how many Nazis go free just because they're anti-communist. Just wait. It will happen."

"That's nonsense," Sabine said. "The Russians are our allies."

"The Russians are greedy. And so are we."

"Take me with you," Sabine pleaded suddenly.

"Are you crazy? Go across Europe now? You can't possibly know what it's like."

"Matt, I don't care what conditions are like. I can stand anything. But I tell you, I cannot rest until I find out about Freddy."

Matt had her travel permits in two days. He was in an extremely powerful position, she realized as she flew to London to join him.

The two of them traveled by jeep across France and into Germany in May of 1945. It was like suffering an intense fever—periods of lucidity followed by periods of nightmare. In France they passed through shells of villages, the people walking slowly out to the fields beyond the towns, attempting to harvest a crop, attempting to continue their lives. Paris, on the other hand, had not been touched; the restaurants were all open and flirtations flourished. From Paris they traveled till they crossed the Rhine, and then they slept in army barracks, and found food in distribution centers. They did not drive at night because there were still little pockets of war left, and life was dangerous.

By the time they had crossed the German border, they were accustomed to the brick and rubble and the bare branches of uprooted trees that should have been flourishing. They saw lines of people forming on either side of the road, refugees, displaced persons, some German, others foreigners,

all of them heavy with weariness, their bundles bulging with
the remnants of their lives. At times a cord would break, a
bundle would burst, its contents littering the road. And then
there would be another fever of sweeping up, of collecting, of
clutching onto suitcases, wheelbarrows, baby carriages. There
were always more women than men, more old than young.
Here and there, incongruously, a neat pinstripe suit stood
out. But more often, wooden shoes or ski boots, sometimes
bare feet, predominated, with men in torn workshirts and
women in men's baggy pants. The lines of people never
looked up: their eyes and their lives all seemed to be contained in the next step, the next piece of earth that lay in
front of them. There were perhaps fifteen million people
struggling to get to a home that perhaps was no longer there.
No wonder they merely placed one foot in front of the other
and did not look up or look beyond. What was there for
them to see, beyond the fact that they still existed?

There were centers for displaced persons, DPs as they were
called, established by the Allied Forces. The first camp Matt
and Sabine visited was near Bamberg in Bavaria. It was a
transient camp, formerly a cavalry barrack, and run by three
U.S. officers, seven enlisted men, and five Allied officers.
They dispensed meat, potatoes, vegetables, and milk to the
transients, who would remain until a train of boxcars was
filled, and then they would leave for Holland, or Belgium, or
France, or Italy. Few seemed to leave for the east. There
were many Abramowitzes there, but none of the
Abramowitzes they sought.

They moved on to Dachau, to view the grotesque mountains of papers and lists of names, bones, wigs, gold, children's toys; they did not close their eyes to the gas chambers
or to the groups of living skeletons whose lives hung by a
thread. Everywhere they went, they were surrounded by staring eyes, bald heads, barracks and barbed wire.

At Dachau the American officers were overwhelmed by
their task. They sat in the Kommandant's office, rifling
through papers, interrogating, trying to answer the questions
of streams of people who themselves were picking through
the remnants of lives that had already been obliterated.

There was no record of Sammy Abramowitz at Dachau.

Matt likened it to the Stations of the Cross. On they went,
camp after camp, fringed by the lovely countryside and Ba-

varian beauty, bounded by barbed wire and outposts and long, long corridors filled with file cabinets.

Then to more DP centers. Wildflicken. Spittal. The journey took them farther east, and the zone of control changed. They were now in the Russian sector, protected by Matt's travel permit and, perhaps, by the jeep and the American flag. Cooperation still existed, if only partially.

The worst was still ahead. There was Auschwitz, there was Birkenau, Maidanek and Treblinka. There was no room left for emotion. A curious thing happened to Matt and Sabine. They no longer touched one another and spoke only to give directions or to order food. There were no "good mornings," no "good nights." It was better to have no feelings. It was bettter just to move one foot and then the other, to go one mile and then the next, to check one camp and then the next.

At Treblinka they were told of Terezin, the "model" camp. At Terezin they were advised that several of the surviving children had been taken to an orphanage. And at the orphanage they were directed to another displaced persons camp near Ratibor. It was there that the jeep broke down, and since there was only one mechanic in Ratibor, and he had never seen a jeep and all the wrenches were the wrong size, it was at Ratibor that they stayed while Matt and the mechanic attempted to make repairs. The village was small, no more than twenty houses. The villagers were friendly, and Matt and Sabine found a room in a farmhouse. It was evening and cool and in the kitchen the farmer's wife had just baked bread. The fire in the old-fashioned hearth radiated heat, and Sabine accepted the bread and the milk, thanking the farmer and his wife for it. She wondered why this village was so untouched, when not twenty miles away so many people had died. *Did this farmer and his wife know? How did they go to church then, how did they care for their own children?* Resentment rose in her, making it difficult for her to swallow.

There was a knock at the door, and the farmer opened it. The woman from the camp had come with a wagon. A new trainload of people had arrived from the north, she said. There were some children. She thought perhaps the lady would like to know.

What was the use, Sabine thought wearily. She could no longer stand to gaze on faces and eyes and rags of clothing; to smell the stench of them. *Please, no more, no more feelings, no false hope, no more disappointments, no more parades. Let me alone. Not one, not one have I been able to save. Not one.*

But the woman was standing there waiting, and the cart and horse were outside. And the woman was looking at Sabine, so she rose, disgusted with her own self-pity, and followed the woman out to the cart. She shivered in the evening breeze. The journey took perhaps a half-hour. The new arrivals had all been herded into one room. Some of them still wore their strange prison stripes. There was a sea of faces and they all looked alike, all starved, all beaten dogs, all fearful eyes. It was impossible to tell them apart.

Sabine found herself looking into another weary face, that of a woman, who looked at her harshly and asked suspiciously, "Abramowitz?"

Sabine nodded.

"Have you papers?" the woman continued.

Sabine produced her passport. The woman looked at the green document, compared Sabine's photograph with the real article, and returned the passport to her. "Abramowitz," the woman said again, almost absently. "Abramowitz." Standing behind her was a child, his head down, wearing a gray shirt and short pants. He had no shoes, and placed one foot on top of the other, to keep at least one foot warm. The stone floor was very cold in the late May night.

"This is Freddy," the woman said. Sabine looked for some recognizable sign. Six years ago the boy had been a baby.

"How do you know?" Sabine asked.

The woman suddenly changed posture, embarrassed. "I was . . . I do not know the words in English. From every film of Sammy's I watch. So it was possible to recognize him from the screen. Although his hair—before they took his hair—his hair was not really black." She brushed her own hair nervously. "He was, you know, taken from Terezin, he was—"

"Yes, I know. His ashes were returned, I was told," Sabine said abruptly.

"The boy speaks no English," the woman said. "I gave to Sammy my word that I keep his son."

"His mother?"

"She died—I can't remember when."

"Does he have things—clothing, belongings?"

The woman smiled at Sabine. "No, he has nothing."

Sabine knelt down beside the child. "Freddy," she said. The boy would not look at her. He was trembling. She hoped it was merely from the cold.

"Tell him that I have come, that I am a relative, that I have come to take him to America."

The woman spoke to the boy, but the only word Sabine could recognize was *America*. When the little boy did not understand and stood there, docile, expecting nothing from life, Sabine reached out her hand and touched his bony little arm. She could feel him tense.

"Freddy," she said, and searched for some word to make a bond. All she could think of was *liebe*. She said it. The boy did not move.

The woman was impatient. She shoved him toward Sabine. *"Geh schon,"* she said. The boy looked back at her, but the woman would no longer look at him.

"Take him now," she said. "Yes, take him. Give him a life."

Sabine suddenly emptied her purse into the woman's hand.

"Here, take money. Take something."

"Money has no meaning yet."

Sabine shook her head. "Money always has meaning. If not today, tomorrow. This is from Sammy and this is from me. Thank you. Goodbye."

Sabine took Freddy by the hand and walked out of the door. No one tried to detain them or question them. No one cared. They only felt relief. Another one gone.

Back in the village she found that Matt had repaired the jeep.

"Let's get out of here," she said. "Right now. I want to get him out of here, out of this."

She made a gesture behind her. To her it meant all the camps and the mud and the marshes, the death, insanity, torture. All the Polish names that had been Germanicized, all the borders and guards and barricades and barbed wire and uniforms, everything that had begun for her on a sunny afternoon in a little Swiss customs house in 1939. And hadn't ended yet.

Matt looked at the child, who was still shivering. Sabine had wrapped her coat around him, but his feet were still bare, and the night was becoming even colder.

"Give him a pair of my socks and stay close to the fire. I'll be back," Matt said. He returned in an hour, having bartered his way into two loaves of bread, a round of cheese, some K-rations (where did *they* come from?), three blankets, and two bottles of brandy.

Sabine was astounded. "Where did you find all this? How did you get this much?"

"I now have no cigarettes. You are about to observe the onset of a nicotine fit."

"Then let's leave *now!*" she said, and they did.

They wrapped Freddy in the blankets and in a jacket and sweater and drove through the night. They were stopped at the Czech frontier. The border guards examined their American passports briefly, saw the letters of transit, and waved them through. Sabine did not find her anxiety diminished. It was only one border crossed, and another to come. At the Austrian border near Breclav, the guards were Russian soldiers. But solidarity still existed. The boy was sleeping; they did not wake him up for questioning. There was a toast to the great Soviet people and another to the Americans, and with great magnanimity Matt left one bottle of brandy behind.

A second frontier passed. They drove through the Russian zone without stopping. In Semmering the jeep broke an axle. Sabine looked around her: Russian soldiers, guards, more guns. She tried to control her hysteria.

"I think I'm going to explode," she whispered to Matt.

"Just talk nicely. They don't understand English. Smile." Miraculously, they found, there was a train heading west: four boxcars and an open coal car with straw in it. The train was returning from Vienna through the Russian zone.

"Come on," said Matt, and they climbed into the coal car. There were maybe forty other refugees huddled in the straw, some of them just returned from foraging for water and bread.

"Any idea when the train is leaving?" Matt asked in English.

"Oh, any minute now," one said, and the others laughed uproariously.

"Three days we have been here," another spoke up. "Three days and perhaps we leave someday. What are you?"

"American.'"

They were shocked. What were Americans doing in a coal

car? They were all-powerful. They were the rich. They could waste water.

A Russian soldier swung over the edge of the gondola car and demanded everyone's papers.

One of the group spoke Russian and explained their position. Not one of them was a Pole or a Czech. They were French or Dutch. They had travel permits. The Russian nodded but said nothing, then pointed to Matt.

Matt produced his passport, then Sabine's. The soldier frowned. At that moment Sabine thought maybe she would just scream. She could not stand the tension. The soldier read the passports forwards and backwards as though they were *War and Peace.*

"*Amerikanski?*" He indicated the three of them.

"Yes," said Matt, grinning.

"Fuck you," Sabine smiled. Matt looked at her, and she kept right on smiling and said to him, "If I don't do this, I am going to scream and this is better than screaming. I don't think I can take more than another minute of this. Oh, fuck you very much!" She smiled again at the soldier.

The soldier pointed toward Freddy. "*Polski?*"

"No."

"*Russki?*"

"No."

"*Amerikanski,*" Sabine said in a cocktail party voice, "and if you touch him I will kill you, bastard, shit-head." Then she turned to Matt, "Why don't you offer him a drink?"

"To the great Soviet people!" Matt said, producing the second bottle of brandy. To the soldier it was better proof than a passport: of course this was an American. There were more toasts.

The Russian knew one word of English. "Cigarettes?" he inquired.

The DPs looked at Matt. Every American had cigarettes. That was common knowledge. Matt paled, then turned to the DP who spoke Russian.

"*Nicht rauchen,*" he explained. "No smoke."

The DP translated as the others looked in shock at Matt. America *was* cigarettes. Matt shrugged his shoulders and kept on grinning. Sabine laughed at the joke. *How funny, how funny, ha, ha.*

"May you live to die in an old age home where they won't

allow you to smoke!" she toasted the Russian with the brandy. Her laughter was contagious. Even the Russian smiled. She pressed the bottle on him.

"Keep it! Keep it and get drunk and fall down and break your neck!"

The Russian soldier nodded, then waved, and climbed out of the coal car.

"I am going to be sick," Sabine said.

"Not yet," said Matt. "Wait for the American zone."

The train jerked forward.

"Is it possible we were waiting for that one Russian son of a bitch?" Sabine said.

"We'll see," said Matt, and clasped her hand to keep it from trembling. The train continued to move. They were leaving the freight yard. Suddenly the DPs began to shout and stand up and wave and dance. Everyone was smiling. Joy unconfined.

"I do have a feeling we should sleep in shifts," Matt remarked in an offhand manner. "It's quite possible any one of them would kill to get his hands on an American passport."

They lumbered across the province of Steiermark and reached the American zone at Radstadt. More Russian soldiers approached.

"What are we going to do? We can't buy our way through Europe on brandy," Sabine muttered.

"Watch!" Matt said. Fifty feet away was the American zone, and there stood American GIs.

"Hey, guys!" Matt yelled.

They looked up, suspiciously.

"Mayday! Mayday!" he yelled sunnily. He had caught their attention. Now they watched as the Russians again checked travel permits, DP papers, and the American passports. These Russians looked at the papers and then waved them on without questioning. They reached the American zone.

"Everything okay?" the American soldier said.

"Yeah," Matt breathed.

"How about you, lady?"

Sabine vomited right in front of him.

Matt made two phone calls and they were given another jeep and enough fuel to get them to Switzerland.

"Oh God bless the *New York World*. God bless the network!" Sabine kept repeating as they drove through Tyrol. Freddy was now awake, and watched wide-eyed as they passed the glorious white-capped Alps. It was spring and the streams were rushing down the mountains, the flowers were a celebration of yellow and blue. The cattle grazed peacefully in the meadow and the earth smelled fresh.

"Don't stop," Sabine said. "Don't stop for anything until we get to Switzerland." They passed Innsbruck. They came to Landeck. She remembered the rainroad station; she remembered Sammy the swell in his elegant Viennese clothes amid all the lederhosen and Tyrolean hats. They drove toward Buchs. Buchs was the border. Buchs and Feldkirch. Now they were in the French zone. *Please God, don't let anything happen. Not a flat tire, or a broken axle.*

They approached the last border. The tricolor was flying. And beyond it, just beyond the barriers, was the Swiss flag. The French guards looked at their papers with scant curiosity. The barrier was lifted. They passed through.

The Swiss were more attentive.

"Your destination?"

"New York."

"Your reason for coming to Switzerland?"

The man spoke excellent English. Sabine had to restrain herself. He might even know what "'fuck you" meant.

"To get to New York." Matt was still smiling pleasantly.

"The child?"

"He is with us. He has no papers. He is my son," Matt said. He flashed three more official documents.

"These papers are for transit only. You understand that?" the guard said.

"Yes," Matt said. "We are going to the consulate in Zurich."

"In order to remain in Switzerland longer than seven days, that is most important," the guard counseled them.

Efficient, wonderfully efficient, deserving of promotion. Who wants to stay here any longer than necessary? Stop talking! We'll get out within the week. I understand. All booked up. Vacate the premises.

But she said nothing. The guard looked at her. "Anything to declare, madame?" And she looked down at the dress she had been sleeping in for a week, the smelly remains of a

cloth coat, and a suitcase that contained dirty laundry. She
looked in her bag and held up a checkbook.

"This, from the Bank of England," she said, continuing to
smile.

"You will find a branch in Zurich," the guard assured her,
not smiling back. Then he let them pass.

They had crossed the border. They were safe. The Swiss
flags flapped in the breeze as they passed. The small bundle of
rags that was the last remains of her family clung to her for
warmth.

One. I have saved one.

They stopped in Zurich for the night. They had forgotten
what the world could be like. The hotel was deluxe: the
lobby understated, wood-paneled, bustling, the clientele well-
dressed, jeweled, coiffed, washed. There were shop windows
displaying diamonds, watches, and furs. There was a staircase
of marble, and three elevators with wrought iron doors. And
there was an American bar. Inside men and women were sitting and chatting, drinking, smoking.

Smoking.

"Do you realize I haven't had a cigarette in three days?"
Matt shouted. "I don't believe it."

"Maybe it's time to quit."

"Are you kidding?"

They grabbed Freddy by the hand and went into the tobac-
conist. There were American cigarettes, Lucky Strikes and
Camels. How incredible. Freddy watched the two strangers
who were now somehow in control of his life puffing and
blowing smoke out of their mouths.

"Oh God, it's good," Matt groaned.

"Better than anything," Sabine agreed.

"Maybe you're right," Matt grinned.

Their room was not really a room. It was a suite. With a
huge bed, heavy draperies, quilts, gilt furniture, carpets. The
bathroom held a gigantic tub. And look—hot water, steaming
hot! And a bidet. And a separate water closet.

Beyond the windows there was a lake with the swans.
Down below there was traffic, strolling people. And a little
garden café with colored umbrellas. Sabine was in such ecstasy she raced around the room with Freddy.

"God, Freddy, look, doorknobs! Polished doorknobs! Sit,

sit in the chair. It's like sitting on a cloud. Look at the bed.
Bounce on the bed." Of course he didn't understand a word.
She tried once more to control her joy. It was impossible. She
swept him up in her arms.

"Never again," she said, clutching him. "Never again."

Freddy had never seen a telephone. That fascinated him. It
fascinated the three of them.

"Will you look what you can get here?" Sabine marveled.
"And in four languages! I want to try everything."

They were dressed like paupers. They decided to eat in
their rooms. They ordered from room service. A parade of
tables and silver-covered dishes arrived, followed by a pastry
cart with chocolate éclairs, strawberry tarts, mousse and
whipped cream, and charlotte russe.

Freddy chose one of each. She let him. He did not know
how to use a fork. Matt showed him. He ate an éclair and
then devoured the strawberry tart.

He guarded the pastries with his left arm as he ate with his
right. He gorged himself on three more, then looked up in be-
wilderment and threw up on the white tablecloth.

"It runs in the family," Sabine said as she started to clean
up.

"Let the maid do it," Matt said.

"No, I'll do it," Sabine said. "I'm his mother. My God,
Matt. Guess what? We're parents."

"Well then, as parents I guess we'll have to say no sweets,"
Matt laughed.

"Tomorrow. We can say all that tomorrow."

Tomorrow. It was the first time in months she had looked
forward, had anticipated the future. What a luxury that was.
She looked at Freddy.

"He is dropping with fatigue. Look at his eyes. I'll give
him a bath. My God, what will we do with his clothes?"

"The same thing we'll do with ours. Get rid of them. Buy
new ones."

She laughed as she took Freddy into the bathroom and
undressed him. She passed her hands over the emaciated little
body. She would give him everything, she promised. Nothing
would be denied him. She would fatten him up, give him
good meat and milk, watch him grow. Off came the shirt and
the pants and he was naked in front of her. She took a bar of
good Swiss soap and handed it to him.

Freddy screamed in terror. He did not try to run for the door. He crouched in a corner and screamed. He did not cry, there was not a tear, just the fear of death in that scream. Matt burst in.

"What happened?"

Freddy's eyes were on the shower. They followed his glance.

"How stupid of me," Sabine said quietly. "Even the littlest ones must have known, they must have heard."

Matt gave Freddy his hand. The little boy hesitated and then obeyed. Matt took the child in his arms.

"Wet the washcloth," he told Sabine. "And give it plenty of soap."

And that was how they washed his face. She washed him so gently, as if she might wash away each scar and every horror. First forehead, then face, then behind the ears to the skinny neck and bony shoulders. And Freddy relaxed. He was not going to die. Matt let him down and Sabine continued to wash, then Matt dried the child with a huge terrycloth towel.

When they returned to the bedroom, the dinner had been cleared away and a maid was turning down the beds. The sheets were so clean and smooth; the room as lovely as a dream of heaven. Freddy looked from Matt to Sabine for permission; they motioned him into the big bed and he disappeared from view, except for his head. His eyes were dropping shut with fatigue. There was no language one could use to comfort him.

"*Geh schlafen*," Matt said awkwardly, and the boy smiled. He was asleep in two seconds, turned toward the light that was by the bed.

The maid looked at the child, and then at them. "*Gute Nacht*," she said softly, and left them. They were alone.

"My God, we're dirty!" Matt exclaimed, observing the two of them in the mirror.

"Very observant. I need a bath."

"I need a drink." Matt telephoned for a bottle and ice and two glasses. The service seemed instantaneous. Matt was still sitting with his shirt half unbuttoned when the buzzer sounded and a waiter entered with their order. Matt signed the bill and the waiter discreetly left. Matt poured them each a drink.

He carried the scotch into the bathroom, where Sabine was standing.

"I don't believe this. It's like a dream," she said. "Look at the size of that tub. Feel these towels!" She turned on the shower. "Hot water!" she exclaimed as though she had invented it.

They stripped off their clothes. By this time the room was full of steam. They looked at each other, and sensuality flooded over them. He reached for her and kissed her. Their bodies joined, slippery with sweat. They slid against one another, and the smoothness of their two bodies aroused them. Still standing there, he entered her, and the moment she felt him inside her she came, shuddering, welcoming him, grabbing his tongue with her teeth and sucking on him, allowing him to cover her body with his, allowing him everything, feeling him everywhere at once on her, but mostly and most beautifully penetrating her again and again.

They washed and dried each other and entered the luxurious bedroom. Sabine looked around at the elegance, the soft lights, and then back at Matt.

"You know what I want?" she whispered.

"Not again!" he whispered back.

"No. I mean, yes, but not now."

They crawled into bed, one on each side of the sleeping boy, and turned out the light. In the dark, Sabine said, "I'll tell you what I want. I want a hotel like this. I want everyone to be able to sample such luxury."

Matt's voice was already heavy with sleep. "Whatever you want, Sabine, you'll know how to get." Soon they were both safe, safely asleep.

Just before dawn, Sabine work up, wondering where she was. Then she heard the steady breathing of her two men. It occurred to her that without marriage and without birth she had acquired a family. It was a pleasant shock. And she immediately went back to sleep.

Chapter Twenty-Two

Matt Ryan was absolutely right, of course.

Sabine had set her mind on learning about luxury hotels, and there was no better schoolroom than Switzerland.

They had two weeks before the *Caronia* was scheduled to sail from Le Havre to New York, and in those two weeks Matt, Sabine, and Freddy sampled only the best. In Zurich, Bern, Lausanne, Evian, Geneva. Sabine noted everything: the name of the maitre d' in Zurich whose dining room functioned with the efficiency of a Swiss watch; the mark on the china in Lausanne; the al fresco lunches in Geneva and Lausanne—she jotted down the recipes on the backs of the menus. She talked to chambermaids and examined the labels on sheets and stuffed her mind with facts while she stuffed Freddy with food. At the end of two weeks he was a different child. The paleness was gone. Only his beauty remained. Black eyes. Curly hair. Ivory skin. Sabine watched him. Freddy resembled her father more than he did his own.

They sailed on the *Caronia* and landed in New York four weeks before two atom bombs dropped on Hiroshima and Nagasaki, ending the war. And four weeks after that, a strange new world was opening up for all of them, without their realizing it.

In the beginnning, everything seemed normal. The poker games, for instance; they still took place every Wednesday night and, for the most part, the players were the same as before the war. Seymour Martin, promoted to vice-president of the network that owned the *World*, had replaced James Price, the actor, in the game. Boseman and Mason from the network also played, as did O'Brien, the newsmagazine publisher. But they were all busy men, and there were alternates: Jack Werner and Murray Lefcourt, whose position in the New York office of the studio had declined as Bernard's star had risen; Sam Mishkin, whose position had risen; and Greg Newmark, who, after all was a lawyer, and flew in from the Coast twice a month.

It was Seymour who one night, who casually asked Sabine about her plans.

"Oh, didn't you know?" she said. "I'm going to reopen Glenrocks."

"But it burned down."

"That's right. But I'm going to rebuild it. And it won't be just a hotel. I'm going to build a resort. I promise you it will be the most luxurious place you ever invested in."

"Who invested?" They all stopped for a moment.

"All of you. You're all going to invest because you can't resist a good gamble. And this will be."

"See you and raise you," Jack Werner said to Matt, as the game continued.

"Call," said Matt.

"I'm in, Sabine," Murray Lefcourt said. By the end of the night, they all were.

The hotel became clearer in Sabine's mind with each passing day. She wanted to combine the luxury of Europe with the fun of the United States. It should be a playground and it should dazzle, the way Mizener had dazzled everyone with those wonderful palaces on the Florida Gold Coast.

Maybe she'd have mirrored bathrooms, ceilings, and walls. And round bathtubs with gilded swans for spigots. And in the bedroom, thick carpets and huge beds. Luxury and sensuality, partly a harem, partly a hotel. A pleasure palace. That was it. There would be balconies off every room, overlooking the valley. Indoor and outdoor swimming pools. An indoor skating rink. And for the kids (because the kids were terribly important) she wanted to create a special environment—bowling alleys and the equivalent of the corner drugstore. (Was she thinking back to her own childhood, she wondered?) Jukeboxes. A place to dance. Tennis courts and a golf course for the parents. And ski trails—skiing was becoming increasingly popular. And a dining room where a thousand people could eat at once, combined with a nightclub that featured big-time entertainment. Ah, if New York State only allowed gambling . . .

All it took was money. No, she decided, it was more than that. It took money plus magic. She had the money, and part of the magic came from Matt and the power of his name. That meant the power of publicity and the people who wanted to know him, who delighted in knowing her: prizefighters and socialites, investment bankers and tennis players. They were a good crowd, a free-spending, fun-loving crowd. A very different generation from Bertha and Simon, for instance.

Bertha had never heard of any of them. Simon did not want to know any of them. They both abdicated. Glenrocks was to be Sabine's child. Her second child, perhaps, since her first was Freddy.

Sabine was impatient. When was all this money and magic going to turn Glenrocks into a real resort, she continually asked the contractor and architect. By 1947, they answered. You'll open by the summer of 1947.

"That's forever. That's ages away. My God, when it opens, Freddy will be . . . eight years old. Practically married!"

"Don't worry," the contractor said in a fatherly way. "Time will fly."

And he was correct. From the beginning of fall, it suddenly turned to Christmas. For the first time in five years lights in Manhattan celebrated the peace—store windows, billboards, streetlights, skyscrapers, Christmas trees all advertised peace, prosperity, good times.

Freddy was already speaking English—his own brand—and his favorite pastime was talking to Jerry Davis on the telephone. Sometimes Sabine thought they were at almost the same emotional age. Jerry had arrived in New York for the Christmas holidays because he refused to spend another holiday in California being depressed.

Sabine found herself suddenly speaking in elliptical phrases. She had no time to finish sentences as she raced around Manhattan buying presents, looking at architects' plans and scale models, and being impatient for time to pass—but also anxious because time *was* passing.

One afternoon in the middle of December she was on her way back to the Village when something in a shop window on Fourteenth Street caught her eye. A menorah.

She walked into the store and bought it.

"Just in time. Tonight's the first night," the store owner reminded her.

"Of course," she said and took the menorah home.

"What is it?" Matt asked her.

"It's a menorah," she answered.

"What's it for?"

"For Chanukah."

"No, I mean what do you do with it?"

"You light candles."

"All at once?"

Sabine stopped. She had no idea. She called her mother.

"Why ask me?" Bertha said. "We never had menorahs. We were socialists. I'll ask Simon." A minute later she returned to the phone. "Simon says no."

"No, what?"

"You do not light the candles all at once, but he wants to know why you have a menorah in the first place."

"It's for Freddy."

"Simon disapproves."

"I don't care. It's Chanukah, and it's for Freddy and it's a time for family. Why don't you and Simon come over? I'll call Jerry." It was such a spontaneous moment that everyone accepted. Two hours later the improvised family was standing around an unlit menorah, arguing.

"There's a special way to light them," Simon was insisting, "but I wouldn't know. I was never religious."

"Well," said Bertha, "if you're going to do it at all, you ought to do it right."

"Why are you doing it?" Jerry asked.

"I just want him to know what it means to be a Jew."

"I imagine he knows that already," Simon said sarcastically.

"What is Chanukah?" Matt said.

"Ah," said Simon, "it commemorates the time the Jews defeated the Maccabees."

"I thought the Jews *were* the Maccabees," Jerry said hesitantly.

"Impossible," Simon said flatly.

"I thought it was the festival of lights," Bertha said timidly.

"It is," said Sabine.

"I don't understand," Matt confessed.

"If the Jews were the Maccabees, who were they fighting?" Simon asked Jerry.

"Greeks, weren't they?"

"Was it Greeks or Romans?"

Sabine stopped the bickering. "Someone must know about this Chanukah business," she said.

It was Dieterl, in California, who informed her long-distance about the ceremony.

"First," he said in his careful way, "it marks the time when the Greeks had defiled the Jewish temples and Judas Maccabeus rallied the forces—"

"Then he *was* Jewish."

"Judas Maccabeus, definitely."

"Jerry was right."

"Now, it seemed that there was only oil enough to last one night, but by a miracle, it lasted eight. That's the reason for the menorah with eight branches. Listen carefully. Light the tallest one in the middle first. That is the *shamas*. Then you light the other candles from that one. But you light one candle for the first night, two candles for the second, and so forth and so on. *And* you place the candles from right to left, *but* you light them from left to right—"

"Oh, Dieterl, thank you," Sabine said.

"—while you say the prayers," Dieterl finished.

"What prayers? There are special prayers? Wait. Let me get a pencil."

Dieterl waited in Santa Monica while Sabine found a pencil. Then he proceeded to spell out phonetically the Hebrew prayer and responses. When she was finished, he said, "Some Jew you are!"

"Oh, it's not for me. It's for Freddy," Sabine answered.

Dieterl's voice changed. "Kiss him for me and wish him a happy Chanukah."

She hung up. Jerry suddenly rose.

"Wait. I remember. It's like the twelve days of Christmas," he said. "Except there's *Chanukah gelt*. And presents you have to hide."

"You never got all that nonsense from me," Simon accused him.

"God, no!" Jerry answered. "I learned it on the street."

Sabine took Freddy out of the room while Matt and the others hid small presents under cushions and chairs. Then Matt went to get an enormous package from the hall, hiding it at the far end of the dining room. Sabine brought Freddy back, took a match, and lit the first candle and haltingly began the prayer as Freddy watched.

"Boruch atoh adonoy eloh-hay-nu . . ."

Uncomfortably the others stumbled behind, awkward with the Hebrew phrases and with the tradition. Sabine was conscious of the boy's eyes watching her but she could not fathom his expression. *Were there services in the camps?* she wondered. *Does Freddy have any idea about Chanukah? He must certainly have seen people praying.* But he did not move. His face betrayed nothing.

She finished the prayers. Then Jerry showed Freddy how to search for the presents. Freddy's eyes lit up. Presents! He was a little boy—he understood presents.

While Jerry and Freddy continued to look under pillows and in corners, Matt and Sabine began to set up the contents of the big box on the dining room table. It was a miniature electric train. There was a locomotive (with real headlights), boxcars, flatcars, passenger coaches, a tunnel, a station, even a genuine whistle.

Without saying a word, Matt set the train in motion and it raced around the track, circling the table, entering the tunnel and coming out on the other side. The adults looked on with amusement. It was an all-American miniature dream, the electric train—what every boy wanted for Christmas.

"Freddy!" They summoned the boy. He was on the other side of the room and he turned, staring at the train. His eyes were intent. Matt adjusted a switch and the train slowed down and stopped at the station.

"Here," Matt said. "You try it." But Freddy remained where he was, across the room.

"All aboard!" Matt called and started the train. Slowly it gathered speed as Freddy watched it.

"What a fantastic machine!" Jerry marveled.

"Look! He doesn't know what to say," Bertha commented.

"American technology. It leaves us all speechless!" Simon contributed.

They looked at the little boy, and his eyes were filled with terror. Eyes that had seen loading platforms and lines of refugees, belongings under one arm, men to one side, women and small children on the other, and then the boxcars packed and stinking and rotten. Eyes that had seen the transports, watching a night filled with nightmares from which you never woke up.

The train whistled.

Death.

"Ich bin kein Yid!" the boy cried out in terror.

It marked the end of Freddy's religious upbringing.

Chapter Twenty-Three

Freddy had no problems with Matt. As soon as he could say the word in English, Matt was Dad. Not Papa—that name belonged to another person. And never Daddy. Dad showed him how to be an American. Dad *was* American. When it was time to take Freddy to school (they had decided to make their home near Glenrocks), it was Dad who took him, to the same school that Sabine and Matt had attended. And it was Dad who announced rather fiercely to his teachers and classmates that this was Freddy Abramowitz. The Irish eyes swept the classroom, waiting for a challenge. But there was none. If anyone made fun of Freddy's English, it was behind his back.

They did not make fun of his English for long. More than anything in the world, Freddy wanted to be an American. He crouched on his bed, concentrating on the dresser mirror, saying over and over, "*The—that—those . . .*"

Within a year his English was perfect. He spoke exactly like an American; he even learned to love baseball. Matt had taught him to pitch, and how to use the bat, how to step *in* to the ball when he swung. Freddy's coordination was good and his body responded. His body also grew. His dad was teaching him how to be an all-American.

He could have been Huck Finn or Tom Sawyer or Penrod. He knew all the ball scores and the new popular songs.

But then the all-American boy began to steal.

The first time it was a piece of fruit, such a small thing that Sabine left it to Matt to explain that it was wrong to steal and that there was no need. They had plenty of food.

Freddy nodded. He understood. He understood that, from then on, he would have to be more careful about stealing. He stole from the other children at school. He took a wonderful knife that had a corkscrew and a bottle opener, with a handle made of pearl. He grabbed whatever spare change might be

397

around. He walked away with cigarettes. He had seen what a cigarette could bring. Trading cigarettes with a guard had brought food, or an additional day of life.

Freddy did not keep his treasures in his room. He found a space—remote but accessible—where he buried everything: money, knives, watches, candy. He watched his collection grow and with each addition he felt a little more secure.

He had to be very careful. He could let nothing slip, nothing that would focus on him. He would be the good kid, the most popular boy in class. Whatever life he had left behind he buried along with the knives and the watches. He would not allow the past to enter his mind. He promised himself that.

One day a schoolyard scuffle with a classmate turned uglier than either Freddy or the other boy had intended. Someone had to either back down or really attack; a crowd ringed the adversaries.

Memory suddenly overtook Freddy. He had seen the submissive backdown under the reign of blows. He had seen heads crack open, blood gushing from the kicks in the face. He knew about crushed hands. He knew they didn't always come from the guards. The prisoners themselves, struggling for that one piece of bread, had often killed for it.

Go for the balls. Freddy, go for the neck and strangle. Gouge out the eye. Get the bread. Win. Or die. Attack.

He did. He played by no schoolboy rules. The first kick was to the balls, and when the other boy crumpled, Freddy went for the neck. He had seen it done before. He watched his opponent's eyes bulge, he recognized the gurgle and the rasping for breath.

The children were separated by a horrified teacher. The next day she told Sabine, in a calm primary education voice tinged with reproach, that a small boy ought to be able to take a joke, that Freddy's reaction was not *normal*.

Sabine carried the message home to Matt. "You're a man. Do something," she demanded.

"What?"

"Show him how to fight."

"It looks like he knows how."

"No. Fight fair. Box."

"Oh, the Marquis of Queensberry rules and all that?" Matt was secretly amused by Freddy's behavior.

"Matt, don't be dense. I don't want Freddy to get into trouble. He's got to know the difference in fighting—he can't just go in and kill somebody."

"Okay, you're right," Matt agreed. "I taught you how to fight—I can certainly teach Freddy." He held his arms open and Sabine found her safety. Always, within his arms, there was a safe place. Hand in hand, they went to see Freddy.

The boy was in the bathroom. He had just taken a shower and was trying to slick down his curly hair, to straighten it. *He wants to be Tyrone Power*, Sabine thought. *Why, when he's so good-looking himself?*

"Freddy, your father and I would like to speak to you."

"Okay. Just a minute."

"No, not just a minute—*now*."

"*Okay* . . ." It was Tom Sawyer's disgust, circa 1946. Sabine was amused at herself and at him. Mother and son, having the age-old traditional argument.

Matt did the talking, earnestly explaining the difference between right and wrong, the differences in degree. The boy, whose curls were already defying his brush, nodded when Matt finished.

"You understand, pal? You got that? Tomorrow I'll show you some tricks about boxing. Okay? Kiss me goodnight."

Freddy was relieved that the lecture was over. He threw his arms around Matt and kisssed the place where the beard didn't prickle. He knew just the spot, between chin and neck.

"Good night, Dad.'"

He kissed Sabine. "Good night, Tanti." *Tanti*, German for "auntie." He had always called Sabine that.

On impulse, she asked him, "Why do you call him Dad and me Tanti?"

Freddy didn't answer.

"Why don't you call me Mother?"

"Because you're not my mother. Good night."

She let it go. What was she going to say—that Matt wasn't his real father? She put it out of her mind. She had too much else to deal with.

She was dealing with architects and contractors and unions. Using the same tactics she had applied to the wholesalers at the Washington Market. She flattered, cajoled, browbeat. She also fired.

Three architects and two contractors (one of whom was later sent to prison for graft) were let go before she discovered Gilberto, a young Brazilian, who finally built her the hotel she wanted. It was shaped in a graceful "S", totally modern, with a great deal of glass and concrete. The New York columnists predicted disaster. Here was an architect who had never seen snow, had never tasted a knish; what would he know about the Catskills? The entire charm of the mountains would be swallowed up in pretension, in a cold, sterile, modern design.

Any number of people were willing—waiting, even—for Sabine to fail.

She was a woman dealing in a man's business. She was outspoken. Her relationship with Matt Ryan was too unconventional. And his views were becoming increasingly unpopular as a cold war rapidly developed between the United States and Russia.

Sabine had turned her back on Hollywood. And Hollywood was outraged. Who was *she* to deny success? In a world where few succeed, she had—and then she had stood up to the industry. Beverly Hills was:

1. Outraged
2. Envious

Still, no one would miss the opening of the new Glenrocks. The rooms had been booked for weeks. The West Coast contingent had chartered planes, the East Coast contingent, limousines.

The opening was scheduled for Memorial Day weekend, 1947. Two weeks before the opening, Matt was sent to Germany on assignment by Seymour Martin, and Sabine was furious, but there was nothing she could do about it.

Her investors arrived to help out. O'Brien from the news magazine brought along his good friend, who just happened to be the editor of the *Daily News*. Aaron Eisen took care of Seventh Avenue and the Hearst papers. And Seymour used his connections with all three networks.

The West Coast group arrived via three different charters. Murray Lefcourt brought Harry Cohn and Darryl Zanuck. Jack Warner arrived on his own.

Surprisingly, so did Bernard Ross. There was a moment of tension when he stood in front of Sabine. They eyed one another. Then Bernard looked around the sumptuous lobby with the dazzling crystal chandelier and asked in a loud voice, "Sabine, you mean you gave up all Hollywood, just for *this*?" and that broke the ice. Everyone laughed and Earl Wilson hurriedly wrote it down as a quote.

And then Bernard began to reminisce about the old Glenrocks and how he had been there from the beginning. He told stories, he even made up some, and the reporters scribbled away furiously. Sabine never ceased to be amazed at Bernard. It was as though nothing had happened between them. He was funny. He was charming. He was insuring the success of her project. Of course, it didn't hurt him any. He was getting more coverage than Zanuck and Warner combined. Let him talk!

Sabine had trained the staff very carefully and now she watched with eagle eye how the limousines were being parked, how the luggage was being handled, how the guests were being greeted, how graciously they were shown to their quarters. She managed a visit to every facility. She saw to it that no one had to wait for anything.

There was to be no formal reception line at dinner, but Sabine and Bertha had agreed to stand together inside the entrance to the dining room. The dining room itself had been decorated in muted colors, spacious but not cold. In the little lobby leading to the dining room, Gilberto had placed three mirrored columns to brighten the eye. Sabine and Bertha found themselves staring at their reflections in the few minutes before the doors opened for the guests.

Sabine wore white. Her dress had been designed by a young Parisian, Christian Dior, whom nobody knew yet. At least, nobody in the Catskills. Bertha was dressed in lilac. Her hair was quite gray now, but she was still a very striking woman.

"How grand we look," Bertha commented, looking at her daughter in the mirror. "I wonder who we are."

"Whoever we are, we are beautiful," Sabine said. "Totally beautiful. And petrified."

"Don't be," Bertha said. "Do you remember our first opening? You were so small then. Your father ran around, improvising everything. My God, there was such a thunderstorm that night. And no electricity. And look, it turned out all right. There's nothing that can't be handled."

"Don't say that. It's bad luck."

"Don't believe *that* either," Bertha said, and did a most extraordinary thing. She kissed her daughter.

And then the doors opened to reveal the governor of New York, followed by Eddie Cantor, who was with Jennie Grossinger. Then came Joe Louis and, behind him, Frank Sinatra. The Hollywood contingent continued to travel in three packs, like wolves: Cohn's pack, Zanuck's pack, and Bernard's pack. Walter Winchell did not stop talking and Earl Wilson did not stop writing; Cholly Knickerbocker did not stop staring, and fortunately nobody stopped eating or drinking or dancing.

It was a miracle. Practically everything worked. For the entire night the only damage consisted of ten glasses, two scraped chairs, and a saxophone player who was too drunk to make it back to the stand after the first set.

Otherwise, it was everything Sabine had dreamed that it could be. It was classy. It was fun. And it was hers.

At three in the morning, feet up on the table by her bed, smoking one last cigarette, Sabine thought about her evening. The phone rang.

"How did it go?" It was Matt.

"Oh God, how I miss you. I wanted you here. Everyone asked about you."

"But how did it go?"

"I think it's okay."

"How about that bastard Winchell?"

"I think okay."

"Well, and the others? Could you tell? What did Seymour say?"

"Seymour was pleased."

Matt could hear the detachment in her voice. "You didn't get the flowers," he said.

"You mean you didn't send them."

"Of course I did. Of course I sent them. White roses. I love you."

"It doesn't matter," Sabine said, "I miss you." She knew him, though, and knew he hadn't sent her flowers, but he was forgiven. It was all right. She loved him.

"When are you coming back?"

"Don't ask that question. This place is a cesspool. Believe me, it isn't just the Krauts, but I don't want to talk about that. I just want to tell you that I love you, and I thought about you all night. Now I want you to go to sleep, and don't let one son of a bitch into your room. Except Freddy. Got that?"

"Got it," she said, and they ended the conversation with a laugh. Sabine, too tired to turn the light off, fell asleep in her slip. At five in the morning she was awakened by a knock on her door. It was Martin, the night clerk, trembling and holding a long red-ribboned box.

"These got delayed somehow," he apologized.

"That's all right, Martin." She opened the box in a stupor. There were two dozen long-stemmed white roses and a card from Matt. He had not forgotten.

She could find no container for them, so she fell asleep with them in her arms, which was probably what Matt would have liked.

Seymour Martin's comment was so casual that Sabine hardly noticed it. They ran into each other the following day by the swimming-pool and she described Matt's call from Germany.

"Is he being careful?" Seymour asked.

"When is Matt ever careful?" Sabine laughed as they walked away from one another. Much later it occurred to her—careful about what? What had Seymour meant? Was it supposed to be some half-humorous reference about venereal fräuleins. No, that was not Seymour's style.

Later that same day, Seymour approached her. "Has Matt made any comments to you about Germany?" he asked.

"He called it a cesspool. No, beg your pardon. What he said was—it isn't just the Krauts who have made it a cesspool. Why? Is that what you meant about being careful?"

"Umm." Seymour looked around and then lowered his voice. "There's a list nobody's supposed to know about."

"What list?"

"From the Attorney General's office. The purpose is to check on the loyalty of government officials."

"What does that have to do with Matt?"

"I don't believe the list stops with government officials. You know the House Un-American Activities Committee had a few meetings in Hollywood, investigating alleged subversion in the film industry."

"Oh, come on, Sy," Sabine laughed. "That committee has been around for years."

"Umm," Seymour said, and left it at that.

The opening weekend of Glenrocks was a total success. On Monday Sabine began to read the papers, but only for coverage of her opening. She was not disappointed. The press was terrific. During the next week the number of advance bookings for the season reflected the good press.

It was only after she had circled both Winchell's and Sullivan's columns that she got around to reading *Ryan's Beat*. Matt was writing from Bonn.

Something stinks here.

As of May 30, 1,300,000 Nazis remain to be tried in the U.S. Zone for war crimes. One third of the Bundestag consists of former Nazis. Every second bureaucrat you meet openly admits to having been a member of the party. Why, my friends, is that?

This is what I'm told.
The Nazis were anticommunists.
The current threat to the world comes from the East, from the socialist world.

Communism is the big danger in Germany now.
Who tells me that? The word does not come from the German vanquished, but from the American victors. The danger, friends, is not in Germany.

Sabine read the column, and put the paper with the others. She thought no more about it.

Throughout the summer she hardly glanced at the papers. She had a hotel to run and a child to raise. She had no time for reading. Matt remained in Europe and she missed him, but she knew he would come back. That was their relationship. Free to come, free to go. For them it worked well.

It was only in September, after Labor Day, that she began to see how much space was being devoted to HUAC and its activities.

Several screenwriters had been subpoenaed to testify in Washington. They had refused to cooperate and were dubbed

"The Unfriendly Ten" by the more right-wing elements of the press.

Then more important members of the Hollywood hierarchy were summoned.

Matt phoned to say he was coming home, and Sabine read him some of the excerpts from the papers.

"It sounds like a Marx Brothers comedy," she concluded.

"I'm afraid you've got the wrong Marx," Matt said slowly.

But Sabine was partially correct. The proceedings did resemble some loony film.

When Bernard Ross was called to Washington as a friendly witness, the newspapers ran excerpts from the proceedings.

CHAIRMAN:	Sir, were you the producer of a film entitled *Storm over Stalingrad?*
ROSS:	I was *a* producer, yes.
CHRMAN:	On the screen the credit reads, "Produced by Bernard Ross."
ROSS:	Well, sir, you know Hollywood.
CHRMAN:	No, sir. I do not know Hollywood. I am endeavoring to discover the amount of subversion that exists. I understand that you have come here of your own accord—
ROSS:	Oh, absolutely.
CHRMAN:	—to give us information.
ROSS:	Yes, sir. I commend the purpose of this committee.
CHRMAN:	Thank you, Mr. Ross. Now, in your estimation, who would you say was responsible for the content of the film, *Storm Over Stalingrad?*
ROSS:	Who? Well, sir, that is difficult—ah,—if I may be allowed to explain—
CHRMAN:	Please do. (*Laughter.*)
ROSS:	What I mean is, no one was responsible. (*Laughter.*)
CHRMAN:	*No* one was in charge?
ROSS:	Well, the film, *Storm Over Stalingrad* was produced because at the time it was felt that the American people should be more aware of their allies.
CHRMAN:	Even if those allies were Communists?

ROSS: We never used that word. That was a word
            that was strictly *verboten.*

CHRMAN: Was that an attempt to deceive the American
            public into believing the Communists were
            just like Americans?

ROSS: No, sir. In the entertainment industry, it is
            important for the audience to identify with—
            to be sympathetic to—the characters por-
            trayed on the screen in order to believe what
            is happening to them.

CHRMAN: Did the writer, Bertolt Brecht, work on this
            film?

ROSS: Only one day. I fired him. I could see he was
            not serious about the project.

CHRMAN: How could you tell that?

ROSS: He asked if we had any footage on happy
            peasants. That was a sarcastic remark, in my
            opinion.

CHRMAN: We found Mr. Brecht to be a most cooper-
            ative witness, Mr. Ross. But now, could you
            tell us of your affiliation with a group, a
            theatrical group, I believe, called the People's
            Theater Alliance?

(The witness conferred with counsel before responding.)

Sabine was still reading when Matt walked through the
door of their New York apartment.

"I don't believe it. Matt!"

"Seymour called me back." Matt hugged her. "It's so good
to be here. You might say that my big Irish mouth has done
it again—asked too many questions for my own good."

She watched him. He looked tired, but perhaps that was
from the long trip.

"I have a feeling people are seeing Red," he said.

"You mean they're angry?"

"No, I wish they were. I think they're scared. You know
about the Attorney General's list? Now Truman has allowed
the Attorney General to hand over this list to the House
Committee."

"Why?"

"I'll tell you why. Truman wants to get the Marshall Plan
through Congress and he feels the only way he can do that is

to scare hell out of the American people. What will scare them? Russia! Why do you think all the Nazis are getting pardoned? Because they're anticommunists."

Sabine nodded and looked at him. Matt was mad, really angry; oh, his Irish was up. His eyes were blazing, he was standing there, fuming, when the phone rang. It was Jerry.

"Sabine?" Jerry said. "I am here in Washington with a group. We have formed the Committee for the First Amendment to fight this thing with everything we've got! I have an appointment tomorrow with Bernard and I intend to tell him that I for one will refuse to name names or incriminate people!"

Everyone seemed to be speaking with exclamation points.

"Jerry, that's good and brave of you, but what has that got to do with me?" Sabine asked.

There was a pause. "Didn't you hear? Bernard named you."

"Me?"

"As the screenwriter of *Storm Over Stalingrad*. Bernard is what you would call a friendly witness. He has named everyone and everything he can think of. It is known as save-your-own-ass time."

"Where is Bernard staying?"

"At the Mayflower."

"And you?"

"At the Shoreham."

"I'll meet you down there tomorrow."

"Another clandestine appointment in a hotel room. A pity nothing ever happens to us."

"Don't blame that on me, Jerry," she laughed.

"Then you are coming down?"

"Yes. As you said, it's save-your-own-ass time."

She got off the phone and faced Matt. "What is all this? The Committee for the First Amendment? Friendly witnesses? Matt, you're going to have to fill me in. I've been very busy opening a hotel."

Matt sighed, and went to pour himself a drink.

"What did Jerry say?"

"That Bernard has given my name. Does that mean I'll have to testify?"

"Maybe. Now sit down. And listen."

It was complicated; as Matt spoke, there was a sadness

about him, as though he were already mourning somebody's passing.

"The First Amendment gurantees freedom of speech. In other words, everyone can say anything. The Fifth Amendment says that you can't be forced to incriminate yourself. Now—if you answer questions about yourself but then refuse to answer questions about other people, their affiliations and so on, you can be cited for contempt of Congress. You can be sent to prison. On the other hand, if you take the Fifth Amendment from the beginning, so that you won't be forced to fink on other people, you automatically become an unfriendly witness, you become known as a suspicious character, a possible subversive, a disloyal American. Does that make sense to you?"

"Of course not, but I don't *not* understand it."

"Oh, you'll be fine on the stand," he laughed.

"Why would anyone want to be an informer?"

"Fear. Nobody wants to lose a job. And then there are those who really believe that communism is the most dangerous threat to this country."

Matt poured himself another drink. He wasn't bothering with ice. Plain scotch was fine.

"And then of course there is revenge. This is a good chance for a lot of people to get even."

"Do you think that's Bernie's reason?" Sabine asked.

"Who knows?"

"Matt," she said, looking at him carefully, "all of a sudden this seems to be a very dangerous time."

He was drinking the scotch, drinking and pouring.

"The *most* dangerous time, I think. Of course, I always did believe that the Constitution was a grand thing, and I have always believed that the American people have sense. I'm also smart enough to know there are crooks and scoundrels and there always will be, and now there are a lot of them who want to take away most of our freedoms. And who knows, maybe there are spies trying to destroy this country. But, Sabine, it's not the Reds who are destroying things now."

He took a last swig and sighed.

"It's not going to be a good fight, this one. It's going to be down and dirty."

Matt did not accompany Sabine to Washington. She thought it better to go alone.

Jerry greeted her at his suite, kissed her, and said, almost excitedly, "I just received my subpoena. I'm being called as a witness. You know, it's almost like the movies. These men come up to the door, like they're from Central Casting, they have these hats, and these somber expressions, ask if I'm Jerry Davis. They act like they never heard of me, like I never made any films, never had my picture in magazines. I say yes, I'm Jerry, and they slip me this piece of paper. Can you believe it? I can't wait to get up on that stand and tell them all off."

"Have you got a lawyer?"

"Of course. Gregory Newmark. He is representing the studio. You know him."

"From poker," she said. "It helps to have a poker player for a lawyer."

"I have an appointment with Bernard at two o'clock."

"Well, I'm coming with you."

"Terrific. Be fifteen minutes late. As usual."

And, as usual, Bernard kept Jerry waiting an additional fifteen minutes. Then he burst through the double doors of his bedroom in the Jefferson suite. He wore a blue pin-stripe suit, a maroon tie, the quintessence of understated elegance.

"Jerry!" His voice was carefully modulated. Had he been taking speech lessons along with tennis? When he saw Sabine, he stopped short, then brushed her cheek with a kiss. "Sabine! What a surprise. What are you doing in Washington?"

"Wondering what you are doing in Washington," she said.

"I am doing my duty as an American," Bernard said.

"Bullshit," Sabine said.

"I feel I was duped. I know now that communism presents a clear and present danger to our American way of life, and I am shocked at the number of subversive elements that have managed to creep into the motion picture industry."

"Stop it, Bernie," she said. "You're trying to save your job."

"Oh, of course," he said. He was always like that.

"But you don't have to do this. You're a powerful man. You could just as easily say no, I won't talk. You could just say no."

His voice was very cool. "It's not as simple as that."

Bernie's voice was cool, but there was a glint in his eye. Sabine realized she was being slightly desperate.

"Why didn't you tell them the truth about me? You know and I know that whatever got tossed into that piece of crap called *Storm Over Stalingrad* came from you. Why didn't you tell them that?"

"They didn't ask me. They merely asked me to name the screenwriter. Believe me, Sabine, if you are innocent, nothing I could possibly say would hurt you."

"*Innocent*? Innocent of what? Guilty of what?"

"Belonging to organizations. Having the wrong kind of friends."

"Bernie, don't do this. Don't do this to us. Please."

"Why?" His voice was suddenly sharp. "Why? If you're innocent, okay. If you're not, and Matt's not—with *his* record—then, well, you have to make your decision. You can defy the United States government. Or you can not."

"You *like* this!" Sabine suddenly yelled at him. "Matt was right. You're doing this to us all on account of some crazy gambling debt and a ripped mohair coat!"

"Cashmere!" Bernard screamed back at her. "It was cashmere, that coat! And you can tell that fuckin' Irish son of a bitch that if he just names all the fucking causes he promoted, and names all the people he knew, he ain't got nothin' to worry about. All he's gotta do is talk! Tell him it's *easy!*"

"Matt Ryan's got nothing to do with the movie business."

"You think it's gonna stop there?" Bernard laughed.

"Listen, Bernie," Jerry said, "I'm not going to have anything to do with this."

"Shut up!" Bernie dismissed him. "I'll get to you in a minute." He turned back to Sabine. "You got anything else to say?"

It was no longer a Marx Brothers movie. And Sabine had no dialogue for what was happening. She looked at Bernard for a brief moment and then shook her head. And left.

It was Jerry's turn. Very casually, Bernard took some photos from his vest pocket and tossed them at Jerry.

"You like pornography. This oughtta interest you—cocksucker." Jerry looked at one of the pictures. He recognized himself, recognized the other man. There were more shots. Same subject.

"Now," Bernard said, "let's discuss your testimony."

Sabine sat in the hotel lobby, too stunned to move. She read the newspaper article over and over. "Nervously fingering a ring on his finger, actor Jerry Davis . . . answering in an unsteady voice . . . close to tears, Davis admitted . . . stammering out . . . hardly audible . . ."

There was a commotion at the revolving door and Jerry came in with a pack of photographers following. He rushed away from them, rushed away from her.

He did not answer his phone or the knock at his door. Sabine went down for a drink in the lounge. Jerry came down an hour later, face drawn, skin pale.

"They play for keeps, Sabine. They play rough," he said when she approached him.

"What was it, Jerry? How could you do it?"

"Blackmail. Ever hear of a fag movie star?" he said, and there were tears in his eyes.

She was silent.

"Say something," he said.

She shrugged her shoulders. They stared at each other. They had known each other for twenty years, had been each other's best friend.

"Say something to me," Jerry pleaded.

"You saved yourself. And destroyed a lot of other people." She got up to leave.

"Wait," he warned her. "Wait and see."

But she was never called as a witness.

They came to her. The men who came were very polite. The meeting had been arranged by Greg Newmark, who was to act as her counsel. It was explained to her that this was an informal session, and, if it were satisfactory, she would never have to testify at the hearings. That depended, of course, as it always did, on her cooperation. They had no desire to involve *her*.

She attempted a smile and agreed that, at least, they had one thing in common. She had no desire to become involved either.

She braced herself for the questions. There was no reason why she would not talk about herself or her own activities, but there was no reason why she should talk about anyone else's. She had a speech all prepared.

She was not at all ready for the first question.

"What is the legal status of the child Freddy Abramowitz?"

She looked at Greg. She was caught off guard. What could she say? They had taken out adoption papers, but only recently, and the papers had not yet been approved.

The men repeated the question.

"I am hoping to adopt him legally."

"Are you married?"

"No."

"Are you living with anyone?"

"Yes."

"But not marrried?"

"No."

"Do you feel you would be a fit mother for this child?"

"Yes."

"Do you feel that the moral atmosphere is a healthy one for a child?"

"I—"

"The Immigration Authorities have been concerned for some time about the disposition of refugee children. Concerned that they grow up to be good Americans. Many have suffered from lack of any upbringing. Their values have been distorted. They do not understand what America is about. There is a feeling among certain members of Congress as well as groups of citizens that these children would be better off in camps, camps that could furnish conditions suitable for these children until the proper foster homes could be provided."

It was very silent in the room.

"What is it you wish to know?" Sabine asked them quietly.

And it began.

"How long have you known Matt Ryan?"

It was very late when she returned to the Waverly Place apartment. Freddy was already asleep. There was dirty laundry all over the place. She had been gone for two days, and her men had not picked up a thing. She was collecting the laundry in a haze when Matt came out of the bedroom.

"Welcome home," he said sleepily. Boozily? Hard to tell. "You want a drink?"

"Yes," she said. "I want a drink." He poured for her, and more for himself.

"What happened? I read the paper. Jerry sang like a bird. Why?"

"You were right," she said. "They play down and dirty."

"Jesus Christ, how is he going to live with himself?"

She drank more, liking the fact that the liquor burned. She looked at Matt and felt herself sinking. She was shaking with fatigue, her eyes burned, she had to close them. She could not face him.

"Jerry had to make his decision," she said, and she waited in the silence. It was a long time.

"And I had to make mine," she said and opened her eyes. She watched him looking at her impassively, the smoke rising from his cigarette. "They asked about Freddy. They said they could take him away . . . they could send him back."

"They wanted to know about me?" Matt asked.

"Yes."

"And you told them?"

"Whatever they wanted to know," she said. "I cooperated. The adoption papers will go through."

They looked at each other a long time. Then Matt rose.

"Let's go to bed," he said. "You must be tired. I am."

They slept with their backs to each other.

Why were they after Matt Ryan?

Because he had criticized the Nuremberg trials.

Because he had criticized the U. S. government's leniency toward the Nazis.

And, mostly, because he was an important syndicated columnist, appearing in one hundred newspapers across the country, broadcasting over a very powerful network, with influence over untold millions of Americans.

Matt's first mistake was to think that he was powerful. *He* wasn't. Before he testified he was told that his column would no longer appear in the papers and that his radio show had been canceled.

His second mistake was that he didn't follow his own cardinal rule: *Never lose your temper. Use your temper.*

Matt was not an unfriendly witness. He was downright belligerent. Before it was his turn to testify, he had watched the proceedings. The bifocaled sons of bitches, he called them, shuffling papers and leaning forward into each individual microphone—leaning forward like obscene birds of prey, asking the question and waiting for the proper response. He hated their dry, flat, deceptive voices. So American—except that none of this was American. This was not a trial, and yet men were being sent to prison on charges of contempt because they refused to answer questions about their beliefs. It was a ritual.

As Matt watched, he could see the creeping paranoia spreading across the country. His country. He knew before he took the stand that he was finished. There were so many people anxious to see Matt Ryan get his. He had known he had enemies. "Fellow-traveler," "dupe," those little phrases blossoming in Kilgallen's column, in Winchell's, in Pegler's. That was no surprise. What did surprise him was to find out how few friends he had.

His name was called. He was summoned to be sworn in. And so it began.

CLERK: Do you swear that the testimony you are about to give is the truth and nothing but the truth?

RYAN: No.

CLERK: What?

RYAN: No.

COMMITTEE: You can't say no.

RYAN: Well, I am saying it. I don't believe in any of this. I believe it's all un-American.

COMM: The witness must comply with the committee's procedures.

RYAN: No. I won't even tell you my name.

COMM: This witness is in contempt!

RYAN: You bet your ass!

COMM: Perhaps the counsel for the witness should advise—

RYAN: I don't need advice. What can you do to me? Take away my job? That's gone. My name? My reputation?

COMM: The witness is not broadcasting *now*.

RYAN: Right! This is the only microphone anyone will let me near. But if the American people knew—

COMM: The American people do know.

RYAN: Like hell they do. You bastards—

COMM:	Restrain the witness. Order! Order! (*Rapping of gavel.*)
RYAN:	If nobody's got the guts to stand up to you—
COMM:	Restrain the witness!
RYAN:	Then we'll all get what we deserve. Maybe one of you sons of bitches for president!

Congressman Richard M. Nixon shuffled his papers while Chairman Parnell Thomas continued to pound with his gavel. In the end, the witness was disposed of and order was restored.

Matt Ryan was sent to the federal penitentiary in Danbury, Connecticut, which was, they told him, a veritable country club.

He left these instructions: he wanted no visitors, he would write no letters, and he would read none.

He spent ten months in the penitentiary.

Freddy blamed Sabine.

He heard in school that his dad was in jail. (Sabine had said Matt was on assignment.) Once again, a person he loved was taken away from him, as his father and mother had been. Somebody was responsible.

Most of his life he had learned to hide. To hide words and feelings along with bits of bread. And hatred.

He said nothing, but he never let Sabine touch him. He did not want the touch of her hands on his shoulder. He wiggled away. She thought it was embarrassment because he was growing up. It was not.

On the day that she received the final papers, making her the legal guardian of Frederick Abramowitz, she was so thrilled she threw her arms around the boy, only to feel him stiffen and turn away.

"Aren't you happy?" she cried. "Now nothing can happen to you!"

Freddy just looked at her. And suddenly she knew that, as surely as her heart belonged to Matt Ryan, she would never have the love of this child. However entangled his emotions had become as a result of the camps and violence and lies, he had learned to trust one person—Matt Ryan. Now that person had been taken away. Now he had learned to trust no one.

Sabine took to creeping into Freddy's room at night when

he was asleep, when the sheets and blanket were all boy-tousled, and she would smooth the sheets and straighten the blanket, looking down at the sleeping boy. Then she would kneel and kiss him, pretending that he was her own child, pretending that he loved her.

When Matt Ryan came back from prison, he came back with the fight taken out of him. He arrived on Monday morning when Freddy was in school, and the man in the shabby coat with very little baggage who got out of the taxi might have been turned away from Glenrocks if Sabine had not caught a glimpse of him as he entered the lobby. He seemed diminished by the great glistening chandelier, out of place. It was the first time she had ever thought that. He did not see her so she had a chance to take a close look at him. He didn't look all that different; there were perhaps a few more lines around his eyes and mouth, but the hair was the same great bristly Matt Ryan red. His skin bore no prison pallor, though he was thinner.

What was the difference? It was the way he carried himself. He was round-shouldered. Caved in. She wanted to shout, "Straighten up! Stand up straight!" He's asking for pity, she thought. She ran up to him.

"Matt, why didn't you phone?"

She gave him a great hug (welcome home, it will be all right, we'll go on, we'll get over all this) but his embrace was wan (whatever you want, it's okay, all right, whatever you say).

"Come on," she urged him, "let's get out of this lobby. I want to see you."

In their private quarters, she gave him a cup of coffee. Signals from the intercom that connected with the hotel interrupted them. Sabine gave instructions that she was not to be disturbed. And then she was sorry she had done that, because nothing disturbed them but their own silence.

He had not kissed her.

"Do you have any brandy?" he asked finally. "To go with the coffee?" She found some and poured, leaving the bottle on the table. He drank the coffee, and then poured more brandy until there was none left.

"I'm glad you're here," she said to his silence. Then, "Let's not talk about—"

He held up his hand.

"Correct," he agreed. "Let's never talk about it."

"Then it's forgotten," she smiled, knowing it wasn't the truth. "What are your plans?"

They were strangers. She was trying to deny it, but they were different people now, not even friends anymore. They had gone different ways. No, she corrected herself, not *gone*. *Sent*, one of them had been *sent*. And it was difficult to look at him.

"I started a novel," he said. "I never wrote a novel before, but I had the time. I guess I have the time now, so why not finish it?"

"There's no better place to write than here. No one will disturb you."

His laugh was like a knife. "I don't have to worry about that. Who would get near me?"

"What's the novel about?" She got up from the chair.

"I'll let you read it when it's finished," he said. "When does Freddy get home from school?"

"Around four."

"I missed him. How big is he?"

"He's tall, there's nothing little-boyish about him anymore. A year can make such a difference."

"I'm anxious to see him," Matt said in the same flat tone.

"Well, there's time. What would you like to do?"

(This was, after all, a vacation resort, with millions of activities. That was the function of Glenrocks. Escape your cares, your worries, your problems. Relax! Enjoy! The brochures all commmanded it.)

"I don't know," he said, "Don't worry. You have work to do. I'm all right."

"No, there's nothing—" she began.

"Don't worry about me," he said. "I'll settle in."

When Freddy came home and found Matt there, he was speechless at first, then crazy with demands. Play ball, come take a walk, look what I made, see me do this. Watch. Dad, look at this. Dad.

Finally, Sabine said, "Freddy, leave him alone. It's his first day back. You'll tire him out." Freddy's eyes met hers, and she looked away.

Before it was dark, in the long June evening, Freddy dragged Matt out for a little batting practice. Over and over in the twilight, Matt tossed the ball and Freddy swung the bat. Once there was a sharp crack and the ball rose in the air and disappeared. Unable to find it, they returned to the house—Matt tired and a little tipsy, Freddy overstimulated.

Sabine put Freddy to bed, and it took sharp words and a slap before he settled down. Matt was already asleep with his clothes on, on top of the bed. He was too heavy for her to undress. She pulled down the bedspread and slept under the covers while he lay on top of them; that was how they spent the first night of their reunion.

Give it time and everything will straighten out, she promised herself. *It takes time to adjust.*

But time was not the answer. The novel Matt was writing did not progress. The hours passed in the morning at the typewriter, and whole pages were crumpled up and thrown away, not even in disgust. As if in waiting.

So Sabine suggested that Matt contact Seymour Martin. "Call him. He's a friend."

"*He* could have called me."

"But he didn't. So you call him. You'll feel better."

Matt was silent.

"Do you want me to call?"

"No. I'll call him."

And he did. Although the conversation was short, Seymour seemed genuinely pleased to hear from Matt.

"I wasn't sure I should call, Sy. You never know who your friends are."

"Are you kidding, Matt? Listen, we have gone through good times and we have gone through bad times. Now, it's time for good times again."

"Well, I wanted to call . . . to say hello."

"When can we see you?"

"Anytime."

"Let me check with Irene. You know me when it comes to social schedules. But I'll get back to you. Where are you anyway? In town or at Glenrocks?"

"At Glenrocks, for the moment."

"Well, send my love."

"You too . . ."

And they hung up. It wasn't exactly what Matt had in mind. He needed a job. He was realistic enough to know he would never—no, never say never—he would not soon be back in the same position as before. When Sy called back, he would ask straight out if there were any openings.

But Sy did not call back. After two weeks, Matt called again—with half a pint of brandy in his stomach—to talk to a secretary who told him Seymour Martin was out of town, had gone to Europe. When he returned, she would leave the message that Matthew Ryan had called.

"Matt. Matt Ryan," he corrected her.

"Oh? Is there a difference?" the secretary asked, with just a touch of acidity in the professional honey.

"Maybe not," Matt said.

The days passed and the weeks passed, and Matt never seemed to change. "Whatever you want" was his answer to everything. Except he never approached her, never made love to her. And she couldn't ask him.

Whatever you want . . .

He knew what she wanted. She wanted his love back. She wanted it to be like before.

"Let's be like everybody else here," she said. "Let's be tourists. Let's have fun."

"Whatever—"

They played tennis. He was good and she was terrible, but they played for an hour and then they swam in the pool. She suggested they go for a walk. They walked by the meadow, past the field to the pond under the maple tree. There were lovers there. Lovers.

"Remember?" she asked him.

"Who would have thought . . ." he started to say.

"What ?"

"How Glenrocks has grown. Look at it. It's gigantic. An empire."

They ate dinner in the grand dining room of that empire. Two orchestras played for dancing, one a Latin band. Latin was very popular. Later there would be a show. Big entertainment. Glenrocks had nothing but the best.

"Do you remember the first show? That horrible Molière?"

"Yes. I remember you and Jerry."

"Do you remember Max whirling my mother around the room?"

Jerry had brought back the wrong kind of memories.

"Do you want to dance?" she asked him.

"Why not?" Pleasant.

Remember? She tried to say it without speaking. *Remember when you took me to Harlem, when you showed me what jazz was all about, when you showed up at Glenrocks, when we went for that ride in that shiny blue convertible, when it all seemed so simple . . . ?*

"Who's on the show tonight?" Matt asked as they were dancing.

"Who cares?" she said. "We're tourists. We only know that Glenrocks has the best!"

"Have you booked Zero Mostel?" he asked her.

"I don't know."

"He's having trouble getting work. What about Paul Draper and Larry Adler?"

"Aren't they kind of high class?"

"You said Glenrocks had the best."

"It does. Listen, that's why we're going to have fun."

"I'll tell you what's fun," Matt said. "Let's go to New York."

"Now?"

"Right now. Let's go see the city."

It was so like the old Matt, the sudden enthusiasm, the spur-of-the moment energy—of course she said, "Okay." He hadn't had too many drinks, so she let him drive. They whirled down the highway, and there was the necklace of the George Washington Bridge and then that fabulous city, New York.

"Where do you want to go?" he asked her, and she could hear the old excitement.

"Everywhere. Let's go everywhere."

But Café Society was closed. Barney Josephson's brother had been named by HUAC and had gone to prison, and the columnists hadn't let go of the fact that the owner of Café Society was the brother of a communist. Business dropped, and in eight months Josephson had gone broke.

So they went on to the Vanguard, and they stood at the bar, and a press agent who was working for one of the acts bought them a drink.

"I want to shake your hand," he said to Matt. "Congratulations. It took guts to do what you did. To stand up to those bastards. You made me proud."

"Hey, thanks," Matt said. "Listen, do you want a picture of me with your client? We could be shaking hands, you know, or the buddy pose . . ." The press agent evaporated.

They moved on uptown, to the jazz joints. It was wonderful to be back at the old haunts, the places where Matt was remembered so well, where the music wiped out every lousy memory. They sat at a table, and everyone came by. But nobody stayed too long. The musicians were called to play, the press agents were called away to the telephone. The owners had other customers. There was no time to talk. Nothing to talk about. But the music was good, though never quite so good as they had remembered. So they hopped from bar to bar, looking for what they had had. Sometime after midnight they dropped in at the Blue Angel, where Max was genuinely pleased to see them and Jacoby's smile, which some took to be chilly, was merely distracted. The place was packed. It was Friday night. Matt asked for a table.

"It's Friday night," Jacoby said. "If you had called up, we certainly—"

"I never had to call before. There always used to be a table."

"Matt, why don't you sit with Sabine at the bar. Sonny will take your coat. We will find a table."

"Sabine, sweetie, you want to sit here?"

"Yes, it's okay. They'll find us a table."

It might have worked.

"Hey, anybody need a reporter?" Matt's voice carried across the bar.

"Ssh, Matt. Don't do that."

"Anybody want to check my *credentials*?"

Jacoby hurried over. "Ssh," he warned. "They can hear you inside."

"No!" Matt mocked. "You mean someone can actually hear my voice? *Anyone want to hire me*? For anything?"

"Ssh! You cannot make this disturbance!"

"*Anyone*?"

Sabine was tugging at his sleeve. "Matt, let's go. I don't want to stay."

"*Anybody. Anybody at all? Last chance*?"

Sabine had hold of one sleeve, Max had his other arm. But Matt suddenly broke away, grabbing a drink off the bar and throwing it at the mirror. He grabbed a stool next and slammed it down on the bar itself. There were screams. Three waiters ran into the inner room, wanting no part of the violence, two others tried to restrain Matt.

"Congratulations!" Matt yelled out, spewing the words into the crowd. "Congratulations, Matt. It took guts! Somebody had to do it! I'm proud of you!"

Then, suddenly, the fight was out of him. Deflated, he mumbled to Max, "Sorry. I'll pay the damages tomorrow. I'm sorry, Max. Tell Herbert?" And he left on his own. Sabine started to say something but Max made a little gesture. It was nothing, the gesture said, it was nothing. Go with him. She did.

They walked the streets again. Such a ghostly walk, because again it was recalling another time when they had been newly in love, when Matt was going off to Spain and a boundless future, when they had walked until dawn, crazy in love with each other and the world and the promise it held.

But everything had turned out differently.

Don't change, that had been the end of the movie Sabine had written. *Don't change.* But it all had. Not the city. Manhattan still glowed and sparkled like the wonderful jewel it was. But the laughter and the jokes had changed, were more bitter now, the jazz too cerebral, the singers a little too facile, as if maybe they didn't mean any of the words.

The two of them had changed as well.

Matt hailed a cab.

"I don't think I want to go on," he said.

"Then we'll go home."

"No, I'm not going on, I said." They were standing on the corner, and it was beginning to lighten in the east. The city was very fresh and he was very tired.

"I can't live like this," he told her, "and I don't want to anymore." He stroked her hair. "I really loved you. And I know why you did it. I honestly thought I could forgive you. I tried to, but I can't."

The cab had pulled up and he got in, then said through the open window, "Either I'd kill you or I'd kill myself. I don't want to do either." He handed her the keys to the car and left in the taxi.

That was on the corner of Fifth Avenue and Fifty-fifth Street, perhaps the most glamorous section of the most glamorous city in the world. Sabine was standing there with a set of car keys in her hand. It was sometime after five in the morning, and she was crying.

So it is true then. You really do have to learn to live with the choices you make in your life.

She drove back to Glenrocks—and Freddy—that night. After all, that was the choice she had made.

Chapter Twenty-Four

It was a secret world Freddy lived in. Nothing showed. He
kept himself to himself. Played baseball, played football, ran
track. By the time he was fifteen, he was a candidate for the
track team. He always handed in his homework on time. He
was a good boy.

He never showed his drawings to anyone; they were too
strange. He wasn't sure why he drew the pictures. Was it for
relief? He drew orange and black figures with no eyes. Men
with outsized hands. Women with no mouths. Silent figures.
Like himself.

When he began to write, not for class, for himself, he did
not remember why he did that either. First it was in the mar-
gins of a school paper, as a teacher droned on. Then he
started writing at home, in a special notebook bought just for
the purpose.

He kept the notebook hidden, the same way the thefts of
his childhood had been put away—secreted close enough for
comfort but far enough from detection. And in this notebook
he committed murder.

He killed her many times. Shot her. Left her bleeding on a
curbstone. Sometimes he was behind the wheel of a car and
she was in his way, and he could have stopped but he did
not. He left her behind him, he could see her body in the
rear-view mirror bleeding, holding up one piteous arm.
"Help! Help! Help me!"

He drew her naked and then wrote about her body. He
fucked her on paper. He had found out about *that*. He liked
the word; there was something so rough about it. He wrote
how he surprised her, how he came into her room, startled
her. He described the fear in her eyes and her black beautiful
hair. He grabbed at the hair, forcing her to her knees, making her kiss him *there*, and then he fucked her on the floor,

and the most exciting thing was to hear her crying out in pain as he *fucked* her. He loved to see her cry. Because she didn't. He had never seen her cry. He wanted to make her sob in fear.

Freddy was fifteen and unhappy at Glenrocks. Sabine had told him to stay out of the lobby, since he refused to cut his hair and he insisted on wearing dirty blue jeans.

Yes, she had seen Marlon Brando in *On the Waterfront* and she knew all about the motorcycle scene, but it didn't belong in the Glenrocks lobby. You still dressed for dinner at Glenrocks, casually, of course, but dressy; ties were required.

Freddy did not defy her.

Instead he found the bars and the roadhouses of the area, the places where the "pickers" played. These were juke joints serving 3.2 beer, and the music was mostly guitar, sometimes accompanied by a fiddle. Hillbilly, it was still called. Old men were playing it, bawling out the lyrics in a flat expressionless voice. Sometimes a young man would sit in. At some places there was a drummer with a painted sunset on his bass drum. Sometimes there was a drum that lit up from inside.

They came from work on Saturday nights, straight from the garages. There was still grease on their hands and dirt under their fingernails. They would play some and drink some, and if they got a hard on for one of the girls who hung around, they would dance or just go outside in the back seats of cars and screw. Then they would come back for some more picking. Picking and screwing on Saturday nights.

Something about it all satisfied Freddy's anger. It was music that kept punching at you. Nothing in the words was nice. People smelled, Love didn't last beyond Sunday. There was talk of broken trusts. He knew about that. These old boys were bawling out the *truth*.

He began to write songs. He listened to all kinds of music: folk, Dust Bowl ballads, old broadsides. He listened, and he imitated.

He was no longer the good boy.

He wheedled a guitar out of his grandmother and then hung around the musicians at Glenrocks, begging for lessons. One of them, bored, taught him chords on the piano, and keyboard harmony. A guitarist showed him fingering.

He took all that, but he wasn't interested in their music.

He didn't sing like the crooners who came up to Glenrocks on Saturday afternoons, rehearsed quickly with the band, did two shows, and left on Sunday morning for another mountain resort. They sang smoothly, smiled, their voices like Brylcream. And each of them, at the end, had an open-armed closing number, which they sang full out and ended on a high note that was guaranteed to bring applause and whistles. Every singer had the same voice, the same gestures, the same finish, the same high note.

Freddy wasn't like that. He wasn't Brylcream. There was a wolfish look to him. His eyes burned with a fierce kind of determination. There was nothing soft there. He played the guitar like steel, and when he sang it wasn't singing; he wailed and growled and bawled and shouted out a kind of cool defiance.

Nothing quite rhymed in the songs he wrote. There was no mention of love in bloom. He was writing about the down-and-outers, the Saturday night boys in the juke joints, the girls in the back seats who got liquored up and forgot the grubbiness of life for a time. And then he began to look around. He wrote about Glenrocks. About the fat and the lonely, the pampered desolation. The pin-ball machines and cha-cha lessons.

For it was the age of the mambo and instruction around the pool. Sabine had brought instructors to Glenrocks to teach. And to mingle. The guests, mainly the women, were trying so hard to be young. To be happy. They smiled and they laughed, and they swung their hips and put their faces up to the sun.

Freddy saw all of this and wrote it down. He contrasted the society he saw at Glenrocks with the workers and girls who filled up Liberty on their Saturday nights.

> Saturday, cha-cha
> Saturday, mambo
> Saturday, ha-ha
> Would you die to dance
> Under the lights
> Out by the pool: The music sweet
> Cha-cha, mambo
> Ha-ha

While, down by the river
They wail
Like coal smoke
Their own lonely tale
Comes a drifting   And curling round
Curling round
The mountains of dreams

Saturday night
   wah-wah
Saturday night
   cha-cha
Saturday night
   ha-ha!
And following Saturday
Yah, then it comes Sunday.

And the more he saw, the more he learned, the more intolerant he became of Sabine.

Sabine decided not to notice, the same way she refused to look in a mirror to see if her face had changed. She lived in a land of no tears, no laughter, and no feelings.

The hotel continued to expand. She considered and had approval on everything. There were now more tennis courts than at Wimbledon. Glenrocks fed more people than the Plaza Hotel in New York. Sabine employed a brigade of chefs, three entertainment directors, a hundred maids, waiters, busboys. Glenrocks had reservation centers in Boston, Chicago, and the West Coast. Everyone wanted to come to the mountains.

Soon there was television in every room. Whether this was due to the impact of the McCarthy hearings or *Your Show of Shows* and Milton Berle, Sabine had no idea. The public wanted TV—Sabine provided the sets.

And then there came a time when the public wanted more than Glenrocks. They knew about Las Vegas; tales came back to the East about the new Gold Rush. El Dorado was not in the mountains of California but the Nevada desert, and the fortunes came not out of the ground but from the tables and roulette wheels.

Sabine visited Vegas. Her investors urged her to build an-

other hotel—Glenrocks West. She looked at the neon and the
desert and the huge billboards advertising superstars like so
many A & P special sales. She looked at the busloads of tourists, the hookers and the sports, the gambling halls with the
free drinks and the free tokes, at more money than she
thought possible spinning around on wheel and slot and deal.
And she left it all. The gambler in her resisted. No Glenrocks
West. Her investors sighed, and suggested Florida.

Florida was another story. She had not been there since
she was a child. Now, it was again the Gold Coast—Miami
Beach and the mammoth hotels all facing the incredible blue
ocean, Sabine returned to Miami with Bertha, fortunately, the
place bore little resemblance to the Miami they had left behind so many years before. From their suite, Sabine could
stare out at the ocean and return to a childhood room, darkened except for the lamp with the lemon-colored shade; she
could hear again the sweet dance music down below.

But then she looked around, and in the neon around her
she could find no traces of the lost little girl she had once
been.

Sabine decided to build a hotel on Miami Beach. She telephoned Gilberto in Brazil. He agreed almost immediately,
thankful there was no snow in Miami Beach (the knishes he
could deal with). Gilberto viewed the expanse of beach,
palms and blue Atlantic, listened to Sabine's vision, and knew
exactly what to design. He was in his element.

Here, there was no waiting for spring to begin work. The
hotel was constructed under the December sun. The concrete
was poured. The steel girders were put in place. Sabine traveled back and forth between Florida and Glenrocks, leaving
Bertha to bask in the sun—for maybe twenty minutes a
day—and supervise everything (including Gilberto) the rest
of the time. Simon came to visit when the weather was good.
But he came less and less often.

Simon was involved.

In the early part of 1955 he had left the union to invest in
a recording company. He had always loved music and he was
knowledgeable about it. This was a new industry. The long-
playing record had made it so. And not all the successful
companies were giants. There were small outfits specializing
in folk music or jazz trios, not-quite-name singers and a

profitable line of classical music recorded cheaply in Europe; these companies were doing well too.

It cost relatively little to turn out an album. Folksingers, for instance, usually required one microphone, two if they used a bass. The record was pressed and released. If it worked, wonderful. Put out another album. If not, forget it. Some of the singers became stars, some drifted out of sight. But it was a new kind of entertainment. Simon spent much of his time frequenting the clubs in Greenwich Village along West Fourth Street. One night he heard a young girl named Helena with the face of a Botticelli angel and a voice like a mountain stream. At nineteen, she was escaping a bad marriage and two abortions. Her appeal to the young was universal. Girls identified with her pioneer spirit (she wore no makeup and drove a jeep). Young men listened to her and fantasized about making love in the great outdoors.

Simon heard her and signed her.

Simon became involved.

Bertha was busy in Florida.

Sabine was just busy. Every moment of her day was filled. She took good care of herself, had a massage and a facial every day. She seemed to grow more sleek. The hair remained jet black, the eyes sparkling, hypnotic sapphire. She was leaner now that she was older. She boiled with energy.

She decided to give up the Waverly Place apartment. Matt would not be back. She had the furniture moved out, sent back to the auction houses where all the chairs and tables and china had been purchased in that first flurry of high hopes and promises, bought by two people who had loved each other since childhood.

Now it was auctioned off again, and brought a fortune. Memorabilia and Victoriana were coming back.

The books were sold to a secondhand book store, the clothes donated to the Salvation Army. At last the rooms were empty.

Sabine took a last look to see that nothing had been forgotten.

Nothing had. The memories came in on her with such force that she had to grasp the door handle. This had been a huge part of her life. And now it was over. No, Matt would never come back. It was the first time she actually accepted it—and she suddenly thought of her mother, that day on Rivington Street. How impatient Sabine had been with Bertha, weeping for her lost lover, weeping for Jacob. She had not known, she had not understood what Bertha felt. She had been too anxious to get on with her own life.

She drove back to Glenrocks, and ordered herself a man. That was very simple. She ordered Paul, the mambo instructor, a slim dark young man with no hips, to come to her room. He was French, a beautiful boy, maybe twenty-one. He was very ambitious, and therefore very anxious to please.

She was lying on the bed when he came in.

" 'Allo!" he said cheerfully. She nodded. He approached the bed. He reeked of cologne.

"Stand over there," Sabine said coolly. He did.

"Strip," she ordered.

He looked at her. There was a moment of indecision, but then he began to undress. She could see him, see that he was watching his own body in the mirror.

Paul divested himself of his shirt in such a way that he could display his torso, which was slim and muscular. Then, watching her with stripteaser's eyes, he unbuckled his belt and slowly unzipped his fly. He was wearing French briefs. He had a huge erection. He turned slightly to look at himself in the mirror. Then he let the briefs slip down to his ankles—and he posed.

"Is beautiful," he said fondly, commenting on his own body. Sabine remained silent.

"Is also beautiful?" He showed her his cock.

"Is silly," Sabine said and tossed him the hundred dollars she was going to pay him. He had to stoop to pick it up. It was extraordinary how graceless he was, squatting to pick up the money.

Paul left, confused. What had he done? What hadn't he done? He was no longer a living statue.

Silly little cocksman, Sabine thought as she watched his tight ass disappear.

But even his humiliation had given her no relief.

In her world of blueprints and construction, of Big Band entertainment and indoor ice rinks, Sabine was unaware of what was happening to Freddy. He forced her to become aware of it.

Glenrocks was still, as always, a family resort. The fathers played cards, as did their wives. The wives also mamboed, and instructors taught the latest steps. Their children tried all kinds of sports.

There were the meals with huge amounts and varieties of food. Every resort in the Catskills vied with the others in that respect.

And there was entertainment. The biggest stars, plus an opening act.

Recently, since her trip to Vegas, Sabine had established another policy—entertainment in the Lounge, a trio, perhaps with a girl singer. The smaller, more intimate form of entertainment was catching on.

But there was another room at Glenrocks she didn't know about. The hidden room, the place where the kids went.

It started with the fifteen-year-old girls. They began to listen to Freddy because he looked so unusual and acted so different from everyone else at the resort. He always wore Levis and a blue workshirt, with work boots and sometimes a pit jacket. He carried his guitar everywhere, and he didn't cut his hair. To the fifteen-year-old girls he was irresistible. Whatever rebellion lurked in their Jewish Westchester County souls began to flower.

Where the girls went, so went their boyfriends. And they discovered their own rebellion. And their idol.

When it finally came to Sabine's attention that there was an "underground" at the hotel, she was first annoyed, then intrigued. She decided to investigate one Saturday night.

The cellar—yes, it was part of the cellar—was thick with smoke and crowded with teenagers. There was a skiffle band playing, a guitar, a fiddle, and a washboard bass. The kids cheered.

When Freddy appeared, they were mesmerized. At first, Sabine thought he possessed no musical gift at all. But then she began to understand what he was doing. She listened to the words he had written. They were scornful and angry. He was as angry as she was. As mistrustful and bitter.

What was he writing about? About hypocrisy. About keeping silent. About injustice. *Oh my,* she thought, *the sophomore topics again.* And yet, as he sang about them, Freddy carried authority. The sarcasm of his humor, the power of his anger was undeniable.

How old was he? Still a teen-ager. How old had she been?

But that had been another world. Her world and his were completely different.

How alike we are, she realized. And how little we know each other. She was beginning to feel pride again, and a sense of excitement. This was something Freddy had done all on his own, of which she had been unaware. Look at him, she thought, and look at me. The typical proud stage mother.

He finished singing, and four or five little girls were hanging onto him. Of course, she thought. Adoration. Then Freddy saw her, and he froze. His eyes grew cold. She went up to him.

"You've been keeping secrets from me," she said. She thought she was being amusing.

"This was nothing you had to know about," Freddy said to her flatly.

"What I meant to say was, I was surprised," she told him.

"At what?" he said, belligerent. She could feel her own anger rising.

"Girls," she said to his little crowd, "I think this is going to be private."

"See ya later." Freddy shrugged them off and they left.

Sabine and Freddy were alone, facing each other for the first time in years, looking *at* each other, not through each other.

"There was no reason to speak to me like that," she said.

"Whatever I'm doing, it's not for you."

"Who is it for, then?"

"For me. It's my own business."

"I said before, there is no reason to talk to me like that. So don't!"

"I won't talk to you at all."

"God, why are you so *angry?*" She was the one who was exploding.

"It's my life. What have you to do with it?" he yelled at her, and without thinking, she raised her fist and struck him.

"Everything!" she screamed at him. "I have everything to do with your life!"

"I don't want to have anything to do with *yours*. I hate you. I hate what you did. You are disgusting, and you are a liar."

"What are you talking about?"

"Who sent Dad away?"

"You don't understand!"

"Sure, I understand. You wanted to keep this miserable fucking hotel, and you decided his life, his place, wasn't worth it. You think I don't have ears? You think people don't talk? Everybody knows who you are, and what you did!"

She didn't know where the strength came from, but she threw him across the room, and he collapsed against a banquette.

"You listen to me," she raged. "You think I did this for a hotel? You think I gave up the one man in my life I loved? I've loved Matt Ryan since I was a child. I loved him more than anything in life—more than you, even. I loved him, and I made a choice. And that destroyed him. And it destroyed the love he had for me. Maybe I could have saved him; at least we could have gone away together. *Or* I could save *you*. Somehow, maybe it was because of your father, I don't know—I chose you."

They were on opposite sides of the room now. She was sobbing and furious, and she could smell the stale odor of tobacco. Oh, the anger! The anger at life, at herself, and at him. She picked up an ashtray and hurled it the length of the room.

"I lost him. I lost him," she said, the tears streaming from her eyes. She had to get out of here. She was no longer in control. All she could see was this kid, this rebel, her beautiful accuser, sitting across from her, sprawled where she had hurled him, stunned by her fury.

"I lost him. And now I've lost you." She fought the tears, but it was no use. She tried to find her way blindly out of the room.

His hands were on her shoulders. Strong hands, almost a man's hands now.

"Tanti," he said in a soft voice, "it's not your fault. Not your fault."

She couldn't see his face, but she could sense that he was crying too. And from that point in their lives, their friendship started.

When Freddy looked back on it later, it was obvious he had gotten what he wanted. He had made Sabine cry.

Chapter Twenty-Five

It was quite an opening in Miami Beach. Sabine brought Freddy with her. He had never been south before, had never seen a palm tree. She thought he would enjoy it.

The hotel was a delight to her. Gilberto had designed the place in four sections, and the sea breeze wafted through the connecting patios. Instead of one pool, there were a number of separate pools. It gave the hotel a more personal, intimate feeling. Once again, Gilberto had combined Continental elegance with a playfulness that was purely American.

The roof of the hotel's Skytop Room restaurant swept back to reveal the tropical night. "Moon Over Miami," that was what Sabine had wanted—the most romantic hotel in Miami Beach. And that's what she had. The individual balconies offered privacy, the foliage offered shade, so that it was like living in one's own personal jungle. In the middle of the lobby Gilberto had created a Brazilian jungle, including a waterfall.

And Bertha had also done her job. The staff had been well trained, the service was impeccable, the cuisine the equal of the original Glenrocks's. Bertha was satisfied. Sabine had provided her with a three-room suite overlooking the ocean. She had her work, and she had made friends. And of course Simon came as often as he could.

It was, however, not quite the opening Sabine had planned.

First of all, Simon arrived—with a tennis racket and a toothbrush. He kept a set of clothes in Bertha's suite. She welcomed him, although she was slightly annoyed at his timing. Simon seemed to have no sense of anyone else's time schedule. The hotel was *opening*. She belonged in the dining room. What was he asking her to sit *down* for? This was no time for a drink. She had work to do.

But she made him a drink. He sat with his back to the

ocean. She faced him. Beyond, she could look out across the balcony and see the rim of the ocean. It was going to be a beautiful night—warm, starry, magical. What *did* he want?

Simon looked up from his drink. He hadn't changed. He was still curly-headed, gray, muscular; he looked better than any other man his age. Since his hair had been prematurely gray, he looked very little different than when Bertha had first met him. Simon was still a charmer.

"I'm in love," he said.

"What?" Bertha was caught off guard.

"I'm in love, and I thought I ought to tell you first. I didn't want to hurt you, and I didn't know how to tell you—except to *tell* you. So, now I've told you."

"Is that why you came down here?" Bertha wanted to know.

"I wanted to tell you I'm moving in with her."

"Who?"

"Her name is Helena. You've heard me speak of her."

"Yes. She's the young girl who sings."

"I manage her."

"Simon, may I ask you a question? What did you bring a tennis racket for?"

"I have a game scheduled in the morning."

Bertha rose. "Simon," she said, "drop dead."

And she left to supervise the service in the dining room.

Freddy was wearing a tie and he looked uncomfortable. But Sabine took it as a tribute to her that he had consented to wear both a tie and a jacket.

He looked around the Skytop Room. Sabine was wondering what his comment would be. The sound of the music, the roof that was open to the stars, the smell of the sea breeze, the entire atmosphere was so much a part of the dream of her life—so bound up in the remembered deluxe hotels of her childhood, her mother and father, the tea dances, the elegance . . .

"Why aren't there any Negroes?" Freddy asked her.

It was Sabine's turn to be taken off guard.

"What?"

"Why aren't there any Negroes here?" Freddy asked again.

"I don't know," was all Sabine could answer. "What makes you ask?"

"Well, I wondered if you kept them out. Or if they just didn't want to come . . ."

"Frankly, I never thought about it." Sabine was disappointed. Freddy hadn't noticed the sliding roof or the stars, or the elegance.

"Where did you go today?" she asked, to make conversation.

"I went to Miami. I took a bus there. I bummed around. You ever been on a bus in Miami?"

Sabine did not want to remember her childhood. She was not going to.

"No. Not recently."

"Back-of-the-bus time."

"What are you talking about?"

" 'Niggers in the back of the bus,' that's what they said. And that's what happened. I think it's shit."

She looked at him with exasperation. She had brought him down here for a good time, and here he was making trouble. First thing he had to notice was Negroes. Back of the bus. He was looking at her with those eyes again. They bore right into her.

"Well . . ." She hesitated. He was waiting for her to say something.

"What do you want me to say?" she asked.

"I don't care what you say. What are you going to do?"

"About *what*?"

"Are you going to let Negroes into the hotel?"

"Yes!" she said, more loudly than she meant to. Then she amended it. "I think. I'll have to see. The hotel is just opening. Let me think about it."

She could have continued, twenty sentences of equivocation. Freddy's look still accused her. Who was he to be her conscience?

Sabine spent a troubled night. She blamed it on Freddy. But then at around four in the morning, after the second sleeping pill had not taken effect and she was staring out at the ocean, it came to her. She had built this hotel to take care of her dreams, to give her what had been taken away from her, to bring her father back.

And, of course, what she had built was merely a hotel. No, a luxury hotel that would bring her a great deal of money, but not her father. And she had a choice to make with this hotel.

She made it before leaving for the airport with Freddy. She stopped in at the manager's office.

"I want to make a policy rule,'" she told the staff. "There is to be no discrimination here. In other words, Negroes are to be admitted as guests. And hired as employees. In all capacities."

The manager was polite, but Southern. "Do you think that's wise?"

"No," she answered truthfully. "I'm not at all sure. But somebody's got to start it. It might as well be me."

When they were on the plane for New York, Freddy turned to her and said, "Thank you."

"Mmm." Sabine looked at him. "That took a lot of guts. How many Negroes do you know who can *afford* Glenrocks?"

It was six months later and they were walking on West Seventy-second Street. Freddy had decided he wanted to live in New York for the summer. He was playing guitar. He was singing. What he wanted was to get to West Fourth Street in the worst way. He knew that was where his life was headed.

Sabine had accompanied him into town. If he was going to rent an apartment, she wanted to supervise. They had looked at some on upper Broadway. Freddy had been dissatisfied.

"What's the matter with them?"

"Hey, I have no idea. But everybody's in like the West Seventies of their lives." What he didn't tell her was that he loathed the people. They were old. And they were Jewish. They bargained over oranges and spent lives bound by the Key Food Market and the television screen.

They were heading for the Villlage, for the subway— Freddy's choice, not Sabine's. And they were talking.

"If it's a job you want, Freddy, you could work anywhere. I could arrange it. Another hotel, if you wanted."

"No. I don't want that. I can look out for myself. I think maybe I can find my own jobs."

"Doing what?"

"Singing."

They had just crossed the street to the triangle where the IRT station was located when Freddy stopped. He grabbed

Sabine's arm. He was staring at an old man who was coming toward them.

"My God," Freddy whispered. "Papa."

Sabine looked, and saw Sammy approaching them. And then she fainted.

Chapter Twenty-Six

Sammy Abrams was holding court in the Glenrocks lobby. Freddy's father was telling his extraordinary story, which he never tired of repeating.

Sabine looked at Freddy, but Freddy was looking at no one.

"There I was," Sammy was telling a group, "crossing Seventy-second Street to enter the subway. And there was this young man, pointing at me. Handsome, this young man, I could tell that immediately. He had an air about him. There was this woman with him. I didn't see much. She collapsed, fell to the ground, and immediately there was a crowd! People gather for anything. I was about to go on my way. Was it my business a woman fainted? But something held me there. Something *forbade* me to move."

Sammy was calculating his audience. His was a practiced eye.

"Then he grabs me by the arm. What am I to think? I think he wants to rob me. That's the first thing on West Seventy-second Street. He wants to rob and kill me. Then he says 'Papa.' Just like that. And I think, Na, na, my Freddy is dead. This is a terrible joke. But then I look. I can see the eyes of my own child."

Freddy never looked up during this recitation. His father had been restored to him. Papa. Sammy.

"Just think," Sammy was saying. "If I had been a minute earlier, or a minute later, we would never have seen each other. One minute's time either way . . . Suppose I had taken a bus!"

"Think of it!" someone in the crowd said.

"I had it in mind, but it was such a nice day. Suppose it had been raining!"

Sammy did not lack for an audience. At Glenrocks, he was

439

recognized. The hair was white now, and the Nazis had knocked out most of his teeth, but the plate fit well. All he looked was older, but he was still the same Sammy. There were those who remembered. The Austrian Jews who had fled after the *Anschluss*, who had come to this country and started new lives, taken the law exams, passed the Medical Boards, opened millinery shops and joined accounting firms, established shoe factories. They had prospered, but they were still Viennese. That meant they still congregated at the Café Éclair on West Seventy-second Street to sample pastries and gossip about love affairs. Middle age had arrived between dessert and coffee, but they absolutely refused to recognize it.

At Glenrocks they crowded around Sammy, a celebrity, their *own*. And they asked him all the questions Sabine refused to.

Where had he been all these years? Had he never tried to get in touch with his family? Did he not know of Glenrocks?

Sammy shrugged. "I was told they were dead. Even Sabine—shot while trying to escape. I accepted it. Canada, first Sweden, then Canada. I came to this New World and worked as a radio actor. It is still possible. There is a Yiddish theater in Toronto."

"You never called? . . . never wrote? . . .," his audience marveled.

He never wrote, Sabine thought. *If he had written, if he had tried just once to get in touch, how different my life would have been.* She realized she was looking at the garrulous old man with resentment, and her eyes caught Freddy's. She recognized the same expression.

The group asked Freddy, "Young man, how did you feel?"

Freddy resisted their questions. "I thought Papa was dead."

"Me dead? No chance. I will never die. Believe *me*. How about my English now, eh?"

Sammy was smoking a cigarette in the Russian manner. He was expansive. In his element. His audience could still recall his films. Remember *Drei Liebe*? Sammy had always been so funny, so funny. Was still as funny as ever.

Yes, everyone has his own road, Sabine thought, watching Sammy do his act over and over to an everlastingly appreciative audience. When Freddy ran off to Chicago a few months later and found a job singing, Sabine made no effort to bring him back, even though he was not much more than a boy.

Whatever was bothering him—and she knew it had to do with Sammy—it would be useless to force him to come home. He had to find his own way.

Freddy wrote from Chicago. His first job only lasted two nights and then he was fired. They didn't understand what he was singing or the songs he wrote. The audiences were used to bouncy crew-cut collegiate cut-ups who sang glib arrangements of American folk songs. They were not prepared for Freddy's intensity.

He sent a card from Denver, from a club called the Exodus. He was not fired from there. He learned his trade. Sometimes they listened, sometimes they did not. He went from the Exodus to the West Coast, where he sang in a small club and was offered a recording contract. An album was released, and reviewed favorably. But the sales were poor and the company did not renew his contract. A year passed, and then he wrote Sabine he was coming to New York. An engagement in the Village. The place was called Gerdes Folk City.

Sabine went alone. She walked inside and sighed. The place was half empty and seemed cavernous, lonely. What else could she expect? Freddy's career was not an easy one.

Surprisingly, she met Seymour Martin there. He was also alone.

"What brings you here?" she asked him.

"An act. A friend of mine from RCA asked me to listen to this boy. Do you know who he is?"

"You mean Freddy? Yes, I know him."

"I didn't know you traveled in such radical circles," Seymour said, making a joke, and then was very sorry he had made it. "What can I say?" he apologized.

"Nothing."

The opening act was a trio, two men and a pretty girl, who sang well, but nobody cared much. During their set, the place began to fill up. Sabine looked at the crowd. Who were they? Kids. All in denim. The girls wore fringed rawhide, sometimes T-shirts. Everything was denim and Army-Navy surplus. What were they here for?

Freddy.

He appeared, wearing his pit jacket, clod-hopper shoes. He turned his back to the audience, tuned his guitar to the bass.

The room was still. Freddy began to sing, and as he did, he turned slowly. The guitar was jangling, the strings harsh. He didn't play, he attacked. Savage strokes. Then silence. And he sang in a jagged way, the words coming out in clusters.

Bone skinny, Sabine thought. *His cheekbones stick out from his face, his hair is savagely curly. Defiant, that's what he is, staring them down, spitting out words and challenging anyone to stop him.*

But what intrigued her most were his songs. Each one of them was a slashing portrait of society. Who wrote songs like that? Nobody. Daumier and Hogarth had drawn like that. But who wrote songs like that?

Freddy did.

And his audience listened in rapt silence and exploded with applause and whistles and cheers and stamping feet. Unruly, that's what they were. Defiant fists were raised in the air.

She met Seymour as he was leaving.

"Well?" she asked him. He was in a hurry.

"God, I think he's awful," Seymour said. "I'm telling RCA no."

Sabine found Freddy standing among the cartons of toilet paper, cases of beer, and boxes of napkins that made up his dressing room.

She could tell by his face that he had already heard about RCA.

"Do you want to talk about it?" she asked.

"What's there to talk about?" he said, and then, "What should I do?"

"You could change." Sabine said, looking at him. "You could wear a tie. You could cut your hair. Shave. Change your style. Write different kinds of songs."

"Uh-huh," he said, looking around at the beer cases.

"Or wait for the times to change. Because they will."

Freddy didn't have to wait. The times caught up with him in about six months.

RCA reconsidered.

He had a manager, signed a contract. The sixties had hardly begun and he was already being called the symbol of those years.

Everything was moving fast. Television was becoming a giant. The recording business was now the recording *industry*.

Both records and TV were big enough to worry Hollywood. So Hollywood did the smartest thing possible—merged.

Parking lots and shoe companies took over the studios. Every enterprise became the subsidiary of something else. Even the hotels.

In the space of three weeks, Sabine had four offers to sell Glenrocks, both the hotel in the mountains and the new Miami location.

She considered the offers. Truly she was not needed. The hotels ran very smoothly with the staff she had acquired. They were not even hotels anymore; they were institutions, a tradition handed down from generation to generation. Go to Glenrocks, "Where your mother and I met," "Where your father and I got married," "Where I've been coming since I was a little girl." The last was said by a stout lady on the far side of thirty. It did not sit well with Sabine.

She considered herself. Forty-seven years old. And no one would say she looked it. Forty-seven was an age to hide. Shame on the woman who reached that age. But Sabine was still beautiful. The rages had died down. She was detached, maybe even aloof. Unattainable, according to most men. Therefore desirable.

But—forty-seven. She had to sit down and think about that for a bit. Nobody needed her. The phrase haunted her. Not Freddy, whose career was in full rush. He was taken seriously—why did she find it so hard to believe this?—not only by musicians, but by poets and politicians. His generation was vocal, passionate. She found herself attracted to these kids. They wanted voter registration in the South. They wanted equal rights. Freddy was in Mississippi now, working with SNCC.

And what did *she* want? She had no idea. She needed nothing, and no one really needed her. Sammy was thriving on the West Side in New York, her mother was busy in Miami Beach. Freddy had his entourage; his manager, his recording people, the band that traveled with him on the road, his *road* manager. His girls.

A twinge there. She had walked in unexpectedly one morning and found him asleep with a woman, their bodies carelessly entwined, the bed a mess of lovemaking. She recognized the girl: Helena. Simon's Helena.

Ah, good, she thought as she discreetly backed out of the room. But she never told anyone, not even Bertha.

Her mind was straying—she had decisions to make. Then she reconsidered. The hell she did. She could take her time. She could do what she wanted. What she wanted was *not* to be getting old. What she wanted . . .

She wanted to spend a couple of weeks and do nothing. She wanted not to make any decisions for a while.

It was the fall of 1963; Sabine finally decided on New York. She would stay in the city and rest, invite Bertha to come up and go shopping.

They went to Bergdorf's, the first time they had ever shopped together without fighting. They were good critics for one another now.

"That's no good around the bust," Bertha said to Sabine. "You should have something that shows more."

"Please don't bring my mother anything with lace on it," Sabine instructed the salesgirl. "The Chanel suit, could we see that? And a Hattie Carnegie or an Adele Simpson. Stop with the lace."

She told her mother about Leisure Corp.'s offer to buy Glenrocks.

"What do you think?" she asked Bertha.

"I think you could still show more bust."

"About selling."

"I think you should wait."

"You know what I'm trying out this weekend? Colored lights and dancing to records. It's the craze in Paris. Who knows?"

"You're right. Who knows?" her mother said, but then had to add, "But I wouldn't bet on it."

Bertha was wrong. In two months the discotheque was the craze at Glenrocks. Hastily Bertha opened one in Miami.

Sammy was humming as he sauntered through the park. "Autumn in New York." He was beginning to remember American tunes.

He looked at the sky. Clouds to the west, or was it the east? He had never been good at directions. Hollywood, however, he knew was west. It was time for him to go there. He was humming because he felt optimistic. The afternoon had been wonderful. Life was wonderful!

Did the clouds mean the possibility of a thunderstorm? Perhaps. As he continued to walk, he noticed the lights in the buildings. Even in the afternoon the skyscrapers were full of light. Beautiful.

"*Man-hat-tan. Electric lights.*" Ragtime. Jacob. How long ago that had been. He could still picture Jacob standing at the crossroads, challenging him. And who had lived to see it—"*Man-hat-tan, Electric lights?*" He had. Sammy.

Because he had paused, because his mind was elsewhere, half a century away, on a plain in Poland, he was not aware of the danger until they were upon him. And then his mind became confused. The men had sticks. *Ka-Zed! Kapos! Truncheons!* They were demanding money, his wallet, his watch. He remembered the lines and the piles of gold, the jewels and the valuables heaped up to the side of the line.

His first reaction was to fight them. But one of them lifted his arm, and the blows rained down on Sammy. He was trapped. This was the end. This was Auschwitz. Before, he had always managed. But now it was his turn. He kicked, but it was no use. They were opening the doors to the *Krema*. They were beating him. He had lived through this nightmare before. And the nightmare had always ended. But now . . .

The hospital room was a corner one, and Sabine stayed by the window, watching the traffic sizzle in the sudden rain.

The police had found Sammy in the park, had found the number at Glenrocks in his discarded wallet; had found Sabine, and here she was in the hospital. She had telephoned Freddy, who was on his way.

Sammy was asleep with his head wrapped in bandages. There was silence except for the sound of the traffic. *Hospitals are quiet places*, she thought. *So little of the agony is evident, but even the silence is agonizing.* There was so much equipment. And so many nurses and orderlies, walking with animal stealth.

She looked at Sammy. How clearly she could remember that summer day at the railroad station in Landeck. The dapper man in white, the phony black in his hair. The boulevardier with the cane and the villa, the wife and the new baby. The classic European *bon vivant*.

The *bon vivant* was now lying in bed. Without his teeth, his face had sunken in. Death was already making a short visit.

The door opened. It was Freddy, wild with the rain, out of breath from running. He looked at Sabine and then at the figure on the bed.

Something—the rush of movement, perhaps—stirred Sammy. He opened his eyes. There was a flash of terror. Then he seemed to recognize Freddy. The son. The baby. The stranger.

The boulevardier remained, right to the end. Sammy smiled at his son, a mocking smile, and said, "Too late."

And he died. It was over, that quickly.

Freddy's reaction was a surprise. He began to run. Sabine ran after him, past the orderlies and the nurses, past the outstretched hands with documents to be signed. Down the stairs and out the door into the boiling rain. And then she saw him two blocks away, pounding his fists on the roof of an automobile, pounding the metal for punishment, for relief, for some way to ease the pain. The pain was physical—she felt it herself, felt it *for* herself, and for him. She wanted to say something but no sound would come out. She ran to Freddy. She reached him just as a policeman arrived to investigate.

"Lady, lady, what is it?" the policeman asked, his voice as soft as a carpet.

She looked up at him, and then around. What could she say to him? How to explain? In the rain, she noticed a procession passing—men wearing black hats. Was it a funeral, at this hour? It was almost six o'clock.

"What is that?" she asked the policeman.

He was surprised by the question. He wanted to know what was going on with her and Freddy.

"What's that? That's Yom Kippur," he said. He was a black cop, and as comforting as a father. "Now, what happened?"

"A loss," she managed to say. "His father . . ."

"I'm sorry," the officer said, "but you better get him off the street."

"Yes," she said, and she took the policeman's advice. In the rain, not really sure where she was going, where she was leading Freddy, she followed the procession. Freddy seemed unaware of where she was taking him.

Once they were inside the synagogue (how strange it all seemed to her—the hats, the ceremony, the tradition of it) a man who was collecting tickets held out his hand.

"We are strangers," she said to him, "but we need to come in. Can we stand in the back?"

The man looked at them with suspicion. Freddy's black curls were hanging down over his face. The two of them were soaked with the rain. But they were in such obvious pain. The man nodded assent.

It took Freddy a moment to realize where he was. He saw figures. He saw prayer shawls. He saw yarmulkes. The men were bowing, swaying . . . He had seen that before. The barbed wire came up in front of his eyes. He heard the sound of chanting.

Together, the men and the boys, the whole group of them, with the eldest standing in congratulatory groups, were shaking each other's hands. After so long, the news was here. Even he—and he was allowed to take his father's hand, to stay by his side—even he knew. The Germans were losing the war.

Freddy looked around. He saw stained glass. He saw candles. He saw men and women, umbrellas. Prayers . . .

"You realize," the younger man was saying, "it has been six weeks now and not one transport has left. What do you think that means?"

"What does it mean? It means maybe—perhaps—look, I'm biting my tongue—maybe it's over. Maybe, who knows, maybe no more transports."

His father was happy, but his father was joking as always. "Oh, the disappointment. How I wanted to see Poland. My birthplace. The Nazis will disappoint me again."

"Shut up, Sammy," they said with affection. Sammy had made them laugh. For years now, the ones who had not been taken off in the transports had stayed around Sammy, who had kept up their spirits, had forced them to perform plays, had read poetry. They had presented little cabarets. All approved, of course. But this was the model camp, this was Theresienstadt. The rest was all whispers and darkness. Freddy had heard the names—Oswiecim, Dachau. He knew about the transports, the trains and the destinations. The train whistle that announced the departure. Another group for

Auschwitz. Another group. For six weeks there had been no whistle.

The rain was beating on the synagogue roof. Freddy stood, clutching Sabine by the arm. The candles were so bright. There were so many things to forget.

"Truly, we can give thanks. Perhaps we have been saved. You know what day it is today? Yom Kippur. It is time for the services."

And the guards with the guns at their chests and their helmets stared at us, whoever was left, standing out here, and then we found a place, a place where the candles could be lit, and we all gathered there, men, women and children. And we thanked God, we thanked God that we had been spared. No more transports. No more death. Soon, no more war. No more barbed wire. Soon, safety. Soon, happiness. The sunset was warm on our faces. The sunset was beautiful.

The rain poured down on the street. Sabine winced in pain, Freddy's grip was so powerful.

"How beautiful, Papa. We're still together, and there are others, old friends, boys my own age, who are still here too. So many have disappeared. But what now? What is the old man doing?"

He is raising the ram's horn. What a sound, how lonely, how lovely. What is it? A cry?

What is it? What was that? I know that sound. I can tell from their faces, it is the sound of the train whistle. The transport—it is to be filled up. Already, they are ordering us into groups. Separating us. Why do I choose my father? Why not my mother, why can't I go where my mother is going? Why do I want my father, why Sammy? He will joke, he will be wonderful. No matter what.

The candles dazzled Freddy's eyes.

Darkness and the smell of piss. The smell of shit. The smell of death. Cries, little cries, whimpers more than anything. Next to me I know that is a dead body. Where are we going, where are we headed? I can tell that next to me is a dead man, a dead body. Stiff with death. But Papa is still there. And then I feel the wind, why is that? There is no wind here. Look, there are stars . . . What happened? What happened? I reach for my papa's hand, but it is no longer there. Stars, I see them, I see night. I am pushed. I feel it. My father; pushing me? I do not want to go, but he pushes

*me and I tumble out of the train. The ground is hard and it
is cold now, the train has passed and I am alone. The train
has passed.*

Sabine looked at Freddy's face, covered with sweat. He
was breathing heavily, his eyes closed, looking like death. She
called his name, but he did not hear her.

"Bury the clothes. Bury them. Steal . . . Run!"

The cantor was approaching the *biene.* The Rabbi faced
the congregation.

*"Do not look at anyone. See, they are shooting down those
who are Jews. Do not look at them. Wait, there is a farm.
Food."*

The congregation closed their eyes, heads bowed in prayer.
It was the Day of Atonement. All over the world, the moment was approaching.

*"Ich bin kein Yid! Ich bin kein Yid! Katholischer Heimat."
Bread. At last, bread. A barn. Sleep. Tomorrow. "Kein Yid."*

To Sabine, the sound was quite extraordinary. The sound
of the shofar rang out in the synagogue.

*I wait for my hair to grow in. I am no Jew. I cross myself.
I learn the prayers. I talk about the dirty Jews. The dirty
Jews.*

Sabine looked over. Freddy was shaking, sobbing, in terrible pain. Tears rolled down his cheeks. He had bitten his lip,
there was blood on it. The sound of the shofar died away.
And then, a terrible echo, a cry of pain broke from Freddy.

"Mama," he wailed, leaning against Sabine, "Mama, I *survived!"*

Chapter Twenty-Seven

When Sabine read the invitation, she could not believe her eyes.

You are cordially invited to attend
the Joseph Hirsch Humanitarian Awards Dinner
this year honoring distinguished producer and filmmaker

BERNARD ROSS

to be held in the Grand Ballroom
of the Glenrocks Hotel
October 15, 1963.

The event will be televised.

When Sabine had approved the Hirsch Award's request for the Grand Ballroom, months before, no one had told her who was to receive the award. At the time she hadn't cared. There had been too much else on her mind. And now it was too late to do anything about it. Could she cancel? No, that would not be appropriate.

A television special, *live* from Glenrocks. *That* had been the result of one of Seymour Martin's two-martini lunches. The network had snapped at the idea, since their recording subsidiary had a few stars who could help the ratings (Freddy being one of them); their film company had a number of pictures that could use the promotion (one a film produced by Bernard Ross); and they could also promote one of their new fall series, starring Jerry Davis.

The idea for the show was simple: to trace the rise of Bernard Ross from his humble beginnings on Manhattan's Lower East Side to his first job as busboy at Glenrocks. (That also made the network happy, since it was part of the conglomerate hoping to buy Glenrocks.) From busboy to fledgling comic—the heroic struggle for success in the hard world of show business. Then, the eventual triumph. And now the charities, the philanthropies that had been helped by Bernard Ross. At the end, an award in the name of human rights to be accepted by Bernard.

Nifty. Seymour Martin set the whole production in motion: the remote units to be set up at Glenrocks, the sound truck, all the entertainment. Afterwards, he called Sabine. After everything had been arranged.

Her first impulse was to hang up the phone. In the end she agreed. Would she appear on this program? Why not?

"After all, let bygones be bygones. That's a lot of water under the whatever," Seymour said glibly.

"Absolutely," Sabine agreed.

So here she was, on the evening of this awards dinner. Jerry Davis was in the suite next to her private quarters, but there was no communication between them. Freddy and his entourage were safely removed from the rest of the crowd. She had let Freddy use her own apartment.

Bob Hope had checked in. Sinatra had come. Most of the biggies had already arrived.

The phone rang. She picked it up. It was Victor Jones, one of Freddy's managers.

"We're having a problem. Same old hassle. The network is giving us the usual. They say Freddy is too controversial."

Sabine sat up.

Victor continued, "It's beautiful, man. He's signed to their label, he brings in more bucks than anybody, but then they want him to sing some dumb asshole song out of the fifties."

"Victor," Sabine said, "tell Freddy I'll be right down."

The cameras were all set up and the floor was covered with miles of cable. The band had run through Sinatra's number and was on a break. Fuming to one side was writer-producer Alan Preskoff with his director. They had an eight o'clock deadline.

It was easy to spot the executives—they kept up their corporate courage. In conference. They were happy when Seymour appeared. "Seymour, we can't get clearance on this material. It's too controversial," Preskoff said.

"May I hear it?" Seymour said. Freddy would be right out, a gofer said.

Freddy appeared, very aware of the situation; and also aware that his presence on the telecast would boost the ratings tremendously. He and his group quickly set up on the stage. Then he nodded to Mason and began.

> "The bums are in the colleges
> The bitches are in heat
> The priests are in the lockup
> The church is in the street
> The trials are all theatrical
> With all the tales they tell
> But who is in the pulpits now
> To keep us out of hell?
>
> "Well it's hard times, rough times
> For the human race
> When no one minds his business now
> And no one keeps his place."

Seymour waved his hand. "Funny. Good. Satirical. Not appropriate."

"I thought this was a program about humanity." Freddy's voice carried across the ballroom. "This song is appropriate."

"Then we disagree," Seymour said.

Freddy nodded. "Then we don't perform," Freddy said, and left the stage with his group.

Seymour turned to Sabine, ignoring his corporate colleagues. "The material is too controversial. Listen to it."

"I did," Sabine said.

"I don't think there's any reason to be offensive."

"You think the songs were offensive?"

"Making fun of the church!"

"But not the priests—"

"Sabine, I'm not going to argue."

"No, you're going to keep silent. Again."

Seymour flushed.

"There's always a reason for keeping quiet, isn't there?" Sabine continued. "In this case, it's good taste."

She started to walk away. Seymour hurried after her.

"You're not bowing out too, are you?"

Sabine looked at him. "I wouldn't dream of it," she said, smiling.

The awards dinner ran smoothly, but for once Sabine didn't notice the service. She was seated at a table where it would be easy for her to rise and address her remarks to Bernard. The camera could follow her, another camera could catch Bernard's reactions. Except for the musical numbers, this was the way the show would run. Various friends and associates would stand to honor Bernard Ross with a speech, an anecdote, a remembrance, a toast. All informal, yet impressive, due to the quality of the performers and speakers. For just a second, her eye caught Jerry's. They looked at each other. Old friends, the best of friends. But neither made a move of recognition. Another one of Bernard Ross's good deeds, Sabine thought sadly.

The performance began. The band was revealed, playing one of its biggest hits, and the audience broke into applause.

Bob Hope made the opening remarks and was, as always, appreciative and *de*preciative at the same time—providing a funny and relaxed way to start the evening.

What was she going to say? Sabine looked up at Bernard, who was sitting at the dais. Balding now, beaming. His wife Carol was at a front table.

The anecdotes went on. Bernard chuckled. Wonderfully amusing and slightly embarrassing facets of his personality were being revealed.

Sinatra sang.

Bernard was praised for his charities, his contributions to the State of Israel.

Sabine closed her eyes. It was going to be very easy. She could tell the story of Bernie the waiter dragging a cow into the dining room, and then turn around and ask him how he liked the food so far. She could do that.

But she would not do it.

She whispered to the man on her left. "Do you have a pen?" He produced one, and she began to write on a napkin.

"You shouldn't do that," the man to her right whispered.

"Why not?" she whispered back. "It's *my* napkin."

Bernard was praised for being a great American. A wonderful example of a Jewish boy, a son of immigrant parents, who struggled to better himself, and ended up bettering the world.

Sabine kept on writing. Scratching out. Correcting. She was out of practice at writing on a deadline.

The evening droned on, livened mostly by Jerry Davis, who did a piece of special material about performing in the Catskills, about improvising material on Friday night for Saturday's show. His homage to Bernard was slightly oblique.

"Bernie," he said, smiling sweetly. "There never was anyone *quite* like you. And I say this from the heart."

There was a break during the proceedings. Time for a commercial.

Sabine noticed Bernard walking her way. They had not yet spoken.

"I want to thank you," he said, "for allowing us to use Glenrocks. It will surely be good publicity for all involved. You are as beautiful as ever."

She did not rise and she did not speak. He didn't seem to notice.

"This is sure a far cry from the old days, huh? Who would have thought *then* what would become of all of us? By the way, you'll be glad to know I am doing your movie."

"What movie?" She was so surprised she spoke right up.

"Oh, the one you were always after me to make during the war. We made it with Poles or some cockamamie thing. It bombed the first time. But now we expect big things. It's my next project."

The floor manager was making frantic signals. Bernard had to return to the dais. She watched him go, and found tears of fury smarting her face. She wiped them away with the napkin, then began to write furiously. Nothing else mattered.

When she heard her name called, she was too involved in her writing to notice. Someone nudged her with an elbow. She looked up. Everyone was looking in her direction. The boom mike was circling toward her.

"Writers are always working against deadlines." She waved the napkin and the pen, and the audience chuckled. "I really didn't know what to say about Bernard Ross. It just came to me now."

Sabine went on, "It's so hard nowadays to know exactly what you can say—when it's better to keep silent, when it's better to speak out. Anyway, to this humanitarian, who has had every accolade heaped upon his humble shoulders tonight, I want to dedicate a poem.

"Now, I have to warn you that Mr. Ross and I have known each other for a very long time, a lifetime. So I should like to propose a toast to an old . . . well, an old friend. I will read it off this napkin."

She strolled toward the dais, carrying the napkin and her glass. The director-producer of the TV film was entranced. This was television. Spontaneous. Alive. He was thinking of Emmys even as she spoke.

She began.

> "To you who kept your silence
> When you could have spoken out
> To you who now give millions
> To the Jewish State
> I give what's due
> To you, Humanitarian
> Whose courage came
> Six million Jews too late."

The director was looking frantically at Seymour. Seymour's face was impassive. No signal. Sabine raised her glass in a toast.

> "To you who spoke so freely
> When you had no need
> To you, whose testimony ruined
> Countless lives
> I give what's due
> To you, Humanitarian.
> As long as we keep still
> You will survive!"

And with that, she threw the champagne in his face—in front of maybe fifty million American viewers. And as she walked out, to find Freddy standing in her way, laughing— laughing hard, she passed Jerry's table. He was beaming.

"That's what I call speaking up," he said, and she nodded.

"At last," she said.

Chapter Twenty-Eight

The airport in Jackson, Mississippi, had never seen such a crowd. And such a strange-looking one. The air was so heavy in the August twilight that Sabine had trouble catching her breath. She looked around her. All these people were waiting for the flight out. There were Northern clergymen and union officials, entertainers, mothers who were carrying babies. There were members of civil rights groups and college kids, and everywhere there were the television camera crews who had followed the march all the way to the capital. For four days some of these people had been marching, their goal the courthouse. And along the sides of the highway there had been the Confederate flags and the signs—"Nigger Lover!" A woman had whizzed by the marchers in a shiny blue car, suddenly stopped, stuck her tongue out, then raced away.

They had all come down here to push for voter registration. The laws had been passed. Now they had to be enforced, no matter what. A president had been shot in Dallas, and still the fight continued. Nothing was going to stop them. Nothing had stopped them, not even the threat of violence or the bombings.

They had been given instructions:

When you march, keep the women and children in the middle, and if there's a shot, make the others kneel down. Don't be hanging around, or you're going to get hurt. Don't rely on the troopers, either. If you're beaten, crouch and put your hands over the back of your head. If you fall, fall right down and look dead. And one last warning—let me tell you—the food is lousy.

Sabine looked at the crowd—ragged, bearded, dedicated, black and white. A lot of young faces. Thousands of them.

456

She wondered what she was doing here. She had come down because it seemed right. It seemed that if ever there were a time to get things *right*, now was the time.

A constant stream of announcements about departing flights came over the loudspeaker. She caught sight of herself reflected in a window. Tired, hair all messy, face muddy. That's how she looked. And why not? She had been sleeping in fields, and standing in line for food (yes, it *was* terrible!), and she hadn't had a bath in four days.

She sat down and lit a cigarette. The surge of people swarmed around her. Had they done any good? It was so hard to tell.

She got up again, restless. Freddy had chartered his own plane. They were waiting for clearance now. She passed her hand through her hair and suddenly found herself staring at Matt Ryan.

He was sitting on a duffel bag, smoking a cigarette, his head down. He looked thinner than he used to be. There was gray mixed in with the red of his hair. He looked up, perhaps because she had been staring at him so intently. When he saw her, when he finally recognized her, he rose and came over.

"Of all people," he said, and she noticed how tired his voice sounded.

"Of all places," she said, gesturing around the crowded airport.

"You look a mess."

"I know."

"And you never looked better. I saw your show," he said, and she looked around nervously. She was always either being congratulated or castigated for throwing a glass of champagne in somebody's face.

"I didn't know you had such good aim. I never taught you that," Matt said and he gave her that grin. It was the grin she remembered from childhood, from schoolyards and play times, from nightclubs and taxis. From jazz and Thanksgiving, and from a flatcar in Austria. It had all been fun, that grin said.

"How are you?" he asked her. "I don't have to ask about Freddy. I can see he's doing just fine."

"Did you speak to him?"

"No, I didn't try. He always has so many people around him."

"But he would have wanted you to."

"I didn't want to."

Newsmen and photographers, FBI men and National Guardsmen passed them.

"What about you? Where are you?" she asked him.

"I'm living in Seattle. I work for the *Post-Intelligencer*. I got a nice house in a nice part of town. It's called Queen Anne."

He was looking at her eyes. Still that electric green-blue, still so full of sparkle.

"You can see the Sound from there," he said.

"The Sound?"

"Puget Sound."

"Oh."

There was the roar of planes taking off. Matt and Sabine still looked at each other.

"Then you came out all right," Sabine said, "in the end."

He laughed. "In the *end*? Good God, it's not over!"

They called his flight, and they only had time to look at one another again in the midst of the ramshackle airport in a hot Mississippi town.

"I've got to take off," he said, and she nodded.

"Can I call you?" she said.

He leaned down to kiss her, on the mouth. "I can't wait until you do. And if you don't, I'll call *you*. At Glenrocks."

"Oh, Matt—can we . . . ?"

Her question was lost in the noise of the crowd. But he was grinning at her. *Oh God, thank God, the grin is back,* she thought, and her tears—the tears streaming down her face were tears of relief.

Up in the air, headed for New York, Sabine glanced out of the window. They were reaching the Atlantic Coast. She could see the edge of land and the beginnings of the Atlantic. Far, far below were little squiggly lines. Roads. Journeys.

From this height Sabine imagined that she could see the whole world. Far off to the east, across the water, the beginning. Jacob's journey. And Sammy's. If she looked behind her she might see the beginnings of Florida. The end of Jacob's journey. To the west, which was still light, Matt was in flight toward Seattle.

So many journeys.

Mark in an English grave. Sammy dying in "Man-hat-tan."

Freddy, with his life spread out like a giant spiderweb encompassing the globe. An international star.

Jerry. She would not think of him.

She considered her own journey. What a strange path she had followed so far. What an adventure it all had been.

Where was she going? She had an answer for that. First, she was going to Glenrocks. She wasn't selling to the conglomerates, not just yet. She had installed a discotheque. It had worked. Now she wanted to see about legalizing gambling . . .

Her mind went beyond that. The *Post-Intelligencer*. Queen Anne. Puget Sound. She tried to imagine Seattle. Matt. She whispered his name.

That was the next step in her journey. To Matt. And where would it lead? Her father had taught her the answer to that.

Who knows?

About the Author

Will Holt was born in Portland, Maine, and attended Phillips Exeter Academy, Williams College, and the Richard Dyer-Bennet School of Minstrelsy in Aspen, Colorado, before embarking on a career that has included performing in nightclubs (The Blue Angel in New York, the hungry i in San Francisco, the Gate of Horn in Chicago); composing "*Lemon Tree*," "*Sinner Man*," "*One of Those Songs*") and writing for the theater (*Me and Bessie, Over Here*, starring the Andrews Sisters, and the award-winning musical *The Me Nobody Knows*). He is married to the actress Dolly Jonah. They have a son, Courtney William, and they divide their time between a Manhattan apartment and a house in Maine.

His first novel, SAVAGE SNOW, is available in a Signet edition.